LEGEND [illegible] RINGS

The realm of Roku [illegible] ers, and mystics, of dra [illegible] d of heroism, magic, and steel.

Through times of peace and war, the samurai of the seven Great Clans have competed for power and influence. But as the trust between them fractures, those struggles turn ever bloodier. Former allies become fierce adversaries, and unlikely pacts are forged between ancient enemies.

While conflict and political intrigue divide the clans, the true threat awaits in the darkness of the Shadowlands, beyond the vast Carpenter Wall. There, in the twisted wastelands, an evil corruption endlessly seeks the downfall of the empire.

As the Shadowlands threat grows, samurai from the warring clans must put aside their differences and unite if they are to save the very soul of Rokugan.

Also Available in Legend of the Five Rings

The Daidoji Shin Mysteries

Poison River by Josh Reynolds
Death's Kiss by Josh Reynolds
The Flower Path by Josh Reynolds
Three Oaths by Josh Reynolds

The Hundred Tales

The Night Parade of 100 Demons by Marie Brennan
The Game of 100 Candles by Marie Brennan
The Market of 100 Fortunes by Marie Brennan

The Legend of Iuchiban

The Heart of Iuchiban by Evan Dicken
The Soul of Iuchiban by Evan Dicken

Clan Novels & Novellas

Curse of Honor by David Annandale
To Chart the Clouds by Evan Dicken
The Great Clans of Rokugan: The Collected Novellas Vol 1
The Great Clans of Rokugan: The Collected Novellas Vol 2

Rokugan: The Art of Legend of the Five Rings
Legend of the Five Rings: The Poster Book

A BITTER TASTE

A Daidoji Shin Mystery

JOSH REYNOLDS

First published by Aconyte Books in 2024
ISBN 978 1 83908 301 3
Ebook ISBN 978 1 83908 302 0

Cover art by Xteve Abanto

Rokugan map by Francesca Baerald

Distributed in North America by Simon & Schuster Inc, New York, USA
Printed in the United States of America
9 8 7 6 5 4 3 2 1

ACONYTE BOOKS

An imprint of Asmodee Entertainment Ltd

Mercury House, Shipstones Business Centre

North Gate, Nottingham NG7 7FN, UK

aconytebooks.com // twitter.com/aconytebooks

For Anna. Thanks for looking after Noah.

Dragon Lands
Unicorn Lands
CITY OF THE RICH FROG
Rokugan
Lion Lands

CHAPTER ONE
Opportunity

Daidoji Shin was sulking.

He lay amid a nest of cushions, his robes in disarray, his hair unbound, and his face unshaven. He stared through the open balcony doors, watching as a gray pall of rain fell across the city, rendering the violet rooftops of the noble district a pale puce. It had been raining for nearly three days now and a better metaphor for his mood he could not imagine.

Shin closed his eyes and sighed, long fingers rubbing his aching temples. He thought he had good reason to be upset. Some weeks prior, he had been informed that he was to at last suffer a fate he had spent a great amount of time and effort avoiding. The first few days after this unpleasant revelation, he had twisted and turned like a fox in a trap, seeking some way to escape the inescapable. Gradually, however, desperation had curdled into resignation. The end had come, and no amount of squirming would see him escape.

Not this time.

Still brooding, he picked up his biwa and plucked idly at the strings. It sounded discordant to his ears and he frowned, annoyed. Fiddling with it, he looked around, taking in the state of his quarters for the first time in what felt like days. They were a mess, much like himself. Almost absently, he realized that he wasn't handling things well at all.

A Daidoji was supposed to be iron, unbreakable and unyielding. But he was neither of those things. He never had been, more was the pity. It was no wonder he was a constant source of disappointment to his family. He sighed and closed his eyes.

The bell hanging near the entrance to his quarters jangled. Shin cracked one eye. "I never should have installed that," he murmured. It had been a suggestion from a merchant of his acquaintance, and it was a good one. A way of alerting himself to visitors early, before his servants needed to announce them. That way, he could always look his best. Except in this instance, in which he did not feel like it.

There was no polite knock at the door. Instead, it was wrenched open and the glowering face of his bodyguard, Hiramori Kasami, peered in at him. "You are not dressed," she said flatly.

"I am not," he said, flicking the biwa's strings. "Tell them to go away."

"Get dressed."

"No. Tell them to go away." More strings were flicked.

Kasami growled low in her throat and marched into his quarters. What she lacked in height, she more than made up for in presence. Even out of armor, she had the bearing of a warrior – a killer. Which was not surprising, given that as a daughter of the Uebe marshes, she had been trained for her duties almost from childhood. The Daidoji had honed her into a lethal weapon, so as to best ensure the survival of her charge – namely, Shin.

When she had first taken up her duties, there had been some… friction. Shin had not particularly wanted a bodyguard and, to her credit, Kasami had not particularly wanted to be his bodyguard. But they had muddled along, and come to an oft-uneasy understanding of each other's peculiarities of character. Most notably, Kasami's utter lack of respect for his esteemed status as a son of the Daidoji.

She snatched the biwa from his hands and raised it as if to smash it on the floor. Shin didn't protest. She hesitated at this lack of response, and then set it down, out of his reach. "Get up, clean yourself. Lady Konomi is here. She wishes to speak to you."

"I am not in the mood to entertain visitors today." He sank back into his cushions, one hand over his eyes. "Send her away, and have Niko fetch me some willow bark tea, please."

Kasami looked down at him. There was concern in her gaze, but mostly frustration. "This is unseemly," she said, as if to a child. "It is unworthy of a Daidoji."

"Well, as I am an unworthy Daidoji, it is the best I can do."

Kasami looked away. "It is not a death sentence, you know," she said, as gently as she could manage. "It is your duty to be married."

"I do not recall agreeing to it," Shin said petulantly. He glanced at the stack of missives he'd been doing his best to ignore. Letters of introduction from potential marriage matches, none of them particularly suitable in his opinion.

He crossed his arms and glared out at the rain, as if it were responsible for his situation. "I was given no choice in the matter, and I strenuously object to the very idea of it." Despite this assertion, he'd always known that his duty was to marry and produce an heir. He had been taught as much when he'd been no more than a child himself. The Daidoji started early with talk of duty, the better to see that it was carried out. That didn't make it any easier, however. Especially when the news had been delivered at the tip of a sword – a metaphorical sword, perhaps, but a sword nonetheless.

The possibilities of his life, once boundless, had now narrowed to two equally unpleasant paths: marry, or be quietly removed. Thus, his current mood. He thought, after all he had done to better society, he was allowed some leeway in how he processed his coming doom. Kasami, however, didn't agree.

"Object or not, it is the only way you will live to see out the year. Lord Kenzō and I agree on that. It is the only way to save your life…"

"Lord Kenzō, is it?" Shin asked acidly. "As I recall, you offered to kill him for me." Junichi Kenzō, an auditor sent by the Daidoji Trading Council, had claimed to be investigating Shin for financial irregularities. In reality, he'd come to deliver the news that Shin was to be married – or else.

"You are mistaken," Kasami said stiffly. She paused. "You asked me if I would, and I said no. Wisely, as it turned out, since he is the only thing standing between you and the fate that befell your predecessor."

Shin hesitated. "We don't know that to be the case." He had his suspicions, of course. His predecessor had died suddenly, under somewhat unusual circumstances. Popular opinion had it that her debauchery had caught up with her. But he often wondered about that, especially given that what he knew of her spoke to a woman who was far too cagey to be caught out by common street thugs. Assassination was the obvious answer, and the Daidoji Trading Council had a long, unfortunate history of removing obstacles to the fiscal well-being of the clan in such a manner.

Kasami didn't reply. Instead, she turned toward the door. "Get dressed. Clean your face. Konomi is impatient to see you." As if to lend weight to her words, the doors opened again – less forcefully this time. Iuchi Konomi stood in the doorway, hands folded before her.

"She's right, I am very impatient," she said. One of Shin's servants, Niko, peered around Konomi, her expression anxious. Shin gestured for her to depart, and she did so hurriedly. Konomi watched her go, and then entered the room. "Niko tried her best, but I was implacable, I fear."

"So I see." Shin glanced at Kasami. "Would you catch Niko and have her make us some tea, please? And where is Kitano? I have errands for him to run."

"Errands can wait," Konomi said, as Kasami left them, carefully sliding the doors shut behind her after sharing a knowing glance with Konomi. "I wish to socialize."

"I don't," Shin said. He rubbed his head. His headache was getting worse.

Konomi smiled sadly. "Oh, Shin, what makes you think you have a choice?"

"I am not in the mood to socialize."

"You are moping."

"I am overcome with despair."

"You are sulking."

"Yes," Shin said, collapsing into his cushion. "Yes, I am sulking. Why should I not sulk? I am facing a crisis of existential proportion, and there is no one to whom I can turn for succor." He raised his fists and shook them at the heavens. "I am alone, exiled to a rock in a storm-tossed sea. Cast out… accursed…"

Konomi pursed her lips. "You are being childish."

Shin glared at her, but it wilted after a moment. It required too much strength to maintain, and he had precious little of that. Instead, he flapped his fan in the direction of the door. "Leave me, I beg you. Let me sink into the mire of despair in peace."

Konomi grunted, shoved up the sleeves of her robes and reached down to grab him by the ankles. Shin squawked in alarm as Konomi dragged him bodily from his carefully built nest and out onto the rainswept balcony. Shin wailed like a cat as he was instantly soaked to the bone. Konomi attempted to pull him to his feet, and he took the opportunity to squirm out of her grasp and scuttle back to the warmth of his room.

Konomi hooked an arm around his midsection and hauled him into the air despite his struggles. They wobbled, off balance, and fell in a heap on the balcony, Konomi atop Shin. They lay in silence for several moments, panting from the effort of their struggle. "You never mentioned you were a wrestler," Shin said, after a moment, suddenly all too aware of her proximity. Not to mention her smell – not flowery or subtle, something wilder. It put him in mind of wildfires and crashing charges across the steppe.

Konomi looked down at him. "The Unicorn encourage their daughters to train both body and mind by whatever means suits them."

"And you chose that?"

"One must work with what one has, Shin." Konomi smiled. "And what I have is…"

"Muscles?"

"I was going to say strength."

"That too," Shin said. He settled back and looked up at the falling rain, at the birds huddled in the eaves of his home, at the shape the smoke rising from the houses around made in the wet air. Really, at anything other than Konomi, whose face was entirely too close to his own. It wasn't that she was unattractive – quite the opposite, really. She had all the qualities the Daidoji valued – physical strength, fortitude, and a mind like iron.

And yet.

And yet, there was something there, in her eyes and her expression, that he found troublesome. A hint of wariness, but more than that. Arrogance… hubris? At times, he feared it was too much like looking at his own reflection in a basin of water.

He wondered if she saw the same, when she looked at him. As she studied him the way he studied her, the way one studied a painting… or the way one might observe an enemy formation about its maneuvers. "I can't breathe," he said softly. Which wasn't totally a lie; pleasant as it was, she was quite heavy.

Konomi blinked, then flushed, and made to push herself off him. Shin winced as she used him for balance, and then again as she hauled him to his feet. She looked him up and down, and let loose a tiny giggle. "You look like a drowned rat."

Shin plucked at his white hair, plastered to his neck and scalp by the rain. His robes were wet through and in even more disarray. He did his best to gather the tatters of his dignity about himself and said, "I have looked better, I admit. But I have an excuse…"

"Yes, sadness," Konomi said pointedly. "That is not an excuse for such as we, Shin. What you are feeling is not true sadness, it is just frustration. I have felt this particular flavor of it myself and more often than you."

Shin flapped a hand dismissively. "Yes, yes, but we are not the same. You have no idea how tight this noose is about my neck, Konomi. It is marriage – or death. Those are my options, and neither is appealing."

Konomi sighed and shoved Shin inside, out of the rain. She began to wring out her robes as she spoke. "Only because you lack imagination. Marriage can be an opportunity."

"Then why aren't you married?"

She fixed him with a stern look. "Because one does not have to seize every opportunity like a child snatching fruit from a tree. Some must be left to ripen, or to rot as fortune dictates." She smiled. "I am waiting for the right one."

"That doesn't help me!"

Konomi sighed and began to unwind her hair. It was quite long, and spilled down in a glossy cascade as she tried to strip the water from it. "If you would shake free of this cloud and think clearly, you might see that it does. Really, Shin… I thought you were made of sterner stuff than this."

Before he could reply, however, Kasami appeared in the doorway. If she noticed their bedraggled condition, she gave no sign. Instead, she said, "Azuma is here."

"Lord Azuma?" Shin glanced at Konomi, who looked equally confused. Kaeru Azuma was the official representative of the governor. The Kaeru were nominally vassals of the imperial Miya family, but only because the Miya paid better than their rivals. Even so, they were inextricably tied to the city, and, in some ways, had as much claim to it as either the Unicorn or the Lion. The Kaeru saw to the continued function of the city, and Azuma saw to the function of the Kaeru. "What does he want?"

"To talk," Azuma said, from behind Kasami. She quickly stepped aside as the tall, whip-thin man entered the room. He had hard features and hair that was steadily going silver. He wore official robes, marked with the sigils of the Miya and the Kaeru. He was also armed, which Shin found somewhat alarming.

"About?" Shin asked sharply, annoyed that people kept barging in on him. Perhaps it was his own fault; he'd made his home open to his acquaintances. He had only himself to blame if they eschewed social decorum.

If Azuma noted Shin's tone, he gave no sign. His expression was stiff and troubled. "There's been a death," he said without preamble.

Shin frowned. "An important one I'm guessing, if you are here to inform me about it." He wasn't surprised that Azuma had come to him. It wasn't the first time, after all. He'd made something of a name for himself as a solver of puzzles, discreet or otherwise. Thefts, disappearances, and even the odd murder or three. A wise man might have avoided garnering such a reputation, but Shin found that besides having a knack for it, he also rather enjoyed it. Yet something felt different this time.

"You might say that." Azuma frowned and glanced at Konomi, as if wondering whether he ought to ask her to leave. Finally, he said, "Junichi Kenzō."

Shin paused, momentarily dumbstruck. "Excuse me?" He barely noticed when Konomi gasped and grabbed his hand.

"Lord Kenzō is dead." Azuma hesitated, which was unlike him. "Murdered."

Shin blinked, unable to process the thought. Kenzō – dead? Murdered, even? It seemed impossible, especially given what he knew of the man. Crane auditors were not simply counters of rice, but trained warriors. They were more than capable of defending themselves, under normal circumstances. "Do you have a suspect?"

Azuma glanced at Konomi again. He swallowed, clearly uncomfortable. Shin gestured impatiently. "Out with it, man – do you have a suspect or not?"

"We do," Azuma said heavily.

"And who is it?" Shin asked.

"You, Shin," Azuma said, with visible regret. "It is you."

CHAPTER TWO
Saibanshoki

Hiramori Kasami frowned as the imperial skiff approached the Saibanshoki. In the gray misty light, the great tree resembled nothing so much as a mountain towering over the two rivers that rushed about it unceasingly. When the sun was high, the shadow of its branches fell on either shore, casting a pall of gloom over the docks unlucky enough to have been built there. The thinnest point of its trunk was twenty yards across, at least.

A manor house hung in the uppermost branches, over the rivers. Other facilities coiled about the lower trunk like a serpent of stone and wood – a courtroom; the offices of the imperial clerks and toll takers; others of various purpose. Servants bearing signal flags stood on the balconies and branch-platforms, communicating with parties on either side of the rivers as well as the many boats and skiffs that blanketed the surface of the water. Kaeru archers patrolled the observation bridges that were scattered like cobwebs throughout the branches, their keen eyes ever in search of threats.

Shin thought of the tree simply as an imperial residence.

But it was a fortress and she viewed it as such. Taking it would not be an impossible task – merely an extremely difficult one. She occupied herself imagining various military scenarios and allowing them to play out across the surface of her mind as their craft bore them across the water to the imperial docks.

Shin was talking, as usual. Trying to pry answers from Kaeru Azuma, which, in her opinion, was akin to trying to force a stone to laugh. "This is preposterous, Azuma, and you know it." He'd been saying as much ever since Azuma had arrived. Kasami had quietly escorted Lady Konomi out as Shin protested his innocence. Konomi, normally eager to hear any gossip, had departed without protest for once. In fact, she'd seemed unusually subdued. Kasami pushed the thought aside and went back to her ruminations on how best to disable the Kaeru defenses of the imperial residence.

"It is," Azuma said, and not for the first time. "And yet, there is a witness."

"Odoma," Shin said, sitting back. "So you said." Kasami frowned. The head of the city's merchant association had borne Shin a grudge for some time, claiming that Shin had swindled him out of some property. The shoyu merchant had come sniffing around for money on more than one occasion. Shin always sent him away unhappy. "I'm sure he was eager to provide testimony."

Azuma nodded. "Apparently."

"He's lying," Shin said.

"I know that as well."

Shin sighed. Kasami glanced at him. He still looked unkempt, if not so much as before. Perhaps Lady Konomi's visit had done some good. He'd even insisted on getting dressed before they left, which Azuma had politely allowed.

"When was he – when did it happen?" he asked. "You can tell me that much, surely."

"The body was found yesterday, though his death itself could have happened several days ago. The brewery has been closed for repairs for the last week. Something about new cedar barrels being installed, I'm told."

Shin paused. "New barrels? That's going to ruin the taste." He shook his head. "Not that Odoma's shoyu was particularly noteworthy. Who found the – who found him?"

"Odoma and his bodyguards."

"How convenient."

"So I said at the time." Azuma smiled. "Odoma was not pleased by the implication."

"No, I expect he wasn't. Odoma is a scoundrel, as well as a purveyor of substandard shoyu," Shin said. "How can anyone take his word over mine?"

"Normally, we wouldn't," Azuma said. "But there are… extenuating circumstances."

"Which are?"

Azuma hesitated. "Perhaps we shouldn't speak of this just now."

Shin fixed him with a look. "Can you think of a better time? If I am to solve this puzzle, I must have the facts. I cannot build a house without wood, Lord Azuma."

"You are not building this house," Azuma said firmly. "Not this time. As I just said, there are… complications. The Crane."

Shin hesitated at the mention of his clan. "The Crane already know about Kenzō's death?" Kasami, alert now, pushed military strategy to the side in order to better listen. Shin, she knew, suspected that Odoma had complained to the Trading Council, thus initiating Kenzō's investigation.

But there'd been no proof, and Kenzō himself had demurred when Kasami had put the question to him. If it were the case, however, the Daidoji wouldn't take kindly to the death of their agent. It would simply confirm any suspicions they might have had.

"They do. More, they are already here," Azuma said.

Shin blinked. "You said you only found him yesterday."

"Nonetheless, they are here. They want you, Shin. In their custody."

Shin glanced at Kasami. She gave a slight shake of her head, indicating that she'd heard nothing of this. That wasn't surprising, however. Since they'd come to the city, her sources within the Daidoji had become uncertain at best. Shin was not favored by his family. Kenzō's presence alone showed that.

"And what do you want?" Shin asked Azuma, carefully. Azuma frowned.

"I want what I always want – the status quo maintained. As does the governor."

"The easiest way to maintain it is to hand me over to whoever has come looking for me," Shin said slowly. Kasami grimaced; she knew that Shin liked Azuma, and she thought the feeling was mutual. But the Kaeru were the loyal servants of the imperial governor, and had watched over the City of the Rich Frog for generations. Azuma had a duty to Miya Tetsua, and the city, to do what was best for them. He would not let his friendship with Shin interfere with that – something she could respect. Nonetheless, it made her wary. "Who is it, by the by?"

"Daidoji Aoto. A cousin of yours, I think."

Shin blanched, and Kasami winced in sympathy. Shin and his cousins were not on the best of terms, and Aoto was the worst of them, to hear Shin speak of it. Kasami, having never met him, often wondered whether Aoto's unpleasantness was simply exaggeration on Shin's part. She supposed she was about to find out. "Aoto," Shin said, after a moment. Azuma nodded, a frown on his face.

"Unpleasant fellow. Not as polite as you."

"No, well, Aoto is not a believer in politesse. He prefers to put his faith in cold steel."

"He dresses like a courtier."

"His mother had high hopes for him," Shin said absently. "Sadly, he preferred the rough and tumble of the practice field." He slid his fan out of his sleeve and gave it a desultory flutter, stirring the wet air. Kasami frowned.

"That is no bad thing," she said. "You could do with some more of that yourself."

Shin frowned but didn't reply. Kasami grunted, annoyed by his lack of fire. Annoying as she normally found him, she didn't care for this dispirited and sullen version of him. She resolved to continue to poke and prod at him until he snapped out of it. She turned back to Saibanshoki and saw that they were nearing the imperial docks. They nestled among the tree's massive roots, emerging from Saibanshoki's base like the spokes of some immense wheel. Despite their size, they saw little traffic, save for the occasional noble visitor or the Kaeru prisoner transports.

The usual Kaeru guards were in evidence on the jetty as they approached, but there were others present as well. "Cranes," Shin murmured.

"Auditors," Azuma said. Kasami studied the quintet of dark-clad newcomers with interest. Kenzō had taken great pains to appear as nothing more than a simple bookkeeper, but these five were doing little to conceal their potential for violence.

They bore the Daidoji sigil on their robes, and all were visibly armed, though they sensibly kept their hands away from their weapons while the Kaeru guards were watching. "They came with your cousin."

"Aoto has always taken a hands-on interest in things," Shin said. There was a hitch in his voice that Kasami doubted anyone but herself would notice. Their craft reached the jetty and they disembarked, Shin more slowly than his companions. Kasami wondered if he was afraid, or merely lost in thought.

The auditors were watching them now, gazes keen like those of birds of prey. One, tallish and narrow, made as if to intercept them, but his fellows stopped him. Azuma made a surreptitious gesture, and several nearby Kaeru moved to cordon off the Cranes. "As I said, they are here to take you into custody," Azuma said. "But Lord Tetsua wishes to see you before he decides whether to allow it or not."

"How kind of him," Shin said.

"It is, yes," Azuma said. He glanced at Shin. "He is taking a risk, Shin. I hope you appreciate it."

Shin paused and Kasami thought something like a shadow passed over his face, but his expression barely flickered. Whatever else, Shin was an excellent courtier. "I will thank him personally," he said. "I wish to speak to Kasami before we go in. May I… ?"

Azuma nodded. "Make it quick. Your cousin is not a patient man."

"Swift as a bird in flight, that's me," Shin said. He stepped aside and motioned for Kasami to join him. She did so, keeping her eyes on the Cranes.

"They're a lethal looking bunch, don't you think?" he murmured.

Kasami grunted, but was quietly pleased. He was trying to annoy her. That meant his mood was improving. "We are wasting time. What did you want to talk about?"

Shin leaned toward her, his fan between them and the scowling Cranes. "I need you to go back to the city, find Doctor Sanki and bring him here as quickly as possible."

"Sanki? Why?" Kasami disliked the old physician immensely. Bad enough he'd once served the Lion as a battlefield surgeon, but he was also disrespectful and acerbic. He had no respect for anyone – not even Shin.

"I will need his expert opinion. Azuma let slip that they brought Kenzō's body here. I'm going to inveigle a viewing and I want Sanki with me when I do it. And if you see Kitano, tell him to fetch Ito and have him meet us at home."

Kasami nodded. That, at least, made sense. Ito was one of the merchants Shin ostensibly oversaw on behalf of the Daidoji Trading Council. In reality, he was a spy, keeping an eye on events in the city on behalf of the Crane, or so Shin had told her. Regardless, Ito and Kenzō had spent much time together of late – too much, in her opinion. Shin undoubtedly hoped Ito might be able to shed some light on the auditor's final hours.

"What if the auditors protest?" she asked.

Shin frowned. "Do as you think best."

Kasami blinked, then nodded. She glanced at the Cranes again, and saw that they were studying her as well. She thought she knew what they were thinking and her hands curled into fists. "Do your best not to provoke them," she said quietly. "I will not be here to intervene if Aoto decides to challenge you."

Shin smiled weakly. "I shall be on my best behavior."

Kasami didn't believe him, but nodded and turned back to

the boat. Finding Sanki wouldn't take long. Convincing him to come, on the other hand, would be more difficult. Even at the best of times the old man was hard to rouse.

She had the distinct feeling that there was no time to waste.

CHAPTER THREE
Daidoji Aoto

The gubernatorial receiving room was as small and sparsely decorated as Shin recalled. The only notable item of furniture was a small, low table set in the center of the room. Atop the table was an intricately carved Go board, complete with two sets of stones – one group white, the other black – in their kitani bowls. Two individuals sat studying the bare board intently, as if preparing a strategy for a game to come.

He and Azuma were not the first to arrive. Daidoji Aoto stood stiffly near the table, trying without success to hide his impatience. Aoto was a slender man, neither tall nor short, with lean features accentuated by his white hair. The hair was dyed, of course. Aoto liked his hair to be the pristine white of new-fallen snow, Shin recalled. He'd always been quite vain about it, even as a boy. Still was, from the look of him. Aoto barely acknowledged Shin's presence, though the two with him openly stared. Glared, rather.

They were not Daidoji, though they dressed the part. Not Hiramori either – too neat. Something about them reminded him of Kenzō. More auditors, then. Come to collect their fallen comrade, or, more likely, to punish his killer.

Which, from the looks they were throwing his way, they'd obviously decided was him. Shin sighed and turned his attention to the Go players.

The first, in his dark, plain robes, was innocuous in appearance and bearing, and might have been a scribe or priest – but he was anything but. Miya Tetsua was a representative of the Emerald Throne and the imperial governor of the city.

Officially, of course, the City of the Rich Frog was a tripartite assemblage. Three clans claimed mastery of it, and had divided it between themselves. The western bank of the Three Sides River belonged to the Unicorn. The Lion claimed the eastern bank, as well as everything south of the Drowned Merchant River. In contrast, the Dragon had ceded their claim to a minor clan – the Dragonfly – and contented themselves with the island-shrines that rose at the junction of the two rivers.

It was the Dragonfly's representative who sat across the board from Tetsua. Tonbo Kuma was a slim, androgynous individual with dark eyes and long hair bound back in a neat knot. They radiated strength, and Shin knew from experience that there was a decided firmness to them, beneath the seeming softness of their face and voice. The priest's presence came as something of a surprise to Shin, but he was careful not to let it show on his face as Tetsua glanced up from the board and gave Shin a lingering gaze. "So glad you could join us, Lord Shin. I trust we are not taking you away from anything important."

"I was sulking," Shin said blithely. "A good sulk does wonders for the soul."

Aoto sucked on his teeth, clearly wanting to comment but resisting the urge. Shin gave him a lazy look. Aoto hadn't much changed since they'd last confronted one another. He still looked underfed and slightly ill, despite his warrior's frame; a result of all the bad feelings simmering within him. Aoto had never met a day he didn't find wanting. "Cousin. What brings you here?"

Aoto bared his teeth. "I think you know."

"I think I don't."

Aoto snorted. "Play the fool if you must, Shin, but do not expect me to take part."

"No, you never were one for a bit of give and take, were you, Aoto?" Shin snapped open his fan and gave the muggy air a stir. When it rained overmuch, the damp of the river crawled up into the branches of Saibanshoki and hung there like some great bat, fluttering its wings, and filling every room with a stultifying humidity.

Not that Tetsua or his opponent seemed to notice. Then, Tonbo Kuma had some affinity for water. Perhaps they were keeping the worst of the damp at bay, through some priestly magic. As Shin watched, Kuma tapped a piece on the board as if considering. Tetsua paid no attention, his eyes on the Crane. "I assume Azuma has informed you of the charges against you, Lord Shin."

"He has."

"Good. That saves time. And your response?"

"Not guilty by reason of the sheer ridiculousness of the charges, my lord."

A quick flicker of something that might have been a smile passed across Tetsua's features. "As I expected. Nonetheless, I am pleased you chose to accompany Lord Azuma here without complaint. It is appreciated."

Shin bowed his head, acknowledging the compliment. It had been made solely for Aoto's benefit, he thought. "I thought, under the circumstances, it would be best to clear this matter up as quickly as possible."

Tetsua nodded and briefly turned his attention back to the board. "As to that, Lord Aoto wishes to clap you in chains. He believes the case against you to be ironclad."

Kuma snorted. Aoto's jaw clenched. Shin allowed himself a thin smile. "I take it that you do not agree, my lord."

"Master Odoma's testimony is somewhat lacking, in my opinion."

"To say nothing of his reputation," Kuma said, still studying the board. "The man is a swindler and a criminal, or so my own people tell me."

"All merchants are criminals," Aoto said primly.

Shin sniffed. "And yet here you are, on behalf of the Trading Council. What are you, Aoto, but a merchant writ large?"

Aoto wheeled to look at Shin, a sneer plastered on his face. "And what are you then, besides a waste of your mother's womb?"

Shin blinked. That was a new one. Then, Aoto had always liked to plumb the depths when it came to insults. He closed his fan and glanced at Tetsua. The Miya seemed utterly preoccupied by the condition of the gameboard. Shin glanced at his cousin. "I am, as I have always been … myself, and nothing more."

"You are a disgrace, Shin. And now, you are a murderer." Aoto's smile was like the edge of a blade. "Finally, you will get the end you so richly deserve."

Again, no response from Tetsua. Shin smiled and decided to take the fight to his cousin. "So – to sum up, you came here with the intent to arrest me, based on the accusation of a dodgy merchant who bears me a grudge, for the murder of a man I had no reason to kill," he said calmly. "You've always been overeager, Aoto, but this is something even for you."

Aoto hissed under his breath and took a step toward Shin.

Azuma tensed, as did the guards posted at the door. The auditors looked ready to defend Aoto, if it came to it. Shin extended his fan, pressing the end against Aoto's breastbone and causing his cousin to stop in his tracks. "I am not surprised to see you here, cousin," Shin went on, noting that Tetsua was listening, now, though still seemingly unwilling to intervene. "But you arrived startlingly quickly, given that he only died yesterday. I suppose you were already enroute, for some reason?"

Tetsua cleared his throat. "It seems your presence is requested at home, Lord Shin. Or was, prior to this… unfortunate occurrence."

"We came to drag you back home, Shin," Aoto clarified, with blunt relish. "You have had plenty of time to do your duty. Now a decision will be made for you – unless, of course, you are executed for the crime of which you now stand accused." He swatted Shin's fan aside. "Myself, I almost hope it is the latter. You disgrace the Daidoji with every breath you draw. If not for your grandfather–"

"If not for him, I would not be here," Shin said sharply.

Aoto gave a bark of laughter. "Exactly! That conniving old man has played the interposed blade for you too often. Now, he can do nothing. Finally, we are free to rid ourselves of you…" He faltered, as if suddenly recalling his location and who his audience was. He swallowed and stepped back. Shin shook his head.

"Interposed blade. That is certainly one way to think of it. Then, you always did lack the ability to see beyond your own spite."

Aoto growled low in his throat. "At least I have the support of my family. What do you have, save a reputation as a fool and a liar?"

"My good looks," Shin said. He heard Tetsua bite off a laugh. Even Kuma looked amused. Aoto, however, looked as if he were about to explode.

"I cannot wait to see your face when you are at last called to account, cousin," Aoto said. He turned to Tetsua. "My lord governor, I call on you to turn this miscreant over to my keeping, until his guilt can be determined..."

"I'm afraid not," Tetsua said, moving a piece across the board. Aoto paused, nonplussed by the reply.

"My lord, I must insist," he began.

"If you feel it necessary," Tetsua said. "It will do nothing to change my mind, however. Lord Shin has proven himself to be useful to me on more than one occasion and I am loath to cast aside such a tool before its use is fully expended."

Shin frowned. He didn't like hearing himself referred to as a tool, though he understood the rhetorical tactic for what it was. Tetsua continued, "Besides, the evidence against him is not the best. It would be embarrassing for all concerned if Shin's innocence were proven after I had turned him over to you. I am sure you see my dilemma."

"I – yes. Of course," Aoto said, grudgingly. He hesitated, and then, as if unable to stop himself, he turned to Shin and said, "Do not think that this is anything other than a momentary reprieve, cousin. You are caught fast, and no matter how much you squirm, you will not escape justice."

Shin knew the wisest thing was not to reply, but he couldn't resist. Aoto had always had that effect on him, and he couldn't, in good conscience, give him the last word. "And who decides what justice is, Aoto? You? If so, the fortunes truly are blind."

Aoto reacted as if struck. "What do you mean by that?"

Shin smiled. "How often, as children, did I save you from the consequences of your own stupidity? How often did I take the punishments meant for you? And, as ever, you repay me with accusation and scorn. That you, of all my cousins, would be the arbiter of my fate is nothing more than a jest by the Fortunes." As he spoke, long-buried feelings of resentment rose up out of the waters of memory.

They'd been friends, once. Companions. But Aoto had chosen a different path. He'd chosen to fall in line and do as he was told, and he'd resented Shin for not following his example. Or so it seemed to Shin, at least. Maybe there was more to it, on Aoto's side. Maybe not. Regardless, they had been on opposite sides for far longer than they'd been close. Aoto flushed as Shin's words sank in, and his hands knotted into fists.

"Enough," Tetsua said softly.

Shin fell silent and stepped back. Aoto bowed his head and did so as well. Tetsua sighed and sat back from the Go board. "As entertaining as it is to watch two Cranes peck at one another, I do have a full schedule for the day. Thus, my sole comment on the matter is this: Lord Shin is not to be taken into custody until such time as his guilt in this matter is determined." Before either Shin or Aoto could comment on this, Tetsua went on. "Further, as I have some vested interest in the resolution of said matter, I have asked my friend Lord Kuma to suggest an outside investigator to handle the matter for us in a civilized fashion."

Shin raised an eyebrow. Outside investigator? That didn't bode well. He'd expected Azuma to oversee things. He glanced at the Kaeru, and Azuma shook his head slightly. Shin deflated slightly. It seemed he was to be cut out of his own defense; to be expected, perhaps, but disappointing all the same. He cleared his throat. "As the accused, might I ask the name of this… investigator?"

Tonbo Kuma stirred from their study of the board and gave Shin their attention for the first time. "Kitsuki Ko," they said. "She is… one of the best, I am told." Their expression was enigmatic. "You know her, I believe."

Shin, feeling as if the ground were about to collapse beneath him, swallowed and forced a weak smile.

"Yes, you – ah – you might say that."

CHAPTER FOUR
Doctor Sanki

Kasami kicked the doorpost. "Sanki! Get out here you old reprobate! Lord Shin requires your aid." Her voice carried well in the narrow confines of the alley where Sanki resided, startling several river birds nesting on the rooftops above. The waterfront was only a street over, and she could hear the creak of anchored vessels, and the shouts of the dock workers as they unloaded cargo for transport to the Unicorn warehouses. The day was wearing on, despite the rain.

She cast a wary look about her, silently counting the seconds. At the five count she kicked the doorpost again. "Sanki!" She broke off into a cough, choking slightly on the river-stink that permeated the alleys closest to the water. The smell eddied in these confined spaces, never fading, only growing stronger.

She had sent a runner to the house, hoping to catch Kitano. The former gambler turned manservant was hard to pin down, even at the best of times. Part of her still expected him to run for the hills the moment he heard about Lord Shin's difficulties, though he'd proven his loyalty more than once of late. Then, maybe running was the right idea.

Angry at herself for such unworthy thoughts, she banged on the doorpost again. "Sanki! I have no time for this today!"

She heard footsteps and a querulous voice said, "Stop kicking my door! I'm coming." Annoyed by his tone, she kicked the doorpost again. Sanki was disrespectful and contrarian. Shin seemed to find it amusing, but Kasami did not.

"Hurry up!"

The door slid open with a rattle and Sanki's wizened countenance peered out at her. "What is it?" he demanded. He had a wispy beard shot through with silver, and his long hair was knotted atop his head in an untidy bun. He was bent with age, but not broken by it; brittle but in one piece, as yet. His robes were clean for once, if utilitarian.

"Lord Shin needs you."

"And I need my lunch," Sanki grunted. He made to close the door in her face and her hand snapped out to hold it open.

"Eat later. It is a matter of importance."

"It always is, with him." Sanki paused and gave her a speculative look. "Is this about that dead Crane they found?"

Kasami frowned. "How do you know about that?"

Sanki snorted and stepped back. "Everyone knows. That fat fool Odoma and his cronies have been crowing about it in every gambling den and sake house in this part of the city. He's quite proud of himself." He gestured for her to come inside. Kasami hesitated, but reluctantly did so. It was easier to humor Sanki than argue with him; she knew that from experience.

Sanki's residence was also his place of business. It wasn't squalid by any means, but nor was it especially pretty. Sanki had a Lion's disdain for the cosmetic. The walls were bare, with not even an illustrated scroll to liven things up. It was almost admirable.

Sanki led her into the back, where a small kitchen overlooked a dingy garden. Sanki grew his own medicinal herbs, she recalled. Not long after they'd first made Sanki's acquaintance, Shin had spent several days enthusiastically grubbing in the dirt alongside the old man, learning about the plants and their various uses.

"What else have you heard?" she asked, as Sanki led her into the kitchen. She stopped abruptly in the doorway, startled by the presence of another familiar face. Captain Lun was another of Shin's strays – those peculiar individuals he'd collected to help him in some way. As ever, she was dressed like a common sailor despite her rank, with bared arms and feet, and her shaggy hair cropped short. She grinned at Kasami and thrust a finger beneath the eyepatch she wore, scratching at the empty socket. "Bodyguard," she said, in greeting.

"Pirate," Kasami replied. "What are you doing here?"

"Having lunch with a friend," Lun said. "You?"

"None of your concern."

Lun's grin widened and her good eye flicked to Sanki. "I told you."

Sanki gave a grumbling chuckle and Kasami looked back and forth between them suspiciously. "Told him what? What are you talking about?"

"That Shin–" Lun began.

"*Lord* Shin," Kasami corrected sharply.

"That *his lordship* would send you to collect the old bag of bones here, for reasons no doubt relating to the death of that auditor," Lun continued, with barely a hesitation. She paused. "Let me guess – the Cranes who arrived with the tide yesterday have decided his lordship is to blame."

"Yesterday?" Kasami frowned. "You know about them?"

She didn't like this. Too many people knew about the auditor's death. What had Odoma been saying? What sort of rumors were spreading through the city, even now?

"I know enough to stay out of their way," Lun said. She rubbed her chin. "Convenient timing, though. Not for Shin – Lord Shin – but for them."

Kasami hesitated. In a previous life, Lun had been a marine in the Crane fleet. She had decided opinions about the clan she'd once loyally served; opinions shared by Shin, though he never voiced them so bluntly or with such relish. "If you knew about their arrival, why didn't you inform us?"

Lun shrugged. "I figured his lordship already knew about it. Why else would he have been in such an almighty sulk for the last few weeks?" She gave Kasami a sly look. "Is it true he's to be married finally?"

"Yes – no. Maybe. If he survives the next few days." Kasami immediately regretted the comment, but it served its purpose as Lun immediately fell silent. Kasami looked at Sanki, who was finishing up a bowl of rice. "We must go. Now. Time is of the essence."

"In my experience, the dead don't much care about schedules."

"It is not the dead that concern me," Kasami snapped. Sanki raised an eyebrow, but set aside his bowl and cleaned his hands on his robes.

"Fine. Let me get my bag. Where are we going?"

"Saibanshoki." Kasami felt a peculiar flicker of satisfaction at the looks of surprise that passed across Lun and Sanki's faces.

"Then the Kaeru did arrest him," Lun muttered. "That's not good."

"Not for him, and not for us," Sanki added. Kasami understood their worries. If Shin was implicated in a crime, all of his associates would come under investigation by the Daidoji. They would tear apart Shin's life, and the lives of those who served him, in search of even the smallest sign of guilt.

"How far has this gossip spread?" Kasami asked Lun, as Sanki hurried to collect his things. Shin's reputation had never been the best, but something like this could utterly destroy it, rendering his position in the city untenable.

"Don't worry, only us poor folks know," Lun said, tapping the side of her nose. "Odoma and his jackals have been boasting, but only to people who can be counted on to cheer. Once the nobles get wind of it, he'll be in trouble, and he damn well knows it. After all, he's nothing but a grubby merchant – right?"

Kasami frowned, but had to agree. Reputation and status often meant more than facts in cases like this. Shin had often decried such himself, but now seemed to be counting on it. Then, she knew for a fact that he hadn't committed the crime in question – couldn't have. Unless he'd somehow slipped out without her knowing. Which, of course, he'd done before and on more than one occasion, despite her many admonishments. She pushed the unhelpful thought aside. "Odoma bears Lord Shin a grudge; that is enough to make his testimony suspect. Especially given where the body was found."

"Yeah, odd that," Lun said, reaching for Sanki's abandoned bowl. She scooped the last of his rice into her own bowl and added, "Maybe Odoma did it himself. It wasn't like he and the auditor were friends."

Kasami paused. "You have proof of this?"

Lun looked at her as if she were an idiot. "Of course not. Even Odoma isn't that foolish. I'm merely stating what everyone already suspects." She blew out a noisy breath. "Your master sure does know how to pick his enemies… Odoma has always been a bad one. If he'd asked me, I'd have told Lord Shin to steer clear of him."

Kasami wasn't really listening anymore. Where was Sanki? She looked around impatiently. "Oh?"

"He's a gangster," Sanki said, coming back into the kitchen. "Or he was, before his uncle drowned in the river. Now he's a respectable man." He looked as if the thought made him want to spit. He held up his satchel. "I'm ready."

Kasami blinked. "Gangster?"

Lun stood. "Yes, of course. I'm surprised his lordship didn't know." Her smile was mirthless. "And here I thought he knew everything."

Kasami paused. Shin had known nothing of Odoma prior to Ito introducing them. Even then, Shin had paid little attention to the man, not until he'd made himself a problem. He'd kept their interactions to a minimum. A wise move, she felt, given Odoma's status as head of the merchant's association. "He knows only what people tell him," she said firmly, giving them both stern looks. "Why keep this to yourself?"

Lun stretched. "It's not my business to keep him informed. I just deliver cargo." She hesitated. "I'm not planning to go anywhere for a few days, so if his lordship decides that he wants to take a trip, I'll be ready."

Kasami nodded. "I will tell him." That was something, at least. Though she doubted Shin would take advantage of the offer. He had too much invested in the idea of himself as a problem-solver to just abandon it so callously.

"Good." Lun grunted and clapped Sanki on the shoulder. "Don't let the Crane talk you into anything stupid, old man," she said, and then was gone, out the back. Kasami watched her go and frowned.

"Infuriating woman."

"But loyal," Sanki said. "We're all loyal to him, no less than you." He indicated the door. "Shall we go?"

Kasami grunted and led the way. But as she slid open the door, her instincts screamed a warning and she paused, one arm braced across Sanki's chest, keeping him back from the entrance. "Wait," she said softly. She tensed slightly, waiting for – what? An arrow? But none came, thankfully. Still, she felt something.

"What is it?" Sanki muttered.

"Something… I don't know. Wait here." Kasami pushed him back and carefully stepped out into the alley, her hand resting on the hilt of her sword. She took her surroundings in at a glance, ignoring the odor and the rain, focusing on the buildings and darkened corners. What was it? What had she sensed?

A splash, from down the street. As of someone moving away very swiftly. Lun? Something told her no. Why would the captain seek to hide her presence? Then, faintly, the sound of bamboo, tapping against wood and stone, as if whoever it was, was using… a cane? There was an unpleasant familiarity to it, though she couldn't say why.

She raced after the sound and slid out of the alley, eyes sweeping the street. People moved in all directions, and the hum of their voices pushed against the falling rain. A few looked at her, and others gave her a wide berth, clearly startled by her sudden appearance.

Slowly, she relaxed. Whoever had been spying on Sanki's place was gone, vanished into the flow of people. Stifling a curse, she turned and gestured for Sanki to join her.

"Paranoid?" Sanki asked, unfurling a much-patched and colorless umbrella.

"No," Kasami said stiffly. She took her hand away from her sword.

"Let's go. Lord Shin is waiting."

CHAPTER FIVE
Kitsuki Ko

Shin waited impatiently on the balcony of Saibanshoki's receiving room, his eyes fixed on the river. It was hard to tell one vessel from another given the rain, but he maintained his vigil, hoping to spot Kasami as she arrived. His fan creaked in his hands as he squeezed it behind his back nervously. Aoto was prowling around somewhere downstairs, conferring with his lackeys, likely hoping to find some pretext to arrest him, imperial decree or no. But he wasn't the one who worried Shin. No, that privilege was saved for Kitsuki Ko.

He closed his eyes and tried to center himself. It wasn't easy, but he felt his racing pulse begin to slow as he forced himself to take deep, steadying breaths. He heard someone join him on the balcony and cracked an eye. Tonbo Kuma stood a small distance away, hands folded, expression serene. "You look as if you're afraid to leave," they said.

"Merely cautious, I assure you," Shin said.

"Yes." Kuma studied him with a measured gaze. "You know her, then."

Shin hesitated. "I… did, yes. Once upon a time."

"Ah. Was the encounter… unsatisfactory?"

"I'm sure she would say so," Shin said. He swept his folded fan along the wooden rail of the balcony, sending a spray of water out across the river. "We were… betrothed. Only for a short time, but there was… anger, on both sides. Afterwards." That was putting it mildly. Ko wasn't the sort to lose her temper, but he'd always been good at reading her face.

Even now, he shied away from thinking about it in any great detail. They'd enjoyed one another's company, and then – not. Things had changed. They had changed. And now they were here. "I have you to thank for her presence," he said.

Kuma smiled enigmatically. Then, they did everything enigmatically. "She was close to hand, investigating a murder just upriver in Three Fathom Village. One of the local merchants apparently drowned his wife for the crime of being older than himself and wealthy. He thought to trade her for a younger woman and an inheritance."

"How foolish of him. I trust she identified the malefactor post haste."

Kuma nodded. "Far more quickly than the local authorities anticipated. Hence her quick arrival, at my request. I knew that she was near, and so reached out."

Shin hesitated. It was difficult to read Kuma at the best of times. The priest kept their thoughts close to their heart. They gestured, and the falling rain seemed to twirl and spin like fireworks. Shin felt his hackles stiffen at the sight. Kuma, like many priests, had some degree of inexplicable authority over the natural elements. Peasants called it magic; priests referred to it as a discipline. Shin tried not to think about it at all.

"Why?" he asked.

Kuma glanced at him. "Why what?"

"Why help me? Last our paths crossed, we didn't exactly part as friends." That was an understatement, Shin knew. Kuma had very nearly killed him, during the Poison Rice Affair. Politics was a vicious game, especially in a city like this.

"Didn't we?" Kuma smiled gently. "Perhaps I simply do not like seeing an innocent person accused of a crime they did not commit."

"Well, I'm glad to hear that there's at least one person who doesn't believe me capable of murder." Shin took a deep breath. "When is Ko – Investigator Ko – to arrive?"

"She should be arriving any time this afternoon, depending on the weather. Possibly sooner." Kuma frowned. "Why do you ask?"

"I want to see the body, if I can," Shin said. "Before she arrives, preferably." Once Ko arrived, he'd be working at a disadvantage.

Kuma frowned. "That might be difficult. Investigator Ko has already claimed all the evidence for her own. The Kaeru have been requested to keep everyone away from it until she arrives."

"She works quickly," Shin said, with grudging admiration. It looked as if Ko was following traditional protocol, just as he'd feared. "What did Aoto have to say about that?"

"He was not best pleased."

"No. Good. The longer we keep them at each other's throats, the better."

Kuma raised an eyebrow. "Surely he knows better than to interfere?"

Shin smiled and shook his head. "He does – but whether he will heed that bit of common sense is up for debate. Aoto is used to doing as he sees fit. And Ko, well… she is not one to be intimidated by a Crane fluffing his feathers, even if they are made of iron."

"You speak from experience," Kuma said.

"Often painful," Shin replied. He paused, sighting a boat docking below. Kasami and a hunched, familiar figure – Sanki. "Ah, excellent! I'll take that look at the body now, if I might, once I've retrieved my bodyguard and my private physician." He turned and headed for the doors without waiting for a reply. Kuma followed more sedately.

An assortment of steps and landings wound down the trunk of the great willow tree, providing access to the docks within the roots. Shin took the steps two at a time, moving with more speed than grace. He wanted to be down to greet Kasami before Aoto noticed her arrival. While Kasami had the utmost respect for clan hierarchy, she also had a Hiramori's devotion to following her master's orders. If Aoto tried to stop her, he'd regret it. And while a part of Shin wanted to see that, it would lead to unnecessary complications.

When he reached the docks, Shin hustled toward the newly arrived boat. Kuma easily kept pace with him, though the priest didn't seem to be hurrying at all. Flowing like water, maybe, but not hurrying. Kasami was just stepping onto the dock when Shin reached her. "Excellent timing," he called out, greeting Sanki with a nod. The old physician grunted in reply as Kasami helped him out of the boat. "We must hurry. There's an investigator on the way and we must…"

Shin's next words died in his throat as he spied another boat arriving, from upriver. It was larger than the usual skiffs that carried people from one side of the river to the other – a proper river vessel. Bells rang as a gangplank extended from the side and thumped against the dock. Crew shouted in greeting to the dockworkers and Kaeru guards, as passengers began to disembark. Including a familiar figure, to Shin at least.

"Oh no," he murmured. His heart fell as if it were sliding into his stomach. "Too late."

"What is it?" Kasami asked curiously.

Shin didn't reply as Kuma swept forward to greet the new arrival. "Lady Ko, you have arrived with all due speed," they said, in greeting. Kitsuki Ko bowed low to the Dragonfly representative. She was much as Shin remembered – a bit older, perhaps, but then so was he.

Kitsuki Ko was not a tall woman, but she had a certain presence to her; a stoicism that lent her an aura of strength. She wore drab robes, marked with the Kitsuki sigil – a dragon encircling a lightning bolt – and bore no obvious weapon, other than a fan. Her round features were not conventionally attractive, yet it was hard not to give her a second, and a third, look. There was something about her eyes, Shin thought. Her eyes were too alert, too active. They saw everything, drew it all in like deep pools, but let nothing out.

"I am honored by your request, Lord Kuma," she said as she straightened. "I expect this shall prove to be a most – oh." Her eyes narrowed as she caught sight of Shin. A shadow passed across her face and then her expression became masklike. "Shin," she said, in a flat tone. "I was not aware you would be here to greet me."

"Ko," Shin said, as he stepped forward, albeit reluctantly. "Pleasant trip?"

"Lady Ko," she corrected, slapping her fan into her palm. Shin winced.

"Ah. Still angry, then?"

Another slap of the fan. "No. Why would I be angry?"

Shin hesitated. Her words were a trap, he was certain of it. But how to avoid it? He decided the direct approach was best.

"Many reasons. I'm told I can be quite troublesome." He smiled as he said it, but she didn't appear to notice. Her expression did not so much as waver. Then, she'd always had the most inhuman composure. When they'd first met, he'd had to go to ridiculous lengths to get her to even crack a smile – a challenge he'd enjoyed, at the time. Somehow, he doubted she'd be smiling much in the here and now.

"You are that, yes. I am told that the Daidoji are quite unhappy with you." She tilted her head toward Kuma, who looked back and forth between them somewhat awkwardly. Even the priest's imperturbable façade had its limits. "Some things do not change, I see."

Shin forced a chuckle. "Yes, well, I live to disappoint. I take it you are to investigate Lord Kenzō's untimely demise?" An obvious question, with an obvious answer. But words were like blades – put them between you and your opponent, and you bought yourself time to think. And he needed as much of that as he could manage.

"I am to render judgement, based on the facts of the matter – nothing more," she said primly. But there was a glint in her eye that he recognized. She was enjoying this, whether she admitted it to herself or not. That might be useful. "If that should happen to convict you, well, it simply cannot be helped."

"As coolly calculating as ever," Shin said, with mild venom. Nonetheless, it stung, as he'd meant it to. Suddenly, it was many years ago, and they were much younger and things had soured; words were exchanged. Her eyes narrowed in annoyance, and he wondered if she were remembering those long-gone days as well.

"What is that supposed to mean?"

"Never let emotion cloud the facts, yes?" Shin said, repeating something she'd often told him. Past her, he saw Aoto and several of his lackeys moving across the dock. They'd spotted Shin and the others, and were hurrying toward them. "Never let context interfere with the story the facts are telling." He snapped open his own fan and gave it a flutter. "You always did think of facts as the sole arbiter of your conclusions."

"Facts are undeniable. Immovable. They cannot be gainsaid."

"Facts are weightless, without context. Why is as important as how and what." It was an old argument, one they'd had often. Once, he'd have enjoyed it. Not now.

Ko tossed her head, a slight sneer on her face. "So you often said, but you'll forgive me if I do not take your opinions on this particular matter into account." She fixed him with a steely look. "The evidence thus far seems decidedly not in your favor."

"And yet context might–" he began.

Ko snapped her fan open. "It won't."

"It might," Shin insisted.

"It will not," she countered firmly. His heart sank at the look on her face. He knew that expression well. Despite all of her training, Ko had already made up her mind. She wanted him to be guilty, and so he was. But she would dutifully gather and categorize the evidence nonetheless. That would take her some time, at least. Especially if he could confuse the trail somewhat.

"Yes, well, we shall see." Shin cleared his throat and then raised his fan, signaling Aoto, who looked startled by the gesture. "Oh cousin, yoo-hoo… have you met Investigator Ko?" Ko frowned, but Aoto hurried toward them before she could respond.

"What are you yammering about?" Aoto demanded.

"Why, I just thought you'd like to meet the person who's going to be doing your job for you. She's very clever, you know." Shin stepped aside, leaving Aoto with a clear path to Ko. She took an uncertain step back as the Crane glowered at her.

"We need no help from a Kitsuki," Aoto growled.

"No? Lord Tetsua seems to disagree. Isn't that so, Lord Kuma?" Shin gestured for Kuma to interject. The priest raised an eyebrow, but nodded, going along with the ploy. Aoto flushed and made to relitigate his unhappiness with Tetsua's decree. Ko, blindsided by this, could do nothing save endure Aoto's brewing tirade. Shin made a surreptitious gesture to Kasami, and they and Sanki left the others to their argument. Kuma would keep Ko and Aoto from killing each other, and hopefully distract them long enough for Sanki to complete his examination.

"That was interesting," Kasami said, as they hurried away from the confrontation. Shin's hope was that by the time anyone noticed that they were gone, they'd already be with the body. "Someone was watching Sanki's place," she added, in a low tone.

"Did you get a look at them?" Shin asked softly.

Kasami shook her head. "Whoever it was, they were quick. As soon as they saw me, they took off." She seemed annoyed by the admission.

"Yes, well, you are very intimidating." Shin frowned. It could be unconnected. But he feared they weren't that lucky. Something was going on, but he couldn't say what just yet. He could feel it, like the headache pressing against the underside of his temples. As if someone or something were stalking him, just out of sight.

"Regardless, that's a problem for later. Right now, we have a dead man to examine."

CHAPTER SIX
Remains

Junichi Kenzō's mortal remains had been placed in a special chamber deep within the roots of Saibanshoki. The chamber was rectangular and made from smooth, dark stone, brought at no small expense from the Anou stone quarries in the foothills of the Seikitsu Mountains. The room was cool, swaddled by the river, but surprisingly dry and utterly lacking in the humidity that crept through the rest of the city.

The chamber might once have had a different purpose, but it now served as a place for the dead, or at least those whose deaths came with questions. Wooden biers lined the walls, with buckets and cloth-piles beneath them. Shrouded forms occupied several of the biers. Covered lanterns hung from the ceiling, casting an unpleasantly eerie reddish glow over the room and its contents. As Shin and the others entered, Kasami took up her post next to the door. Despite being responsible for her share of dead bodies, she had a rather traditional outlook when it came to the dead.

Shin shivered slightly as the chill of the stones rose up through his sandals and into his legs. Beside him, Sanki shifted his worn-out medical satchel beneath his arm and rubbed his skinny hands together. "It's always as cold as a frog's backside down here," the old man muttered.

"How do you know?" Shin asked absently. Sanki looked at him.

"What?"

"How do you know how cold a frog's backside is?"

Sanki grunted and changed the subject. "Which one?" he asked loudly. Sanki had seen too many bodies to have any reverence for the dead. Nor was this the first time he'd visited this particular part of Saibanshoki alongside Shin.

Shin gestured to the nearest bier with his fan. He recognized Kenzō's sandals and robe, sitting folded neatly next to the body. If they'd timed things right, they would have at least a few minutes. Hopefully that would be enough for Sanki to make a thorough examination. If not – well. He'd do what he could, with what he had.

"I heard the Kaeru brought in another investigator – a proper one," Sanki said, conversationally, as he pulled back the shroud and studied Kenzō's slack features with a critical eye. Shin studied them as well, but less dispassionately. "Was that her out on the docks? Good looking woman. Strong face."

"Yes. Well, a second opinion is always helpful," Shin murmured. Ko was a seasoned Kitsuki investigator. He'd kept abreast of her career with some interest. She was as dogged as they came, and had the sort of analytical mind that the Kitsuki favored. But she'd never had the greatest imagination. She would follow the evidence wherever it led, and never ask why the path took her in that particular direction.

He shook his head and turned his attentions back to the dead man. The auditor's body had been cleansed and arranged on the bier by Kaeru servants, prepared for whatever fate awaited it. Shin wondered whether they would transport the dead man home, or simply dispose of the body here. He knew that the Junichi had their own funerary customs, though not the particulars of them.

It wasn't the first time he'd seen a body up close – far from it – nor was it the first time it belonged to someone he knew. But something about this time was different. Kenzō had not been a friend, or even an acquaintance, but nonetheless, in an odd way he'd been family. Or at least the representative of such. While Kenzō had not come out and said it, Shin knew the auditor had been sent by his grandfather.

As to why, he still wasn't certain. Ostensibly, Kenzō's job had been to root out any financial irregularities on Shin's part, but he'd also been clear that he'd come to save Shin's life… by seeing him safely married off. Shin wondered whether that was still the plan. Aoto certainly didn't seem to think so; then, Aoto had never been one to follow anyone else's plan.

In a way, Shin almost admired him. Aoto was, in many ways, the perfect Daidoji: utterly loyal to his family and the clan, brave, ruthless, and traditional to a fault. Aoto was everything he wasn't. Perhaps that was why they'd fallen out.

Sanki whistled softly and Shin glanced at him. "You found something?"

The old man had lifted Kenzō's head slightly and was feeling around the base of his skull. "We need to turn the body," he said. Shin's skin crawled at the thought.

"Are you certain that's absolutely necessary?"

"Do you want me to make an examination or not?" Sanki growled, fixing him with a beady stare. The old man had learned medicine in the military camps of the Lion, sawing off shattered limbs and sewing up spurting wounds. The social strictures against touching the dead held little sway with him. He saw Shin's expression and sighed. "Fine. Get his shoulder, we'll just pull him up so I can get a better look – is that suitable, your lordship?"

"Just make it quick," Shin said, ignoring Sanki's rudeness. The doctor was irascible and unconcerned with social niceties, but he was good at his job. Gingerly, hands wrapped in his sleeves, he hauled up on Kenzō's shoulder, tilting the body toward him. It felt at once stiff and boneless, and he was unable to repress a shudder.

Sanki had unrolled his satchel on a nearby empty bier and retrieved several metal tools. With them, he probed something on the back of the corpse's head. "There's a clean perforation at the base of skull – looks like someone stabbed him with something long and thin… steel, obviously."

"Why obviously?" Shin asked, through gritted teeth.

"No splinters or chips left in the wound. Whatever went in, did so without leaving anything behind. So, steel."

"A knife?"

"Wound's too narrow. More like a… needle, say. Or a woman's hairpin."

Shin frowned. "Could a hairpin do that sort of damage?"

"I said like a hairpin, not that it was a hairpin," Sanki grumbled. He probed the wound with his tools. "It was a single thrust… smooth and clean. Angled to kill."

"The murderer was shorter than the victim, then?"

"Or crouching," Sanki said. He sucked on his teeth in an unpleasant fashion. "Do you want my opinion?"

"That is why I snuck you in here," Shin said, in some exasperation.

"Whoever did it knew what they were doing. This wasn't

some accident or spur-of-the-moment killing. This was planned and executed by a professional."

"An assassin?"

"Maybe. Not for me to say," Sanki said. "But whoever it was didn't have to bother."

Shin blinked. "What do you mean?"

"Lay him back down," Sanki said. "Look at this." He directed Shin's attentions to Kenzō's hands. "Discoloration in his fingers. Did he have problems with his circulation?"

"Not that I was aware of," Shin said, peering down at the dead man's hands. His previous revulsion was forgotten, washed away in a tide of curiosity. The discoloration was faint, but there. He'd taken it for the early stages of decomposition. "It looks like bruising."

"He was suffocating," Sanki said flatly. "I've seen this before. A type of poisoning that comes from consuming bad soybeans or fish or wheat. It starts in the extremities, and then spreads. Death usually occurs in a few hours."

"Soybeans," Shin murmured. Kenzō had been found in Odoma's shoyu brewery – there would have been dozens of barrels of fermenting soybeans close to hand. "Accidental?" He could imagine any number of ways that something unpleasant might have wound up in Kenzō's stomach. But so close to his demise? Surely it couldn't have been a coincidence.

"Possibly," Sanki allowed. Then, "But maybe not. Certain teas… I could tell you more if I could open him up. See the condition of his insides."

"You will not," Kitsuki Ko said, sharply, from the doorway. "You should not even be here, let alone touching the body." She was flanked by Aoto and an apologetic looking Azuma. Aoto shoved past her.

"Trying to cover up evidence of your crimes, eh?" he said. He was smiling as he said it, as if he'd caught Shin red-handed. But the expression faded as Kasami smoothly interposed herself. She said nothing, and didn't so much as gesture to her sword, but her intentions were plain. Aoto stopped and grimaced.

"If you mean trying to prove my innocence, then yes," Shin said, stepping between Aoto and Kasami. Sanki was quickly packing up his tools, his expression sour. Aoto glanced at the old doctor, and then dismissed him immediately, his focus on Shin.

"You have never been innocent a day in your life," Aoto said.

Shin smiled and tapped Aoto in the chest with his fan. "Flatterer."

Aoto swatted the fan aside. "I am taking you into custody."

Azuma coughed discreetly. Aoto glanced at him in annoyance. Azuma straightened. "Governor Tetsua did say that Lord Shin could examine the body before he departed." A bending of the truth, but Shin had no intention of questioning it. Between Azuma and Kuma, he had some allies as yet.

"Did he also say that Lord Shin could bring along an accomplice?" Aoto demanded, indicating Sanki. "Who are you, old man?"

"My private physician," Shin said smoothly. "I wished for him to make a professional examination of the deceased. To determine cause of death."

"This? This is your doctor?" Aoto asked, incredulous. He looked Sanki up and down, as if expecting him to crumble and blow away at any moment. "He must be a century old!"

"My hands are still steady," Sanki said, giving Aoto a glare. "What about yours?"

Aoto frowned and made to reply when Ko said, "I would like a copy of his findings, if I might have them. I will compare them to my own conclusions, as well as those of the Kaeru physicians." She had moved to the body, and her eyes flicked across its hands. Shin wondered if she'd noticed the darkening in the extremities as well.

"What is there to examine?" Aoto growled. "He was murdered. By Shin."

"That is yet to be determined," Azuma said. Ko nodded.

"Lord Azuma is right. While Lord Shin undoubtedly had motive, the evidence is inconclusive. Answers will be found, but I must have time."

"Perhaps if you had some help," Shin began, annoyed by her little crack about motive. He didn't really want to work with Ko, but if he could convince her of his innocence, it would not be an entirely wasted effort.

"She has help – me," Aoto said. "I have already offered Lady Ko the aid of my auditors in this matter, and she has graciously accepted." He gave Shin a smug smile. "So, you see, you are surplus to requirements... as well as being a suspect." He glanced at Ko, as if expecting her support but to his chagrin she didn't seem to be paying attention to them at all.

Shin cleared his throat. "What I meant to say was that I am something of an investigator myself and–"

"I am aware of your latest... hobby, Shin," Ko said, still looking down at the body.

"I would hardly call it a hobby," Shin protested. "I have successfully concluded a number of private investigations – the Cedar Barrel Killings, the Poison Rice Affair, that nasty business down under the docks two months ago..."

Ko did not rise to the bait. "You fancy yourself an investigator without the responsibility. But that means you are no investigator at all."

Stung, Shin hid his frown behind his fan. "You are welcome to your opinion, I am sure." He glanced at Azuma, and the other man looked away. "Though I might be an amateur by your lights, I assure you that I am not merely play-acting." More softly, he added, "I did not forget your lessons, Ko."

"Lady Ko," she said, not looking at him. Her tone was mild, but he sensed the anger behind the imperturbable front. "And if you had actually listened, you would know better than to touch the body."

"Given that it had been moved and cleansed, I saw no reason not to," Shin protested.

"Something might have been missed," Ko said. "In fact, I suspect something was. But to learn what, I must have privacy." She fluttered her fan without turning. "See them out, if you would, Lord Azuma."

"But–" Shin began.

"Wait–" Aoto started.

Azuma indicated the door. Shin noted that Sanki was already gone. The old man was no fool. Aoto looked as if he wanted to protest, but Azuma's expression made him think better of it. Shin was the last to leave. He paused and looked back at Ko, bent over the body, her expression one of intent concentration.

Then he was out in the corridor, and Aoto was rounding on him. "You will not interfere in this, Shin. I may have to put up with this playacting from her, but we both know how this affair ends. Show some dignity and cease your attempts to wriggle free."

Shin matched his cousin's glare, waving Kasami back as he did so. "Why is it that for men like you, dignity is always equated with surrender?"

"If you try to interfere again, I will arrest you – governor or no," Aoto said, glancing at Azuma. The latter frowned, but said nothing. Shin understood. Tetsua had, in some ways, exceeded his authority by allowing an outside investigator to take over. Aoto would accept it, but only until such time as he decided that the Crane's interests could be best served otherwise.

"I wouldn't dream of it," Shin said, with forced mildness. It was an effort to stay calm. Tension thrummed through him, demanding an outlet. But not here. Not yet. "In fact, I'll just go home, shall I?" He pushed past Aoto and gestured for Kasami and Sanki to follow him.

"Where I can await the inevitable like a good Daidoji."

CHAPTER SEVEN
Ito

It was still raining when they arrived home.

Shin and Kasami had parted ways with Sanki at the Unicorn docks, paying the doctor well for his services. Kasami had remained silent throughout the walk home, her expression flat and stiff. Shin wondered what she was thinking, but knew better than to ask. She would no doubt share her thoughts at the most inopportune time. Until then, all he could attempt to do was gather his own and come up with a strategy.

He felt at odds with himself; too much was happening, too quickly. First Aoto, then Ko… he was under siege, and he hadn't even realized that war had been declared. He pushed the morose thought aside when he spied Kitano waiting for them in the front garden. At least some things could be counted on, Shin reflected.

The former gambler turned manservant looked nervous as he greeted them. He scratched at his cheek with his prosthetic finger – a gift from Shin, to make up for the one Kasami had taken from him, on their first meeting. "I found Ito, master," he said, falling into step behind Shin. "He's waiting in the reception room. I've had Niko brew some tea as well, and gather some willow bark." He glanced at Kasami, but she ignored him. Shin nodded gratefully.

"Thank you, Kitano. I have another errand for you, if you're willing." Despite his words, his tone ensured that Kitano knew it wasn't a request. "I need you to go and find the shoyu merchant, Odoma. Don't let him see you, but keep an eye on him. I want to know when and if he goes back to the brewery. I need to speak with him and that will be the best time."

Kitano hesitated. "Are you … certain about that, master? Is that really the – well – ideal thing to do, under the circumstances?"

"Are you arguing with Lord Shin?" Kasami asked, in a low tone.

"No, no! Not arguing, per se … more clarifying," Kitano said quickly. He gave Shin an apologetic look and bowed his head. "It's just … maybe we could do something else."

Shin stopped, and Kitano nearly collided with him. "Like what?" Shin asked, not looking at his manservant. He wasn't surprised that Kitano was aware of what was going on. Servants had access to different channels of information; Kitano often knew things well before Shin himself. It was one of the reasons Shin tried to remain on good terms with his own subordinates. "Flee?"

"We could call it a holiday," Kitano said, in a small voice.

Shin smiled and shook his head. "I appreciate the thought, Kitano, but that would only give my foes the excuse they need to escalate matters. No – better to treat this as we would any other problem that has come to my attention. As a mystery to be solved, rather than the end of the world." He paused. "But if you wish to leave my employ before matters … come to a head, I will understand."

Kitano blinked, startled by the offer. "No, master," he said, bowing his head. Kasami grunted in approval. Shin allowed himself a small smile. Kitano had made great strides since their first, inauspicious meeting. The former gambler had become something of a dogged investigator in his own right, taking Shin's tutelage to heart. He had become Shin's left hand, as Kasami was his right.

"Oh good, because honestly I don't know what I'd do without you," Shin admitted. Kitano straightened, looking pleased. "Can I count on you to keep an eye on Odoma, then? I have a feeling he's tied up in all of this somehow." Given what Lun and Sanki had said to Kasami, as well as Shin's own history with the man, Odoma was the obvious suspect. He had the most to gain by Shin's arrest. Even so, something about it seemed odd. But until he knew more, he wanted to have eyes on Odoma.

"I will do my best, my lord," Kitano said, and bowed low. He slipped away as Shin started up the steps. Behind him, Kasami cleared her throat. Shin paused and turned.

"You have doubts as well?"

"You told Lord Aoto you wouldn't interfere."

"I'm not interfering with the investigation into Kenzō's death. Rather, I am simply conducting a… parallel investigation, into those matters that the esteemed Investigator Ko will no doubt deem unimportant."

"You're interfering," Kasami said bluntly.

Shin threw up his hands in a gesture of annoyance. "And so? Do I not have the right to defend myself?"

"There is a difference between defense and offense, which you would know if you practiced more," Kasami said, raising her voice slightly. "If you – if we – are caught, they will have all the excuse they need to arrest you."

"Then we had best not get caught, eh?" Shin said. He turned away before she could respond and continued up the steps. Her words stung, but he understood her concern. The sad fact was, there was no good way to handle this sort of situation. Sitting and waiting was anathema to him. But she was right – interfering only increased the likelihood that he'd be arrested. He was caught fast in a trap, and the more he struggled, the worse its grip became. Yet what could he do but struggle?

He had to investigate because only he had his best interests at heart. More, he had to do so quickly, else he would be found guilty before he knew it. Enemies were all around him; he thought of traps again and wondered at the appropriateness of the word.

He tried to push his worries to one side as he stepped into the receiving room. It was sumptuously decorated in hues of blue and white. Scrolls depicting the great triumphs of the Crane hung against the far wall, while more sedate decorations illustrating the natural beauty of the Crane lands clung to the other walls. Lanterns burned in the corners, throwing back the gloom of the rainy day.

The paper merchant, Ito, was waiting in the center of the room, even as Kitano had said. He was one of three vassal merchants that Shin was obliged to oversee in his duties as trade representative for the Crane. The other two were utter non-entities as far as Shin was concerned; dull-witted and lacking in even the smallest entertainment value.

Ito was different, however. He was a short man, stout and as bald as an egg. His robes were well-made but utterly lacking in ostentation. Ito preferred to keep to the background, where possible. He maintained a profitable paper import-export business, and provided materials necessary for the keeping of toll and cargo records. An important cog in the machinery of trade, if not a flashy one.

But it was not just his vast knowledge of the paper trade that had drawn him to Shin's attention. Instead, it was Ito's other predilection: the gathering of information. Mostly on behalf of the Crane, but some on behalf of Shin himself. Ito, simply put, was a spy and a very competent one at that.

He abased himself as Shin greeted him, and Kasami took her usual seat near the door. "My lord, I can but deliver my most exceeding sympathies for your recent loss. Lord Kenzō was a fine example of an auditor…" He paused as he took in Shin's expression. "Or perhaps congratulations are in order, instead?"

Shin sighed. "No, Master Ito. This is a sad thing – and an inconvenient one. Thank you for coming, though. I know you must be busy."

"Never too busy to help, my lord. I am at your service, as always." Ito situated himself into a more comfortable position as Shin sat opposite him. He paused. "Though I am at something of a loss as to what sort of help I can provide in this instance."

"I wish to know what Kenzō was up to when he met his end," Shin said. "Since he was ostensibly here to go over my records, I want to make certain that there are no discrepancies that could come back to haunt us."

"Surely he found nothing, or so I was given to understand," Ito said hesitantly.

"So he said, but – something got him killed."

"Then it was murder," Ito said softly.

Shin nodded slowly and touched the back of his head. "A single blow to the base of the skull. Quick and efficient."

"The work of an assassin?" Ito asked.

"Possibly. Either way, Master Odoma has been dining out on

the story of how he found the body and accused me of murder." He paused. "Is it possible that he might have … ?" He trailed off. Ito caught his meaning and sighed; he braced his hands on his knees.

"Killed Kenzō? Why would he?"

"That is what puzzles me. I certainly had no motive, but Odoma… well. Who can say, with him?" Shin paused. "Tell me, how much have you heard about it?"

Ito frowned. "Not so much as all that. The Kaeru are very good at keeping secrets and they've been bullying everyone into silence. The only one really speaking about it is Odoma, and given the rumors he's attempted to spread about you in the past, few of us in the merchants' association are inclined to give him credence." He hesitated. "But that won't last, my lord. Even the Kaeru cannot keep a lid on this for long."

"No. Which is why I feel confident in saying that time is of the essence. Anything you can tell me about the last time you spoke to Kenzō would be appreciated."

Ito gnawed his lip. "It wasn't recently, I can tell you that. More than a week ago, in fact. He wanted to look at some of my financial records, which I dutifully supplied him."

"Which records were these?"

Ito hesitated. "Just some of my business dealings with other merchants in the city. A dealer in dyes, and an importer of leather goods, among others. Nothing untoward."

Shin retrieved his fan and snapped it open. "Did he say why?"

Ito shook his head. "Not to me. You told me to cooperate with him, so I did."

"Have you spoken with any of those merchants since?" Ito hesitated. Shin made an impatient gesture. "Out with it, Ito. What is it?"

"Regrettably they are no longer with us."

Shin paused. "Dead? All of them?"

"The city is dangerous and not all of us can afford bodyguards. One was caught in a house fire. Another was killed by robbers. A third went missing on the river." Ito gave a fatalistic shrug. "Things happen."

Shin slapped his fan into his palm. "Yes, they do… but one must question the timing." Dead merchants? What did that mean, if anything? What had Kenzō stumbled onto? Again, his senses screamed "trap." But a trap for whom? Kenzō or himself – or even some third party? "It all seems very suspect, don't you agree?"

Ito tapped his chin with a finger. "Have you considered that he might simply have been in the wrong place at the wrong time?"

Shin had, but it didn't seem to fit. "But why would that place be Odoma's brewery?"

Ito shrugged. "It seems to me, my lord, that you must put that particular question to Odoma himself."

"I intend to at the soonest available opportunity," Shin assured him. "But for now, I would like to know if there is anything Kenzō might have said that lingers in your memory. A statement, an intimation… even an offhand comment. Something that might explain why he wanted to talk to Odoma of all people."

Ito sat back, expression considering. "It is all but certain that Odoma is – was – the inciting factor in his investigation. His complaints about the purchase of the Foxfire Theater were likely enough to give the Daidoji Trading Council cause to open an investigation into your finances. Perhaps Kenzō went back to clarify something in that earlier complaint."

"Due diligence, you mean?"

"If you like. I spent little time with him, but he – Kenzō – struck me as a thorough individual. If he'd found some… discrepancy, say, he might well go back to ask the obvious questions, even if the matter was otherwise settled. To satisfy his own curiosity, if nothing else." Ito scratched his chin. "It could be that that discrepancy is what killed him. Or perhaps he was killed to prevent him from telling you about it."

"But why? What would be the point?"

Ito shrugged. "Again, it depends on what it was that he learned. You must consider that it might not have anything to do with you at all. Kenzō might simply have stumbled across something that proved inimical to his health."

"Illicit doings by Odoma, you mean."

Ito inclined his head. "He has been known to… engage in certain activities."

Shin glanced at Kasami. She'd filled him in on her conversation with Sanki and Lun, regarding Odoma's reputation as a criminal. "So I understand. I must ask why you didn't see fit to tell me that before I bought the theater from him."

Ito gave a somewhat sheepish smile. "I felt you might hesitate to make such an investment if you knew of Odoma's history. And it is history; whatever he once was, Odoma is a legitimate businessman. Not a very good one, but a legitimate one."

"So you don't believe him capable of killing someone?"

Ito shook his head. "Capable – yes, certainly. Willing to endanger himself? No. Not unless there was good reason for it."

Shin sighed and sat back. "I suppose that would be too simple. Nor, I suspect, will it satisfy my cousin and his auditors, who are even now champing at the bit to take me into custody."

"More auditors?" Ito seemed startled. "So quickly?"

"They were already coming for me," Shin said absently. "But Kenzō's death has put a new wrinkle into the fabric. It's not just my freedom on the line now – but my very life." He leaned forward. "I fear that if I am to have any hope of seeing out my natural span, we must solve Lord Kenzō's murder – and bring the true killer to justice."

CHAPTER EIGHT
Investigator

Kitsuki Ko stood in the center of the chambers she'd been given in Saibanshoki, the Kaeru reports on the crime scattered on the floor about her in a rough circle. It was a pleasure to have such reports available. The Kaeru were thorough; they had made sketches, noted the dimensions of the scene as well as catalogued everything in the brewery, right down to what the victim had been carrying on his person.

"Junichi Kenzō, auditor for the Daidoji Trading Council," she murmured, cementing the information into her mind. One of her talents was to remember anything she heard or saw with almost perfect recall. "Victim was carrying an impressive array of weaponry, most of it of an illicit nature – none of it apparently useful." Kenzō's death was ostensibly due to a single thrust to the base of the skull with something sharp; not a knife, but something long and thin, like a hairpin. Not the weapon of a thief or a common hired murderer, in her opinion. An assassin, then.

She knew of half a dozen other murders committed in such a fashion, scattered across the empire. None of them connected.

Most murders were, in her opinion, crimes of passion and of opportunity. Assassinations were rare, but did occur. But why would someone go to the trouble of assassinating a man like Kenzō?

Possible motives ran down the surface of her mind like rain. None of them stuck. She let them pool in the underside of her mind, for easy access later. She had learned early on that an investigator's mind should be full of nooks and crannies, into which information could spill and wait for when it was needed.

Her initial observations were slim – at the moment, she was simply building a picture of who the victim had been in her mind. It was obvious that Kenzō had trusted, or at least known, his killer. She could not imagine him letting them get behind him otherwise. She flicked open her fan and gave it a flutter, stirring the muggy air.

It was hot here, especially given the season. There was snow in the mountains and the lowlands. But the rain seemed to collect in the skies here, as if it were part of the river. When she'd arrived, she'd had trouble telling where the river ended and the rain began. The noise, the smell… the humidity. It was oppressive. She plucked at her robes, uncomfortably aware of the sweat beading on her flesh. She wondered how anyone could stand it.

Outside, through the open window, she could hear the song of commerce, underneath the steady thrum of rain. Boats rode the river, their crews calling out to one another in jocular fashion, or in anger. Competition for berths on the docks was rife, even with the weather. She'd seen at least three fights break out, upon her arrival.

The City of the Rich Frog was an economic hub of the empire. Three clans claimed ownership and only the presence of an imperial representative kept them from each other's throats. The Crane, however, was not one of those clans. Their interest in the city was primarily related to the paper trade, rather than more lucrative imports or exports. A nothing assignment; unimportant. That was why they'd sent Shin here.

So why send an auditor? Obviously, Shin was suspected of malfeasance. But Kenzō had clearly found nothing otherwise Shin would have been arrested – so what was it? She pushed the thought aside. It was unimportant. She was here to investigate a murder, nothing more. She would stick to the facts, and leave the mystery for someone else to untangle.

She thought of Shin and felt a frown crease her features. Would he – could he – murder someone? Kill them, certainly. Shin was as lethal as any Daidoji, especially with his back to the wall. She knew that better than many.

"I wish to speak with you."

Ko looked up from the reports. Aoto stood in the doorway, looking annoyed. She wondered if that was his default expression. She'd only met a few Daidoji in her time, and besides Shin, they all seemed to regard smiling as some sort of breach of etiquette. "Speak," she said simply. "But be quick. I am not staying long." She still had to visit the scene of the crime before night fell. Azuma swore that his men were watching it, but she knew better than to assume it would remain untouched for long.

"You embarrassed me, earlier. I will not be treated like a servant and dismissed at your whim. Like it or not, we are allies in this."

"We are not. I am investigating a murder. I am not yet certain why you are here."

Aoto sniffed and entered without invitation. He gave the

room a brief inspection, and then his gaze fell upon the reports on the floor. "You appear to have dropped something."

"I did not drop them. They were very carefully placed." Ko turned back to the reports. "What do you actually want, my lord? Not to chide me, I think."

"You are rude."

"I am busy."

"One is not an excuse for the other."

Ko frowned. "My apologies. Not all of us learn to wield civility like a blade."

"A poor education, then." He looked around. "I am surprised. I would have thought you would have encamped yourself among your own kind, rather than in the imperial residence. A sign of favoritism, perhaps."

"No. Despite your earlier assumption, I am investigating jointly with the Kaeru, thus I must have access to them at all hours. If I am ensconced in the Dragonfly quarter, there will be inevitable delays. Here, I am at the heart of everything." She paused. "What do you mean, favoritism?"

"It seems to me that Lord Tetsua would prefer that Shin be found innocent."

Ko shrugged in annoyance. "Perhaps. If so, he has said nothing of it to me."

"Mmm." Aoto nudged one of the reports with his foot. "These are the Kaeru reports, from the scene of the crime?"

"Yes."

"We already know what happened. You saw the body, as did I."

"No. We merely have a theory. That is why I will be visiting the scene shortly. The evidence might tell a different story."

"That would be unfortunate," Aoto said. Ko glanced at him. In her opinion, there were two sorts of courtier – foolish and cunning. The foolish ones, like Shin, were only troublesome if you allowed them to be. The cunning ones, however, were always a problem. Aoto was a cunning one. Ambitious. He saw opportunity in this death. Given his earlier behavior, she could already tell he was going to be underfoot the entire time.

"The truth is never unfortunate," she said.

"Truth is as malleable as clay, under the right hands." Aoto said it as if it were a good thing. Ko disliked him intensely. The Kitsuki investigative method was still regarded as something untrustworthy by the majority of the clans. Despite the self-evident flaws in the traditional methods of criminal investigation, a more thorough inquiry was regarded as an inherently worthless expenditure of effort by all but a few far-sighted individuals.

"That is an opinion, certainly," she said, diplomatically. From the look on Aoto's face, however, she might as well have slapped him. His gaze hardened, and he deliberately stepped on the reports, hiding them from her sight.

"I do not think you understand me," he said firmly.

"I believe I do. You wish me to rule on this matter in your favor. You have a grudge against Shin, and you want to see him punished whether he is guilty or not." It was not uncommon for people to attempt to sway the judgement of an investigator, though it was unusual for it to be done so bluntly. Then, the Daidoji publicly disdained subtlety.

Aoto paused and then went to the window. His hands were clasped behind his back – calloused hands; the hands of a swordsman, or perhaps someone skilled in use of the yari. Aoto was a warrior first and a courtier second. "I am not the only one with a grudge," he said, finally. "I remember you. I remember your betrothal. It lasted all of – what? – a few weeks?"

"One month, seven days," Ko said.

"It must have felt like an eternity," Aoto said, sympathetically. She thought that he meant it as well. There was no ploy here, no condescension. He genuinely felt sorry for her. That annoyed her even more than his previous haughtiness.

"I was happy," she said. And she had been, though she'd known Shin had felt anything but. Even now, she was not certain whether his dissatisfaction had been with her – or himself. Aoto turned.

"Shin is like a sweet confection," he said. "The first taste is heaven... but eat too much, and your belly ties itself in knots." Was he speaking from experience? It was hard to say. Aoto and Shin were cousins, but that meant little. Cousin was a term with many definitions. Aoto continued, "He gets bored, you see. And when he gets bored, he does something stupid and selfish and self-destructive... and inevitably those around him pay the price. But I am not telling you anything you don't already know."

Ko said nothing. Aoto was correct: she did, in fact, know that. Her betrothal to Shin was a painful memory, but pleasurable as well. She had been surprised by it, at first, and then pleased. A good match, if not the best for either of them. All because of a chance meeting.

And then, it had all gone wrong. Somewhere along the way, the spark had gone out and then – Shin was gone. She had her theories, of course. Familial pressure was the obvious culprit, but perhaps Aoto was right, and Shin had simply become bored. For a time, she'd believed he'd only spent time with her in order to learn her investigative methods but that was ridiculous. He'd also wanted to sleep with her.

Aoto smiled sadly, taking her silence for assent. "He is

dangerous when left to his own devices. He takes risks, threatens stability – better for us all if he were kept on a shorter leash."

"Or executed," Ko said. Aoto looked away.

"I do not want him dead," he said, after several moments. "I want him tamed; humbled. I want him yoked to the wheel of duty as all of us are. You understand?"

"I do."

"Then you will do it?"

"I will not."

Aoto turned, expression incredulous. "Why not?"

"Because I must be impartial," she said. "Whatever my – our – feelings on the matter, justice must be delivered fairly or else it is not justice at all." She felt heat rise to her face as she spoke. "Shin is… an irritant. A gadfly, stinging horses to amuse himself. And if he committed murder, he will be punished. But if he did not, I will not say he did in order to soothe my injured pride. To even suggest it is reprehensible." She swallowed. "We are better than that, Lord Aoto. We are better than him."

Aoto stared at her for long moments. Then, "Speak for yourself, Lady Ko. I came here with one task, and I will see it done, whatever others might think of me." He strode past her, scattering the reports as he went. An act of petulance, or simply a heedless one, she could not say. She said nothing as he left, for she saw no use in it.

He was going to be trouble, she could tell.

Crane courtiers always were.

CHAPTER NINE
Brewery

The Red Gull was a teahouse of little repute and nothing Shin saw as he entered gave him any reason to reassess it. It sat on a wide street, amid others of its kind. Across the way, the shoyu brewery owned by Odoma loomed.

The latter was a large, squarish building and it occupied a good deal more space than Shin had first assumed. Barred windows overlooked the street and the doors were tightly sealed. It reminded him of a fortress, readying itself for a siege. Kaeru guards loitered near the doors, doing their best to stay out of the rain. At least Azuma was taking no chances that someone might interfere with the scene of the crime.

As Shin and Kasami entered the teahouse, the proprietor bowed and scraped and showed them to a back table, where Kitano was waiting, huddled over a pot of tea and some barley cakes. The rain made a staccato sound on the roof as Shin sat, and a young woman was crouched along the far wall, softly playing a shamisen, her head bowed. Kasami took up an unobtrusive position in the corner, where she could observe the other patrons. "Kitano, you look like a drowned rat."

"Thank you, my lord," Kitano said wryly.

Shin checked the teapot and winced. It was a house blend and smelled like the stuff one found beneath the docks. For the life of him, he couldn't say why Kitano liked this place. It certainly wasn't the tea. Maybe it was the barley cakes. He tasted one and immediately regretted it. His eyes strayed to the shamisen player, and he felt a sudden quiver of uneasiness, though he couldn't say why. "We should invest in an umbrella for you."

"I think I prefer the rain, my lord," Kitano said. He took a gulp of noxious tea. "Odoma is here, but he's not alone."

Shin nodded in satisfaction, forgetting all about the shamisen player. Kitano had sent a street urchin to bring word about Odoma's return. He'd left Ito with his ledgers and brought Kasami to speak with the soy merchant. He suspected Odoma was going to be difficult about it. "Bodyguards?"

"A few. I know most of them – of them, I should say. Haruko, Masa, Itachi…" Kitano paused. "Bad sorts, my lord. Gamblers and killers. Odoma's been splashing around a lot of money and there's a certain sort that sees that as blood in the water. Sharks, my lord, every one of them." Another pause. "There's something else…"

"Oh?"

"He's got a – a woman. Fancy. Lots of jewels. A courtesan." Kitano frowned. "She's new. Never seen her before. Out of town talent, got to be."

"Meaning?"

Kitano grimaced. "Courtesans, you have to understand, my lord. They're… territorial. They don't like new faces in their profession. And they gossip. But I haven't heard so much as a whisper about her."

Shin frowned. "And what does this imply to you?"

"That she's dangerous, my lord," Kitano said simply.

"In what way?" Shin implicitly trusted Kitano's opinion in regard to such matters. The gambler had an almost instinctive grasp of such things, likely honed by his years walking the crooked path. If he said a person was dangerous, they were.

Kitano shrugged. "Who knows, my lord. You pay me to observe, so I observed."

"Very well." Shin considered the time. Dusk was fast approaching. "We won't be long. Keep an eye on things after we leave. Report back tonight. Kasami…" Kasami rose without a word and they left Kitano to finish his tea.

Protected by his umbrella, Shin crossed the street, Kasami trailing in his wake. "This is a bad idea," she said.

Shin didn't turn. "So you keep saying. But I want to get a look at the scene of the crime, and speak with the witness."

"The witness who insists that you did it."

"Yes, well, we both know that's wrong. Odoma is playing some angle, and I intend to find out what it is."

"And if we are interrupted in the process?"

Shin shrugged. "We run."

"Run?"

"Very quickly."

Kasami grunted unhappily, but Shin ignored her. The Kaeru on guard duty had spotted them and were moving to intercept. "My lord, I'm afraid–" one began, but Shin cut him off with a smile and a gesture.

"Lord Azuma knows I am here," he said blithely. "He has given me permission to observe the scene." It wasn't strictly the truth, nor was it a lie. The guards looked at one another and then, as Shin had hoped, they stepped aside. Azuma's name carried weight. It was more than their pay was worth to risk angering him. Shin beamed genially at them and continued on, up the steps of the brewery.

At the door, he fluffed his umbrella, scattering raindrops. Kasami slid the door open for him, and Shin stepped inside. He'd been in breweries before, but this one was larger than most. The interior was practically cavernous, with a great deal of its space taken up by the immense brewing vats and the wooden platform that extended across their tops and acted as the brewery's second floor. Stacks of straw mats, for the fermentation process, lined the far walls. The air smelled thick and sweet, and Shin drew out his fan to keep from being overwhelmed.

"We're closed," someone growled. A lanky shape stepped out from among the vats, one hand resting on the hilt of a sword. He was dressed in threadbare robes, and he scratched an unshaven chin as he studied them. Kasami slid smoothly between Shin and the newcomer, but didn't touch her own blade. Instead, she kept her hands folded within her sleeves.

"I expect you are," Shin said. "And yet, I find myself here regardless. Quite the pickle, as they say."

"Who says?" a new voice called down, from atop the platform.

Shin looked up. "Someone, somewhere, I'm sure. Is that you, Master Odoma? Might I have a bit of your time?"

Odoma looked down at them from the edge of the second floor. He was a short man, but heavily built, who looked all the rounder for the thick, brocaded robes he wore. His round, bald head gleamed in the glow of the paper lanterns that hung from the support beams above. A woman, no doubt the one Kitano had mentioned, stood at his side. She was pretty, Shin thought, but in that too-precise way that removed all character from her face, as if she were a doll. "You shouldn't be here," the merchant said.

"Not the first time I've heard that," Shin said cheerfully. "May we come up?"

Odoma rubbed his nose. "If you must, though I don't have anything to say to you."

"That's a first," Shin said, as he climbed the flat, wooden steps that led to the space above the vats. Kasami followed, and the guard trailed her, though at a cautious distance. "Normally, you talk my ear off."

"Yes, well, hasn't done any good, has it?" Odoma said, as he crossed the platform to meet them. "What do you want?"

"To talk, nothing more. But we are being rude. Introduce me to your friend." Shin gestured to the woman with his fan. Odoma glanced at her and smiled.

"You like her?" He stroked the young woman's painted cheek with a knuckle. "Isuka is expensive but worth it. She's been my comfort in these long weeks since that actress of yours threw me over."

"Chika," Shin supplied. Odoma had had a brief fling with the actress, a member of the Three Flower Troupe to whom Shin acted as patron, but she'd had more sense than to link her fate to his permanently. Odoma frowned and nodded.

"That's the girl. Wicked tease. Abused my generosity and then withdrew her affections on a whim."

"Is that what you call it?" Shin murmured. He studied Odoma's new consort. She was lithe and graceful, to all intents and purposes a professional concubine. But there was something off about her… something in her flat gaze, he thought. It was like locking eyes with a shark. Worse, he could tell that she was studying him as well. Sizing him up, perhaps. Was she considering his potential as her next patron… or her next meal?

"How is the theater, by the way?" Odoma asked. He waved Isuka away, and she swayed toward the stairs without a backward glance. "Regretting it yet?"

Shin watched as Isuka descended the steps. "In some ways."

"I could take it off your hands, if you like. Given the trouble you're in, it might be a benefit to you. One less thing for the Cranes to pick over, eh?" Odoma smiled again. "Shouldn't have murdered that poor auditor, my lord. And to leave him here, no less. That's just not the proper way of doing business, you know."

Shin allowed himself a small smile. "You would know all about that, I expect."

Odoma's eyes narrowed. "Are you accusing me of something?"

"No. I was merely making an observation." Shin took in the interior of the brewery. "I'm told you recently had work done. New vats and all."

Odoma nodded. "The old wood was moldy. Unsightly."

"I'm also told mold is good for the taste." The timbers of a good soy brewery were often covered in a shroud of yeast and bacteria; that covering gave the brewery its own unique characteristics, including smell and taste.

Odoma snorted. "Nozomi tell you that? That old reprobate would say something that foolish." Nozomi was one of Odoma's rivals in the shoyu trade, and, like the theater troupe, another of Shin's recent investments. Nozomi was old, a traditionalist. His brewery was smaller, but his product was, in Shin's humble opinion, superior. Odoma's soy sauce tasted bland in comparison. But blandness had its place, especially when sold cheaply, thus undercutting rivals.

Odoma indicated one of the new cedar barrels. "These cost me, but they're worth it. The cedar will infuse the mix, and lend it some class."

"Class," Shin repeated. "Was your sauce lacking, then?"

Odoma sniffed. "Things can always be improved." He peered at Shin. "How much do you know about the process?"

"Not much."

"Nozomi didn't explain it, then?" Odoma smirked. "He used to talk about it incessantly, when I was younger. He and my uncle both." He gestured to a smaller vat. "That old bag of bones even taught me how to steam the beans, and mix in roasted wheat."

"And yet you seem determined to ruin his business." Nozomi had been all but reluctantly retired when Shin had made his investment.

"That's the game we play," Odoma said. "Nozomi is old, and he should yield ground to those of us with the strength to prosper." He gave Shin a stern look. "And he would have, too, if you hadn't stuck your nose in. That's twice now you've cost me money."

"That's the game we play," Shin replied.

Odoma snorted again. "So it is." He gestured to the vats. "I found him there, down below, but you probably already know that."

Shin fanned himself slowly. "I didn't, actually. Do me the courtesy of acknowledging that much in my presence, at least."

Odoma chuckled. "I don't believe you're due much courtesy at all, frankly."

"Why was Kenzō here? What did he want to talk to you about?"

"Who knows?" Odoma said, with a shrug.

"Presumably you. You were here, were you not?"

"I was. But I did not see Kenzō… not until he was… well…"

"I find that hard to believe." Again, Shin looked around. There were plenty of places to hide, if one was of a mind. He glanced over his shoulder and saw that Isuka was watching them from the floor. Her gaze was cool, calculating. Shin gave her a friendly wave, but she gave no sign that she'd noticed.

Odoma laughed. "I don't care."

"You should." Shin looked at Odoma. "I am not the only one who doubts the veracity of your accusation. In fact, there isn't a single person who believes you."

Odoma grunted. "Doesn't much matter though, does it?" He licked his lips. "The Crane want an excuse, and I gave them one. What happens now is up to them. I have no say in what comes next."

"True. Unless you were to retract your accusation."

"And why would I do that?"

"Common sense."

Odoma laughed. "It seems to me that common sense would dictate that I get rid of you at the first opportunity, my lord. A man in my line doesn't get far, sparing his enemies."

"What line is that exactly? Soy sauce… or something else?"

Odoma's smile faded. "Another accusation. You should watch yourself, my lord. I am the head of the merchants' association." He snapped his fingers. "I can ruin the Crane's trade in this city like that."

"You have never lacked for hubris," Shin said, in a mild tone.

Odoma sneered. "The same might be said of you." He leaned close. "Did you think you would get away with it? That I would just let you take it all from me?"

"I'm certain that I have no idea what you're talking about," Shin said, puzzled. "Take what? Is this about the Foxfire Theater? Or perhaps my investment in Nozomi's brewery?"

Odoma glared at him. "Don't play the imbecile. We are both men of the world, though we come from different strata. We both know how the game is truly played. When we first met, I thought you just another rich fool but you proved me wrong." He looked away. "This is my city, Crane. And your time here is done."

"I think I am the best judge of my own time, thank you," Shin said, wondering where this venom was coming from. Odoma was about to reply when the lanky bodyguard suddenly appeared at the top of the steps. The merchant rounded on his servant impatiently.

"What is it, fool?"

"The Kaeru – they're coming!"

"On second thought, you might be right, Master Odoma," Shin said. Ko was as punctual as ever. "Perhaps it is time to go. Shall we, Kasami?" He hurried toward the stairs, Kasami at his side. Thankfully, no one tried to stop them.

As they reached the floor, Shin glanced back to see Odoma glowering down at them. Nor was he the only one. Isuka was watching them as well, and of the two, it was her gaze that gave Shin the most pause, and brought something Sanki had said to mind. "A woman's hairpin," he murmured, as they stepped back out into the rain.

Kasami looked at him. "What are you muttering about?"

"Something Sanki said." Shin unfolded his umbrella. "Kitano was right. That woman is dangerous… far more so than her employer. Come. Let's go."

"Home, hopefully."

"Not just yet. First, I want to visit an inn." Shin lifted his umbrella. "I want to inquire about a room."

CHAPTER TEN
Scene of the Crime

Aoto made an impatient noise, and Ko paused in her examination of the cedar vat. "Yes?" she asked, fighting to keep her tone even as she studied the spot where Junichi Kenzō had died.

"This is a waste of time."

"I do not recall asking for your help," she said pointedly. The brewery stank sweetly; she found soy sauce to be an extravagance, and it impinged on her senses. She wanted to be out of here as quickly as possible, but she could already tell that Aoto was going to cause a significant delay.

The Crane had insisted on coming, despite having no interest in aiding her in her investigation. Thankfully, he'd left his auditors behind. There were already enough heavy-footed officials stomping all over her crime scene as it was. Not to mention the raggedy looking bodyguards of the building's owner, Odoma. She'd counted three of them on the way in, and had been told that there were more scattered unobtrusively about the property. Though she wondered why a simple soy brewer needed so many hired swords, she had not voiced the question, as it was largely irrelevant. Instead, she had focused on the scene itself.

The body had been found among the vats, facedown. She had recreated the scene as best she could with a length of ribbon and several pegs, marking the body's location. There was still a bloodstain where Kenzō had fallen, and she'd duly taken samples from the floor to compare with those taken from the body.

At the moment, she was in the process of taking samples from the vats to compare with those found on the dead man's robes. After being stabbed, Kenzō had staggered away from his attacker. While death was likely instantaneous, it had taken time for the body to realize what the spirit knew. She'd already backtracked a small blood trail on the vats and floor to a point some distance away – the true site of the murder. It didn't change much as far as the official report, but it was good to have the facts.

"I thought he'd be here," Aoto muttered, knocking on one of the vats.

Ko paused again. "What?"

"Shin. I assumed that we'd catch him here… interfering."

"If that's what you wanted, you should have shown up earlier," Odoma interjected. "He was here, asking all sorts of impertinent and frankly insulting questions."

Aoto turned to fix the merchant with a sharp look. "Is that so?"

"Yes. If I'd known you wanted him held, I'd have detained him for you." The merchant's tone was obsequious, but Ko could read the annoyance in his expression. He didn't want them here. Nervous – or something else?

"If you had touched him, I would have removed your hands personally," Aoto said, with a mirthless grin. "Guilty or innocent, he is still a Daidoji and you – well. You are nothing at all, merchant. Just a brewer of sauce."

Odoma's eyes narrowed, and Ko read barely restrained violence in the way his big hands twitched. Odoma was deceptively round; there was muscle there, underneath the fat. The calluses on his hands spoke to some familiarity with a blade, just as the scars on his knuckles implied a willingness to use his fists. She wondered if Aoto noticed such things. If he did, he wasn't overly concerned about it.

Then, Aoto himself was no stranger to violence. She could read it in the way he moved. For all that he came across as an officious courtier, he was as well-trained as any Daidoji warrior. Better than Shin, in fact. Of course, Shin had never been interested in swordplay – not the kind that involved steel, at least.

"I expect you will be the one to replace him, my lord," Odoma said, bowing his head. An attempt to curry favor, or a veiled insult? Shin would have known. Ko dismissed the thought and began an examination of the floor.

"As if I would lower myself to even contemplate such matters," Aoto said haughtily. "Tell me, what did Shin want with you?"

"He threatened me," Odoma began.

Aoto laughed. "I doubt it! Shin isn't the type. No, he came here to bribe you, I expect. How much did he offer you?"

"Nothing," Odoma said, looking slightly bewildered. "He threatened me, I tell you! Him and that bodyguard of his!"

"Hiramori Kasami," Ko said, rattling the name off from memory. She finished her examination of the floor and stood, wiping her hands on her robes. "I will need to speak with her at some point."

Aoto glanced at her. "Why?"

"For the same reason I will need to question Shin. To

ascertain their guilt or innocence." She looked at Odoma. "I will need your bodyguards to turn over their weapons."

Odoma blinked. "What?"

"The deceased was killed by a blow to the base of the skull with something sharp – a blade of some kind. Likely not a sword, but even so." She slapped her fan into her palm. "You will ask them to turn their weapons over. They will receive a receipt, and the weapons will be returned once they have been ruled out as the murder weapon."

"But you already know who did it," Odoma burst out. "I told you!"

Ko kept her tone even. "You told the authorities. The authorities have engaged me to investigate. Are you refusing to cooperate?"

Odoma stared at her. His guards tensed, and the Kaeru edged closer. Aoto loosened his sword in its sheath. "Do as the investigator asks, merchant, or I will remove your head."

"This isn't right," Odoma muttered.

"It is neither right nor wrong," Ko said gently. "It is protocol. Now, while we are on the subject… are you armed, Master Odoma?"

Odoma gawped at her and then convulsively shook his head. "Of course not! That's what these fools are for!"

Ko's attentions turned to the young woman standing behind the merchant. "And what about you, Isuka, was it?"

Isuka bowed her head. "I am not armed," she said, in a soft voice.

Ko nodded. To her ear, the woman's silken tones hid a core of steel. "Of course. May I have one of your hairpins, please?" Would the victim have noticed such a woman, or would he have disregarded her as unimportant?

Isuka's hands fluttered to her ornately styled hair, and her eyes widened in obvious alarm. "My… hairpins?"

"Yes."

"But – surely you cannot think…" She glanced at Odoma, who purpled in rage. Something there, Ko thought. She couldn't say what, but something.

"This is preposterous," he said. He was fighting the urge to bellow, Ko thought. A wise choice, given Aoto's own short temper. "Insulting," he went on. "Outrageous!"

"Protocol," Ko repeated. "You found the body. Therefore, you must be ruled out as a suspect. To do that, I will need to examine your weapons and match them against the wound. The more swiftly we accomplish this, the quicker you will see the return of your property." She paused. "Speaking of which, we will need to maintain a cordon around this building until I have determined that there is no more evidence to be found."

"What about my business?" Odoma asked.

"You will have it back in a few days," Ko assured him.

Odoma stared at her for several moments, then rounded on Aoto. "I was assured that my business would not suffer," he growled. Aoto frowned.

"I gave you no such assurances."

"Yet I have done a favor for the Crane, have I not?"

Aoto's eyes narrowed and he glanced at Ko before replying. "Think carefully about your next words, merchant. This is not some grubby business transaction. Whatever bargain you think you made, it was not this one."

Odoma's face had taken on an unpleasant hue. He seemed to be choking on his own anger. "I – this is unfair! I was promised protection!"

"By whom?" Ko asked quickly.

"The Daidoji Trading Council!"

Ko hesitated. An unexpected accusation. She glanced at Aoto, whose eyes had gone flat. "How dare you," he said. "You are not one of ours, soy merchant. And we do not make bargains with such as you."

Odoma didn't retreat from the threat in Aoto's tone. Ko noticed that the merchant's bodyguards had begun to spread out, cutting off potential avenues of escape. One of the Kaeru sidled toward her, and, in a whisper, said, "My lady, it might be best if we were to leave. Before someone says something that will precipitate a response."

Ko nodded, still pondering Odoma's outburst. The Kaeru were outnumbered, even with Aoto. She snapped open her fan, startling both Odoma and Aoto. As the two men looked at her, she said, "On second thought, we can simply take measurements of the weapons. There is no need to confiscate them. And I do not foresee any need to return here. Nothing I have found has thrown doubt on Master Odoma's testimony. However, I must ask: why was the deceased found here, of all places?"

Odoma hesitated. "He wanted to discuss something."

"I see. Of a personal nature?"

"No. Business."

"Yours?"

"No," Odoma said.

"Lord Shin's?" Aoto broke in, intently. Ko shushed him with a gesture.

"Was it Lord Shin's business he came here to discuss, Master Odoma?"

"I assume so."

"You say you found the body… how did you know he would be here?"

"He sent me a message. Asked me to meet him." Odoma's reply was reluctant, grudging. Ko wondered why. Was it simply a reluctance to appear guilty, or something else? She filed the thought away.

"And you agreed? Why?"

"I thought it was about my complaint."

"Your – ah." Ko glanced at Aoto, who was pointedly looking elsewhere. That might explain the outburst. Did Odoma believe he was owed recompense? "This would be the same complaint which originally brought the deceased to the city?"

"Yes," Odoma said, bobbing his head. "That's the one, my lady."

"But Lord Kenzō was dead when you arrived."

"As I said, in my testimony," Odoma grunted, glaring at Aoto.

"Curious. How did he get inside without anyone seeing him?"

Odoma blinked. "I… am not sure."

Ko nodded. She had been half-expecting some pitiful attempt at explanation. This was almost refreshing in its simplicity. "Were there no guards on duty?"

Odoma looked around, as if dazed by the unceasing flow of questions. "N-no. Who would rob from a soy brewery?"

"I'm told arson is a common business practice among certain merchants," Ko said, in a genial tone. "Are you not worried about rivals?"

Odoma straightened. "I have no rivals."

That was a lie. There were three soy breweries in the city. While Odoma's was the largest, the other two did nearly as much business. And one of them had Shin as a patron, according to what the Kaeru had told her. "You must be pleased. If you have no concerns regarding security, why do you have so many bodyguards?"

"I didn't say I had no concerns," Odoma said. He took a step back, and she could sense the walls going up. He'd recovered his equilibrium now; common sense was reasserting itself. Odoma, she thought, was a man so used to blustering his way through confrontation that he'd never developed the vital strategic sense needed to deal with people above his station. It was no wonder he seemed to bear Shin a grudge; Odoma was exactly the sort of fool that Shin most enjoyed humbling.

"Explain," Aoto barked. He looked intrigued now, despite his earlier annoyance. "What were these concerns of yours?"

Odoma smiled sourly. "The same as yours, I imagine." A sly look came into his eyes as he added, "You might not be a merchant, my lord, but Lord Shin certainly knows how to play the part. He's quite good at it."

"What do you mean?" Aoto demanded.

"Just what I've heard, my lord – and what I've seen with my own eyes." Odoma was trying to look aggrieved, but only succeeded in looking smug. "He's a cagey one, is Lord Shin. Clever. Perhaps he sent me that message so that I would discover the body and… well." He shrugged. "But unfortunately for him, the odds have turned against him at last. Always the way, for degenerate gamblers, of course. I heard his predecessor was much the same…" Odoma trailed off, as if realizing he'd gone a step too far.

Aoto's expression was cold. "I have asked you to watch your words and tone, merchant. I will not do so again. You think that because you have some grievance against Lord Shin that it entitles you to speak freely of your betters? Disabuse yourself of that notion, lest you come to an unfortunate end."

Odoma blanched. "Is that a threat?"

Aoto smiled. "Yes."

"I am the head of the merchants' association!"

"And I am Investigator Ko," Ko interjected. She fluttered her fan in Odoma's face, catching his attention. "To sum up, then: Lord Kenzō asked you to meet him, presumably to discuss your grievances against Lord Shin. When you arrived, however, he was dead. You believed this to be an attempt to implicate you for the crime, so you struck first – accusing the party you believed responsible. Am I correct?"

"Y-yes," Odoma said, somewhat taken aback. "That is correct, my lady."

"Good." Ko paused. "Where is the woman?"

"Woman? You mean Isuka?" Odoma and the others looked around. The courtesan was gone. Vanished, Ko suspected, while everyone was preoccupied by Aoto and Odoma's squabbling. But why? Frightened – or trying to avoid having her hairpins tested?

Odoma bowed apologetically. "She must have fled. You know courtesans, my lord… no stomach for violence."

"That has not been my experience," Aoto muttered. He looked at Ko. "I would speak with you. Outside."

"Very well. I am finished here, for the moment." Ko could already hear his next words. He would seek to reinforce Odoma's theory, despite his harsh words for the merchant. It served his ends. She decided to strike first.

As they stepped out onto the steps of the brewery, sheltered from the rain by the overhang of the roof, she said, "I still need to check Kenzō's rooms at the inn he was staying at. Will you accompany me there?"

"No," Aoto said. "I have already wasted too much time on this."

"Again, I did not expect you to accompany me."

Aoto grunted and scratched his neck. "When do you plan on questioning Shin?"

"Tomorrow. Today is for evidence – tomorrow is for suspects."

He looked at her. "And is Shin still a suspect, then?"

"Of course," Ko said, taken aback by the question. How could he think otherwise?

Aoto grunted again, in satisfaction this time, she thought. "Good. Tomorrow, then." He descended into the rain and departed. Ko watched him go, and turned to go back inside. As she did so, she caught a glimpse of two people watching the brewery from across the street. The first was a seedy looking fellow; unshaven and one hand deformed – no, injured. He wore what appeared to be a prosthetic finger. The second, a young shamisen player, who felt her way along with a bamboo cane.

The man hurried off down the street, followed at a distance by the young woman. Ko frowned, and hurried back into the brewery to inform the Kaeru it was time to leave. Something told her she needed to get to Kenzō's lodgings, and quickly.

CHAPTER ELEVEN
White Frog Inn

The White Frog Inn sat back from the main thoroughfare that led to the city's commercial district, separated from the noise of the street by a thick wall and a substantial gate. It was one of the larger inns, and its clientele were almost exclusively high-status merchants or out-of-town nobility. As far as Shin was aware, Junichi Kenzō had made it his home for the entirety of his time in the city.

Kasami prowled ahead of him as they entered the courtyard. It was surprisingly tidy, despite the rain. Shin studied the inn from beneath the shelter of his umbrella. It was three storied, with the front rooms open to the courtyard. Direct entry, however, was barred by a sturdy wooden lattice. White lanterns, already lit against the encroach of evening, hung from the corner-posts, and willow branches were strung from the roof-beams. Several serving girls sat in front of the lattice; they perked up as they caught sight of Shin.

"Room for the night, my lord?" one called, fanning herself.

"Best rooms in the city," another added, giving Kasami a

sultry glance. Kasami scowled, but the young woman didn't seem to mind.

Shin gave the group a friendly smile. "I am not here for a room. I wish to speak with your proprietor, please."

"I'll get her. Fees are nonrefundable, though," a third server said, as she rose languidly from her seat and ambled inside. Shin chuckled.

"I'm starting to see why Kenzō chose this establishment."

"That, and it's a Crane front," Kasami murmured. Shin nodded.

"Yes, that too."

While the Crane had no real influence in the city, divided as it was between the Lion, the Unicorn, and the Dragonfly, they did have myriad business interests. Mostly import-export, but some few businesses as well.

As a Crane representative, he was aware of them all, though he had no authority over them. There was a farrier in the Unicorn district, a kite-maker in the Dragonfly district, and a handful of inns, scattered throughout the city.

The White Frog was the largest of these, and many visiting Cranes patronized the establishment. Not Aoto, thankfully – he and his auditors were encamped at the Iron Lamp, on the waterfront, according to Azuma.

It was a risky thing, visiting the inn. Ko was certain to pay a visit to Kenzō's residence sooner or later. But he intended to get the first look in, if possible.

"If we are caught here, it will not help your case," Kasami said, echoing his thoughts. She ignored the rain, and stood beside him, arms crossed. Shin sighed and adjusted the umbrella so that it protected them both.

"No, but doing nothing is equally unhelpful. Ko is clever –

observant – but she is a traditionalist at heart. She will go where the facts lead her, and never consider another path." He paused, gnawing his lip. "I fear Odoma's accusation is just the first signpost. There will be others, positioned so that Ko will find them."

"A conspiracy?" Kasami frowned. "Why do you think that?"

Shin hesitated. "A feeling. Nothing more." And that was the truth; it was just a feeling. But it was one he couldn't shake, and it was growing stronger the more he turned things over in his mind.

"Does it have something to do with what Odoma said?"

Shin frowned. "Possibly. He seemed… angry. As if I had attacked him, somehow. But that doesn't make any sense. I've done my best to limit my contact with him." He shook his head. "But more than that, it's a question of timing… Kenzō's death, the arrival of my cousin, it's all too perfect to be a coincidence. It's as if someone is trying to box me in."

A conspiracy, as Kasami had said. The city was no stranger to conspiracies; neither was Shin, for that matter. But this one was vast and tangled. He had come to believe that someone was working against the city and its rulers for reasons he had not yet deduced.

It had begun with a shipment of poisoned rice, and continued, most recently, with an attempt to ruin a Lion wedding, at which he had been a visitor. But there had been other incidents, before his time. He had made a careful study of them, noting places and times, trying to discern possible reasons. But of late he'd felt as if he'd stumbled into some immense spider's web – and the strands were beginning to tremble.

The spider, he was beginning to fear, had noticed him at last.

He shook that gloomy thought aside as the proprietor of the

White Frog finally arrived. Mistress Agito was a small woman, shrunken by age, but still sprightly in her movements. Snowy hair was bound atop her head in a tower, and her robes were of fine quality. "Lord Shin, to what do I owe this unexpected pleasure?" she asked.

"Mistress Agito, as youthful as ever." Shin respectfully bowed his head. "I require a favor of you, if you are willing." It galled him somewhat to use his status as a cudgel, but needs must and time was of the essence.

"For you – anything," Agito simpered. "Come in, come in, out of this dreadful rain." She scattered her servers with a flap of her hands and led Shin and Kasami into the inn. Swallows chirped in the eaves; innkeepers encouraged the birds to build nests among the rafters, in the hope that they might help keep the mosquito population under control.

The common room was full of travelers, and they all looked up as Shin spun his umbrella free of water and closed it with a snap, before handing it to one of the servers. "Don't mind us," he said. "Just passing through." The patrons took it as a command and resolutely returned their attentions to their meals.

Agito led them through the room to her offices in the back. They were small and cramped. Shelves holding the inn's records, bills of sale and invoices dominated the walls. Agito carefully closed the door behind her and said, "What can I do for you, my lord?"

"Junichi Kenzō. I wish to see his room."

Agito hesitated, frowning. "That is… highly irregular, my lord. My clientele pay well for my discretion…"

"He will not complain, I assure you," Shin said.

"Oh?"

"He is dead," Kasami said flatly. Agito's eyes widened.

"If we could see his rooms, I would be in your debt," Shin said softly. Agito looked at him and her expression turned sly.

"A worthwhile trade. Come. He had my finest room. Paid for it in advance."

"Did he? He seemed a frugal man."

Agito laughed. "Oh yes, my lord. And flirtatious. He even offered to look over my record books for me." She giggled. "As if that would be at all proper, him a lord and me – well." She patted her hair and led them to the narrow wooden stairs that provided access to the upper levels of the inn.

Kenzō's room was on the top floor, overlooking the rear of the inn. There was a fine view of the river, and Saibanshoki rising over it all. The paper walls had been decorated with soothing scenes of frogs rollicking among lily pads and rushes, with watchful cranes lurking in the background. As was to be expected there was no furniture save a sleeping mat, a low table for meals and a writing desk. "All of his luggage is still here," Agito assured them. "Nothing has been touched, I assure you."

That you know of, Shin thought but didn't say. Instead, he nodded gratefully and indicated that they would like some privacy. Agito retreated with all due haste, leaving them alone. Kasami looked around. "Now what?"

"Start with his things. I will search the room." Shin went to the mat first. It held no surprises, save for a thin, flat blade concealed beneath the spot where someone's head would lay. He retrieved it and weighed it thoughtfully, wondering whether a similar blade might have been used to make the wound in the base of Kenzō's skull. He placed it back where he'd found it and continued searching.

The dining table was nothing more than a plank of wood. But the writing desk was a curious thing; it didn't belong to the inn.

Instead, it was decorated with the Daidoji sigil, and made from a dark wood sourced from the Uebe marshes. He ran his fingers along its corners and seams, looking for hidden catches and false panels. When he found one, he gave a sigh of satisfaction and slid it open. Unfortunately, there was nothing in it save a single letter, the wax seal broken. He carefully unrolled the letter and bit back a hiss of surprise.

"What is it?" Kasami asked.

"A letter… from my grandfather, to Kenzō." He slid the letter into his sleeve without reading any further. He had some idea of its contents, given Aoto's boasting earlier. Regardless, it could wait. He closed up the writing desk and set it aside. "Find anything?"

"Perhaps." Kasami brought him a small stack of folded reports – copies of reports, rather. They did not bear the seal of the Kaeru, but Shin knew them for what they were, nonetheless. He took them from Kasami and flicked through them. Each concerned the death of some poor unfortunate. Shin recognized none of the names.

"How did he get these?" he murmured. It didn't make any sense. What did these deaths have to do with his finances? "Anything else?"

"Yes." Kasami handed him a small blue ledger, like a miniature version of the ones he used to keep track of his finances. He flipped through it. Kenzō had been keeping his own books, likely to compare to Shin's. Certain entries had notations attached, or their dates marked. He glanced at the records again, and saw that the dates matched those in the ledger.

"What is this?" he murmured. "What did you find, Kenzō?"

"Does it mean something?" Kasami asked, peering at the ledger in confusion.

"I believe so, though I cannot say what just yet."

There was a soft knock at the door. Kasami slid it open to reveal one of the servers from outside. She bowed low and said, in a low voice, "Mistress Agito wanted me to tell you that there's a troop of Kaeru coming down the street, heading our way. She said you might want to be gone before they arrive..."

Shin hesitated. Clearly Agito knew more about recent events than she'd been letting on. He nodded in thanks to the young woman. "Tell her she has my thanks. Is there a... discreet exit from this establishment?"

The young woman smiled and nodded. "End of the hall, behind the wall hanging. It'll take you out behind the bathhouse. No one will see you, if you're quick."

Shin thanked her and as she vanished, he turned to Kasami. "We'll take one set of records, but leave the others – and the ledger."

"Why?"

"Because we already have our own, remember? Besides, Ko will be expecting to find something. Better we let her think that she's succeeded, yes? Else she might come calling on us, and in a foul temper."

"Because she's all cherry blossoms and sparrows now," Kasami said.

"It can get worse, trust me. Much worse. Let's go. Quickly."

As they stepped into the hall, Shin heard Mistress Agito loudly protesting as the Kaeru entered her establishment. He heard Azuma's stern tones, and Ko's softer ones. He gestured silently to the end of the corridor, and the wall hanging. Kasami pulled it aside to reveal a narrow aperture, and set of cramped stairs, heading down.

Shin gestured. "After you."

Kasami grimaced, but went. Shin waited until he could hear the stomp of feet on the main stairs and then followed, ensuring that the wall hanging was still as he went. There was a tiny doorway at the bottom, covered by a moveable lattice. Kasami shifted it aside and they stepped out into the rain. It was only as they passed through the service gate at the side of the courtyard that Shin realized he'd left his umbrella behind.

He paused, wondering if he ought to go back. Then, with a sigh, he dismissed the idea as foolish. Hopefully no one would notice another umbrella, sitting among the rest of the rainwear. But as he and Kasami left the White Frog Inn behind, Shin couldn't help but feel he'd made a mistake. It wouldn't be the first.

Hopefully, it wouldn't turn out to be his last.

CHAPTER TWELVE
Shadows

Kitano Daichi ducked down a side-street, moving quickly, following Odoma's courtesan at a discreet distance. As he walked, he rolled a pair of dice in the palm of his hand. He took comfort in the feel of them, worn smooth by a lifetime of fortune; not all of it good, but he broke even more often than not.

He'd taken to carrying them again only recently. They were the same dice he'd been using the night he'd met Lord Shin. He'd lost the game and his finger, and almost his life. At the time, he'd cursed them and imagined them to be tainted somehow. But of late, he'd begun to reconsider. Maybe that night had been his salvation. After all, what sort of life had he been looking at? Being a professional gambler had its perks, but it was a precarious existence.

Then, he'd grown up on the knife-edge. His parents had been wave people; vagabonds and mercenaries, hunting paid sword-work in whatever town they wandered into. They'd been good parents, as far as it went – he and his siblings had never gone hungry, and they'd learned how to fight and steal early, both useful professions. But there'd been too many cold nights with empty bellies for his liking. Too many evenings spent sheltering in roadside shrines or cleaning out stables, too many uncertain days.

They'd been blown on the winds of fortune for so long that it had seemed only natural to make it a way of life. He'd learned early that he had a talent for dice and other games of chance. He had luck, and when he didn't have luck, he had quick fingers. He glanced at his ruined hand and smiled ruefully. Had, being the operative word.

But if the fortunes took with one hand, they gave with the other. He was no longer his own man, but the one he served was a good one. They helped people; even people like himself. Maybe especially folk like himself. Lord Shin never let an innocent person suffer, if he could help it. He was frivolous with his money, but in a good way; he gave it away to anyone who needed it, without expecting anything in return.

Shin was a fool, but a good fool. There were times that Kitano was even proud to serve him. Other times, he wondered if maybe it wasn't time to find a new game. There'd been a few too many close calls. The Poison Rice Affair, the Cedar Barrel Killer, Shonji the Toymaker… the Fox-Wife. Kitano shuddered at the thought of the last one. She'd nearly drowned him in a bathtub; would have, if Kasami hadn't gotten there in time.

Now here he was following another killer. And she was a killer. He was certain of it, though he couldn't say why. Something about the way she walked, the way she studied her surroundings. He couldn't tell whether she was armed or not, but he'd have wagered money on the possibility.

He was acting on impulse, following her like this. She was going somewhere in a hurry, and he figured Lord Shin would want to know about it – even if he didn't know that he wanted to know, just yet. That was the problem with Lord Shin… he didn't know what he needed to know, until he needed to know it. Which, inevitably, was too late.

Kitano knew Odoma – a gangster, pretending to be a merchant. He'd even worked for Odoma a time or two, though he doubted the other man would remember him. Odoma had courage and fire aplenty, but no foresight. Like Kitano, he was a wave person. He moved from opportunity to opportunity, never thinking ahead. Just going where the river took him.

Lord Shin didn't – couldn't understand. He played at being that sort of person, but really, he was meticulous. He planned things, kept a ledger in his head. Men like Odoma and Kitano just acted. They rolled the dice and went with the results, good or bad.

That was why Kitano was suspicious of the courtesan. Odoma wasn't the sort to keep a woman on his arm. He didn't see any value in that. So why her, why now? Because – and it was that simple – he'd rolled the dice. Now, they just had to figure out whether the result was good or bad. Lord Shin, he figured, would want to know either way.

The courtesan took a left, down a long stretch of dirt path, bounded on either side by loosely arranged stones and crowded with pedestrians. The stones were for the water, when the river slopped its banks in the rain. There'd be sacks of dirt and straw bales in the better parts of town, but here, on the waterfront, it was stones. Anything dredged from the mud of the river, that was big enough to make a water-break. The establishments to either side didn't advertise what was for sale, which was, to Kitano's mind, the best sort of advertising.

Men and women lounged in doorways, watching the

passersby for any sign of interest. Carts splashed along the muddy track, as rain sheeted down and gathered in dirt runnels. The courtesan was easy to follow; she was the only one with an umbrella.

Kitano stayed on her tail until she reached the end of the track, where a single establishment made a dead end. He stopped and sidled back, under a bit of roof, out of the rain. From somewhere nearby came the sound of someone idly plucking the strings of a shamisen; the sound of it danced through the curtain of rain and sent a shiver along his spine, though he couldn't say why.

He knew where she was going now, but he didn't understand why a courtesan for a soy merchant would visit the headquarters of a gang of waterfront extortionists like the Snakeheads. "What is she doing here?" he murmured to himself.

The Snakeheads had been waterfront bullies for almost as long as Kitano had lived in the city. They were little more than amateur extortionists, and they kept their coercion to independent merchants and captains. They were smart enough to stay well away from anyone associated with the clans or the Kaeru, and in return, the Kaeru let them conduct their business with little in the way of harassment. That was, until someone had planted a length of steel in their chief's gut.

Taoko had been his name; a rough man, even for a gangster. And dumb. Word was, he'd fallen into line behind someone even worse, but that was how things worked on the waterfront. The bad served the worse, and the good suffered. But ever since Taoko had died, things had gone downhill for the Snakeheads.

From what he'd heard, there'd been the usual squabbles over leadership afterwards. Then someone had put their foot down, and that had been that. The Snakeheads now mostly just bullied fishermen and ferry-crews. Maybe Odoma had been the someone. He'd hired an awful lot of sword-dogs of late. Was that why?

That made a sort of sense. Odoma liked to be the boss. He was still turning that over in his mind when he realized the street was suddenly empty, save for him and three men at the far end. He cursed himself for his inattention and tried to make himself inconspicuous, but it was a vain effort.

"Get out here, gambler," one of them called. "No use hiding."

Kitano cursed again, more loudly this time, and stepped out. He had a knife, but they had weapons, too, and already in their hands. Had the courtesan seen him? He didn't think so, but maybe she was more observant than he'd assumed.

They were an odd group. The tallest, in yellow robes, had his hair pulled up in a messy topknot and a face that would have been handsome if not for the scarring and the length of willow bark he was chewing on. He smirked as Kitano stepped into the open. "Where's your master, Kitano?" he growled. He rested his blade across his shoulders. "Tell us, and maybe we'll leave you with enough fingers to feed yourself."

"Haruko," Kitano said, in greeting. "You look as sour as ever. Murder-for-hire business not been going well?" Haruko was a thug who fancied himself a swordsman. There were a lot of those in the city these days. Some were looking for mercenary work, others just wanted to skim off the spoils of any conflict that arose between the powers-that-be.

"It's picking up," Haruko said. "You know my friends?"

Kitano swallowed and glanced at the other two. "Dogi and Taj, yes. You still owe me money, Taj. I don't suppose you have it on you?"

Taj grinned, showing off a mouthful of brown teeth. Hygiene was not a primary concern of Taj's. Kitano could almost see the fleas hopping in the folds of his mud-stained robes. Like Haruko, he had a sword in his hand. Taj scratched his chin and said, "Nope."

"Fair enough," Kitano said. "What about you, Dogi? Last I heard, you wanted to cut Taj's ears off. You two friends now?" He glanced back toward where he'd last seen the courtesan. It was odd that no one was coming out. Maybe the Snakeheads had better things to do. Or maybe they'd been told to stay out of it.

"Bounties make for strange bedfellows," Dogi grunted. He was a thickset man, built like an ox and about as smart. He hefted the studded club he carried. "If you try to run, I'm going to break your legs. It's not personal. Just business."

"It feels a bit personal, seeing as they're my legs," Kitano said. He glanced around, trying to spot something – anything – that might be of help. "Why are you after Lord Shin?"

"Money, why else?" Haruko said. He took the willow bark out of his mouth and pointed it at Kitano. "Help us, and maybe we'll cut you in. Or we can just cut you up… your choice."

"My loyalty is worth a lot more than you can afford, Haruko. Though maybe if I talk to your boss, I might change my mind. You're still working for Odoma, right?"

Haruko twitched a finger chidingly. "No, no. We're the ones asking questions. Guess we'll just have to hurt you until you cough up some answers, eh?"

"Suits me," Dogi grunted. He took a threatening step toward Kitano and brandished his club. Kitano whipped out his knife and bent his knees, ready to move. Three against one was bad odds, especially when the one was him. But if he could break past them, make it to the street, he might have a chance.

But it wasn't Dogi who came for him. Taj was quicker off the mark. Only a split-second realization saved Kitano from losing his head as the ronin lunged and made a wild swing. "Don't kill him, fool!" Haruko called, as Kitano retreated and the two killers closed in. Taj went low, for his second attempt, forcing Kitano to hop back from the slashing blade. Unfortunately, it put him into the path of Dogi's club.

Kitano managed to avoid most of the blow, but it glanced off the side of his shoulder and he found himself rolling across the ground, his shoulder screaming in agony. No blood, nothing broken, he thought, but it definitely hurt. And he'd lost his knife. He flailed blindly, trying to find it as Taj closed in. "Stop embarrassing yourself, Kitano," the ronin said, in visible amusement. "It'll only hurt worse."

Then – a sound. A voice, querulous and wheezy. A hunched, stooped figure was behind Haruko, muttering something. Haruko turned, an annoyed look on his face. "Get out of here, old man, before I–" His threat faltered as the newcomer produced an arm from within his rags – an arm that ended in a wooden cap, concealing the stump of a hand. Then, with a quick gesture, the cap popped off, revealing a short, wide blade.

Another quick flick of the wrist, and that blade opened Haruko's throat to the bone. Haruko stumbled, dropping his sword, clutching at his neck, as the newcomer sprang past. He snatched up the ronin's fallen blade and parried Taj's attack, as the remaining two ronin turned to confront the new threat.

Kitano found his knife and rolled awkwardly to his feet. He didn't think – just acted. He leapt onto Dogi's back and rammed the knife into the base of the big man's skull. Dogi stiffened and toppled without a sound, dragging Kitano down with him.

Taj was down as well, twitching and gurgling as the rain carried his lifeblood into the gutters. The ragged figure of

Kitano's rescuer threw back his hood and gave a crooked smile. "Still in one piece, gambler?"

"Cho-Chobei?" Kitano asked, in surprise. The one-handed man smiled grimly as he wiped his blade-hand clean on Taj's robes and rose to his feet. At first glance, he was a short man, but the longer you looked at him, the taller you realized he was. To most, he appeared as nothing more than another fisherman, bent and stooped by a lifetime pulling in nets. But he was anything but that. Like Kitano, he'd once tried to kill Shin and wound up serving him, albeit at a remove.

"I was following you when I spotted these three doing the same. You should be more observant. Yui would be upset if you died."

Kitano smiled at the mention of Chobei's daughter – at least he thought she was his daughter. She was a fierce one; as lethal as Chobei, despite having a child on her hip. "Would she?" he asked, rubbing the back of his head. "Never mind – why were you following me?"

"Our master is in trouble, gambler."

"Tell me something I don't know."

"These fools were just the first." Chobei slid the cap back onto his prosthetic with a hollow clack, concealing the blade. "There'll be more by tomorrow. And worse than these." He kicked Taj's corpse and looked at Kitano.

"There's a bounty on Lord Shin's head, and every sword-dog in the city will be aiming to collect."

CHAPTER THIRTEEN
Representatives

Ko settled herself on her heels as her guests sat themselves opposite her. She had returned from the inn to find them waiting for her. She'd sent runners to request their presence after taking a brisk perusal of Kenzō's records. While questioning associates of the accused was not something she normally found useful, given the paucity of material evidence in this case, she was forced to make do with circumstantial.

This in mind, she took stock of the first of her guests. Ichiro Gota was a short, burly man whose every movement was made with great weight and force. The Badger Clan trade envoy was a human avalanche, wrapped in robes that did not suit him. His Ujik bodyguard lounged near the doors, looking bored. Ko studied the bodyguard for a moment, taking in his lean, scarred features and the flatness of his gaze.

She turned her attentions to the second of her guests, Akodo Minami. The commander of the Lion garrison was sturdily built – a warrior, rather than a courtier or merchant. She looked uncomfortable in her formal robes, and she made small telltale gestures that spoke to being more used to the weight of armor.

Her bodyguard, an older Lion samurai, knelt near the Ujik, and gave the latter disapproving glances every so often.

Ko had expected a third guest, Iuchi Konomi, but the Unicorn noblewoman had made her apologies, claiming a previous engagement. Ko was annoyed about this lack of etiquette, but took pains not to show it. She could always pay a visit to the Unicorn later, if it proved necessary. "Thank you for coming," she said, as a servant poured their tea. "I know it was short notice, but we are on something of a schedule..."

"You mean the Crane are impatient to drag Lord Shin off," Minami said. Ko peered at her. The history of the Lion and the Crane was a fraught one; it seemed improbable that Shin would have had any dealings with Minami. Yet, by all accounts, they were acquaintances if not friends. One of Shin's great strengths was his ability to charm those people otherwise predisposed to dislike him. Ko reluctantly included herself among that number.

"They are impatient for a solution to the murder of Lord Kenzō," Ko corrected.

"The way I hear it, the soy merchant Odoma did the deed," Gota said, leaning forward, hands braced on his knees. "Never liked the man. No manners. No respect."

Ko glanced at him. "Be that as it may, he is the one accusing Lord Shin of the murder. Until such time as I find other evidence, that is the theory I must work from."

"He is not a murderer," Minami said.

"Until proven otherwise, he must be considered as such," Ko said.

"Ridiculous!" Minami sat up. "Lord Shin has never been anything but circumspect in his dealings with myself and the Lion. Indeed, he has been of great help to us–"

"So I have heard," Ko interrupted. "Recently, he had some

involvement in the wedding of your cousin, I believe. There was some trouble on the day of the ceremony, I'm told. Lord Shin was involved in the death of a prominent Akodo vassal…"

"That man was a murderer and would have killed others, if Shin had not stopped him," Minami said sharply. "He has my gratitude, and that of my superiors."

Ko accepted this with a nod. "Were you acquainted with Lord Kenzō?"

Minami frowned. "Not well, no. I knew of him, of course."

"Oh?"

"For a time, he was the talk of the city," Gota interjected. "The auditor come to unravel the fortunes of the city's favorite Crane." He chuckled and clapped his hands to his belly. "Only, he never seemed to get around to doing any such thing. An easily distracted fellow, in my opinion."

"Then you knew him?"

"We met, yes. He came to nose about my dealings with the Crane. Paper, before you ask. It's the one thing we can't easily get in the mountains. Shin cut me a deal, exclusivity in exchange for a smaller return. Not unusual, as these things go."

"I was given to believe that Lord Shin rarely showed interest in business."

Gota chuckled again. "Oh no – lazy as the river is wet, that man. But sometimes even the laziest warrior must pick up his blade, eh?" He glanced at Minami. "Cut you a deal as well, eh?"

Ko looked at the Lion commander. She sighed and nodded. "Paper, fish and iron."

Ko examined her notes, perplexed. "I see no record of that."

Gota snorted. "You wouldn't. Middlemen are the lifeblood of this city. Given the history of hostility between them, the Lion would never openly trade with the Crane. So, they do it through independent merchants, or third parties such as myself. The Crane sell their goods to some unaffiliated businessman, who, in turn, sells it on to the Lion. The Lion sell to the same fellow, who, well, you can guess." He tugged on his beard. "Clever, no? All perfectly legal, perfectly acceptable – but discreet."

"And open to abuse," Minami murmured.

Ko looked at her. "What do you mean?"

"Trade at a remove relies on the participants being scrupulous in their dealings. But a simple alteration to a ledger or a schedule can create a – a gap of sorts. A wrinkle in the fabric. Things go unaccounted for. Deliveries, cargo – time. Criminals often make use of these gaps in order to smuggle goods…"

Gota laughed. "No disrespect intended, my lady, but the Lion are overconcerned about such things. Records are not sacrosanct; they are… suggestions." The Ujik snorted at this, and Gota paused to shoot him a glare before continuing. "A mistake or two is to be expected."

"What about three or four or five?" Ko asked. Gota frowned.

"Then, someone might need to hire a bookkeeper."

"What is your opinion of Lord Shin's bookkeeping?"

"I wouldn't know," Gota said. He looked at Minami, who shook her head. "Not proper, looking at another man's books." He paused, a speculative look on his face. "Though, there is someone you could ask about them: Iuchi Konomi."

Ko sat back. "Lady Konomi was not able to attend this meeting, though she was invited. Are she and Shin… close?"

Gota grinned. "The way I hear it, there was talk of them being wed."

"Gossip ill becomes you, Lord Gota," Minami said, in disapproval. She looked at Ko. "Assumptions were made by many. Lady Konomi is… often seen in Lord Shin's company.

There was some rumor of her marrying Tonbo Kuma last year, but they seem to have been replaced by Lord Shin, of late. They are just friends, however."

"Lord Shin makes friends easily," Ko said. "Do you consider him a friend?"

Minami hesitated. "I do, yes."

Gota nodded. "Insofar as men like us can have friends, yes."

Ko nodded. "Answer me this, then – could Lord Shin have killed the auditor?"

"No," Gota said dismissively. "No stomach for it. Oh, he'd have done it if the man had come at him with a knife but in cold blood? No."

"His bodyguard might have, if she thought he was in danger," Minami said, with visible reluctance. "She takes her duties quite seriously."

Ko considered what she knew of Hiramori Kasami, and found that she agreed. The Hiramori had a well-earned reputation for pragmatism. "I still say Odoma did it," Gota said. "That man has never met a situation he couldn't make worse. He ran that theater of Shin's into the ground, sold it for scrap and then had the temerity to complain when Shin made something of it. There's your – what does he call it? – motive."

Ko frowned. "The theater?"

"Envy," Gota clarified. "Odoma has been head of the merchants' association in this city since the last one – well. You hear things. Anyway, along comes Shin, buying up worthless properties and investing in failing businesses and always, somehow, turning a profit. The theater, the soy brewers, that little wharf of his… he's made quite the little nest for himself, our friendly Crane." Seeing Ko's expression, he hurried on. "What I mean is, Odoma prides himself on his cleverness, his acumen, and here comes Shin, showing him up at every turn. And worse, he has the ear of the governor, of the Tonbo, of the Iuchi… of the Akodo. For a man like Odoma, I expect it's like having a bellyful of scorpions."

Ko glanced at Minami. "And what do you think, Lady Minami?"

The Akodo commander was silent for a time. Then, "I do not listen to gossip."

Sensing she'd learned all she could from the pair, Ko thanked them both and saw them out. She paused, and then sent one of the servants to request Lord Aoto's presence. She didn't have all that much desire to speak with the man, but it was necessary for the next stage of her investigation.

As she waited, she thought about what Gota and Minami had told her. The Shin they described was not the Shin she remembered. Not wholly. Change was inevitable, but still somewhat startling. The Shin of her youth had been good with his tongue but little else. But he seemed to have come into his own here.

Her brief encounter with Odoma had convinced her that he was hiding something. Guilt? Perhaps. Then, Odoma did not seem the sort to feel guilty about anything. But it was a loose thread in need of a strong tug, nonetheless.

Shin might have been adept at making friends, but he was equally skilled at making enemies. Kenzō might well have been one of them.

Aoto came in some time later, as she was organizing the papers she'd recovered at the White Frog Inn. She made a note to request Shin's personal ledgers, in order to compare the two sets. If Shin were attempting to hide discrepancies of some sort, it might explain why Kenzō had been killed.

"Are you finished with the body?" Aoto asked, without preamble. "Only it must be prepared for the journey home." He glanced at the doors as they were shut. "What were the Lion and the Badger doing here?"

"I was questioning them."

"Why?"

"To learn about Shin's interactions with Lord Kenzō. They seemed to be at odds, at least until recently."

"Then he did do it," Aoto said, eyebrow raised as if in mild surprise.

"You sound as if you find that hard to believe."

Aoto waved this aside. "It doesn't matter. The end result is the same, guilty or innocent. Shin will be taken home, to Mura Sabishii Toshi, where he will face the ire of the Daidoji Trading Council."

"And then?" she asked. She assumed a decision had already been made in regard to Shin's fate. Oh, there might be some form of mock trial to assuage the concerns of various interested parties, but, in truth, Shin had already been tried and found guilty. Of that, she was certain. "Will he be executed?"

"Of course not! Shin is no low-ranking servant to be so casually disposed of. No, he will be wed to a suitable spouse, and sent to oversee a country estate. His future is one of rice quotas and grain tallies. His only entertainment will be whatever traveling performer deigns to visit such an isolated locale, or puppet shows put on by the village children."

"He would consider that torture, I think," Ko said, amused despite herself. Aoto gave a wide, pleased smile.

"I know." He paused. "I hope that he resists. It has been some time since he has been humbled on the training field, I suspect. He could do with a good beating or three. Perhaps on the journey home." He sounded hopeful on that last point.

"Do not plan it just yet. I have not determined his involvement, if any, with your auditor's death." She considered her next question carefully. "How much do you know of why Kenzō was here? Were you his superior?"

Aoto hesitated. "No. Does it matter?"

"Perhaps not. But his papers paint an interesting picture of the situation. His examination of Shin's finances reveal few irregularities – less, in fact, than I had been led to believe." That wasn't strictly true, but she wanted to see Aoto's reaction.

"I have no doubt his books are spotless. That doesn't mean he's not up to something."

"Agreed," Ko said. "For that reason, I would like your permission to question the merchants Shin was overseeing. There are three of them, I believe. A dealer in… fish, an iron-seller and a purveyor of paper."

Aoto sniffed. "Dotards, all three." He gestured airily. "I don't know their names. I doubt Shin does either."

"Meaning?"

"They are elderly," he clarified. "In the twilight of their careers. That is why they were sent here, rather than someplace more important. It is a… reward, for their service. An easy post, where money comes easily."

"Is that why Shin was sent here?"

Aoto gave a bark of laughter. "Hardly. Shin was sent here because – well. He is Shin. Useless and irresponsible. The merchants would have known better than to bother with him, save when absolutely necessary."

"And his predecessor?" Ko asked, without quite meaning to. Aoto turned, his expression one of wariness.

"What about her?"

"Was she the same? Useless?"

"I do not know," he said, and she believed him. "Why ask me about her? What part does she play in Shin's guilt or innocence?"

"None, that I can see," Ko said. Like herself, his picture of Shin did not quite align with that of Gota and Minami. However, she doubted Aoto would even consider that Shin was capable of change.

"Then I would suggest that you focus on what matters." Aoto paused. "I am done for the evening. I and my auditors will be returning to the inn. We have business in town tomorrow. If you should wish to reach us…"

"I will not," Ko said. She retrieved one of Kenzō's ledgers and turned her back on him. "I will be focusing on what matters, as you have suggested." She paused, and selected from among Kenzō's possessions the red umbrella she'd found at the inn. It was too nice to belong to any of the other guests, but had still been wet when she'd spotted it. "One last question – do you recognize this umbrella?"

Aoto looked at her as if she were insane. "Should I?"

"No. I suppose not." She set it aside. He departed without replying.

She hoped Aoto was wise enough to refrain from doing anything rash. But if not, she would just have to hope that his foolishness didn't endanger her investigation. She sighed and picked up a blue record book. Hopefully, it contained the answers she needed.

"Or at least the right questions to ask," she murmured.

CHAPTER FOURTEEN
Ledgers

Outside, the rain fell and the city settled down for the evening. Inside, Shin and Ito pored over the former's official ledgers. Tea steeped on the table between them as they combed the books for commonalities with the dates and notations that Shin had found in Kenzō's lodgings. "I must remember to send Mistress Agito a thank you gift," Shin said, as he turned a page. His servant, Niko, wandered the edges of his perceptions, lighting the lanterns that provided illumination for the receiving room.

"Mistress Agito is a clever woman, though she'd deny it if you accused her of it." Ito smiled fondly. "I helped her set up her business, you know."

"Is there anyone you haven't helped in some fashion, Ito?"

"A few, my lord." Ito watched Niko depart. "She's not very skilled at eavesdropping, is she? These young people today – no professionalism."

"I keep Niko around because of her lack of ability, not for her professionalism." Shin was fairly certain, if not absolutely, that Niko was a spy. Perhaps for the Trading Council, perhaps for his grandfather. What mattered was that she wasn't very good at it.

Ito snorted. "I could teach her a few tricks, if you like. At the very least I could show her how to read a document upside down without making such obvious contortions."

Shin smiled piously. "Lady Konomi has offered much the same, but I think it is important that Niko learn such things on her own."

Ito frowned. "Tell me, have you ever thought of confronting her? Perhaps suborning her loyalty?"

"No. In the first place, she is an adequate servant and getting better. And secondly… well." Shin gave an elegant wave of his fan.

"It's better to know which of your servants is reporting back on your activities, eh?" Ito asked slyly. Shin nodded.

"Exactly. A spy in the hand is worth two in the net, as my grandfather says."

"An intriguing man, your grandfather. Have you considered that this might all be some strategy of his?" Ito posited the question carefully. Shin shook his head.

"Given my cousin's comments, I suspect other parties at work." The Trading Council was as riven with factionalism as any other body; coups were commonplace, and circumstances shifted with alarming frequency. It was likely that Shin had inadvertently become a pawn in some game being played.

His finger traced a latticework of dates, names and amounts on the pages before him. His entire history, assembled numerically and chronologically. These numbers were him, in a sense. In the view of the Trading Council, at least. They determined his worth, whether he was a good man, or a bad one. Whether he was deserving of life… or death.

Would they kill him? Aoto might, in the heat of the moment. Others certainly would. He could not run to his parents for protection; his father was iron to the core and his mother would take his head herself, if she thought it might advance her own ends.

Something on the page caught his eye, and dismissed all thought of family. He compared the ledger with the notes he'd recreated from Kenzō's books. The dates for quite a few of the deliveries didn't match Kenzō's version. What was going on?

Ito noticed his frown and looked up. "Is something wrong, my lord?"

"Maybe. Maybe not." Shin had filled out the ledgers himself, according to reports given to him by Ito and the other merchants under his authority. So where had Kenzō gotten his dates from, if not there?

Shin decided to say nothing of it to Ito. Not yet. Instead, he asked, "Tell me what you make of Kenzō's notes, if you would. Specifically the reports he got from the Kaeru."

"They seem like the expected travails of city life to me. Then, I am but a humble seller of paper." Ito paused. "I do wonder how he came by them. The Kaeru are normally quite tight-fisted when it comes to their paperwork."

"Speaking from experience?" Shin asked.

Ito's smile was fleeting. "Perhaps."

"Did you recognize any of the names?" Shin asked. There had been six names to go with the reports: Hiroto, Dari, Taoka, Shaiban, Osho and Sato. All dead within a few days of one another, and all within the last month. Not unusual, given the nature of the city, but something about it pricked at his instincts. "They weren't all merchants, were they?"

Ito frowned and flicked through the ledger he was holding. "No. Shaiban was a known smuggler. And Taoka was – hmm." He paused. "Odd, that."

"What?"

"Taoka is – was – a gangster. Leader of some petty gang or other. He extorted independent merchants on the Unicorn docks. He did work with Shaiban, on occasion, but I can't see either having a connection to the others."

"Tell me about the others. You had dealings with them?"

Ito nodded. "Often. Hiroto and Dari were minor merchants – fish and rice, respectively. Osho imported leather goods. Sato was a dealer in dyes."

"You mainly trade in paper, I thought."

Ito smiled thinly. "Some seasons, it behooves a wise man to plant more than one type of seed. Besides which, merchants need paper, too."

Shin nodded slowly. "Were they… sources of information?"

Ito hesitated. "Sometimes. The only real connection they all had–"

"Besides you," Shin interjected. Ito grimaced.

"Besides me, was that they dealt primarily with the Lion. Which is, of course, the opposite side of the river from where Taoka conducted his business…"

"What about Shaiban?"

Ito grunted. "Hard to say. Smugglers are wave people, they go where the money takes them. Shaiban no doubt had business on both sides of the river. I never had dealings with him myself, so I can't say."

"What about Odoma? Would he have had dealings with Shaiban? Or Taoko?"

Ito scratched his chin. "I couldn't say. Not that he's above using the services of such men, but he has his own hired killers. And he used to be a smuggler himself, before he decided to become legitimate, so I can't see him needing a fool like Shaiban to help him."

Shin paused. That corroborated what Kasami had told him. "I had heard that." He looked at the ledgers again, lining up the dates with those he'd seen on the reports. The latter, he thought, corresponded with the ones that struck him as wrong. As if… no. He dismissed the thought even as it formed.

Ito chuckled. "Why do you think he bought that theater in the first place?"

Shin looked up, momentarily forgetting about dates. "The theater?"

Ito nodded. "The cistern. You went down into the tunnels below it?"

Shin blinked. He had, once. It hadn't been a pleasant experience. "Surely they don't extend that far?"

Ito shrugged. "Far enough. There are portions of those tunnels that lead to the riverbank. Most of them are blocked off by false panels, mind. You wouldn't see them, unless you knew they were there. And if one knew about them, one could avoid the docks entirely – at least in this part of the city." He chuckled and shook his head. "Half the smugglers in the city wept when you bought the place and cut off their access to the tunnels."

Shin considered this for a moment. "And the other half?"

Ito looked away. Shin laughed softly. "Ah. Is that why you advised me to buy the theater in the first place, Ito? Were you cutting Odoma out of his own web?" Suddenly, Odoma's anger was starting to make a bit more sense.

"Anything I have done, I have done on your behalf and for your benefit, my lord."

"Ito, has anyone ever told you that you have a way of answering a question without actually answering it?"

Ito smiled. "I take it as a compliment, my lord."

Shin waved this aside. "Did Shaiban ever use those tunnels?"

"I assume so. Anyone could – or can – if they pay the toll."

"Taoka, the gangster… did he know about them?"

Ito hesitated. "It wouldn't surprise me, but his business was on the docks."

"Is that why Odoma has been so insistent in attempting to regain possession of the theater?" Shin asked, already knowing the answer. He'd been a fool; he'd assumed Odoma had just been one more greedy merchant, but instead it seemed as if the man were at the center of a vast conspiracy. More and more, it was looking as if Odoma was the one behind his recent troubles, and not simply because he'd made a ridiculous accusation.

Ito nodded slowly. "Possibly. When he went legitimate, use of the tunnels was limited to a trusted few – those who could be counted on not to get caught, or who were bringing in high value goods on which Odoma would receive a substantial percentage for providing."

Shin tapped his lips with his fan, turning the accumulated facts over in his mind. "Then why sell the place at all?"

"Ah, there you'd have to ask him," Ito said.

"But at the moment, I'm asking you."

Ito sat back. "I can think of one good reason. The Poison Rice Affair threw a sharp light on the local smugglers. Many of them left the city, at least for a time. The Kaeru were cracking down on those who remained. Lord Tetsua was flexing imperial muscle in an effort to reassure the clans that matters were in hand."

"So, Odoma decided to cut ties with all of it."

Ito set his ledgers aside. "He's an impulsive sort. Likely he made the decision in an instant and immediately regretted it."

"You mean when the Kaeru turned their attentions elsewhere, he tried to buy it back."

Ito tapped the side of his nose. "You have the right of it, my lord."

Shin arranged the ledgers into a tidy pile. "Tell me, why was he made head of the merchants' association? I have often wondered about that. You yourself said he wasn't particularly successful, or well-liked. Was it access to these tunnels that cinched it for him?"

"In part. He also threatened people. As I said, he was a bit of a rogue before he inherited his uncle's soy brewery." Ito frowned thoughtfully. "Thinking on it, it is not… inconceivable that Odoma and Taoka knew one another. Or that Shaiban was one of his… clients. But the others?" He shrugged again. "Who can say?"

"It would be helpful if you could find out," Shin said. There was something Ito wasn't saying. But he thought now wasn't the time to press the merchant.

Ito made to reply when Kasami interrupted. She slid open the doors and said, "You have a visitor." Her tone implied they were an unwelcome one. "Outside," she added.

"It's raining outside," Shin said, as he rose to his feet and smoothed his robes.

"They didn't ask to come in. And I didn't invite them."

"Ah. Forgive me, Ito – won't be a moment."

Ito bowed low. "Of course, my lord. Take your time."

Shin stepped out of the receiving room, and followed Kasami to the garden doors. She slid them open, exposing Shin to the chill of the rain and the flickering glow of the lanterns hanging to either side of the doors.

At the bottom of the steps stood two figures. One held an umbrella over the head of the other. Shin cleared his throat and Aoto looked up at him, from beneath the brim of his lackey's umbrella. "Shin."

"Cousin."

"I am here as a courtesy."

"How delightful. Would you and your companion like to come in?"

Aoto sniffed and looked around. "Plenty of time for that later. We'll be confiscating this place tomorrow. All your records, all your possessions… they were gifts of the Daidoji and we are taking them back. I trust you will not resist."

Shin, who'd expected something like this, sighed and looked up at the night sky. The stars were hidden by the rain. "I know how disappointed you will be to hear this, but I wasn't planning on it."

"Why not?" Aoto growled. "I would. Any Daidoji worth the name would. Why not you? Why are you so… so…"

"Cowardly?" Shin offered. "I prefer pragmatic, myself."

"We are taking your home!"

"Yes."

"We are taking your money!"

"Yes." Shin smiled down at his cousin. "And, when this matter is settled, you will no doubt return them with all due contrition."

Aoto snorted. "It has nothing to do with that, and you know it. You murdered an auditor? Fine. He wasn't a Daidoji, Shin. It doesn't matter to me, or to the council." Shin glanced at the auditor next to Aoto, wondering how he felt about his superior's assertion. To the man's credit, he appeared not to be listening at all.

"Then why are you here?" Shin asked.

Aoto waved the question aside, and went on as if Shin hadn't spoken. "What matters to us is your constant refusal to do what is expected of you. You are to be married. You will be moved elsewhere. Somewhere quiet. Where you will not get into any trouble, and where you will concentrate your… sociability on doing the work of the Crane."

"The work of the Crane," Shin repeated. Of course it would be this. Death was too quick, and he was too useful. "And what have I been doing, then?"

"That is my question, Shin. What have you been doing? A theater? A soy brewery? You were sent here to oversee the paper trade – nothing more. Yet you have collected a slew of businesses and bestowed the patronage of the Crane without regard for proper protocol. You knew there would be repercussions. And yet you did it regardless. Same old Shin."

Shin looked down his nose at Aoto. "And here you are, chastising me though you know it won't do any good. Same old Aoto."

Aoto's expression went through several amusing shades and contortions. Shin could tell that his cousin wanted nothing more than to give him the beating he believed Shin deserved. He'd done so in the past, of course. But always in appropriate surroundings. On the training field, or under the watchful eye of their elders.

Finally, he relaxed. "Very well," he said, as if to himself. "I have warned you. What happens next is up to you, Shin. If you run, I will drag you back in chains. If you attempt to hide, I will root you out. If you resist…" He left that part unspoken as he turned away and made for the garden exit, his lackey hurrying after him.

Shin watched him go, annoyed and infuriated in equal measure. "I hate him so very much," he said absently. "He's always been a bully."

"I think the feeling is mutual," Kasami said. "But if so, why bother to come?"

"It was a warning," Shin said softly. "A bit of familial courtesy. Aoto is convinced of my guilt, so he is giving me the chance to hide any evidence before tomorrow."

"I thought he wanted you dead," Kasami murmured.

"No. He wants me to suffer. The more quickly I'm in custody, the sooner my suffering can begin. But if I'm found guilty, there's only one way it ends – and that's too swift for his liking. Or maybe he's simply trying to provoke me into making a run for it." Shin ran a hand through his hair. "He always was a sadistic little bird." He looked at Ito, standing unobtrusively behind them. "Did you get all of that, Master Ito?"

Ito nodded. "I did. The ledgers … ?"

"Take them. And any notes we've made. Get it all out. The longer we keep it out of their hands, the more chance we have of actually figuring out what's going on here." Shin held out his hand to catch the rain.

"Hopefully, before it's too late."

CHAPTER FIFTEEN
Patterns

Ko stood on the balcony of her rooms at Saibanshoki, and studied the city. Night was rising and the sun was no more than a red strand stretched across the rooftops. She sipped a mug of tea as she watched the fading light dance across the waters, and listened to the incessant croaking of frogs. "How does anyone sleep here?" she asked Azuma.

He stood in the room behind her, hands clasped behind his back, every inch the stolid official. A mask, she thought. Azuma was no less a warrior than Aoto, though he played the role of administrator better. "What do you mean?" he asked.

"The frogs are very loud."

"They are singing Saibanshoki to sleep," he said. "The tree is very tall, you know."

Ko snorted. "Is that what you tell children here?"

"No, our children prefer gorier tales." Azuma smiled. "You asked to see me?"

"What did you make of the victim's room at the White Frog earlier?" Ko took another sip of tea. Azuma frowned in puzzlement.

"It was tidy enough. Then, Lord Kenzō struck me as that sort of man."

"Tidy?"

"Yes."

Ko nodded. "Had you been there before? After he was found, I mean."

"No. Why?"

Ko frowned. The Kaeru had many good qualities, but diligence in regard to ancillary inquiry was not one of them. They made good observers, but bad investigators. It was no wonder Shin had been able to make a name for himself as he had. "Someone searched the room before us."

Azuma's frown deepened. "You are certain?"

"As I can be, without having witnessed it. Whoever they were, they were careful. Efficient. But they left traces, nonetheless."

"Such as?"

"An umbrella," Ko said. "I noticed it as we entered. Fine quality, finer than any of her patrons could afford… and still wet. Its owner had only come in recently, and there was a slight trail of water leading upstairs, as might have dripped from the hem of a robe. Someone went up to the room and entered before us. We did not see them leave, so presumably the proprietor warned them of our approach and they availed themselves of the secret exit at the end of the hall."

"The secret–?" Azuma spluttered. "What?"

Ko took another sip of tea. "There was a distinct draft from the direction of the wall hanging at the far end of the corridor. Most large inns have some means of subtle egress, largely to avoid the embarrassment of regular patrons engaged in illicit activities. A hidden stairway or door is the most common."

Azuma grunted. He was doing his best to pretend to be

shocked, but Ko could read his expression well enough to see it was annoyance, not surprise. "I suppose you have a theory as to who it might have been?"

Ko made to reply – but stopped. Why make trouble when it wouldn't help her investigation? "No. It doesn't matter. I found what I was looking for. Are these names familiar to you?" she asked, holding out the records she'd found in Kenzō's room to Azuma. He scanned the reports, frowning.

"How did he get these?" he growled. "These are Kaeru records!"

"Bribery, I expect. Are they familiar to you?"

He hesitated. "Yes."

"What is their significance?"

"Nothing, save to the victims themselves." Azuma flipped through them. "We note every reported death in the city, accidental or otherwise, for future reference and examination. Experience has taught us that sometimes things are not what they seem."

"And these, then, were determined to be all that they appeared to be?"

"For the most part." He lifted one. "Taoka was a gangster – an extortionist who ran up against someone more dangerous." He selected two more. "Hiroto and Dari were merchants, both deaths by misadventure. Fire, in the case of one, and the other died to a robber's blade. Osho, another merchant, drowned in the river. Sato, a dealer in inks and dyes, ate something that disagreed with him."

"And Shaiban?"

"A common smuggler. Likely killed by someone who didn't want to pay him."

"No obvious connections between them, then?" Ko asked. Outside, the rain was beginning to slacken. Lights from the

Unicorn district cast their reflections across the river, like fireflies dancing above a puddle.

Azuma sniffed. "If there was, it would be noted in the reports."

"And yet, Kenzō thought there was something." Ko turned away and finished her tea. It was as she had observed. The Kaeru were good at records, but not at seeing patterns in those records. It was obvious to her that the strongest link between the dead men was the timing. They had all died within a few days of one another, and only a few weeks ago. "Perhaps it is what got him killed."

"You think Lord Shin had something to do with their deaths," Azuma said.

"I have come to no conclusions as yet. Since the murder weapon has not been located, we have only the shoyu merchant's word to go on and that is suspect." Ko sighed. None of the weapons they'd confiscated had matched the wound. "The body provided little information, and the scene was of almost no help."

"Then tell me what you think," Azuma said.

Ko looked at him. The chances that Azuma was feeding information to Shin were too great to dismiss. Shin had friends in high places. He always had. This was no different. Would they seek to help him, if it turned out he were guilty? Of that she could not be certain. Finally, she said, "I believe that Kenzō knew his killer, and did not consider them an active threat. That is why he turned his back on them. It may be that there was more than one of them. That one distracted him while the other struck. I believe his death was premeditated rather than a rash act – a matter of opportunity, perhaps, rather than in-depth planning, but deliberate nonetheless."

Azuma scratched his chin. "You think he found something in these reports related to Shin, and that is why he died?"

"Why he was killed, yes." Ko paused. She considered mentioning the signs of poisoning she'd noticed on the body, but decided to leave it for the moment. She wasn't sure what to make of it just yet. "Shin's predecessor – she was also a victim of misadventure, or so I was told."

"Yes. Drowned in the river by thieves."

"Did you catch her killers?"

Azuma sighed. "No." There was something in his tone, a hesitation. As if he were not telling the whole truth. Ko considered asking him about it, and then decided to let it lie. She was only investigating one death. Even so, it nagged at her.

"What do you know of Shin's business?" she went on before he could protest. "He is a trade representative for the Crane; surely you must keep an eye on what he's been spending his money on, while he's in your city."

"Perhaps one or two eyes," Azuma admitted.

"I would like to see any reports or records you might have, relating to it. I will compare them with Kenzō's findings, as provided by Lord Aoto. Where is he, by the way?"

Azuma frowned. "Finishing up their evening meal, I expect. I am told that tomorrow they will confiscate Lord Shin's property in the city, pending your investigation."

Ko frowned. "I did not tell them to do that." Aoto was being rash, as well as a fool. His determination to publicly humiliate Shin was endangering the sanctity of her investigation.

Azuma gave a bleak chuckle. "I have the feeling that Lord Aoto is not one to wait for permission. Or make apologies afterwards."

"I will need to go with them. If there is evidence to be had at Shin's home, I must be there to take custody of it." She hesitated. "It is not that I do not trust him, but..."

"You don't trust him," Azuma said.

"No."

"Because he wants Shin dead... or because you do?"

Ko blinked at the boldness of the accusation. "I do not want him dead. Nor does Aoto, I think. From what he said, he wants Shin humiliated rather than executed. Some family squabble, I believe."

"Lord Shin has that effect on people."

"You?" she asked, curious.

"No. I find him to be a... good man. Better than most of his status, worse than some. He has helped the governor on numerous occasions."

"Has he?" Ko asked, in such a way as to dismiss the comment. The idea that someone like Azuma, or even Tetsua, might like and respect Shin, was disconcerting. She changed the subject. "Tell me about Master Odoma. What is your opinion of him?"

"He used to be a smuggler before his uncle fell off a pier," Azuma said. Ko blinked. The river seemed to be a common cause of death here. Something to keep in mind, perhaps. "Odoma took over the family business, cut ties with his old criminal associates and became head of the merchants' association."

"You make it sound as if this is to be expected," Ko said, looking askance at him.

"In a city like this? I'm surprised when it doesn't happen." Azuma paused. "How much do you know about how a city like this works, investigator?"

"I assume all cities function along the same lines," Ko said.

Azuma smiled, not unkindly, and said, "Cities are like wild beasts. Some hunt the high places, others prowl the grasslands. This city is not like any other, and not just because of the politics involved. Trade is our lifeblood, but so, too, is smuggling.

Most independent merchants have been or are smugglers. The fishermen are smugglers. The boatmen who transport passengers to either bank are smugglers."

"And the Kaeru?"

Azuma laughed. "My mother, ancestors watch over her, was quite adept at getting certain goods past the Lion inspectors in her youth. Smugglers smuggle until they make enough to pay others to take the risks for them."

"I see. Illicit but not illegal," Ko said.

Azuma shook his head. "Oh no, very illegal. Still very illegal. But we tend to… overlook it, for the most part. Unless it causes consternation." He didn't sound ashamed by this admission, or even embarrassed. It was what it was.

"The Poison Rice Affair." Ko had read the reports. A batch of poisoned rice had nearly set the Unicorn and the Lion at each other's throats. Shin had, reportedly, been instrumental in alleviating tensions, though she found herself doubtful he had been as much help as the reports claimed. 'Helpful' and 'Shin' were not two words that often went together. Yet she was coming to learn that the Shin she'd known had matured somewhat.

"That was one such incident, yes." Azuma stroked his chin. "Since he became head of the merchants' association, Odoma has cleared up most of the worst problems on the waterfront. If it's not clan business, we tend to let it sort itself out. The merchants' association protects its members by whatever means they can afford – bodyguards, mostly. Roughnecks from Lion country, or down from Crab territory. Ronin, all of them, and not dependable long-term, but effective when it comes to little gangs of bottom-feeders."

"What about larger ones?" Ko asked.

Azuma frowned. "There are none. We keep them out."

"How?"

"Aggressively," he said. "Big gangs are often made of little ones. Someone steps up, takes charge, makes two into one and then just... keeps adding territory. Only we make sure it never gets that far. We keep the little gangs at each other's throats, and away from ours."

"This Taoko led a little gang, then?"

"Snakeheads. Waterfront extortionists; some smuggling, a bit of vice."

"Shaiban was a smuggler."

Azuma nodded slowly. "Wrong part of town, though."

Ko dismissed this with a flick of her fan. "Perhaps he decided to move."

"Hard to do for a smuggler. They have contacts, safe ports, a web of information and bribes. Not something you give up on a whim."

"What if someone made him?"

"What does this have to do with Lord Shin, exactly?"

"Nothing," Ko said, with a sigh. "I am merely speculating."

Azuma grunted and looked at the reports again. "Earlier, you asked me about Lord Shin's business interests... well, he had interest in all of these merchants."

"What do you mean?"

"The merchants under Lord Shin's patronage did business with all of them."

Ko snapped open her fan. "That is to be expected, isn't it?"

"Possibly. But it is odd. Sato makes sense – paper and ink go together like fish and rice. But leather goods? It's possible Lord Shin was simply looking for new ways to make money, but..."

"That doesn't sound like him at all," Ko said, before she could stop herself.

"It doesn't," Azuma agreed. "Lord Shin is many things but ambitious and greedy are not among them. Money is not among his interests."

"No," Ko said softly. She closed her fan and tapped her lips with it. Shin's ledgers would be among the first things Aoto confiscated. She needed to get her hands on them before they vanished into the custody of the Crane. She doubted that there were answers to be had there, but she could sense a pattern stirring and possibly a thread or two to tug. She looked at Azuma. "Who do you think killed Kenzō?"

He looked taken aback. "Odoma, of course."

"Why?"

"Simplest answer."

Ko smiled. She liked Azuma. "I meant, why would he have done it?"

"Lord Kenzō was diligent, thorough. If he was visiting Odoma, it was for good reason. That reason probably got him killed." Azuma shrugged. "He wouldn't be the first man whose meticulousness led him into trouble."

Ko nodded and turned back to the river. Azuma's words rattled in her head. Something told her that he was right, and yet wrong at the same time. "I will need some of your men, tomorrow. Aoto will not be pleased to see me."

"You think there will be trouble?"

Ko sniffed. "If he is wise, there will not be."

"Which one are you referring to?" Azuma asked. "Aoto… or Shin?"

"Yes," Ko said simply.

CHAPTER SIXTEEN
Custody

It was morning when Kitano returned, and not alone. Shin was having breakfast when Kasami showed Kitano and Chobei in. Though surprised by the presence of the latter, Shin didn't let it get in the way of good manners. He had more tea brought out and said, "You had me worried, Kitano. It's not often you stay out all night."

"Someone tried to kill me, my lord," Kitano said, bowing low. He looked as if he hadn't slept all night. His robes were spattered with something dark – not mud, Shin thought.

"Odoma?" Shin asked, sitting up.

"In a way," Kitano said. "I thought it best not to come home until I could be sure we weren't followed. Chobei let me stay with him." He winced and rubbed his eyes. Evidently his night had not been a restful one. "Told him you'd pay him, my lord."

"And so I will," Shin said. He studied Chobei, waiting for the other man to speak.

Chobei sipped his tea and said, "There's a bounty, my lord."

"A what?"

"A bounty," Chobei said calmly. "A price on your head, my lord."

"I know what a bounty is, thank you. Who's paying this no-doubt exorbitant fee?"

"The merchant, Odoma."

Shin blinked. While it wasn't exactly unexpected, it was still something of a surprise. It was so blatant. Foolish, even. Was the merchant really that much of a fool? He forced himself to focus on the facts. "Someone was watching Doctor Sanki's place yesterday. One of yours?" he asked quietly. Chobei shook his head slowly.

"No. Odoma has deep pockets, but not that deep." He paused, and Shin felt a flicker of relief. Chobei's cadre of shinobi had nearly killed him once upon a time. He had no wish to repeat the experience of being hunted by them. "Whoever it was, was likely waiting for you. You've never made any secret of your habits, and some would rather wait for you to come to them than waste time looking for you."

"How many people exactly are… pursuing this bounty?" Shin asked, with a sinking feeling. Bounties weren't uncommon, but he'd never been the subject of one himself. From what he'd seen, they tended to bring out the worst in a certain sort of person.

Chobei's expression was grim. "All of them. Every wave person in the city will be weighing their chances."

Shin closed his eyes and tried to staunch the sudden rush of fear that ran through him. Chobei wasn't the sort to exaggerate. If he said all, he meant it. While most killers might think twice about attacking a member of the nobility, desperation might blind others to the potential danger of pursuing such a contract. "When did he place this bounty?"

"The day before yesterday," Chobei said promptly. Shin wondered, idly, whether Odoma had actually approached

Chobei about taking on the job. He doubted it. Odoma wasn't the sort to hire shinobi, too subtle for his tastes. The timing was interesting, however.

"The day Kenzō was discovered," Shin murmured. It didn't make sense. Odoma had already struck a blow – why go to these lengths? Especially given the possible consequences to himself, and his business, if his actions were found out. The Crane would punish him for his temerity. Odoma had to know that.

Shin paused. Unless – there was something he wasn't seeing. Some other motivation. He thought of what he and Ito had discussed about the tunnels beneath the theater. About Odoma's past, and the list of names. He straightened. "If I said the name Shaiban, would it mean anything to you?"

Chobei frowned. "He was a smuggler. Dead now."

"What about… a fish-merchant named Hiroto?"

Chobei's frown deepened. "That one? Bad news." He glanced around, as if searching for a place to spit. Thankfully, he refrained. Shin leaned forward.

"Why do you say that?"

"He had dealings with Shaiban."

"Smuggling fish?"

Chobei smiled. "Smuggling things in fish."

Shin grunted. "Another name, then… Osho."

Chobei shook his head. "Never heard of him."

"Sato?"

"Dye seller. Also a smuggler."

"Hiroto… Dari…"

"Smugglers."

Shin threw up his hands. "Is anyone in this city not a smuggler?"

Chobei smiled. "You, my lord."

"Except apparently I am. Though I didn't know it." Shin sat back on his heels. The last thing he needed at this point was to have to look over his shoulder in case some random fool decided to try and remove his head. "Is there any way to cancel the bounty?"

"Odoma can," Kitano said helpfully.

"Yes, I had gathered that," Shin said, more sharply than he intended. He stared at his tea for a moment, letting all the facts tumble over and over in his mind. Kenzō had been murdered, that was obvious – but why?

Something Sanki said suddenly came to him: poison. Kenzō hadn't just been murdered, he'd been poisoned as well. Why would Odoma poison someone, only to kill them not long after? Unless… Odoma hadn't known about the poison.

Shin straightened. "Oh my." It had been staring him right in the face, and he hadn't seen it. He could blame the distractions of the day, but the truth was he'd simply forgotten until just now. He ran his hands through his hair, mind working now. Perhaps for the first time all day. Kenzō had been poisoned. Then, he'd gone to Odoma – why? Supposedly to talk to him about a discrepancy… but what if Odoma had misinterpreted Kenzō's request? What if he'd simply… panicked and killed the auditor? And what if… *what if* that had been the poisoner's intent? What if Odoma wasn't *the* culprit? What if he was *a* culprit?

"Oh my," Shin said, again. Things were starting to snap into focus. He didn't have the whole picture yet, but he could feel the edges. "Oh my, my, my. Isn't this interesting?" he murmured to himself. There was someone else in this game. Some unknown player, watching him scramble blindly as the trap closed in.

The same person, perhaps, whose shadow he'd been treading on for some time. The person behind the Poison Rice Affair – not those who'd taken the blame, but the one who'd given them the idea… the same one who'd recently tried to set the Lion growling, again through other parties. In both cases, only Shin's quick thinking had kept things from spiraling out of control. Somewhere in the city, there was a spider in a web, and Shin had the feeling it had decided to make him its next meal.

"My lord?" Kitano asked, trading glances with Chobei.

Thinking fast now, Shin pointed his fan at them. "Kitano, I have a task of utmost importance for you. I need you to get to the merchant Ito's residence and stay with him. Tell him it is at my request. He has something in his possession I want you to watch over. Guard it with your life. Chobei…"

"Are you paying me, my lord?" Chobei asked, in a mild tone.

"Yes." Shin reached into his robes and produced his money pouch. He weighed it on his palm and then tossed it to the shinobi. Better to give it to Chobei than to surrender it to Aoto, when he finally arrived. "Consider this a retainer. I need you and your cadre to keep an eye on Sanki, Lun and anyone else connected to me. If anyone tries to do to them what they nearly did to Kitano, I want you to see to it that they have cause to regret their actions."

Chobei smiled. "As you wish, my lord. A good opportunity for Yui to show her boy how certain things are done." He rose smoothly to his feet, but paused, a speculative look on his face. "I believe you are about to have visitors, my lord."

Shin looked at Kasami, who had only just risen to her feet, her face expressionless. He wondered what she made of the bounty. He would have to keep an eye on her, and make sure she didn't decide that the simplest answer was to remove Odoma's head. As Kasami headed for the garden, Shin gestured for Kitano and Chobei to go out the back. "Take the side exit. Chobei, make sure he gets out and there'll be something extra in it for you."

Chobei nodded, grabbed Kitano and the two men hurried for the other side of the house. Shin heard raised voices from outside. Aoto had always been an early riser. He finished his tea, sighed and rose to his feet.

Once more, Aoto was in the garden, but this time he had more auditors with him. Kasami stood between them and the house, her hands at her sides but her expression stony. "You didn't run," Aoto said, when Shin made his appearance.

"The thought never crossed my mind," Shin said, opening his fan and giving it a flutter. The rain had slackened some, but had not ceased. He wondered what the state of the river would be, if it continued. "My house is open to you, of course. Let it never be said that I am one to make trouble. But I hope you will remember that this is my home."

"Nothing will be damaged, Shin," Aoto said, with a sneer. "After all, it is all property of the Crane. Your belongings will no doubt go to repay the funds you have so frivolously wasted." He gestured to Kasami. "Tell your woman to stand aside."

"Kasami," Shin said.

She didn't move. "They broke the front gate."

"It was locked," Aoto said.

"To keep out intruders," Kasami replied. She looked at the auditors, one after the next. "How do we know that they are not here to kill you?"

Aoto looked insulted. "He is a Daidoji. We do not murder our own."

Shin laughed, loud and long. All eyes turned toward him and he slapped his fan shut and tapped it on his palm. "Let them in, Kasami. Aoto is right – and frankly, there is nowhere safer than under the protection of the Daidoji."

"Do you need protection then, cousin?" Aoto asked, as his

auditors filed past Shin. "Who would ever want to hurt so pathetic a specimen as yourself?"

"I've just been informed that there's a bounty on my head."

Aoto paused. "What? Who would dare place such a thing?"

"Odoma. The merchant."

"Him? Pah." Aoto dismissed this with a wave. "Ridiculous. What purpose would it serve? More likely some fool you've insulted playing at investigator." He looked at Kasami. "Still, I suppose the Hiramori has to earn her keep, eh?"

Kasami said nothing, but her expression spoke volumes. Even Aoto seemed taken aback by its intensity. He hastily changed the subject. "You will have to stay out here, of course. And you will be allowed to keep the clothes you are wearing, as well as any items on your person. For now."

"You wish us to wait in the rain?"

"Protocol, cousin."

"I seem to have misplaced my umbrella," Shin said.

"Take mine," Aoto said. He snatched it from the auditor who was holding it and tossed it to Shin. "With my compliments. This shouldn't take more than a few hours."

"And I am just supposed to sit here, am I?"

"If you're as smart as you think you are." Aoto paused. "I suppose you could leave, if you wished. In fact, yes – go. Leave, Shin. You no longer have any right to be here." He gestured toward the broken front gate.

Shin opened the umbrella and descended the steps. "In time. For now, I will sit and supervise. Just to make sure nothing else gets broken."

Aoto pushed past him and up the steps. "Do as suits you, Shin. You always do."

"Aoto," Shin called out. Aoto sighed and turned.

"What?"

"What did you mean, earlier? About my grandfather? Is there something I should know? Only, he and I do not trade letters as often as we should, or at all, really." Shin didn't actually expect an answer; rather, he wanted to keep Aoto distracted for as long as possible. He had no doubt that Chobei and Kitano could avoid the auditors, but Aoto was a different story. Shin prided himself on being the only thing truly capable of making Aoto lose focus.

"You ask this now?"

"I have been preoccupied."

"You are selfish, you mean," Aoto said sternly. "You've always been selfish."

Shin lifted his chin, accepting the accusation. "So people say. But I am asking now. Has something happened?"

Aoto glanced at the house and then looked back at Shin. "Changes are afoot, Shin. Your grandfather is old. People are beginning to question his… suitability, especially given his inability to see you safely dealt with. Married or otherwise." His smile was mirthless. "You see, it is as I have always said… it is not just about you."

Shin stared at him, not quite able to process what Aoto was saying. The thought of his grandfather being vulnerable in any sense of the word was impossible to comprehend. "And you, Aoto, are you one of the ones who question him?"

"If I was, I wouldn't be here," Aoto said flatly. "Enjoy sitting in the rain, Shin. Maybe take the time to think over the choices you've made." With that, he turned and went inside, leaving Shin standing speechless in the rain.

CHAPTER SEVENTEEN
Intimations

When Ko arrived at Shin's residence, accompanied by several Kaeru guards kindly provided by Azuma, she found everything in a state of uproar. Aoto had wasted no time in herding all of the servants into the garden so that his auditors could have free rein in the house. Shin and his bodyguard were seated near the far end of the garden, away from the servants, with Shin sheltering beneath an umbrella.

Aoto saw her arrive and hurried to intercept her. "Ah, Investigator Ko. Come to join in the fun?" He seemed unduly pleased with himself, radiating the sort of smugness that only a Crane in full feather could manifest.

"Are you mad, or simply a fool?" Ko asked, without preamble.

Aoto took a step back, clearly startled by the question. "What?"

"What is the point of this – this nonsense?" Ko gestured to the house. "What do you hope to accomplish with such a display?"

Aoto drew himself up. "I am doing as protocol demands. Lord Shin is guilty–"

"Accused," Ko corrected.

"Guilt or innocence are immaterial. He shames us with his failings, and thus we take back all that has been given to him." He clasped his hands behind his back. "I intend to take a full accounting of his possessions and records, so that we might know exactly how much he has debased himself at our expense."

"As I understand it, he purchased the house himself, using private funds," Ko countered, her annoyance growing by leaps and bounds.

"Funds paid to him by the Daidoji. As a plant rises from a seed, so, too, does all of this come from us, and so we take it back." Aoto made a sharp, grasping motion. He glanced at Shin. "I'd strip him naked as well, if it weren't for that Hiramori attack dog of his."

Ko followed his gaze to Kasami, who stood protectively near her master. The bodyguard was intimidating and brooked no argument, despite her relative lack of size. Even standing in the rain, she had the poise of a killer, something many warriors lacked. "Your restraint does you credit," Ko murmured. She thumbed through her mental files, drawing up all she knew about Hiramori Kasami. "The Hiramori are famed for their… efficiency in battle." A polite way of saying that they blithely disregarded any rule of war that they found less than useful.

"She is too good for him," Aoto muttered. "That woman should be guarding one of our best. Instead she is shackled to a clown."

"Perhaps she finds him amusing. Your auditors are to remove nothing from these premises without my express permission."

Aoto sneered. "Who are you to give me orders?"

Ko gestured to the Kaeru who'd accompanied her. At a flick of her fan, they scattered across the property, moving to see that her orders were obeyed. "I am Investigator Ko, and my protocol supersedes your own at this moment and time. When this affair is settled, you may compose a letter of complaint to my superiors, if that is your wish. Until then, you would be advised to do as I ask."

Aoto watched the Kaeru go about their task with barely concealed annoyance, but didn't protest and gestured for his auditors to allow the interference. "Fine. Though I find your high-handedness distasteful. I still maintain that this is a matter best handled within the clan, and not by outsiders… even ones who might once have joined our family."

Ko didn't react to the jibe. "How long will your assessment take to complete?"

"A day or two at least," Aoto said dismissively. "I hoped it would be quicker, but he collects possessions like a dog collects fleas."

Ko didn't reply. Her eyes were on Shin and Kasami. She needed to question them, and now seemed as good a time as any. She took her leave of Aoto with a nod, and made her way over to her chief suspect and his bodyguard.

As she'd expected, Kasami moved to intercept her. "I wished to speak with you, if I might," Ko said, before the bodyguard could attempt to warn her off. Kasami peered at her.

"You phrase it as a request."

"It is."

"Then no." Kasami looked away.

Ko sighed and followed the bodyguard's gaze to the house, where the auditors swarmed like a flock of hungry birds. Shin watched placidly from his place in the garden, his expression unreadable. The perfect mask of the courtier. He might have been watching a play, rather than the destruction of his life. Kasami, however, had no such mask to hide behind. They had not been so foolish as to attempt to disarm her – Aoto had some sense, it seemed – but Shin had clearly forbidden her from touching her swords. So, instead, her hands twitched.

"Let me restate: I must ask you a question. Will you answer?"

"This is unseemly." The comment, Ko knew, was not directed at her, but at Aoto's actions. And it was unseemly, rude, even. Spiteful and childish. Then, Aoto was both of those things, however much he protested.

"Yes. But temporary, provided that Shin is innocent."

"Lord Shin," Kasami said automatically.

Ko accepted the correction with a nod and went on. "I am told that Lord Shin has a propensity for sneaking away from you."

"He is never out of my reach."

Ko paused. A lie? No – a sincere belief. Kasami was intelligent, not just a blunt object. She was cunning enough to have methods for keeping an eye on someone as slippery as Shin. Informants and spies came in many forms. "Then you will swear that he did not meet the deceased at Master Odoma's shoyu brewery on the date in question?"

"I would swear that regardless," Kasami said.

Again, Ko nodded. In her experience, questioning bodyguards and servants was rarely useful. If they were loyal, they could be expected to reinforce their master's assertions. And if they were not, they could not be trusted. But even so, there was inevitably a grain of information to be had, if you were keen enough to spot it. "Yes," she said. "You are a good bodyguard. It makes me wonder, however, whether you decided to take the initiative in this case. For his own good."

Kasami glanced at her. "Are you accusing me, now?"

"No. I am making no accusations as yet, merely gathering facts. Would you have killed Kenzō, if Shin asked?"

Kasami hesitated. Then, "No. But he did not ask. He would not."

"Would you have done it if you decided it was the only way to protect him?"

No hesitation now. "Yes."

"And was it?"

"No."

"Why?"

Kasami gave a sour smile. "Lord Kenzō was not an enemy."

"Meaning?" Ko asked, in a clipped tone. Kasami gave her a long look.

"How much do you know about Lord Shin's relationship with his family?"

It was Ko's turn to hesitate. "I do not see how that's relevant."

"Lord Shin believes context is the key to any investigation."

"Lord Shin also believes that he can play the biwa," Ko said pointedly, but not loudly enough for Shin to hear.

Kasami turned away. "Lord Kenzō was not our enemy. He was attempting to save Lord Shin's life, at the behest of Shin's grandfather. Why would Lord Shin kill him?"

Ko frowned. Mention of Shin's grandfather took her back to those heady weeks when they were betrothed. The old man had been a looming presence, even then. Shin had feared him in a way that he feared no one else. Unlike many, the old man was immune to Shin's varied charms. "What do you mean 'save his life'? Was he under threat?"

Kasami indicated the auditors. "You tell me."

Ko shook her head. "No. This is immaterial. Only the facts matter. Kenzō was killed by a single blow to the back of the skull – something thin and strong. A knife, perhaps. Wielded by a skilled hand."

"I would not have stabbed him from behind," Kasami said pointedly.

Ko hesitated. "No, I do not think you would have."

"Neither would Lord Shin."

Again, Ko hesitated. "No." She gnawed her lip, considering the statement. Her eyes strayed again to Aoto's auditors. Then, once more to Shin, sitting so peacefully. Resigned, perhaps, to his fate. Something about it struck her as a pose designed to irritate. It was clearly working on Aoto, who was glaring at his cousin from the opposite side of the garden. "I must speak with him," she said, tacitly asking for permission. Kasami hesitated, but only for a moment. She led Ko over and Shin stirred himself as they came to a stop before him.

"Lady Ko," he said in greeting, with a slight smile. She remembered that smile well, infuriating but informative. It meant Shin had something to tell her.

"Lord Shin. I apologize for Lord Aoto's indiscretion."

"You mean you are sorry that he's ruined any chance you might have had to snoop about my home, searching for a murder weapon or incriminating documents?"

Ko paused. "Yes," she admitted. She considered asking him if he'd left his umbrella at the inn the previous evening, then decided against it. If he had, he had left her the information she needed. A courtesy, perhaps. Or simply pragmatism.

Shin chuckled. "You know he's going to destroy anything incriminating he finds."

"The Kaeru will see that he doesn't."

"I wish them luck."

Ko looked away. "Is there actually anything in there for them to find?"

"Not to my knowledge. Then, I am coming to realize that

there is a good deal I do not know about this matter and others."
Shin's grin faded. "I did not kill Kenzō."

"Someone did."

"But not me."

Ko looked at him. Before she could reply, he said, "Poison."

Ko frowned. "What of it?"

"Kenzō was poisoned. I suspect you took note of the signs yourself, when you viewed the body. Doctor Sanki concurs."

"I have not yet received his reports," Ko said stiffly.

"Then I should go see him, were I you. Sanki is a rough cob, but he knows his business. He was a battlefield surgeon for more years than ours combined, and has helped me on several occasions."

"I will make a note of it," Ko said. "If he was poisoned, why bother stabbing him?"

"Why indeed? May I make another suggestion?"

"No."

Shin went on as if he hadn't heard her. "The two things may be related, but not in the way you think. What was that famous case you told me about, once… the one with the two brothers, in the mountains?"

Ko's frown deepened. It was one of the more famous cases; a murder committed over an inheritance. There had been two killers – a brother and the dead man's lover, both of whom had, independently, sought to take the heir out of the line of inheritance. One had used poison, while the other had stabbed the poor man, and claimed it to be the work of bandits. An object lesson for investigators – not all crimes were things of linear simplicity. "Are you saying there are two murderers here?"

"Yes. Neither of them is me, by the way."

"So I am coming to realize," Ko admitted. She paused, noting his pleased expression. "That is not to say that I have exonerated you, Shin. You are still the most likely suspect."

"What about Odoma?"

Ko acknowledged the point with a wave of her fan. "Azuma said much the same. But as you have pointed out, there may be someone else. So, who was the last person to see Lord Kenzō alive?"

"Not me," Shin said, a considering look on his face. "I haven't spoken to him in some weeks. Not since… well."

"Not since it was announced that you were to be wed."

"No," Shin said grudgingly.

"Have you made any decisions in that regard, yet?"

"No," Shin said. She recognized the warning in his tone. He clearly didn't wish to discuss this particular matter, which only made her want to pry further. He cleared his throat. "How have you been?"

Ko's eyes narrowed. "What do you mean?"

"A simple question, Ko." Shin looked at her. "Are you well?"

Ko turned away, folding her hands inside her sleeves. "As can be expected."

"That is good to hear. I have followed your exploits, you know. You have achieved some renown in our field…"

"Our field?"

"Amateur investigation."

"I am not an amateur, Shin."

"Of course, forgive me. Even so, you have quite the reputation."

"Yes," Ko said. She didn't believe in false modesty. Then, reluctantly, "So do you."

Shin nodded. "Our field," he said again. His eyes strayed to the house. "Ah, looks like Aoto is coming to yell at me again. I think I shall take my leave."

Ko saw Aoto discussing something heatedly with one of his auditors at the front door. The latter looked apologetic. Aoto, in contrast, appeared apoplectic. "Where will you go?"

"I'm sure I'll find somewhere," Shin said. "This city can be quite welcoming to penniless vagabonds, such as myself. Come along, Kasami." He rose to his feet and hesitated. "You should visit Doctor Sanki, Ko. Then perhaps have another talk with Odoma. Ask him about the names you found in Kenzō's records. It might prove illuminating."

A moment later, he was hurrying away, Kasami following dutifully in his wake. Ko turned as Aoto reached her. "Where is he going?" he demanded. "Why didn't you stop him?"

Ko kept her expression neutral. "He is not currently under arrest. If he wishes to leave, he is free to do so. You appear agitated. Is something wrong?"

"Yes, something is wrong! The ledgers are gone!"

Ko blinked. "Shin's ledgers?"

Aoto shook his head. "What other ledgers would I be talking about?" He glared toward the front gate. Shin and Kasami were nowhere in sight. "He's made a fool of us, investigator." He turned his glare on her. "So, what are you going to do about it?"

Ko sighed. Of course. Shin was too clever to leave anything valuable laying around where intruders could find it. She looked at Aoto.

"I suppose I am going to speak with a doctor about poison."

CHAPTER EIGHTEEN
Barley Cakes

"What I still can't figure is why she'd be visiting the Snakeheads," Kitano mumbled around a mouthful of barley cake. Ito proffered the tray, and Kitano eagerly took another. He had to admit, the merchant put on a good spread.

Ito hadn't seemed all that surprised when Kitano had arrived at his shop in the Unicorn District. Then, he was a smart one. Almost as smart as Lord Shin, Kitano figured. Smarter, maybe, in certain ways. Ito had a gambler's soul and a merchant's brain. A good combination, sometimes.

"No, that does seem rather odd. Tell me – could she be an assassin?"

"Like, professional?" Kitano asked, chewing. He wiped at some crumbs on his robe and looked around, taking in the merchant's private quarters, set above his shop. Usually, merchants slept elsewhere, but Ito was apparently a traditionalist. His home was small; three rooms and little in the way of decoration. One room for sleeping, one for working and one for receiving. "Could be. She's got that sort of way about her. Not that I know many assassins, mind," he added, quickly.

"But you know plenty of killers, I expect," Ito said, with a thin smile. "So do I, come to that. We are both men of the world, you and I. We have seen the mountain, as the Badger are wont to say."

"You were a soldier, then?" Kitano asked, sneaking another barley cake. He was ravenous. Anxiety did that to him. "My parents were soldiers, too. Ronin."

"I was, in a way."

"Did you serve the Crane?"

"No." Ito selected a cake for himself and pulled it into two pieces. "Not until much later." He studied the pieces and said, "I grew up in the Hida border country. My father was overseer at the local iron mine." His voice softened. "I fancied I could see the Carpenter Wall from the highest tree in the village, but that was probably nonsense." He took a small bite and chewed slowly. Thoughtfully.

Kitano felt an uneasy tingle on the back of his neck. "You grew up near the – the Shadowlands?" he asked, in a hushed tone. The Shadowlands were half-myth, half-nightmare. A place all children knew to fear, even as they speculated as to what or who might live there. He'd heard his parents speak of them only once, when something had managed to get past the wall and come up into the Crane lands. He still wasn't certain what sort of thing it had been, but his parents had participated in the hunt and they'd never spoken of it, despite the pleas of their children.

"Close enough," Ito said. He refilled their cups. "Then, one day, the Crab came and burned the whole village. Killed everyone." He paused. "Almost everyone."

Kitano stared at him. "Why?"

Ito shrugged. "I don't know. Who can say? I'm sure they had their reasons. I was in the trees when it happened. I did so love the trees. I watched as they dragged my father into the street and… well. You can imagine." His voice was hoarse. "When they left, I went north. We had family in the Uebe marshes. I nearly starved on the road. Then again, in the marshes." He finished his cake. "I fell in with a group of bandits. We raided over the border and took sanctuary in the marshes when the Hida sent troops after us."

"You were a bandit?" Kitano said, in some surprise.

"I was an excellent bandit," Ito said, preening slightly. "Bandits make the best merchants, you know. And smugglers, too. A good merchant has a crooked mind – rather like a gambler."

Kitano chuckled. "I knew I liked you, Master Ito."

"And I you, Kitano. We are both crooked men, in service to a crooked man."

"Never thought of Lord Shin that way," Kitano admitted, scratching his chin.

"But he is. His mind doesn't travel on straight paths." Ito smiled. "That's why I do not fear for him, in this instance. The Crane – the Daidoji, in particular – see the world as a selection of set values. This, worthwhile, the other, worthless. Lord Shin, however, understands that value is fluid. A thing's worth is determined in the moment, not by tradition. It is why he is able to see the patterns that bind others, and side-step them." Ito chuckled. "He is a dancer, our lord, and a fine one."

"He is that," Kitano said, though he wasn't certain that he entirely followed Ito's thinking. He looked longingly at the remaining barley cakes, sighed, and clapped his hands against his knees. "So, where do you want me?"

"What do you mean?" Ito asked.

"Lord Shin sent me here to guard his ledgers. I assume you're keeping them up here. Where do you want me to sleep?" Kitano looked around the room. "The Daidoji will come knocking eventually, I figure, but not for a few days. That gives us some time together." He added the last somewhat apologetically.

Ito frowned. "You're planning to stay here?"

"If the ledgers are here, so am I."

Ito nodded slowly, and finished his tea. "I was planning to study them today, while my assistants run the shop. You could help, if you like."

"Me?"

"Well, you might spot something neither I nor Lord Shin noticed." Ito rose. "First, however, I have some letters to write. There's a merchant in Hisatu-Kesu I've been doing business with, and I need to let him know about our current difficulties, in case it impacts our dealings."

"Hisatu-Kesu … that's Unicorn territory," Kitano said, hastily rising to his feet.

"It is indeed."

"You do a lot of business with the Unicorn?"

"I do business with everyone – save the Crab." Ito paused, his eyes on the window. "Hmm. How odd."

"What?" Kitano turned, following the merchant's gaze.

"We're being watched." Ito swept to the window, but didn't stand in front of it, thankfully. Instead, he stepped to the side, so that he could see the street, but not be seen. Kitano followed his example.

At first, he saw nothing. Just the late morning crowd, going about their business as best they could in the rain. Then, two familiar faces lurking in the shadows of a sake house doorway across the narrow street. How Ito had seen them, he couldn't say. Maybe his past life as a bandit had left him with just enough paranoia to notice such things.

"You recognize them," Ito said. It wasn't a question.

"Masa and Itachi. Friends of Haruko." Kitano peered at them, his memory filling in details that his eyes couldn't catch. Masa was the taller of the two, with an ugly scar on one cheek and a tendency to think dousing himself in perfume was a good substitute for a bath. Itachi was red all over, like he was suffering from a permanent sunburn, and liked to chew ginger to cover his foul breath.

"The fellow your associate Chobei killed?"

Kitano nodded. Ito frowned. "What sort of fellows are they?"

"Bad," Kitano said. "I know them both. From the good old days. They used to work for the Snakeheads." Kitano frowned as something occurred to him. "So did Haruko, come to that. I should have told Lord Shin."

"It's probably not important," Ito said. "How bad are they?"

"They work for anyone with coin to spend. Worst sort of ronin. Not skilled enough to sign on with a reputable lord, but just skilled enough to be trouble. Between them, they've killed half a dozen people. Two of whom deserved it."

Ito raised an eyebrow. "And the rest?"

"Didn't," Kitano said flatly. He paused. "I'm no innocent. I've sunk my share of bodies. But Masa and Itachi – they're rotten to the core. They're street-curs with airs. They'd murder each other if you paid them enough."

"I trust your judgement in these matters, Kitano," Ito mused. "Though, I doubt they're here for you. More likely they're watching my place, hoping for Lord Shin to show up. How distressing." He didn't sound distressed, however. Just annoyed. "Master Odoma has really set the hound among the oxen, hasn't he?"

"He was never one to think farther ahead than his next

wager," Kitano said, dismissively. Odoma was a fool, and always had been. Declaring war on a member of the Daidoji was the act of an idiot – or a desperate man. "Want me to get rid of them?"

"Can you do it without spilling blood?"

Kitano grimaced. "Probably not."

Ito sighed. "What are the odds they'll get bored and leave?"

"Pretty good. Neither one is known for their patience." Kitano rubbed his chin. "But you're right. They're probably just – ah." Masa had lurched into the street, Itachi at his heels. "Spoke too soon. They're coming this way."

Ito frowned. "Stay here. I'll deal with them."

"Are you sure?"

"Better they don't know that you're here, I think. I expect they just want to deliver a few threats. It won't be the first time." He went downstairs, leaving Kitano alone. Kitano hesitated, and then slowly, quietly, followed his host. If anything happened to Ito, Lord Shin would be quite upset.

The stairs were narrow and cramped, like everything else in the shop. They creaked alarmingly as he descended, but Ito was already out in the shop. Raised voices reached Kitano as he got to the bottom. He slid the door open a few inches, just enough to see what was going on.

Masa and Itachi loomed large in the shop, their topknots nearly brushing the low ceiling. Masa took the lead, as usual. "Master Odoma wants to talk to you, merchant. Best you come with us."

"I have nothing to say to him," Ito said. Kitano frowned. Why would Odoma want to talk to Ito? To threaten him? Or was he looking for more leverage against Lord Shin? He pushed the questions aside. That was the sort of thing Lord Shin could figure out later. Kitano's job was to make sure Ito survived the next few minutes.

Masa grinned. "I was hoping you'd say that." He took a step toward Ito, but the merchant didn't retreat. Kitano was impressed. Ito had more sand than he'd expected. Then, given what he'd just learned about the man, perhaps he shouldn't have been surprised.

"What is your strategy, exactly?" Ito asked, in a deceptively gentle voice. "To drag me out of here by my heels? That won't go unnoticed."

"What do we care?" Itachi grunted. "Who's going to stop us?"

"The Crane."

"I don't see them here, paper-seller," Masa growled. "Just you – and us."

Kitano decided he'd kept quiet long enough. "And me," he said, stepping down into the shop, dice in hand. "Masa, Itachi. Long time since we last tossed dice."

Masa took a step back. "What are you doing here, gambler?"

"I followed the smell, Masa." Kitano sniffed the air. "Still wearing that cheap perfume, huh?"

"Watch your mouth, Daichi," Masa snarled. "Wouldn't be the first time it's gotten you in trouble." He gestured to Kitano's missing finger and chuckled.

Kitano rubbed his cheek with his prosthesis. "I'll keep that in mind, Masa."

Masa grimaced. "Remember who you're talking to!"

Kitano bared his teeth. "And you should remember that my boss outranks your boss, whatever he might believe. Which means I outrank you two – just like always."

"You piece of…" Itachi began, his florid features turning an even brighter shade of red. His hand twitched, as if he wanted to go for his weapon. "We're still samurai, gambler. You speak to us with respect."

"I lost all respect for you the first time I saw you play dice, Itachi," Kitano shot back. He leaned back against the wall and grinned. "Shame about Haruko, eh? Still, couldn't have happened to a nicer fellow."

The two thugs shared a look. "We heard he, Taj and Dogi came out the worst in a back-alley fight. Was that you, then?" Masa asked. "If so, maybe we should teach you a lesson about killing Master Odoma's valued employees."

"You could try," Kitano said, with a bravado he didn't truly feel. Two against one wasn't as bad as three against one, but it wasn't much better. He needed to keep them talking until they decided it wasn't worth the effort to press the matter. "Or, maybe you could tell me why Odoma wants to talk to the paper-seller, here."

Itachi gave a gurgling laugh. "How's that your business?"

"Well, if you don't want to talk about that, we could talk about why Odoma's new courtesan was visiting the Snakeheads. Remember your old friends? Who's in charge of them these days, anyway?"

Again, Masa and Itachi traded looks. "You should learn not to talk about such things, gambler," Masa said slowly. "It could get you in trouble."

"Wouldn't be the first time," Kitano said. He clacked the dice in his hand and added, "You know, if you two ever get tired of smelling like yeast, I could put in a good word for you with Lord Shin – his bodyguard is always in need of a good pair of training dummies. Though you might need to wash first, Masa."

Masa growled wordlessly and Itachi hissed. Both of them took a step toward Kitano, who tensed even as his hand fell to his knife. The shop was small and cramped. No room to swing a sword. Ito cleared his throat.

"I believe you two should leave, now."

Masa looked at the merchant. "Odoma…" he began.

"Tell Odoma that if he wishes to talk, he can come here. Otherwise, we have nothing to say to one another." Ito faced Masa head on, and the ronin looked away first. The latter swatted Itachi, and the two men slunk out of the shop with baleful stares and muttered imprecations. Kitano loosed a breath he hadn't known he'd been holding.

Ito peered at him. "That was risky."

"Not really. They're all swish, no steel." Kitano scratched his cheek with his false finger and grinned. "Not like Lady Kasami, that's for sure."

Ito smiled. "Few are."

Kitano laughed. "That's the truth." He clacked his dice. "Now, we were going to take a look at those ledgers, weren't we?"

CHAPTER NINETEEN
Foxfire Theater

The Foxfire Theater was silent and dark when Kasami and Shin arrived. While there were undoubtedly members of the stage crew flitting about, hard at work maintaining the theater, the building would otherwise be empty.

There were no performances scheduled for the day or the week, thankfully. While Kasami's opinion of actors had improved somewhat of late, she still regarded the great mass of them as useless butterflies, flitting about and getting in the way. Even so, the leader of the Three Flower Troupe, the theater's resident kabuki players, was waiting on them at the doors.

Wada Sanemon was a large man, bulky and broad like many former soldiers, of which he was one. His robes were ill-fitting, but clean and well made, and he was sweating despite the chill in the air. Sanemon was perpetually anxious, especially when it came to dealing with Shin. Kasami sympathized, somewhat. "My lord, I have seen to the preparation of your box as you asked. Tea has been prepared, and I'll bring it up myself while you situate yourselves."

Shin nodded gratefully. "Thank you, Master Sanemon. Your

kindness is much appreciated as is your offer of sanctuary." Kasami frowned. The theater wasn't the ideal refuge; too many ways in and out and Aoto knew about it. He would come eventually, if only to shut it up and send the crew away. But not for a few days at least. It would take them that long to go through Shin's possessions.

Sanemon bobbed his head and shut the doors behind them. "Not kindness, my lord. Merely repaying the debt we owe you. Without your patronage, we wouldn't have survived all these months." He paused. "Besides, you do own the building."

"That is true, though perhaps not for much longer," Shin said. At Sanemon's puzzled look, he laughed and tapped him on the arm with his fan. "Never mind. Before we settle in, however, I would like to take a look at the tunnels."

Sanemon's look of bewilderment deepened. "Tunnels, my lord?"

"The ones running under the theater."

"The – the cistern, my lord? The sewers, you mean?"

Shin gave Sanemon another gentle tap with his fan. "The very thing, Master Sanemon. The very thing. Lead on, if you please!" Shin spoke with false joviality, but Kasami could sense the strain under the mirth. He was upset, on edge. It worried her.

Members of the crew stopped what they were doing and watched them as they passed backstage. Murmurs ran through the little knots of onlookers; whispers… worries. Kasami had no illusions that word of the auditors' raid on Shin's residence was spreading through the city. If the troupe didn't know yet, they would soon enough. There was no telling how they'd react. Panic, was her suspicion.

Then, as if to prove her right, she heard the familiar voice of the troupe's lead actor, Nao, calling out from behind them.

"Sanemon! Have you heard? He's – oh. Ah." Nao was tall, slim, and effete. In the right light, from the right angle, he could pass for either a man or a woman, a talent he'd employed to great effect in his time with the Three Flower Troupe.

He paused as Shin and Kasami turned. A low bow followed. "My lord, a pleasure as always–" he began, but Shin cut him off with a flick of his fan.

"Hello, Nao. I must compliment you on your performance as Lady Asano in *The Goblin and the Calligrapher,* two weeks ago. I'm told it was singularly affecting."

Nao smiled at the compliment. "I was not aware you saw it, my lord."

"How could I resist?" Shin slapped his fan into his palm. "But I interrupted you… what were you about to say?"

Nao hesitated. "I… nothing, my lord. Nothing important, I mean."

"Oh, that's fine, then. Master Sanemon here was just taking us to the cistern."

Nao blinked. "The… why?"

"The tunnels," Sanemon said. Nao frowned.

"The sewers? Why?"

"That is the question," Shin said, turning back to Sanemon. "Lead on, Master Sanemon! The day runs on, and time is of the essence." Nao fell into step with them as they went, clearly curious and not inclined to pretend otherwise.

"Forgive me, my lord, but I'd heard you were suffering some… difficulties of late," Nao began, cautiously. Kasami realized at once that the comment was anything but innocent. More likely, Nao was trying to feel Shin out and determine whether the troupe needed to prepare for the worst.

"Nothing to concern yourself with, Nao. A simple

misunderstanding which will no doubt be cleared up directly. Ah – here we are." The backstage area was a maze of wooden walls and paper screens, dividing the small space into rooms. But the labyrinth had a center: a cramped, circular room of damp wood, nestled far beneath the stage. It was here that water for the theater was drawn up, and some types of waste disposed of. Kasami grimaced at the smell – river mud, mingling with standing water as well as more human odors – and Shin pressed his sleeve to his nose.

"I thought I asked everyone to dump their waste elsewhere," he said.

Sanemon frowned apologetically. "I did tell them, my lord, but – well. The nightsoil box is on the far side of the building and the stage crew… lazy, the lot of them."

Shin waved this feeble explanation aside. Kasami had no doubt that the troupe felt obliged to ignore as many of Shin's edicts as possible; she had often chided him for not taking a firmer hand with them. Actors could not be allowed to think themselves above their patrons. She was just about to mention this when Shin stepped forward and heaved the wooden cap off the cistern. He let it fall to the floor and stepped back as a rush of noisome air gusted up. Kasami could hear the rush of water below.

"Are you sure this is wise, my lord?" Sanemon began, hesitantly.

Shin frowned. "I first saw these drainage tunnels when Okuni and I were being chased by Chobei and his cadre. I thought little of them at the time. A city like this must have some way of transporting water and waste, and these tunnels were obviously part of that. But they are more than just drainage. They are transport as well. Isn't that so, Master Sanemon?"

"My – my lord?" Sanemon asked. Kasami studied his face. He knew exactly what Shin was talking about, though clearly he wished he didn't.

"Smuggling, Master Sanemon. Apparently, we have been playing host to smugglers. And for some time."

"I told you," Nao murmured. "He was bound to figure it out."

Shin turned. "You knew?"

"Knew enough to pretend we didn't," Nao said, somewhat defensively. "Sanemon here assumed they were acting on your orders. I told him otherwise, but… well. You know how it is."

"No. We do not," Kasami said. "Tell us."

Nao gave her a pouty look. "So humorless. I don't know what Chika sees in you."

Kasami blinked and flushed. "Chika? I…" The actress was a friend, of sorts. Kasami had spent some time teaching her the rudiments of swordplay – purely to help her with stage combat, of course.

Thankfully, Shin saved her from her embarrassment. "How often?" he asked, sharply. Sanemon swallowed and dabbed at his pate with a rag.

"A few times a month, at first. Then every few days. It's stopped of late, however."

"What was being brought in?"

Sanemon and Nao looked at one another. Sanemon made to reply, but Nao beat him to it. "We don't know, my lord. We assumed you knew about it, so we kept quiet. And we didn't poke our noses in where we weren't invited."

"We don't even know where they were storing it!" Sanemon burst out. "I searched every inch of the theater, but – nothing. All I know is that the cistern cap was left off on moonless nights, and the stage crew reported hearing voices sometimes."

"That doesn't sound like staying out of it," Kasami said. Shin waved her to silence.

"No. From what Ito said, it's likely there are storage areas of some sort below." He sighed. "Well, the only thing for it is to take a look for ourselves."

Kasami looked at him in shock. "You can't be serious!"

"Do you have a better suggestion?"

"Yes. We tell Lord Azuma. Let the Kaeru handle it."

"No." Shin drew himself up. "This is my theater. It is my responsibility." He took a deep breath and glanced at her. "Well? What are you waiting for?"

Kasami sighed and peered into the cistern. It wasn't a long drop; easily done, if you knew how to do it. The water was rising, thanks to the rain. But it wasn't overflowing yet. That made for a soft landing. She rucked up her sleeves and vaulted over the side. She heard Shin cry out, but ignored him. Water lapped at her waist; cold, but largely clean. River water, carrying with it the faint scent of mud and rotting vegetation. One hand resting on the hilt of her sword, she swept her gaze across the irregular stones. "We'll need a light," she called up.

"And a rope," Shin shouted down. "How did you intend to get back up?"

"I leave such considerations to you, my lord," she retorted. "Be quick about it. It's cold down here."

"I will. In the meantime, tell me what you see," Shin called down. Kasami gave an exasperated grunt.

"Water and shadows," she replied.

Shin leaned over the edge of the cistern. "The Hiramori are infamous for their traps and tricks, Kasami. More than once, your people have turned those marshes of theirs into a killing ground, full of hidden caches and murder-holes. So, what do you see?"

Annoyed, Kasami took a longer look at her surroundings. There was some light, thanks to the cistern. She studied the way the water flowed and moved against it, in the direction of the river. Wooden boards overhead gave way to stone. She heard a soft sound, like water moving against cloth. She drew her sword and traced the wall to her left with the tip. Metal scraped against stone, until–

Shin splashed down behind her with a muffled yelp and a despairing groan. "My robes!" She turned to see him half-crouched in the water, a candle in hand, its wick shielded from the damp by a paper hood that also concentrated its glow. A knotted rope hung down from the mouth of the cistern overhead. He thrust the candle toward her and spent several fruitless moments trying to squeeze water out of his robes, despite standing hip deep in it. "I knew I should have removed them."

"They were already wet from the rain," Kasami said dismissively. "I believe I've found it. This way." She gestured with her sword, and he obligingly swung the candle up, focusing its glow on the area. Kasami splashed toward it, tracing the stones lightly with her blade. When she reached what she was looking for, she took a two-handed grip and slashed. The backdrop had been expertly painted to resemble part of the wall, but one touch of her blade and it crumpled away from the wooden frame, exposing the wide aperture beyond.

"Ha! I knew it!" Shin crowed. Kasami gave him a steady look. "Good work," he added, hastily. "What I meant was, I knew you could locate it."

Kasami grunted and stepped through the aperture. It smelled as damp as the rest of the tunnels, but care had been taken to keep the interior as dry as possible. It wasn't a large space; barely the size of one of the theater's private boxes. Short barrels of sawdust and grit had been situated in the corners to absorb damp, and the floor was covered in a carpet of woven reed stalks. The walls were slatted with timbers painted with pitch, so as to stabilize the storeroom.

Shin followed her in, swinging his candle about carefully. "Ingenious," he murmured. "The sounds of the water would be enough to disguise any noise." He used his candle to light one of the handful of lanterns stored on a wooden shelf at the far end of the room. The sudden, ruddy glow revealed bushels of cargo, draped in protective cloth, stored around the edges of the room. Most contained rice – now moldy – or salted fish – definitely on the turn. But there were other things as well: rolls of cloth for dyeing and leather goods being the most prominent. Kasami caught a gleam out of the corner of her eye and went to one of the rice barrels. There was a crack in the side; small, but wide enough that she could see something metal within it. With a flick of her blade, she cut the ropes securing the top. Then she plunged her hand in, searching.

A moment later, she stepped back, holding her prize: a small sword in a plain leather sheath. Nothing like her own, save in its general shape. She whistled, catching Shin's attention, and tossed her discovery to him.

Shin caught it awkwardly. "Weapons being smuggled onto the Unicorn docks – why?" He held up the sword and slid it partially from its sheath. It was a common blade, meant for a foot soldier, but no less deadly for its inelegant lines.

"We don't know that they're going to the docks," Kasami said. Shin looked at her and she fell silent. He gestured for her to continue. She frowned and said, "We know only that they're passing through. Why would they go to the trouble of crossing the river, just to travel from a different set of docks?"

"I can think of several reasons. But you believe they're being transported overland?"

"Inland," she corrected, studying the contents of another barrel. Hidden among the rice was a selection of spearheads, all stamped with the sigil of one of the vassal families of the Akodo. She extended one to Shin. "Do you recognize this sigil?"

"The Itagawa," Shin said, as he took the spearhead. "Why send Lion weapons into Unicorn lands?" He weighed the spearhead in his hand and tossed it back into the barrel. "Unless you wanted it to be used – and found. My, my… this is becoming more unpleasant by the moment."

Kasami looked at the other barrels. She imagined the sort of people who might find a use for weapons like this. Shin met her gaze and nodded. "I was thinking the same thing," he said, as if she'd spoken. "You remember that nasty bunch we ran into when we visited Hisatu-Kesu last year? When we helped out Batu with that little problem of his?"

"I do," Kasami said, though calling it a little problem seemed something of an understatement. It had involved dealings with an anti-imperial revolutionary cell, and the attempted assassination of several important members of the Unicorn clan. "What was it they called themselves?"

"The Iron Sect," Shin said softly. "I hoped we'd seen the last of them."

"We do not know it is them," Kasami said.

"If not them, then someone like them." Shin scraped a loose strand of hair out of his face. "It is clear to me that this is what got Kenzō killed. He found out about it, somehow – but why go to Odoma? Unless… information." Shin stepped away from the barrels. "Of course. Kenzō was a diligent man. Of course he would investigate the matter."

"So Odoma is behind it?" Kasami asked.

"No. No, Odoma is a criminal, not a revolutionary. Whoever it is must have realized that Kenzō was on the hunt, so they started tying up loose ends, like Shaiban and the others. Kenzō saw the pattern – but why not tell me?"

"Because you were distracted," Kasami said bluntly. Shin looked at her, and then away. Ashamed, or maybe just annoyed. But he was thinking again, and that was good. That was what was needed.

"I am sorry," he said. "I never imagined…"

"You didn't think," Kasami said flatly. "You never think. You plan and scheme and imagine. But you do not think." She looked at him. "This – all of it – could have been avoided if you had taken but one moment, one single moment, to think. To consider the ramifications of your behavior."

"Now you sound like Aoto," Shin said.

Kasami cut him off with a glare. "I do not care about propriety… at least, not so much as I once did." She took a deep breath. "This is not about the Crane – just you. You have made yourself a target, and now you moan because arrows have been loosed in your direction. It has been weeks since you agreed to be wed. Weeks of dithering, of sulking, of yielding ground when you should have been taking it. If you had just–"

"Just what?" Shin interrupted. He slapped one of the barrels with the flat of his hand. "Just married some stranger, chosen for me?"

"Yes!" Kasami shook her head. "A choice is not a wedding. A choice is simply a choice. You could have chosen and then delayed. Or perhaps even learned to enjoy the idea. Instead, you gave your enemy an opening to strike – and they have."

"I am aware," Shin said. "I agree with your every

recrimination. But knowing I have made a mistake is not the same as correcting it."

"So correct it, then." One of Shin's admirable qualities was how he responded to stress. Put him in a corner, take away all of his options, and his mind began to work at a far greater speed than normal. There was a warrior there, underneath all the frippery. Just a lazy one; slow to react, unless properly provoked.

For a long time, she had thought one of her duties was to do the provoking. Now, she knew better. It wasn't just provocation Shin needed, but a shoulder to lean on. Someone to speak with him as, if not an equal, then a friend. To help him find the right path to take. She took a deep breath and said, "We will not be secure here for long. We must consider other options."

"Like leaving the city, you mean?"

"Yes."

"And where would we go?"

"You have friends. Lord Batu would surely welcome a visit."

Shin looked away. "No. I will not bring my trouble to Batu's doorstep. That much good I can do." He ran his hands through his hair. "But there are other options." His expression was as sharp as a knife. Kasami smiled. He'd been reacting since Azuma had escorted him to Saibanshoki the previous day. Scrambling to stay one step ahead of Ko and Aoto and all the rest. But he'd found his footing now. She was almost proud.

Shin looked at her. "I need to talk to Lady Konomi. She and I have some things to discuss."

CHAPTER TWENTY
Medicine

Ko looked at the shabby little house belonging to Doctor Sanki with disapproval. In her experience, reputable physicians lived in better accommodations. Water was slopping across the cramped street, pressing against hastily erected breaks of sandbags and lumber. The rain wasn't falling heavily, but steadily.

The Kaeru with her, a young warrior named Ina, looked around warily. "The river is angry," she said, as if intoning a prophecy. It seemed to be a habit with her.

"Is it?" Ko asked, not looking at her. Ina, she suspected, had drawn the short straw. The other Kaeru under her authority were still watching over Aoto's confiscation of Shin's property. They would ensure that any evidence was set aside for her, when she returned.

"It will break its banks soon." The Kaeru shifted her weight, dipping excess water off the umbrella she was holding over Ko's head.

"Will it?"

"This area will flood. It has before."

Ko gave her a sidelong glance. "Would you like to leave?"

Ina stiffened. "Lord Azuma said I was to guard you. I go where you go."

Ko snapped open her fan. "I am glad to hear it. I am told this city can be quite dangerous." Tales of the city and its myriad troubles rode the river into the lands of the Dragon. Every merchant and traveler told stories of the raucous and lawless port, cloven into three and controlled effectively by no one.

Only, it wasn't quite as simple as that. The city was under control, but it was a subtle thing. The authorities rode the tides of mood and trouble the way sailors rode the river. Shin did much the same. He rode conversations wherever they took him. His ability to start in one place and finish someplace completely different was one of the things that had simultaneously infuriated and attracted her, in their youth. But she feared it wasn't going to help him this time. As Ina said, the river was angry.

Ko thought again of the list of names she'd found in Kenzō's room. All dead, all connected, though she couldn't say how. It nagged at her, even though it had nothing to do with the facts before her. She reminded herself that she was here only to determine the cause of the auditor's death, and whether Shin was involved.

And yet, here she was, acting on a suggestion from her chief suspect. Her teachers would be very displeased. But despite everything, she found herself trusting Shin, and his observations. He was smarter than he let on.

As she made to knock on Sanki's door, she wondered how Aoto would react to her findings. Would it change his plans any, or simplify things for him? Without the murder charge to complicate matters, the governor's edict would no longer hold weight. Aoto would be free to take Shin into custody, and back to whatever fate awaited him – forced marriage, perhaps. Or a quiet execution. The Crane had a reputation for such things. They liked to tidy away their embarrassments and pretend they had never existed.

Her thoughts were interrupted as the door slid open and the wizened features of Sanki peered up at her. "Well? Are you going to stand out in the rain all day, or come in?" The doctor retreated, giving Ko and her companion room to enter.

Once inside, Sanki proved to be a consummate, if somewhat irascible, host. The tea he provided was a battlefield blend, harsh but warming. As he poured, she considered how best to approach the matter. She studied him with an investigator's eye. Sanki was old, but not beaten down by age. He was like a nut, dried and shrunken into a nugget of hardness. There was no give in him, no fear.

"I am told you were once a battlefield surgeon," she said.

"I was in the service of the Akodo, for more years than I care to count." Sanki swirled his cup, watching the loose strands of tea clump and part. "I cut out arrows, staunched wounds and sewed them. I set bones and broke them, when they needed setting properly. I saw death in every form." He paused. "Burning was the worst. Nothing you can do with it, when it's bad. Except pack them in mud and salve and hope for the best."

"Do you know anything about poison?"

Sanki eyed her. "Right to it, then? Fine by me. Yes, there was significant discoloration in his extremities indicating interference with his circulation. An indication of certain types of poisoning…"

"Yes, I've seen it before," Ko agreed. "A natural poison that occurs from consuming bad fish or wheat. Perhaps he ate something that disagreed with him."

"Or drank it," Sanki said, tapping the teapot that sat on the tray between them. "Fermented soybeans can be ground up and mixed with alcohol or tea. I saw that a time or two, as a young man."

"You think it was intentional," Ko said. Sanki nodded.

"So does Lord Shin."

"But how could he survive so long?" Ko asked, curious now. In the cases she'd seen, death had taken only a matter of moments. An hour, at most.

Sanki shrugged. "I'd guess he only had a small amount. If I could have opened him up, I could have told you." The way he said it sent a clammy shiver along Ko's spine. While she had conducted her share of internal investigations, the bodies had always suffered convenient ruptures at the moment of death. To cut open a corpse intentionally was anathema to her, as it was to most Rokugani. Yet Sanki spoke of it as if it were the most natural of activities.

"Do you do that… often?" she asked. She glanced at Ina, who had a queasy look on her face. Clearly her feelings mirrored Ko's. Sanki seemed not to notice.

"Not often. You can tell a lot about what a man's been up to by the contents of his stomach. As I said, Kenzō probably got a light dose. Not enough to kill outright, but ultimately fatal."

"Was it, though?" Ko murmured. Her first thought was that the poison had been on the blade, but that made little sense. Why go for a killing blow if a scratch would be enough? "Kenzō was poisoned elsewhere, and then killed in the brewery."

"Not a knife," Sanki said. "Something thin. Round, no edges."

"A hairpin," Ko said. Sanki nodded.

"Or something similar."

"Your conclusions match my own," Ko said, oddly pleased.

At the very least, Shin was no fool when it came to employing specialists. Something that might have been pride flickered in her breast, if only briefly. "Could the killer have been a woman?"

"I don't see why not," Sanki said. "Though if I were you, I'd talk to Odoma."

Ko smiled. "Everyone seems to be in agreement on that point."

Sanki snorted. "He doesn't have many friends, that's true."

An understatement, Ko thought. "Do you believe he killed Lord Kenzō?"

The old man gave her a calculating look. "I think he thinks he did. But that Crane was dead well before Odoma stuck a blade in the back of his skull. In my opinion, whoever poisoned Kenzō is the real danger."

"Why would someone poison him?"

Sanki sighed and sat back. "That's a question for Lord Shin, not me. I just deal with the dead. But if you want another opinion of mine… ?"

"I would not be here otherwise."

"I think you should find out who Kenzō had his last meal with. That type of poison would need to be ingested, and the taste hidden by spices or sauces. Ginger, perhaps."

Ko nodded. "Have you told this to Lord Shin?"

"I haven't had the chance, but he knows enough about poisons to… ah." Sanki hesitated, a look of chagrin on his face. Ko almost laughed, but managed to restrain herself.

"You may relax. My thoughts had already turned to that possibility and dismissed it. By his own admission, Lord Shin had not seen the deceased for some weeks. His bodyguard corroborated his statement. I intend to question his servants as well, but it seems that Lord Kenzō's final meal was with an unknown party."

"Find them, find the poisoner," Sanki said confidently.

"Of course, that is easier said than done, I fear." Ko rose. "We have taken up too much of your time, doctor. Rest assured that it was appreciated."

Sanki climbed creakily to his feet as well. "No trouble. Lord Shin told me to expect you sooner or later. He's a clever one."

"Yes. So I'm told."

Sanki paused. "Is it true?"

Ko frowned. "Is what true?"

"Are the Crane here to take him away?"

Ko hesitated. "Yes."

"Because of this murder?"

"No."

"So, they'll take him regardless, then?"

Ko sighed. "I do not know. Perhaps."

Sanki said nothing as Ko and Ina departed. Ko felt as if she'd somehow done the old man a disservice as she stepped out into the rain. She'd wanted to comfort him. To tell him it would all be fine. But there was no guarantee of that. Ina opened the umbrella, protecting Ko from the light downpour. "They are frightened," Ina said softly.

"Of me?"

"No. Of what the Crane will do to them." Ina fell silent. Ko gestured for her to continue. She thought she already knew what the Kaeru was going to say, but she wanted to hear it regardless. Ina looked away. "If the Daidoji believe Lord Shin to be guilty, that guilt will also stain any who have served him. And in a city like this, the reach of the Daidoji Trading Council is long indeed."

Ko nodded. The ways of the Crane were still something of a mystery to her, even now. In their own way they were as ruthless as the Lion. They had made Shin, and now they wished to punish him for doing as he had been taught. Then, that was the danger of a good student – they often learned more than the teacher intended. She decided to change the subject. "Tell me about Master Odoma," she asked, watching the rain. Thanks to Azuma and Sanki, as well as her own brief interaction with the man, she thought she had a clear picture of the soy merchant in her head.

Ina hesitated. "What is there to tell, my lady?"

"I know how those above think of him. That he is a sad necessity. I wish your opinion. Is he the kind of man who would kill a Crane auditor in cold blood?"

"No," Ina said.

"No, he is not a murderer?"

"Yes, but not a cold-blooded one. Odoma is no different from the little gangs on the waterfront. He strikes when threatened or frightened – or when he has something to prove. But he only worries about tomorrow when it comes."

Ko nodded slowly. That jibed with her estimation. Odoma was cunning, but not clever. He was not a poisoner, but it was likely he'd murdered Kenzō without considering the consequences. Or had him murdered. None of the weapons they'd confiscated from Odoma and his people had matched the wound, but given its nature she had a suspect in mind – Odoma's courtesan.

As she turned what she'd learned over in her mind, something surfaced. Earlier, Odoma had claimed that he was under the protection of the Daidoji Trading Council. Aoto had clearly disagreed, but why would Odoma claim such a thing unless he had reason to believe it? Perhaps someone had told him that the Crane would approve of his testimony against Shin.

Perhaps Sanki was right. Perhaps she needed to have another conversation with Master Odoma. Perhaps, perhaps.

Ko clasped her hands behind her back. "I think we should pay another visit to Master Odoma's brewery. There are some questions I must ask him."

CHAPTER TWENTY-ONE
Konomi

Shin poured his guest a cup of tea. "Your opinion then, Nao?" They sat in his private box, high above the stage at the front of the theater. Shin had decorated the box himself; curtains of blue paper separated the front of the box from the foyer, and soft cushions occupied the floor, for use by guests. He also kept a ready supply of extra clothing, books and writing materials inside, for his personal use.

Nao smiled slyly. "The Scorpion? No, my lord. We – they – have their own methods of moving contraband. This business of tunnels, well… not for them." The actor gestured airily about the box as he sipped his tea.

Shin returned Nao's smile. He liked the actor. Nao was clever and acerbic, and just respectful enough to avoid being irritating. He was also a product of the infamous Acting Academy, trained not just in theatrics but in espionage. Though he would never admit to the latter, save in Shin's presence. Nao, like Kitano and others in Shin's employ, heard things that Shin did not, and thus was always worth consulting in regards to certain matters. "Ah, well. I had hoped for a simple explanation."

Nao waggled a finger in a chiding gesture. "The Scorpion are anything but simple, my lord. But this sort of thing is too dangerous, even for them. This smacks of – well – politics. And not the sort they'd find profitable."

"And that is your opinion on the matter?"

"My learned opinion? Yes, my lord." Nao laughed softly and set his cup down. "The Scorpion have nothing to do with this. I doubt any of the clans do, frankly."

"A good assumption," a new voice interjected. Shin looked past Nao and saw the welcome figure of Konomi standing in the doorway, Kasami just behind her. The newcomer nodded respectfully to Nao, who hopped to his feet and bowed low with florid grace. "This is bad business, Shin. But you know that, I think."

"Bad and getting worse," Shin said. Nao saw himself out quietly, leaving them alone. Kasami slid the door shut. Konomi sat opposite Shin, her expression grave.

"The city is abuzz with rumor and gossip, Shin. Darkly feathered Cranes haunt your places of business, and poke their beaks in wherever they please. Your servants have been released, your finances are under investigation… your house, Shin. They took it. And you sit here, atop a secret that, frankly, could start a war."

Shin leaned forward and swept an empty cup from the tray to his side. He poured her a cup and extended it to her. "Which is why I asked you here," Shin said cheerfully. "Now, how do we get out of this?"

"We?"

"Well, yes. You are my friend, and you are an accomplice."

Konomi frowned and snatched the cup from his hand. "You have a funny definition of friendship, Shin." She took a sip of tea. "What is your plan?"

"I do not have one, as yet."

"Then I suggest forgetting about it for the moment, and setting your sights on a more easily solved problem."

"Such as?"

"Your nuptials."

Shin sat back. "I do not think that is the most important thing at the moment."

"Then you are not as intelligent as I have always believed," Konomi said flatly. "The fact of the matter is, Shin, that even if that auditor's death was the result of some grand conspiracy, your fate is already sealed. This matter of weapons and smugglers is, at best, a distraction from the very real problem facing you."

Shin sighed, annoyed but aware she was correct. Konomi was almost always correct. It was one of the things he found most infuriating about her. She looked at him. "Don't you sigh at me, Shin. You know I'm only speaking truth. You are a desirable commodity. I suspect you already have a wealth of potential partners vying for your attentions."

"You might say that," he allowed, grudgingly, thinking of the letters he'd abandoned at his home. There was a small stack here as well, mixed amongst the papers and records that always cluttered up his box, and his gaze strayed to it.

Konomi followed his gaze and chuckled ruefully. "Well, if it makes you feel better, that stack is twice the size of my last one."

Shin decided to mention the other stack. "Was this before or after you stabbed one of your suitors?" he asked instead.

"You'd be surprised at how willing some people are to ignore such a thing," Konomi said primly. She picked up several of the missives and began to go through them, without waiting for an invitation. "Dreadful… boring… too young… too pretty…"

"Too pretty?"

"Trust me, Shin. You need someone with a bit more character." Konomi sent the letter in question sailing out over the side of the box. She held up an engraving of a young man. "What about this one?"

"He doesn't read," Shin said.

Konomi dropped the engraving as if it were a snake and chose a letter smelling of jasmine. She scanned it and said, "She sounds lovely. Wonderful penmanship."

"Too proper."

Konomi nodded and dropped the letter. "Can't have that, I suppose." She held up a paper decorated with carefully shaped red trim. "Is this a poem?"

"Yes," Shin sighed.

Konomi studied it, frowning in puzzlement. "From Bayushi Isamu?" Isamu held a position equivalent to Shin's own among the Scorpion contingent in the city.

"Yes."

"Really?"

"Yes!"

"I never would have guessed," Konomi said, sounding genuinely startled. "Still, it does have a certain sort of logic – relations between the Scorpion and the Crane could use some improvement and–"

"He's taunting me," Shin interrupted flatly. "That's the fifth poem he's sent me since word about my situation got out. Each more elaborate than the last."

"That makes more sense," Konomi said. "He really doesn't like you."

"Can we get back to the matter at hand, please?" Shin asked. "Hidden weapons? Murdered smugglers? City in crisis?"

Konomi waved this aside. "Boring, Shin. And frankly, not something I can help you with. What I can help you with is the Crane."

"I don't need help with the Crane. I need help with the murders."

"No, you don't. You'll figure out some elegant solution as you always do. But what we need to do is concoct some way of getting the Crane off your shadow. A marriage would do that handily, I think." She got a sly look on her face. "My cousin Yasamura is still available… no?"

"No." Handsome as Shinjo Yasamura was, he was too political for Shin's tastes. Shin desired nothing more than to stay out of politics – especially those that guided the fate of the clans. He ran his hands through his hair.

"He'll be crushed." Konomi smiled as she said it, and he wondered why. She fell silent for a moment, and then said, "I am serious, Shin. Joking aside, I want to help. And talking about one problem might free your wonderful mind to work on the other." She reached over and poked him in the center of his brow – hard. "I can see the distraction in your eyes. It's nagging at you. So let me help." Konomi sipped her tea. "Tell me about Lord Aoto. He seems to bear you some grudge."

"Aoto has had it out for me ever since I stole one of his toys when we were boys," Shin said dismissively. "In my defense, he's never been very good at sharing."

"No, I can see that." She paused. "Could this all be some scheme of his, to discredit you?"

"Aoto? No. Well, yes. He's lethal, when it comes to sticking sharp things into people, but not a natural schemer. He's a very good Daidoji… except when it comes to me." Shin paused, trying to think of how best to explain. "I'm a bit of grit in his craw, you see. The mere mention of my name gets him all worked up and forgetting the lessons of his youth. Aoto would chase me to the very gates of hell for the privilege of momentarily inconveniencing me."

"And this is who your family sent to bring you home?" Konomi asked, a startled expression on her face. Shin smiled.

"Oh, I expect he volunteered. Very keen, Aoto. Especially when it comes to making my life miserable." His smile faded. "I expect there was some calculation in it, as well, of course. There are more than a few cousins who'd be pleased to hear that I fell overboard and drowned on the way home. Aoto is exactly the sort to shoulder such a potential burden, for the good of the family."

She frowned. "You think he intends to murder you?"

"He probably dreams of it every night. But no – not unless I gave him some provocation. Which, now that I think of it, I have very neatly done." Shin sighed. "It would be simpler for the Daidoji if I perished here and now. Aoto knows this. But, as I said, he is a good Daidoji. Cold-blooded murder is a bit beyond his capacity."

"I hope for your sake you're right," Konomi said. "Drink your tea before it gets cold." She waited until he'd done so, before she asked, "What about this Kitsuki – Ko? Is that her name?" Shin choked and coughed. Konomi smiled. "You do know her, then."

Shin wiped tea from his chin and said, "In a manner of speaking."

"What manner might that be?"

"We were… betrothed."

Konomi paused. "What?"

Shin shrugged. "Not for long, or very seriously, but yes."

Konomi sat back, clearly startled. "Are you mad?"

"Not to my knowledge." Shin looked at her in confusion. "Have I said something wrong?" he asked, carefully setting his cup down. Konomi was staring at him as if he were a stranger.

"You… were betrothed?"

"I was."

"To her?" She sounded outraged.

"Yes. Why is that so hard to understand?"

"You hate marriage! The very idea of it sent you into a sulk!"

"I was young. People change." Shin paused. "I changed."

"Because of her?" Konomi asked softly. Shin studied her. Was that a hint of envy he detected in her tone? Or simply surprise? Either way, it made him somewhat uncomfortable. He cleared his throat.

"No. Not because of her."

"Your family, then," she said. Not a question this time. Shin's lips quirked.

"They are… complicated."

"No, they wanted to control you, as my family wished to control me," she said, with more vehemence than he'd expected. "Do not confuse idiocy for complexity. Tradition is a bucket, Shin. And the other crabs in the bucket do not like when one of their own gets a taste of freedom. So, they pull them down… and sometimes they tear them apart."

Shin could think of no reply, and so stayed silent. Konomi leaned toward him and put her hand on his. "They intend to tear you apart, Shin. If they catch you interfering with this, they will. You should leave the city. Go somewhere else. Let this Ko woman handle the investigation – we can tell her about these weapons of yours. My servants can keep an eye on things for you." She smiled. "My people will make certain that your cousin and his lapdogs do not unduly damage your home."

Shin laughed softly. "A gracious offer, but I have nowhere to go." He smiled sadly. "I made this city my home, and all I value is here."

Konomi didn't let go of his hand. "I once offered you the use of my private estate outside of the city. I offer you its use again. It is small, nestled in the hills. Private, save for the servants. I go there when I need to get away from the city." She brightened. "We could go tomorrow, in fact."

"We?"

Konomi hesitated. "Well, I thought…" She trailed off as she took in his bewildered expression. Sighed. "Oh, you are the most – most pestiferous man!" She thumped her fists against her thighs and looked away, laughing softly. "Investigator? Ha! Solver of mysteries? Double-ha!"

Shin blinked at her in confusion. "Konomi?"

"All this time, and you – you… ha!" She laughed again, and there was an edge of sadness to it. "Never mind, Shin. Never mind. But yes, I am going with you. If only to make sure you don't get into any trouble."

Somewhat taken aback, Shin frowned. "It is a kind offer, Konomi, but they would simply follow me – us," he began, then paused. He pushed aside Konomi's unusual outburst and focused on the opportunity she'd offered him. "Or would they?"

Konomi frowned. "You have that sly look on your face again."

Shin sat back, his mind working fast now. "I need to get a message to Captain Lun. Tonight, if possible." He smiled, pleased with himself. "Despite your metaphor, my cousin isn't a crab… he's a Crane. And if you show a crane a fish, it will pursue."

"What is that supposed to mean?"

Shin snapped open his fan.

"Why, I'm going to show him a fish, of course."

CHAPTER TWENTY-TWO
Snakehead

Odoma sat back and looked around the brewery as Isuka made her report on Lord Shin's movements. For the longest time, it had been everything he'd desired. Now, it was starting to lose its appeal. Some of that was the Crane's fault; he was moving quickly for a man running out of room to maneuver. With his home confiscated, he'd gone to ground at the Foxfire Theater, which only made sense. When Isuka had finished, he said, "What about the bounty?"

Here, Isuka frowned. "We've had some… difficulties."

"What sort of difficulties?"

"He anticipated us."

Odoma leaned forward. "What do you mean?"

"He's hired his own killers. We've lost half a dozen people since last night."

Odoma clenched his fists. "How is that possible?" he snapped. From somewhere out on the street, he could hear the sound of a shamisen. The tune wasn't one of his favorites and he was tempted to send someone to find and smash the instrument, but refrained.

Isuka's eyes narrowed. "Don't blame me because you decided to hire fools and drunks to do your killing for you. I handled the auditor, didn't I?"

Odoma grunted and waved her comment aside. "Because that's turned out so well for us. I should have stopped you."

"And if you had, we would be dead," Isuka said flatly. "Just like Shaiban and those other fools. Just like those idiots trying to claim the bounty." She looked as if she wanted to slap him. "We are at war, you fat fool – start thinking like a warrior!"

Odoma sucked on his teeth and said, "Careful, woman. You have your uses, but you are not irreplaceable."

Isuka leaned forward, a sneer on her painted face. "Neither are you, Odoma. We're in this together now, whether you like it or not."

Odoma considered his hands. Big hands. Rough. Even now, rough. The hands of a worker and a fighter. He studied Isuka's neck: a slim neck. Fragile. She wouldn't be the first person who'd died with his hands around their throat. He curled his fingers into fists and saw that her eyes were on them. She knew what he was thinking, because she was thinking the same. Cut losses and run for the hills.

"Is that little nest egg of yours still hidden beneath the pallets?" she cooed prettily.

"Is yours still concealed under the platform?" Odoma countered, patting the wooden floor of the brewery's second level. Isuka grimaced and sat back.

"We could leave together," she said. "Let him have the city, if he survives."

"And if Lord Shin comes after us?" Odoma asked, heavily. "What then? Because he will come after us. He's not the fool he plays at being. I'm a loose thread, just like Taoko and the others. And so are you, now. The Crane hold grudges as well as the Lion."

"If he does, we'll kill him," Isuka said. She touched her elaborately pinned hair and Odoma knew she was checking to see if the tools of her trade were still in place. Isuka wasn't a courtesan, or, at least, she wasn't just a courtesan. When Taoka had introduced them, Odoma had thought her just another pretty face. It hadn't taken long, however, for him to see the fox hiding beneath her beauty. She was hungry in a way he recognized.

But hunger wasn't enough. You needed smarts as well. And strength. All things he'd thought he possessed in abundance. But now he was beginning to wonder if he'd ever had them at all. He was caught in the shadow of the Crane's wings, and no matter how fast he ran, he couldn't escape them.

He decided to change the subject. "How'd your talk with the Snakeheads go?" Taoka and the Snakeheads had been the key to his rise from the gutter. The gang threatened independent merchants, and those merchants sought the protection of Odoma and the merchants' association, who charged them for protection. A good scheme, and profitable. But Taoka was dead, a victim of the Crane. Like Shaiban and the others.

Isuka shrugged. "With Taoka gone they've got no steel. The Crane knew what he was doing when he gutted the fool. It'll be a while before they choose a new leader. And even longer before their reputation recovers."

Odoma wanted to groan and curse, but didn't. Instead, he said, "What if we told them we knew where the man who'd killed their leader was hiding?"

Isuka frowned speculatively. "They'd probably investigate."

Odoma cracked his knuckles. "And when they found him,

they'd do what they do. Problem solved." The more he talked, the more he liked the plan. It solved two problems with a single stroke. Even better, it had nothing to do with him. Isuka seemed to like it as well.

"Sometimes, I forget you're an idiot," she said.

He grinned mirthlessly. "Sometimes, I forget that I ought to kill you."

They smiled at one another, two opportunists bound together by ambition and hunger. The moment was interrupted by one of his guards. "Masa and Itachi are back, boss," the unshaven ronin said, with an apologetic glance at Isuka. His guards were wary of her, after seeing what she'd done to the auditor.

"Send them up," Odoma said curtly. He sat back and reached for the bottle of rice wine he habitually kept close to hand. Isuka frowned at him.

"You need to keep your wits," she said sharply.

"I'm not planning to get drunk," he said. "I just need a taste." He poured himself a cup and knocked it back as Masa and Itachi clunked up the stairs. Masa's smell preceded him, as always. Odoma didn't particularly like either of the ronin, but they knew their business. Or at least, he'd thought so. But when he saw that they were unaccompanied, he grimaced. "Well? Did you stash the paper-seller somewhere?"

"He refused to come," Masa said. Itachi grunted in agreement.

"What do you mean, he refused?" Odoma growled. He'd wanted to speak to Ito. If anyone might know what the Crane was up to, it was Ito. The paper-seller knew more than was good for him.

Masa looked away, scratching his scarred cheek. "He said no."

Odoma lurched to his feet, nearly spilling his wine. How dare a nothing like Ito say no to him? It was just another example of the damage that the Crane had inflicted on his reputation. "Then you should have dragged him here!"

"Daichi was there," Itachi protested.

"Who?"

"The Crane's servant," Isuka said, her eyes narrowed. "The gambler."

Odoma grunted. He vaguely recalled the man, a seedy looking sort. He remembered hiring him a time or two for disposal jobs, but not for a long while. Of course he'd be working for the Crane. Like called to like. "You should have killed him."

"You told us not to make a scene."

"I told you to bring me the paper-seller!" Odoma slammed his fist into a nearby support beam. A shudder ran through the platform and he jerked his hand back, cradling it to his chest. Isuka sidled up to him and ran soothing fingers along the nape of his neck.

"It doesn't matter," she murmured. "Ito is just another patsy. Anything he could tell us we'll find out ourselves after the Crane has been hauled off by his kinfolk – or killed. We just have to be patient. One way or another, it'll all work out."

Odoma grunted. He didn't share Isuka's confidence. Shin clearly trusted Ito. Why else would he meet with the paper-seller so often, or allow him to conduct business on his behalf? To Odoma, that implied the merchant knew something. And, given that Ito was the one who'd gotten him into business with the Crane in the first place, Odoma figured he had some explaining to do. The servant complicated things, but he could be dealt with.

"You're right," he said, finally. He ran his hands over his head, rubbing his scalp. "You're right. We need to be clever about this.

Calm." He went back and retrieved his bottle of wine and took a long slug. "Last thing we need, is more trouble."

Even as he spoke, his guard returned, looking unhappy. "Um… boss?"

Odoma didn't look at him. "What now?"

"The – uh – the Kitsuki investigator is here. Outside."

Odoma turned, looked at the hapless ronin, and then at Isuka. "Get out of here. Go tell the Snakeheads where the Crane is. Offer them double the bounty if they get it done tonight."

"Maybe we should go with her," Masa said, as Isuka hurried toward the rear exit.

Odoma snorted. "You two are being paid well enough as it is. You stay by my side until this is done." He looked at the guard. "Well, what are you gawping at? Let the honored investigator in, eh? Fool." The guard hurried to obey, and Odoma glanced at Masa and Itachi. "No provocation, no mouthing off, no talking. Understand?" They both nodded. "Good. There might be something for you later. For now, just do what I say."

Down below, the doors were opening, and the investigator was being shown in. She had a Kaeru with her – not one of the ones stationed outside. "What can I do for you, my lady?" Odoma asked, as he descended the steps to meet her. Masa and Itachi trailed after him.

The Kaeru with the investigator tensed slightly at the sight of them. Odoma restrained a smile. The investigator might be too arrogant to see, but the Kaeru's eyes were wide open. She knew who he was; she understood that he was a dangerous man. That was all he asked, really. A little respect from his lessers.

Ko met his greeting with a placid gaze. "I would like to speak with your companion… Isuka is her name, I think. Is she here?"

"Sadly, no."

"Where is she?"

"Not here, as I said," Odoma said, fighting to keep his tone even. "Maybe I can be of help to you. I can vouch for her, if you wish."

"Irrelevant," Ko said. "Of course you can, and would. She is your accomplice, after all." She snapped open her fan and looked about as she fluttered it. "These are the facts, as I see them. Lord Kenzō came here for a meeting with you. He wished to discuss the activities of a certain group of individuals. While here, he was murdered."

"I don't know anything about any… individuals," Odoma said. "I told you, his reasons for wanting to meet me were a mystery. I assumed it was about my complaint against Lord Shin."

"Yes. Your complaint. What was it, again?"

Odoma sucked on his teeth. "He cheated me."

"How?"

"I don't see why it matters."

"Humor me, please," Ko said firmly. Odoma ran his hand over his head. He felt uneasy. Not intimidated; never that. But she was acting like a player who already knew how the dice were going to land. He didn't like that.

"The theater. He bought it from me, but didn't pay me a fair price. I wanted to buy it back, but he refused. I wrote a formal complaint to the Crane." He hesitated, wondering how much to say. He settled for defensiveness. "I thought Lord Kenzō was here to help me."

"Perhaps he was," Ko said, her eyes on Masa and Itachi. "I do not recognize these men. Have their weapons been checked?"

"No, but I'm certain they had nothing to do with it," Odoma began.

"Even so, it would be for the best if they were to hand them over." She gestured to the Kaeru, standing silently behind her. Odoma paused and then gestured sharply.

"You heard her. Hand over your blades."

"What?" Masa began. Odoma spun and fixed him with a fierce glare. The two ronin shared a glance, and then grudgingly handed over their swords. The Kaeru accepted them cautiously, and Ko examined both swords for a moment.

"It wasn't a sword that killed him," Odoma said. "Even a fool could see that."

"All possibilities must be considered," Ko said politely. She glanced at him. "Earlier, you implied that the Crane had promised you protection. What did you mean by that?"

"Obviously I was mistaken," Odoma said.

"Obviously. But how did you come to have such an erroneous idea?"

Odoma frowned. He didn't like her tone. Like she was smarter than him. Maybe she was, but he was clever, too. He rubbed his hand – still aching from where he'd smacked the beam – and said, "The paper-seller. Ito. You know him?"

She blinked. "No. Who is he?"

"He works for the Crane. He brokered the deal in the first place. Told me to file a complaint. Told me the Crane would see that I was fairly compensated."

"Did he? How curious." Ko turned. "And so you did, and then Lord Kenzō came. You said you thought he was here to help. What changed your mind?"

Odoma grunted. "The fact I don't have my theater back was reason enough, but… our talks were not friendly ones. He thought I was a criminal."

"You are," Ko said bluntly.

"I am a legitimate businessman!"

"You are a smuggler. Two of the names on Kenzō's list were also criminals. It does not take an intuitive leap to guess that the others were as well. I have been told that this city is rife with smugglers, many of whom are merchants by day. But why does a smuggler want a theater?"

"It was mine," Odoma said. He felt as if he were standing on sand. Was it possible that she knew? If so, what did it mean for him? He glanced at Masa, who gave a slight shake of his head. They were unarmed, and the Kaeru was watching them closely. They'd stand no chance. Odoma wondered if that was why she'd wanted to look at the blades in the first place. She was smart, maybe even smarter than the Crane.

"Perhaps." She flicked her fan dismissively. "You made your complaint; why did you assume it would be heeded? The Daidoji Trading Council is not known for its even-handed treatment of independent merchants."

Odoma hesitated. There it was. She thought it had something to do with the Crane, after all. He tugged on the collar of his robes and took a breath. "I was... told by someone on the Trading Council that the matter would receive the utmost attention. That Lord Shin had been of some concern to them for a long time." He allowed himself a smile. "He doesn't have many friends among his kin. I guess birds of a feather don't always flock together, eh?"

Ko's gaze sharpened. "Who told you this?"

Odoma frowned. "I don't have to tell you that. In fact, I think you've reached the limits of my hospitality." He swung his big hand out, indicating the doors. "I'd like you to leave now, please."

At first, he thought she was going to argue. Then, she gave a small bow and turned to leave, gesturing for the Kaeru to return

Masa and Itachi's weapons. Odoma stared after her for long moments, then turned to Masa and Itachi. Masa checked his sword and nodded. "It's too bad, really. She's quite pretty in a way, that one."

Odoma grunted and looked away.

Isuka was right about one thing. It might be time to consider leaving the city.

CHAPTER TWENTY-THREE
Raid

"So, what's in it for me?" Lun demanded as she leaned forward. She hadn't been difficult to find; true to her word, she was sticking close to the city. Shin had asked Sanemon to send a theater page to pass along his invitation. She'd made her way to the theater, eventually, as the sun began to set and the rain slackened. She didn't seem cowed by Konomi's presence, but then, Lun was hard to impress. "I'm going to need more than your pretty smile if I'm going to risk my boat."

Shin smiled. "Money is the traditional compensation."

"Word is, they took your money." She tapped the inside of her wrist, where a faded tattoo of the Crane clan sigil sat atop her sun-browned skin.

"I will pay," Konomi said, from beside Shin. She placed her hand on his; somewhat possessively, Shin thought. Though he doubted she meant it in such a fashion. "Unless you have some moral objection to taking money from someone other than your employer?"

Lun smiled widely. "I've got whatever morals I'm paid to have, my lady." She sat back. "Fine. How long do you need?"

"As long as you can give me," Shin said. "I need Aoto delayed indefinitely – at least until I can figure out what's going on here." He dipped his finger in his tea, and used it to draw a rough approximation of the river across the low table between them. "The plan is simple – I need Aoto to believe I am fleeing downriver. It doesn't matter where. Away from the city will do. Any destination you like."

"Willow Quay," Lun grunted, tapping the line of tea. "It's the obvious place. Especially if you're trying to avoid the authorities."

Shin nodded. The spot in question had sprouted like mold on a bend in the river; a haven for criminals, smugglers and travelers looking to avoid pernicious tolls. He'd visited the crooked little village a few times himself, and had long wondered if some proper investment in the businesses there might turn it into something more… amenable to the social niceties. "An excellent idea. Aoto will be beside himself at the thought of me seeking sanctuary there. It fits nicely into his biases."

"And while the captain is doing that, we will be going upriver – to my estate," Konomi said. "I think you will like it there, Shin."

"I do not expect to abuse your hospitality for long," Shin said, not quite meeting her eyes. "Once this affair is taken care of, I will no doubt be free to return and resume my duties without interference. Hopefully."

"But if not, I am more than happy to give you sanctuary from the Crane," Konomi said quickly. "For so long as you require it. Aoto might be determined, but even he isn't foolish enough to cross the Iuchi."

Shin winced. "I fear you do not know my cousin. He is indeed that foolish… but that is a worry for tomorrow. Today, all that concerns me is distracting him long enough for us to get out of the city without him noticing." The act of leaving would be seen as provocation, of course. Aoto would eventually come after him, but at this point it was simply a matter of employing delaying tactics.

Shin felt certain that if he could discover what was going on, it might help his case with the Crane. At the very least, it might buy him some time before the inevitable. He still wasn't entirely certain how he was going to escape the trap closing about him. Aoto didn't care about the murder, and likely wouldn't care about the weapons. Nor would his superiors. To them, Shin was the problem. Murder and skullduggery were worries for the local authorities.

"I can do it," Lun said. "Those auditors have been watching the wharfs, and my boat, since they got here. I figure they're expecting you to make a run for it – or they're waiting for his lordship to order the confiscation of my sloop." She grinned fiercely. "That won't end the way they expect, I can promise you that."

"If it comes to that, I will make restitution," Shin assured her. Lun waved this aside.

"Pah. Wouldn't be the first time. Besides, this will be a pleasure. Tweaking the feathers of the Crane always is."

Shin smiled at her bravado. In her own way, Lun was as brave as Kasami, though her courage took a much rougher form. He cleared his throat. "Well, with that settled, we come to the second reason I asked you here… the tunnels. You have used them before?"

"Oh, you've finally found out about those, huh?" Lun leaned back, clearly amused. She thrust a finger beneath her eyepatch and rubbed the empty socket.

Shin blinked, startled by her candor. "Is there a reason you never told me?"

Lun chuckled. "Because Ito warned me that you might… well. He said you might take it the wrong way. Besides, what's a bit of smuggling here and there? Everyone does it."

Shin flicked his fan in annoyance. It didn't surprise him that Ito had so effectively misled him. He'd never paid much attention to the financial side of things; he'd trusted others to do that for him, Ito among them. But he couldn't help but feel that it lent some veracity to his family's complaints. Would a more diligent approach to such matters have prevented this embarrassment?

Would Aoto, or his grandfather, have allowed someone like Ito to take such liberties? Shin doubted it. In his grandfather's opinion, merchants only prospered by the sufferance of their betters. He'd thought himself so clever in taking a different path. Now, it seemed that like the fox in the folk tale, it had turned in his hand and bitten him.

He resolved to discuss the matter with Ito before they left the city. At the very least, he needed to check his account books, and question Ito about the changed dates – and why someone might have changed them.

The truth of it was, only a handful of people had access to those books, beside himself. Ito was one… and Konomi, another. He glanced at the latter, wondering suddenly whether her sudden display of feelings was simply the result of the situation, or something else. Even as the thought crossed his mind, he clamped down on it savagely. Suspicion was one thing; paranoia, another. If he started down that path, where did it end?

After all, Kasami or Kitano or even Niko, could have made changes to the books. Ito's own records could have been altered, leading to him making an erroneous report. Shinobi could be involved, perhaps in the pay of Bayushi Isamu, who still bore Shin some enmity for his part in the blackmail affair of the year before. He felt as if he were standing on a field of ice, watching cracks run in all directions.

Konomi's grip on his hand tightened, breaking him from his reverie. He glanced at her. "The captain is right," she said. "Smuggling is as normal as breathing in this city. As much to dissuade pirates as to avoid tolls. Ito is to be commended. The profit he made went into your coffers."

"That is irrelevant. What I want to know is where the weapons are going."

Lun frowned. "Weapons – what weapons?"

"The ones sitting in the tunnel as we speak. Lion weapons, hidden in barrels of rice and fish. Where are they going?" He'd considered contacting Akodo Minami about it, but decided against it. The fewer people who knew, the better.

Lun shook her head. "I don't know. Weapons – that's not the sort of business I'm in."

"What about the others?" Shin leaned toward her. "What about Osho or Sato?"

Again, Lun shook her head. "We don't exactly keep in touch. Or trade names."

Shin paused. Then, "Shaiban."

"Him I know – knew, rather. Dead now, I think." Lun traced the scars on her cheek, good eye narrowed. "Big smuggler on the Unicorn docks. He was one of the first to use the tunnels, back when Odoma owned this place. He threw his lot in with Ito pretty quick, though."

"Would Odoma have taken that as a challenge – perhaps even killed Shaiban to make an example of him?"

Lun grunted and scratched her ear. "Sounds like something he'd do. Though as far as I know, Shaiban got knifed over a dice game."

"What about a gangster named Taoka?"

Lun shrugged. "Throat cut by someone who didn't like him."

Shin paused. "Two more names – Hiroto and Dari. Both merchants. Ito claimed to have done business with them, what about you?"

Lun frowned again. "Dari, no… but Hiroto… rice dealer, right?"

"Yes. You knew him?"

"Carried some rice for him once or twice. He's dead, too, isn't he?"

"Very." Shin waved his fan slowly. "Did he use the tunnels?"

"Definitely."

"Recently?"

Again, Lun shrugged. "If you're asking whether he was the one smuggling weapons, I don't know. I can say that nobody has used them in a while."

"By a while, you mean… a week? A month?"

"A month, give or take," Lun said. Shin nodded, filing the information away. There was something there; some link that he wasn't seeing yet. A quintet of dead men, a load of weapons… and Odoma.

"Was Ito the one who told you not to use them?"

Lun hesitated. "Yes."

"Did he say why?"

She sighed. "Not in so many words, but I figured he was worried about Odoma. Or about the auditor snooping around."

"Sensible," Shin murmured. He needed to have another chat with Ito. It was clear that the merchant was hiding something –

but why? To save his own skin, or to spare Shin possible embarrassment, should Kenzō have discovered the subterfuge? And how did Odoma figure into things? Was he responsible for all of it? Was this nothing more than a turf war between smugglers? But if so, how to explain Kenzō's poisoning?

No, there was something he wasn't seeing. Some hidden angle upon which all of this pivoted – and it had everything to do with the weapons. He felt it in his bones. He snapped his fan closed and opened his mouth to speak – when a crash from the front of the theater interrupted him.

Shin was on his feet in moments. Kasami and Hachi, Konomi's lanky bodyguard, entered the box. "Someone's just smashed through the front doors," Kasami said.

"Lots of someones," Hachi added. He looked at Konomi. "My lady, we should–"

"No," Konomi said, as she rose to her feet. She looked at Shin. "Do you think it's the Crane? Perhaps your cousin grew impatient…"

"No, I don't think this is Aoto," Shin said. He could hear shouts, cursing. Whoever the newcomers were, they were spreading through the theater, and fast. Shin went to the front of the box, where it overlooked the stage and twitched aside the privacy curtain. Several figures prowled across the stage. All were armed, all were dressed in threadbare or tattered clothing. What bare flesh was visible bore tattoos that coiled and flexed colorfully. Lun joined him.

"Oh, that's perfect," she muttered.

"Who are they?" Shin asked, letting the privacy curtain fall back into place. Lun thrust a finger beneath her eyepatch and grunted.

"Snakeheads. Waterfront gang."

Shin frowned. He had the feeling that the gang hadn't come to talk. Given what Kitano had told him, he suspected they were here on Odoma's behalf.

He heard cries from the backstage area, and the sounds of scenery being smashed. Anger warred with concern within him. Sanemon and the others would be easy prey for the Snakeheads. They needed to act quickly before someone got hurt. He glanced at Konomi and Hachi. "Hachi, take your mistress to safety. One of the other boxes, perhaps. They won't be looking for you. Lun…?"

"It'll cost you extra," Lun said, tapping the hilt of her blade.

"But of course," Shin said swiftly. He glanced at Kasami, who frowned.

"You don't have a sword," she said.

"Then I shall just have to acquire one." Shin tapped his fan against his thigh. "I have no doubt that they are here for me. So, let us give them what they want."

"No," Konomi said sharply. "This is foolish. Shin…!"

"What's the plan?" Lun asked.

Shin smiled. "I need to get to the drum tower."

CHAPTER TWENTY-FOUR
Drum Tower

The entrance to the theater's drum tower was located at the rear of the structure. Kasami led the way, moving with lethal grace. Backstage was a morass of confusion. Theater crew ran in all directions, shouting questions to one another. As Shin and the others hurried to the tower, they caught a glimpse of the gangsters, moving room to room, toppling scenery, or shoving hapless workers against walls in order to question them. Shin counted at least a dozen Snakeheads. The chaos, unpleasant as it was, worked in their favor.

They were only confronted once. Two men, clad in ratty robes, with tattooed faces and bared weapons made to intercept them. They died with their demands unfinished on their lips. Kasami barely slowed, save to clean and sheathe her blade. Shin stepped over one of the bodies, marveling, and not for the first time, at the lethal efficacy of his bodyguard. Once, it might have given him pause, but at the moment he was nothing but grateful.

When they reached the rear of the theater, Shin spotted the heavy wooden steps past a quagmire of props, rope coils and folded curtains. No one ever went up into the tower but the drummer, Chizu, and she wouldn't be here today since there was no performance. Shin looked at Konomi, who'd insisted on coming, despite protests from both himself and Hachi. "Now is the time we part ways, I think."

"No," she said firmly. "Where you go, I go. Now get up there so we can get this ridiculous scheme of yours underway."

"It's not that ridiculous," Shin protested. "I'll sound the drums, the Snakeheads will come to investigate – or silence them – and we will confront them."

"Our guards and the captain will confront them, you mean," Konomi said.

"Yes, yes." Shin turned to Kasami. "You and Lun stay out of sight until our guests have arrived. Let a few of them get up the stairs. Then…"

"We show them the error of their ways," Kasami said.

"That's one way of putting it," Lun said. "What about him?" She indicated Hachi. He frowned and gripped the sheath of his sword.

"I stay with my mistress. Always." He glanced at Kasami, who met his gaze expressionlessly. Shin knew that Hachi hadn't meant it to sound like a criticism, even as he knew that Kasami would take it that way.

"That's fine," Shin interjected. "One sword up top won't go amiss." He paused. "I want one of them alive, at least. I want to know who sent them, and why."

"Isn't it obvious?" Konomi asked.

"Yes, but confirmation is always appreciated." Shin led the way up the steps, Konomi following and Hachi bringing up the rear. The drum tower was a simple wooden structure, with a curved, flared roof of blue tile. It had four walls with circular windowlike apertures on each side, allowing the sound of the drums to reach the streets below. Startled birds, nesting among the joists, took flight as Shin flung the trapdoor back and clambered up into the drum chamber. The drums sat on a raised dais in the center of the small room, and Shin hurried toward them. "Leave the trapdoor open," he said, as Hachi made to close it.

"Why?" the bodyguard asked.

"We want them up here, remember? Some of them, at least. Besides, the sound will carry better that way." He picked up the drum mallets and twirled them experimentally. "I suggest you both stay out of sight for the moment."

"Are you certain that this is the wisest course?" Konomi asked.

Shin shrugged back his sleeves. "Not really." Then, with a quick, steadying breath, he began to pound the drums. Not lightly, or with any particular rhythm in mind. Rather, he was simply trying to make as much noise as possible. As he struck the drums, he could hear shouts of alarm from somewhere below. They were faint, at first, but grew louder and were soon accompanied by the clatter of running feet. He prayed that Kasami would follow his directive and let a few past before she pounced.

Moments later, the ascent to the tower echoed with curses and the rattle of weapons. Impossible to tell how many were making the climb, but Shin suspected there were at least six of them. If they were after Odoma's bounty, none of them would want to miss potentially being in at the kill. At the very least, they'd want to silence whoever was sounding the drums before someone summoned the Kaeru to investigate.

The first Snakehead to poke his nose through the trapdoor was a heavyset man with a tattoo of a long, serpentine fish coiled about his bald head and neck. He held a sickle in one thick hand and he pointed it at Shin. "Hey – you! Stop that!"

"Make me," Shin said blithely.

The Snakehead growled and squeezed the rest of the way through the trapdoor. Shin sidled away from him, but continued to strike the drums. The gangster lunged for him, planting his sickle right through one of the drums. Shin struck him on either ear with the mallets, causing him to stagger back, clutching his head. "Do you have any idea how expensive instruments like this are?" Shin asked, pounding on the still-intact drum.

The Snakehead shook himself all over and came for Shin again. Behind him, a narrow-faced woman was climbing up through the trapdoor. Upon sighting Shin, her eyes widened. "Kill him, Bota – that's the Crane who murdered Taoka!"

Shin had no time to process this accusation. Bota roared and swung his sickle at Shin's head. Shin jerked back and smacked the weapon from his attacker's hand with a mallet. Bota cried out and retreated, cradling his bruised hand. "Help me, Sato," he whined.

"Do I have to do everything?" the woman hissed, drawing a short, square-tipped sword from the sheath on her hip. But even as she stepped toward him, Hachi was in motion. His sword sprang into his hand, and the woman crumpled, a bewildered expression on her slackening features. Bota squawked and made for the trapdoor, but Shin reached him first and brought a mallet down on the back of his head, dropping him senseless to the floor.

Shin looked past Hachi and saw a third Snakehead already rising through the trapdoor, hatchet in hand. He made to cry out a warning, but Konomi beat him to it. She slammed the trapdoor down atop the gangster hard enough for something to crunch and he gave a yell and tumbled back down the steps. A cacophony of crashing and banging followed.

"Quick thinking," Shin said. Konomi sniffed.

"It is a good thing Hachi and I were here," she said.

Shin didn't reply. From below, he could hear the sounds of swordplay. He looked at Hachi. "They might need your assistance below. I believe I can handle our bald friend here." He gestured with a drum mallet for emphasis. Hachi glanced at his mistress, who gave a terse nod. The bodyguard flung back the trapdoor and paused. Nothing emerged save the sounds of fierce combat below. He hurried down and Konomi turned to Shin.

"What now?" she asked.

"Now I take the opportunity to question our friend here." Shin crouched beside the dazed gangster and prodded him with the mallet. "Now then … Bota, was it?" he said, conversationally as the man blinked blearily at him. "Let us discuss why you're here, eh?"

"I'm not saying nothing," Bota grunted, squirming back against the wall, away from Shin and the mallet in his hand. Shin nodded agreeably.

"Good man. Always best to say nothing until the situation is clarified. To that end, your friends downstairs are no doubt discovering that the bullying tactics of waterfront extortion are no match for sharp steel." Shin paused, allowing this to sink in. Bota swallowed and cut his eyes toward the trapdoor. A scream rose up, piteous and soon cut off.

"Why did you come here?" Shin asked, gesturing with the mallet.

Bota grimaced. "You killed our chief."

"Taoka," Shin said, glancing at Konomi. "So, this is about revenge, then. Only I had nothing to do with that fellow's death."

"Lies," Bota snarled. He flexed his injured hand. "A Crane killed him and you're a Crane! Our honor demands vengeance!"

"Not exactly honor, I think," Shin said softly. "Your reputation, more like. As well as settling certain other questions. Let me guess – whoever takes my head gets to be in charge. Who told you I was here?"

Bota swallowed. "What does it matter?"

"It doesn't. I already know it was Odoma. Or one of his people. He sent you to kill me by feeding you a lie. I had nothing to do with Taoka's death."

"Odoma said–" the gangster began.

"He lied," Shin countered. "My question is, why? What offense have I caused him? Any insight, Bota?"

Bota's eyes narrowed. He licked his lips. "You – you want to take over. Everyone knows that."

Shin sat back on his heels. "Everyone knows what, exactly?"

"Everyone knows that a Crane is trying to muscle in on Odoma."

"Not everyone, since I had no idea." It was starting to make sense now. Odoma thought he was engaged in a battle against a rival. It seemed that all this time, Shin had been embroiled in a war without his awareness.

Bota stared at him, and Shin felt a prickle of warning. Daidoji training never went away, no matter how much you ignored it. The gangster's injured hand darted into his robes and emerged with a small blade. Konomi called out a warning, but Shin was already swinging the mallet down to intercept the knife. He slammed it down, driving the blade into the floor. Bota howled and lunged for him with his good hand, as if hoping to throttle Shin.

But before he could reach his target, a shuriken sprouted from between his eyes and he collapsed face down. Shin turned and saw a young woman crouched in one of the tower's round windows. "Hello, my lord," she said. "Chobei sends his regards."

Shin tossed the drum mallet aside. "Yui. How is your son? Getting tall now, I expect." Yui was Chobei's niece, and a member of his cadre. It seemed the shinobi were doing as Shin had asked, and were keeping an eye on things.

"Tall, yes... but he still needs me to wipe his bottom for him," Yui said, with an easy smile. She gestured down toward the theater. "Things are under control now, my lord. You can come out, if you wish. It was clever of you to sound the drums."

Shin gave Konomi a triumphant look. "Yes, I rather think it was."

Konomi hit him on the shoulder with a fist. "Idiot!"

"What?" Shin asked, startled.

"Fool! Dunderhead!" She hit him again. "Why would you do that?"

Shin shook his head in confusion. "Do what?"

"He nearly killed you!" A third blow, but a gentle one. Konomi paused and glared at him, panting with emotion. Shin blinked, made to speak and–

She kissed him.

Shin hesitated, and then leaned in, returning the gesture. After a moment, Yui cleared her throat and Shin reluctantly broke away from Konomi. "I – ah..." he began, flustered. Konomi pushed away from him and headed for the trapdoor. Shin turned helplessly to Yui, who was grinning. She laughed at his expression and vanished back through the circular window.

Shin heard the soft clunk of her feet on the roof and then she was gone. Shin ran a hand through his hair and started down the steps after Konomi.

He was confused, and yet not. But he pushed pleasant thoughts aside and tried to concentrate on the matter at hand. Odoma wasn't going to give up; the Snakeheads might have failed, but the bounty was still up. Shin knew that he and his people would be in danger so long as it was in effect.

He took the steps slowly, trying to tease the pattern into a sensible shape. It was starting to look as if Kenzō's death was simply collateral damage in Odoma's grudge against him. But if so, what did any of it have to do with the weapons in the tunnels below the theater? Had that been another scheme of Odoma's – or something worse?

Downstairs, bodies littered the area – four, at least, though with some of them it was hard to tell. Kasami was cleaning her sword with the crook of her arm, and Lun was going through one of the dead Snakehead's pockets. Hachi stood near the steps, looking pale. Shin wondered whether he'd ever actually had to kill anyone before, or whether the Snakehead upstairs had been his first.

Kasami looked at him. "We killed a few, the rest fled."

Shin nodded. "There are two more dead upstairs, one courtesy of Yui. Remind me to pass along my compliments to Chobei when next I see him."

Lun stood, a few coins in her hand. "Not much on them. Then, the Snakeheads have been on the slide since Taoka died. Wonder what got them riled up."

"Odoma told them that I had Taoka killed," Shin said. Lun laughed.

"That'd do it!" She bounced the coins on her palm. "Still

want me to lead your cousin downriver? Because it seems like you might need the help."

Shin hesitated. Lun made a good point. If he threw himself on Aoto's mercy, it might serve to dissuade Odoma somewhat. But he dismissed the thought almost immediately. He had no intention of surrendering his freedom so easily; not when he'd worked so hard to claim it in the first place. "Yes. Stick to the plan. I need time to figure this all out."

Lun nodded. "As you say." She looked around. "I'd best get to it, then. We'll set off with the evening tide." She started away.

"Don't be shy about it either," Shin called after her. "Let them see you going."

Lun waved a hand, but didn't stop or reply. Shin sighed and looked at Kasami. "Go find Sanemon. I want to make certain the troupe is taken care of before we go. And there's some last minute orders I need to give him."

"After that, I think it is time to leave the city as we discussed," Konomi said, Hachi at her side, attentive as ever. She had an odd look on her face, Shin thought. He wondered if she regretted the kiss. Part of him hoped not. He shook his head.

"Not quite," he said. "First, I think I need to have a talk with Ito. He has some explaining to do about all of this."

CHAPTER TWENTY-FIVE
Records

"He's in the wind," Aoto said harshly. Ko looked up from her examination of Shin's correspondence – mostly marriage proposals, as well as some rather sour poetry. It was the third day of the investigation.

"Meaning?"

"The coward is on the run. That disreputable pirate in his employ set sail from his private berth last night." Aoto's hands balled into fists as he spoke. "No cargo, only passengers. He's not even attempting to pretend he's not fleeing the city."

"And what do you intend to do about it?"

"Pursue him, of course!"

"I wish you luck," Ko said, turning her attentions back to the papers. It was a trick, of course. Anyone not blinded by rage could see that. So, obviously Aoto was going to fall for it. Shin was just as clever as she remembered; he knew Aoto wouldn't be able to resist pursuing if he gave him something to chase. And that freed Shin to do… what?

"You don't wish to accompany me?" Aoto asked, looking

startled. "Surely this proves his guilt! Only a criminal flees in these circumstances..."

"Or someone who believes that they will not receive a fair trial," Ko said, not looking at him. "You have made it quite clear to him that you intend to drag him back regardless, Lord Aoto. Why shouldn't he flee?"

Aoto grunted. "Are you saying I shouldn't chase him?"

Ko frowned. "Not at all. Innocent or not, he needs to be in custody until this matter is settled. Besides, it is not my duty to pursue fugitives – merely to investigate the crime." And a few days without Aoto looking over her shoulder would be a good thing.

The Daidoji was proving just as troublesome as she'd feared. He was a distraction, and it was becoming tedious. Perhaps Shin had inadvertently done her a favor as well.

Aoto snorted. "Fine. I will go alone. And when I catch him–"

"If you catch him."

"*When* I catch him, you will see that my suspicions were correct." He picked up a pillow book from the stack that teetered near Shin's sleeping mat. "He always did read too much. It rots the brain, you know."

"Does it?" Ko asked, in a bored tone. She could feel him staring at her.

"Is that why you liked him?" he asked slyly. "The reading? The pretensions of wit?"

Ko sighed and gave him her attention. It was clearly what he wanted. "The circumstances of our relationship are none of your concern. Your questions verge on rudeness."

Aoto tossed the book over his shoulder. "I am starting to wonder if you do not still have feelings for him. You seem to have no real interest in punishing him for his many crimes..."

"I only care about one crime," Ko said sharply. She turned to face him and straightened. Aoto wasn't tall, so it was easy to look him in the eye. He didn't like that. "A good investigator does not allow their personal feelings to interfere with their search for the truth. That is something Shin never understood. I thought it was a personal failing, but now I see that it is a cultural one. You Daidoji are more emotional than I was led to believe."

Aoto's expression was thunderous. "I – how dare – I will – I…" he blustered, before visibly composing himself. He stepped back, expression stern. "Now it is you who are verging on rudeness," he said, after a moment. "But I take your point. You believe I am blinded by some petty grudge. Let me assure you that I am as clear-headed as it is possible to be, when dealing with Shin. He has driven the most placid of monks to madness with his insouciance. He is a demon, disguised as a jester."

"Why do you hate him so?" Ko asked, without thinking. "I know why I dislike him, but you are his cousin. What could he have done to you that was so unforgiveable?"

Aoto turned away. "I am going. I will leave you two of my best, to aid you in your… interrogations."

"To watch me, you mean."

He paused and she caught the flicker of a smile on his face. "Yes. That too."

"You haven't answered my question."

"I loved him," Aoto said, after a long moment's contemplation.

Ko paused. "Shin."

"Of course, Shin. Who else are we talking about?"

"When you say love…?" Ko began. Aoto snorted.

"Not like that. We were kin. Brothers, or as good as. Or so I thought. But he walked away from me, away from our duty.

Because he could not trouble himself to be what he was meant to be."

"Which was?"

"A Daidoji, in service to the Daidoji and the Crane. Instead, he wanted to fly free. And look where it has gotten him he should be thanking me. Instead, he seeks to thwart me even now." Aoto gestured, as if to the city beyond the walls. "I hate this place. It is a festering boil on the river's bend. I hate what it has done to him."

"And what is that? He does not seem much different to me." Ko heard the lie even as she spoke the words. The truth was, Shin was different, albeit in strange and subtle ways.

"It has made him arrogant; he sees himself as greater than his duty." Aoto paused. "He must be shown the error of his ways. He must be reminded that he is Daidoji, and that a Daidoji's first loyalty is to their duty – not themselves."

Ko paused. Then, "Earlier, I spoke with Odoma…"

"Who?" Aoto asked.

Ko paused again. "The merchant who accused Shin. He said that he had been promised protection. By the Trading Council. Is this true?"

"Obviously not," Aoto snorted. "He is a common criminal. They lie as easily as other men breathe."

"Are you certain? Do you speak for the Trading Council in this?"

Aoto drew himself up. "Are you questioning me?"

"Yes. Would the Daidoji Trading Council offer protection in exchange for testimony implicating Shin? Especially if, as you have said, his grandfather's influence is waning?"

Aoto grimaced. "No."

"Are you certain?"

Aoto hesitated. "No," he said, more quietly. "But it does not matter. Guilty or not, when this farce is done, Shin will be going home."

"Which is exactly what Odoma wants." Ko paused. "Are you familiar with someone named Ito?"

Aoto grunted. "Ito? One of the merchants under Shin's authority."

"What do you know of him?"

"A seller of paper, I think," Aoto said, in a bored tone. "One merchant is much the same as another, I've found." He hesitated. "I will leave you two of my best, as I said. Use them as you see fit. I wish you luck, Lady Ko."

"And I, you, Lord Aoto."

Then, he was gone. She stood for a time, marshaling her thoughts, trying to sift emotion from fact; something, she thought, Aoto had never bothered to do in his life.

During their short time together, Shin had barely spoken of his family, save in the vaguest of terms. The Daidoji seemed content to keep him at arm's length, and he, in turn, was content to remove himself from their influence. Some of that, she knew, was due to his grandfather. At the time, the old man had been the head of the Daidoji Trading Council – an esteemed position and a powerful one. Perhaps it was his influence that had kept Shin cushioned from any repercussions for his repeated bad behavior. Maybe he'd had some affection for his grandson after all.

But now, according to rumor, the old man was no longer in charge. Someone new had taken up the burden, and that meant any protection Shin might once have had was now gone. Was that what this was all about? Old grudges, finally being settled.

She looked again at the marriage proposals. Marriage was

anathema to Shin. So why was he now considering it? Aoto and his auditors had been on hand too quickly for their arrival to be due to the murder. They'd been coming to the city for another reason, that was obvious. Why – to arrest Shin? Or to ensure that he did as he was ordered to do? And if he hadn't, what then? Would they have executed him?

At its heart, that was why she doubted that Shin was responsible for the auditor's death. There was nothing to gain from it. The damage had been done by the time the fatal blow had been struck. So, what was there to gain?

She looked around Shin's quarters, searching for something she couldn't name – a sign, a clue, some puzzle piece that was out of place. She aligned the facts in her head, like a Go player laying down tiles. Kenzō had been sent to spy on Shin; he'd found nothing. Yet Shin was being pressured into marriage nonetheless. Did that mean her assumption was wrong, and that Kenzō had, in fact, found something?

Ko pulled out her fan and flicked it open, thinking. Investigations were like water, pouring down a rocky path. Sometimes they trickled in odd directions. Had that happened here? Had Kenzō, in investigating Shin, stumbled across something else – something that got him killed? And if so, what? The answers, she was certain, lay in the dead man's notes.

Annoyed with herself, she snapped her fan shut and smacked her palm. It had all seemed so clear on her journey to the city. So precise. She would investigate and see to the apprehension of the correct party. A slight sound behind her caused her to turn. Shin's servant – Niko, she recalled belatedly – was standing in the doorway, looking upset. "Mistress, I- I am sorry to disturb you. I- I would like to…" the young woman began, anxiously. Ko silenced her with a gesture.

"You wish to speak with me?" She wondered about the timing. Servants made excellent spies; few members of the nobility even noticed them. The Daidoji would not be the first clan to enlist household servants to eavesdrop on their own members in order to ferret out any potential wrongdoing.

Niko nodded, remembered herself, and bowed low. "Yes, mistress."

"About what?"

The young servant swallowed and said, "Lord Shin's financial records." She wondered how much of this lack of guile was a put-on, and how much was real. The way Niko's eyes flashed told her that at least some of her haplessness was feigned.

Ko's eyebrow rose. Aoto had mentioned the records were missing. Had Shin's servants hidden them? "I had heard that they were missing. I had thought perhaps Lord Shin took them."

"Oh no, he never touches them. He says numbers make him ill." Niko smiled slightly as she said it, and Ko heard affection in her words. Shin had a talent for making his subordinates care about his well-being. Idly, she wondered if that might be the answer – some servant of Shin's, taking matters into their own hands and Shin attempting to cover for them – before dismissing it. Even Shin wasn't that loved, or so foolish.

"I see. Then who did?"

Again, Niko paused. A flicker of calculation passed through her gaze. "Master Ito," she said softly. "He was the only one – besides Lady Konomi – whom Lord Shin trusted with them. And – and Lord Kenzō, of course."

Ko paused. Ito, again. "Is that so?"

Niko nodded and smiled slyly. "Before he… left, Lord Shin asked me to tell you that Ito took custody of the records. Kitano is with him. Lord Shin's manservant, I mean."

Ko frowned, but waved her fan. It was obvious that Shin was still investigating, albeit at a remove. The thought annoyed her. "You may go." As Niko departed, Ko turned back to her study of the marriage proposals and tried not to think of what might have been. Instead, she focused on the record books and this man, Ito.

It was becoming clear to her now that the answers she sought might well lie in those books. Had Kenzō found something in them that had gotten him killed? At the very least, it might provide her with a list of possible suspects – other than Shin, that was.

Ko snapped her fan open and gave it a flutter. She needed to see those books, and soon. Before Shin suffered the fate of all scapegoats. She closed her eyes and sighed.

It seemed she was investigating a mystery after all.

CHAPTER TWENTY-SIX
Discussions

Shin sat comfortably in Ito's receiving room, sipping lukewarm tea. Kasami knelt near the door, Kitano beside her. There was still blood on her robe and the hem of Shin's own, and he regretted not taking the time to change into one of his spare outfits from the theater. But the theater was no longer safe – nor the city, come to that – but certain matters had to be dealt with before they could even think of departing, even if only temporarily.

"Well, Master Ito?" Shin asked. The tea was a common blend. Good quality, but with an acridity Shin associated with the blends that came from Unicorn lands. He gave the cup a swirl, watching the eddies of color wash against the sides. Outside, rain made the evening light watery and diffuse, and the shadows deeper than was entirely pleasant.

Ito looked uncomfortable. "I… am not certain what you're asking me, my lord."

Shin sighed and put his cup down. "Who has been using the tunnels? The ones below the theater. The ones you told me about. Why tell me, unless you wanted me to look?"

Ito looked into his own cup, as if attempting to divine the future. Then, with a soft grunt, he said, "The dead."

"What?"

"It was Shaiban's plan. He longed to get out from under Odoma's heavy hand. He was willing to pay, so… well."

"And the others?"

"All of them, yes. And others, as well."

"I asked you before if you'd suggested buying the theater as a way to cut Odoma off at the knees. You didn't answer then. Do me the courtesy of answering now, please."

Ito bowed his head. "As my lord wishes. The truth is no, and yes. Both and neither."

"Do you bear him some grudge?" Shin asked softly.

"The same grudge any honest merchant would bear such a man." Ito ran a finger around the rim of his cup. "Odoma is… bad for business. Bad for our business, I should clarify." He looked up. "Odoma was in the process of forming a syndicate. Have you…?"

"I understand what a syndicate is," Shin said. A mercantile syndicate was a loose group of parallel business interests, formed in order to control a market. Ink and paper sellers, dye and cloth sellers, so on and so forth. "Odoma's syndicate was different, I take it?"

"Yes. Odoma intended to control the waterfront – the Unicorn waterfront, I should say. The Lion docks being largely impenetrable to those of us unlucky enough not to be born into the Akodo family." Ito dipped his finger in his tea and drew a line on the table between them. "Odoma thinks like a gangster. So, when he took over the merchants' association, he wielded its authority like a cudgel. Any merchant without clan protection was extorted into signing on with Odoma."

"How do the Snakeheads figure into this plan of his?"

"They were the cudgel." Ito hesitated. "This is all hearsay, you understand. Things I have gleaned from others. According to Osho and a few others, Odoma used the Snakeheads as the stick, and his protection as the carrot."

"And if he controls the waterfront, he also controls the smuggling," Shin said softly. "Why didn't you tell me this earlier?"

Ito looked down again. "As I said, it was hearsay. And I thought the less you knew, the better. The truth of it is… this is the sort of thing I am here to do. To facilitate trade, and ensure that the coffers of the Crane are not shorted. Odoma's plan threatened the equilibrium of things, so I acted as I thought best."

"And you used me to do it."

Ito bobbed his head. "I did. Yes." There was no apology in his tone, no regret. Merely agreement.

"Shaiban and the others were using the tunnels with your knowledge," Shin said. "Did Odoma know?"

"I expect so."

"Would he act against them?"

Ito paused. "Possibly." He frowned. "Do you think that is why he killed Lord Kenzō? Perhaps Lord Kenzō discovered some link between Shaiban and the others, and traced it back to Odoma. Odoma would not have taken that well."

"No, I don't expect that he would have." Shin hesitated. "Ito… there were weapons hidden among the smuggled goods."

Ito blinked. "What?"

"The goods that were in the tunnels. Who was responsible for them?"

Ito shook his head slowly. "I'm not sure. For obvious reasons, we didn't keep records. It could have been any of them. Of course, now I suppose they'll rot…"

"Is there any way to figure out where they were going?" Shin asked. Ito looked confused. Shin leaned forward. "The goods smuggled through the theater. They invariably go inland, don't they? Into Unicorn territory. Isn't that right?"

"I – yes. I suppose. I have never given much thought where it goes." Ito rubbed his face. "Why smuggle weapons though?"

"Lion weapons, Ito. Ones with identifiable forge markings."

Ito's gaze sharpened. "Ah. I see. That implies… something unpleasant."

"And familiar."

"Yes," Ito said. He sat back on his haunches, shrewd eyes turned inwards. "I cannot say with any certainty which of them was responsible, but I can say that none of them were fervent revolutionaries. Strictly middlemen."

"And now they are all dead."

"Yes. Likely by Odoma's hand."

"As I almost was, earlier."

Ito blinked again, clearly startled. "What?"

"Yes, it seems Odoma told the Snakeheads I was the one who'd killed their leader. They attacked the theater. Nearly killed Lady Konomi and me."

Ito paled. "What happened?"

"We are here," Kasami said. "Judge for yourself, merchant."

Ito glanced at her and nodded. "Yes, a silly question, I suppose. It won't take long for word to get out. I expect Odoma is already panicking, my lord. He may well do something foolish – more foolish, I should say."

"More foolish than sending the Snakeheads after me?"

Ito hesitated. "If Odoma is behind this somehow, it is possible that he has been trimming loose ends. Killing those who might reveal something, anything about his doings. Perhaps he still had contact with Shaiban or one of the others; perhaps the weapons were some scheme of his... but now, his schemes threaten to bring him down. So, he seeks to cut all ties to them. That includes us, I fear."

Shin nodded slowly. Ito was still holding something back. Shin wondered if the merchant had realized that there was something wrong with the ledgers. He decided to leave the question for later. There would be time to unravel that knot when Odoma had been taken care of, and the bounty called off.

Decision made, Shin pushed himself to his feet. "Stay out of sight, Ito. You too, Kitano. Until I tell you both otherwise."

"And what about you, my lord?" Ito asked.

"Lady Konomi has kindly offered me use of her estate outside the city. I will be there, until further notice."

"A good plan." Ito paused. "And what of Odoma?"

Shin paused. "I intend to see to him now. I want to hear his confession from his own mouth. After that, well... I will leave it in the capable hands of others."

"Like the Kitsuki investigator, per chance?"

Something in Ito's voice caught Shin by the ear. If he didn't know better, he'd have sworn it was amusement. Or perhaps annoyance. "Possibly. What of it?"

"She has been buzzing about the city, my lord – industrious and clever. She wishes to speak to me, you know." Ito paused. "I believe she wishes to see the ledgers."

"Then let her, Ito. Unless... there is some reason you think she shouldn't?"

Ito frowned. "I... no. No, my lord. I will be happy to show them to her, if she should come asking about them." It was clear that he didn't care for the idea, but Shin was certain Ito would do as he asked. He didn't doubt the man's loyalty.

"Oh, I have no doubt that she will. You see, I have ensured

that she knows where the ledgers are, and she will know about the tunnels under the theater before the day is out. She will find the weapons and then, likely, come here. Tell her what she needs to know."

"And then?"

"Then, hopefully, this matter will be resolved." Shin smiled. "All will be well, Master Ito. Have no fear." He went downstairs, Kasami following him. Konomi and Hachi were waiting for them downstairs.

"Did you learn anything?" Konomi asked, as she set a handful of paper samples aside.

"More than I hoped, but less than I wished," Shin admitted. "I fear there are two games being played here, and I must end one before I can concentrate on the other. Still, most of the threads seem tangled together, if in an unsatisfying manner."

Konomi caught his arm. "Perhaps we should leave it, Shin. You were almost killed today. We were almost killed. Let us leave, before something else happens."

Barely listening, Shin continued to talk, but mostly to himself. "The only loose strand is Taoko. The leader of the Snakeheads. Why kill him? Unless… his death was some form of punishment?" He tapped his lips with his fan, thinking. If Odoma had killed Taoko and the others, and Kenzō had discovered the link, somehow… but why would Kenzō confront Odoma? Unless there was something he still wasn't seeing.

"Maybe this Taoko was threatening to go to the authorities?" Konomi said speculatively. "Or maybe he simply decided to blackmail his partner? It would not surprise me. A man like Odoma would no doubt take that poorly." She touched Shin's arm. "It doesn't matter, though, does it? He's dead. They are all dead, Shin. As you might be, if you continue to pursue this."

"Are you worried about me?" Shin asked, startled. Konomi shook her head.

"Of course I am worried, Shin. We are… friends, yes? You are allowed to worry about friends, aren't you?"

"Are we friends?" Shin asked softly. Konomi frowned.

"Yes."

"Friends and only friends?" he asked, thinking about the drum tower and the kiss. Her invitation… all of it. It was all tangled up in surprise and suspicion. Convenient and inconvenient, all at once. He wanted to believe it, to surrender to it. But that wariness was still there, in her eyes. That strange distance.

Konomi looked away. "Shin, I…"

"My lord?" Kitano asked, from the stairs. Shin gave Konomi an apologetic smile and turned to his manservant.

"Yes, Kitano?"

Kitano glanced nervously at Konomi. "Are you sure that you don't – well, I could go with you. You might need me."

"I need you here, Kitano. Someone must look after Ito, in case Odoma acts rashly. Chobei and his cadre cannot be everywhere. Besides, I trust you to ensure that Lady Ko receives my ledgers." Shin glanced upwards. "While I have every faith in Ito, his loyalties are, ultimately, to the Crane. He might decide those ledgers should not be seen by outsiders."

"I've seen them," Konomi said. Shin looked at her.

"So you have." He turned back to Kitano. "Watch him. Keep him alive. When I return, you will be rewarded."

Kitano grinned. "I do like the sound of that."

"I thought you might," Shin said, with a chuckle. As Kitano returned upstairs, Shin turned back to Konomi. "My apologies. Where were we?"

Konomi studied him for a moment, and then left the shop,

Hachi trotting in her wake. Shin sighed. "That answers my question, I suppose." He felt a flicker of what might have been regret. Konomi was a constant in his life, and had been since they'd first met. He could always count on her for advice or companionship. And he fancied that she felt the same about him. The memory of their moment together at the theater would have to be enough. He looked at Kasami, who was watching him with a frown on her face. "Ito was right. Odoma is the key, and if I were him, I would be fleeing the city."

She grimaced. "Which is what we should be doing. Lun will only be able to distract your cousin for so long. When he realizes what you've done, he'll come storming back here, and no one will be able to stop him from taking you into custody."

"Then we'd best go now," Shin said. He snapped open his fan, mind working over the problem. There were still too many unanswered questions. "I must speak with Odoma again. And this time, I'm not leaving until I get the truth."

CHAPTER TWENTY-SEVEN
Panic

The rain had increased in tempo by the time Shin and Kasami reached the brewery. They'd parted ways with Konomi and Hachi, the former intent on preparing for their departure from the city. Shin felt somewhat queasy at the thought; he had no illusions as to the limits of his own courage, but even so, abandoning what he'd built felt wrong.

Then, perhaps it was simply that, for the first time in a long time, he couldn't see what was ahead. There was no course to chart, no guiding star. Just a mist of possibilities, most of them bad. He extended a hand from beneath his – Aoto's – umbrella, catching rain drops. The street was clear. Darkness and rain stifled even the most exuberant spirit. Even the Red Gull, across the street, was shuttered up against the weather. "The rain isn't letting up," he said, more to hear himself speak than because he was interested in the weather.

Kasami grunted. Then, "Lady Konomi is a good friend to you."

Shin looked at his bodyguard. "Yes, she is."

"If you would like my opinion…"

"I would not," he said firmly.

"She has feelings for you," Kasami continued, relentless. "That is clear to anyone with eyes and a brain." She stopped and turned, facing him. The rain ran down her sharp features in clear rivulets. "But how do you feel about her?"

Shin looked away. "I do not wish to talk about this just now."

"She is the answer to your problem."

"She is my friend."

"And the answer to your problem," Kasami repeated. "If you were to wed her…"

"This is not the time," Shin said sharply. He started walking, leaving her behind. She did not give up, however. She strode after him, still talking, despite the drumming of the rain.

"Why do you hesitate? Do you doubt her affections?" She stopped. "Or, are you thinking of someone else?"

Shin stopped and turned. "What do you mean?"

Kasami gazed at him through the shifting curtains of rain. "The actress, Okuni."

Shin stared at her. "What?" Okuni had been a member of the Three Flower Troupe, as well as a mercenary shinobi; thief and saboteur, she had become entangled in a deadly conspiracy, the same conspiracy that had started Shin on his current path. With Shin's help, she'd managed to extricate herself and flee the city. He had not heard from her since, though, for a brief time he had hoped – but that was then, and this was now. He chuckled softly and turned away. "No. I assure you, it is not that."

"Then what is it?"

"I am frightened," Shin said, more loudly than he intended. He turned back to glare at her. "I am frightened of her, of what it might mean, of all of it. I do not want to change, or to be changed. I wish to be who I am. I have invested much of myself in being myself." He thumped his chest with his free hand. "As has Konomi. We are two of a kind – would we be happy, or would we rub against one another until we crack, like stones caught in a millwheel?" He hesitated. "More… there is something about her. Something I, at times, see in myself. A sort of uncertainty; a wariness." He saw by her expression that she did not understand.

Shin turned back to the brewery. "As I said, I do not wish to talk about this now. Come, the brewery is just… wait." He stopped. Something was wrong. "Where are the guards?" he murmured. The Kaeru who should have been on duty were missing. Perhaps they'd been ordered elsewhere, but he couldn't imagine Ko allowing that.

Kasami grunted. "Blood."

Shin followed her gaze and saw, in the weak light of the covered lanterns that illuminated the street, something dark splashed across the mud. And there, under the stairs leading into the building, as if it had been kicked there – a sword. He looked at her. "I think Ito was right. Odoma is panicking. Planning to run. Come on."

"Would he be so stupid as to kill two Kaeru?" she muttered. The Kaeru had a reputation for dealing harshly with those who dared raise steel against their warriors. It kept the waterfront gangs in line, and caused even bravos from the Lion district to hesitate. But Odoma was clearly beyond worrying about such things.

The doors were slightly open, as if someone had eased them apart in order to slip through. Shin and Kasami gently slid them the rest of the way open, as quietly as possible. There was a smell on the air – the mingled pong of wet straw and fermenting soy and something else. Acrid and metallic. Kasami retrieved a paper lantern from a hook on the door beam, and lit the candle within.

In the watery light, Shin spied the two Kaeru guards. Both were dead and laying in a careless heap near the doors. "Someone dragged them inside after killing them," he said. Kasami nodded and looked around.

"They might still be here," she said quietly. "Stay close to me."

Together, they moved deeper into the brewery. Nothing leapt out at them as they moved through the vats. "Something is dripping – one of the vats?" Kasami murmured, indicating a spot on her robes. Shin touched one of the droplets and gave it a sniff. It was not soy sauce.

"No," he whispered. "I think we must go upstairs."

Kasami frowned, but nodded. She gestured with the candle, and Shin stepped past her, moving as quickly as he could in the gloom. He climbed the steps slowly, his skin crawling with every creak of the timbers.

He was not used to silence. The city was always talking, often at high volume. The river rumbled, the waterfront hummed with a commercial chorus and the city itself had a multitude of songs, for those with the ears to hear. There was nothing like it, really. But it was absent now; shrouded by the rain and the stout walls. He didn't care for it.

At the top of the steps, he paused. Still nothing. No hum of breath, no rustle of cloth. Absolute stillness. But even so, there was something. And as Kasami crept up behind him, the reach of her candle extended past him and across the platform, revealing–

Kasami hissed softly. Shin stared in disbelief. Three bodies lay before them. Two men and a woman. One of the men lay close, in a pool of blood; he had been of lanky build and clearly a ronin – one of Odoma's guards, no doubt. He'd died without drawing his sword, his body slashed almost to ribbons.

In the candlelight, Shin spied a set of bloody footsteps – those of the killer? He glanced at Kasami and she loosened her sword in its sheath. The other two bodies were at the center of the platform. Neither was Odoma. One was another guard; stocky and red-veined, beneath all the blood. He'd gotten his sword out, but it apparently hadn't done him much good. He was in as sad a state as the other.

The remaining body belonged to that of Odoma's courtesan. She seemed to have put up more of a fight than the guards; a steel hairpin, roughly the length of a knife, was loosely clutched in one of her hands. Shin took the light from Kasami and stooped to examine it. There was blood on the tip. She, at least, had drawn blood – but whose?

Kasami grunted softly, and he followed her gaze. A splash of blood marked the floor near a second, smaller set of steps. There were signs of a struggle; scrape marks on the wood, chunks missing from the rail. And, of course, more blood. Most of it on the steps.

Kasami crouched at the top of the steps. "Injured – then escaped downstairs?" she murmured. Shin nodded.

"Reminds me of that unpleasant business with the Tortoise courier a few months ago," he said, absently. "Poor fellow was determined to escape his captors, despite the absence of his legs… and most of his fingers." He shivered slightly.

Kasami started down the steps without replying. Shin hurried after her, keeping the lantern raised. The blood trail wound down and through the vats beneath the platform. As if whoever it was had been searching for something. Kasami paused and indicated something on the ground. Shin stooped and retrieved a koku. The coin was smeared with red. There were others, here and there. As if a lockbox had been spilled.

Something lurched into the light. Kasami shoved Shin behind her. "No farther," she growled, warningly. The shape stumbled against a support beam, wheezing. Shin raised the lantern and hissed in surprise.

Odoma glared at them, blood staining his brocaded robes and running down his heavy arms to puddle on the floor. In one hand, he held a heavy burlap sack. In the other, a knife. He squinted against the light. "Who's there?" he croaked.

"It is me, Master Odoma," Shin said. "It seems we have caught you at a bad time."

Odoma gave a wheezy laugh and dropped his sack. It rattled as it hit the floor. "You could say that," he said. "Should have – should have run, like Isuka said. Couldn't leave debts unpaid, though." He shook his head, wearily. "Couldn't…"

"What debts?" Shin asked, carefully. "What happened here?"

"I think it's fairly clear," Kasami said. "He killed them, just like Ito said."

"Two armed men, and with only a knife? No." Shin shook his head. He glanced at the sack. It was full of koku. Some of the coins spilled out and rolled across the floor. Odoma didn't seem to notice. His gaze was unfocused, and he didn't seem wholly cognizant of where he was. He was clearly in a bad way. Shin was fairly certain that the blood on his robes was his own. "No, he is as much a victim as those upstairs."

"He's still alive," Kasami pointed out.

"Not for long, if we can't get him help," Shin said. "Odoma…" he began.

"Shut up," the soy merchant barked. He pointed his knife at them. "You won't get away with this, Crane. I know what you are. I'll tell them all and they'll pluck your white feathers for me…"

Odoma swayed on his feet as he spoke, and Shin saw blood

on his chin. Odoma wiped his mouth with the back of his hand. Shin took a step toward him. "You are injured," he said, in a soothing tone. "We can help you."

Odoma stumbled back, swiping at the air with his knife. "Get away from me!"

Shin froze and Kasami readied her blade. "Odoma – who did this to you?"

"You did," Odoma snarled. He jabbed the air with his knife. "You killed the others, and now you've come for me."

Shin hesitated. "The others? What others?" But he already knew the answer to that. Odoma was undoubtedly referring to the slain merchants.

Odoma gave a hollow laugh. "They were mine – my earners – and you took them – and then you killed them when that stupid auditor started sniffing around. Trying to hide what you were up to, eh? But I know who you are."

"So you said," Shin began. "How did I take them, exactly? What do you mean?"

"You took everything," Odoma slurred, shaking his head. "Took my theater… took my business… but you won't get all of it!" He reached down for the sack, swayed again, and nearly collapsed. Shin made to help him, but Kasami jerked him back. Odoma gathered the sack to his chest and tried to stand, still muttering.

Then – from somewhere in the brewery came the sound of a shamisen being played. Odoma jerked upright, dropping the sack, spilling the no-doubt ill-gotten gains across the floor. He raised his knife. The music continued, drifting between the vats.

Shin felt the hairs on the back of his neck prickle. There was something unpleasantly familiar about that sound. Something unwelcome. Odoma's eyes bulged and bloody froth gathered at the corners of his mouth. "No – no – *no!* You won't! I am Odoma. This city is mine – *mine*!" He lunged wildly toward them, knife slicing the air.

Kasami cursed and shoved Shin back against a vat, hard enough to drive cedarwood splinters into his back. Her sword flashed in a silver arc, and Odoma fell with a strangled squawk.

The sound of the shamisen ceased abruptly and there came the soft clatter of someone departing. Shin and Kasami gave chase, but whoever it was, was gone. Vanished into the rain. Kasami cursed, and Shin quietly agreed. "We should go," he said. "There's nothing more to be done here."

As they ducked out into the rain, Kasami said, "He was mad. But there was someone else there. The killer?"

"I believe so." Shin paused, trying to make sense of Odoma's mutterings. "Odoma thought I was his enemy, but he was mistaken. I fear I was merely a convenient distraction… a blind to keep him occupied, striking at shadows. And now the shadows have claimed him at last. Poor fool."

"He tried to kill you. Us."

"Yes, there is that." Shin glanced over his shoulder. He could not help but feel as if they were being followed by some dark spirit. Perhaps the same one which had haunted the edge of his perceptions for the last year. "What matters now is that with Odoma dead, there is no reason to keep me alive." He looked at Kasami, fear humming through him like a wasp.

"I think it's time we got out of the city. The sooner the better."

CHAPTER TWENTY-EIGHT
Shamisen

Ko rose from beside the body of the dead gangster and peered down the corridor of the theater's backstage area. More bodies lay at the other end. A dozen dead, maybe more. Some from obvious causes – missing heads, blood loss from lopped-off limbs, spilled intestines – others from less visible means... darts in the neck or base of the skull, throats crushed by strangling cords and one poor fellow had fallen through a trapdoor in the stage and seemingly died of fright.

"As you can see, it is most distressing," Master Sanemon blubbered, wringing his heavy hands. He glanced warily at Ina, who stood protectively nearby, as well as the two auditors left behind by Aoto. Ko had not learned their names, and they had not offered them. "Most distressing indeed, my lady!"

The massacre had been reported a few hours after Aoto's departure. A suspicious lapse, given the probable time of death estimated by the Kaeru physician who had accompanied her. No doubt it had occurred not long before her talk with Shin's servant. "Yes." Ko fixed the master of the Three Flower Troupe with an even stare. "This was not of your doing, then?"

"Oh no, my lady! We are – are performers and thespians. Not brawlers!"

Her hand snaked out, catching one of his. He was strong, but surprise kept him from pulling away. She examined his hand, noting the calluses, the old scars, the wideness of his fingertips, indicating blows sustained at some point in the past. A soldier's hand. "So I see," she said, letting his hand drop. Like his master, Sanemon wore a mask. Old skills and furies, buried beneath the anxieties of a theater manager. "Where is he now?"

"Who, my lady?"

"Do not play dumb, fool," one of the auditors snapped. The taller of the pair, with a sharp face and cold eyes. Intimidating. Ko waved him to silence.

"You know who I mean. Do not insult us both by pretending otherwise."

Sanemon blanched. "He – he left. With the others."

"What others?"

"C-Captain Lun, and – ah – L-Lady Konomi. My lady."

Konomi. Ko frowned. Out of the corner of her eye, she spied the two auditors look at one another. They had unhappy expressions on their faces. Then, the fact that their superior had been so clearly fooled by Shin's ruse had to be somewhat galling. "He told you to report this after a certain amount of time, didn't he? Why?"

"You'd have to ask him, my lady."

"I would, if I knew where he was."

"The last I heard, he was going to talk to Master Ito, the paper-seller." Sanemon paused. "There… was something else, my lady. Something for your ears only." He glanced at the auditors, who visibly bristled. The shorter one gesticulated at him.

"You have no say in that," she snapped. "Talk or be punished."

Ko waved her fan, interrupting the auditor before she could say something unfortunate. "Speak. Whatever you tell me I will tell them in time. This merely simplifies things." Sanemon seemed unhappy, but nodded.

"Better, I think, that I show you." He led them backstage, to the cistern room. The cap was off the well, and someone had tied up a rope dangling down into the running waters below. Sanemon spoke quickly, nervously, outlining what he claimed Shin had told him about the tunnels and the smuggled cargo hidden in them. When he'd finished, Ko sent Ina to gather the other Kaeru. They needed strong backs, and she had no intention of going down there herself. There were limits to an investigator's responsibilities, and wading through sewage was one of them.

The next few minutes were tedious ones. Warriors descended carefully into the shallow darkness. Moments filled with muffled voices and splashing followed. The voices faded alarmingly. Ko glanced at Sanemon. "How far do these tunnels of yours extend, exactly?" she asked.

"Lord Shin claimed they stretched to the river," Sanemon replied, hesitantly. Ko nodded. She could see it, in her mind's eye: a small, concealed wharf, hidden perhaps beneath camouflaged tarps… then, an aperture, covered by a bamboo grate, perhaps, in order to prevent the tunnels from being filled with detritus during storms such as the one now pelting the city. It would be easy to bring in goods, especially at night. The Kaeru patrolled the river, but by Azuma's own admission, they often looked the other way when it came to such things. No one would notice goods being moved out of the theater, given the daily comings and goings. Ingenious, really.

When one of the warriors who'd gone down shouted up about what they'd found, Ko decided to retrieve it all. "Bring them up. Slowly. Make sure nothing is damaged," Ko ordered, and then stepped back as the first cargo was brought up. It was several weeks old, judging by the condition of the perishables. The weapons were cleverly concealed, but someone had already exposed them. Shin, she knew. She accepted one of the swords from Ina and studied it. She tapped the mark etched into the base of the blade. "This is a Lion sigil. One of the forge families, I believe.

Ina peered at it. "Itagawa."

Ko set the weapon aside. The others were the same. "Itagawa weapons. I wonder what they are doing here?" The implications were unsettling.

"Isn't it obvious?" the taller auditor asked. "It is clear that Lord Shin is involved in a smuggling operation of some note. It is no surprise he killed Lord Kenzō, if his secret was discovered. He must have been trying to hide his involvement."

"Lord Aoto was right; Lord Shin is clearly guilty," the shorter auditor echoed. "We should have the Kaeru issue a warrant for his immediate arrest. Especially if he is still in the city, as it seems he must be." She thumped a fist into her palm. "If we were to capture him–"

"Silence," Ko said sharply. She snapped open her fan, startling them. "If Lord Shin is profiting from such an enterprise, why would he inform us of its existence?" Was this the discovery that had led to Kenzō's death? More, what did Shin expect her to do about it? She turned to Sanemon. "Where are they going? Did Lord Shin say where he believed these weapons were being delivered to?"

Sanemon shook his head. "He said something about Unicorn lands. That's all I know. Maybe that's why after he spoke to Ito, he was going to Lady Konomi's estate upriver, along the Ide trade-road." He paused, glancing again at the auditors, and Ko suddenly had the impression that Sanemon had been coached in what to say – to deliver the location perfectly, at the proper time. And like a good actor, he delivered.

Another crumb of information Shin had seen fit to deliver to her, she knew. Is that why they'd waited so long to report the attack? To give Shin the opportunity to flee, and continue the investigation on his own terms? Was Konomi helping Shin? Or was there some other game being played here? What trail was he following – and where might it lead? She shook her head, annoyed. There were too many questions and precious few answers, and she did not much care for the feeling of being led around by the nose.

She wanted to question Sanemon more about Lady Konomi and her estates, but was interrupted by the arrival of a runner from Saibanshoki: a Kaeru apprentice. He panted as he came to a halt before Ko. "My lady – Lord Azuma sent me – the soy merchant, Odoma – he's…" He broke off, wheezing. Ko waited impatiently for him to catch his breath.

"He is what?" she asked. She thought she already knew the answer. Odoma was fleeing the city. He had to realize that his schemes were undone.

"Dead, my lady. Murdered. Him and the men we had on guard outside the brewery. And there's a – a witness." He gestured back the way he'd come. "They're escorting her here now. A shamisen player from the – the Red Gull. She says she knows who did it!"

Ko shook her head, trying to reorient her thinking around this new, unwelcome information. "Bring her in as soon as she arrives. I want to speak with her." She glanced at Ina, who shook her head slowly.

"I told you. The river is unhappy."

Ko grimaced and looked away. Thankfully, they didn't have long to wait. The young woman was led in, tapping her bamboo cane against the floor. Blind, Ko realized. And a musician. A not unreasonable combination, given the limited opportunities available to someone who had the misfortune to be both poor and sightless.

"You are the shamisen player for the Red Gull teahouse," Ko greeted her. "I am called Ko. What is your name?"

"E-Emiko, my lady," the young woman quavered. She bowed low, shaggy hair covering her useless eyes. She was dressed in plain robes that had seen much repair, by blind fingers. She wore her shamisen slung across her back, and clutched her cane to her chest. She tilted her head at every whisper of sound, tracking it with an odd, almost serpentlike oscillation of her neck.

"You are blind," Ko said.

"Yes, my lady."

"Yet you claim to have witnessed a murder?"

Emiko tapped her ear. "I… heard them, my lady. Heard their voices. Heard the hiss of steel and the sounds of – of pain." She hesitated. "I… often play the shamisen for Master Odoma. He does love it so… or, he did."

Something about the way she said it made Ko narrow her eyes. Almost as if she were amused. Then, maybe she was. Odoma did not seem to have been the sort to be a generous employer – or a kind one. "Were you playing for him today?"

"Yes, my lady. But then, he told me to stop. That he had guests."

"Did he say their names?"

"One of them. A Lord… Shin, I think. He had a very fine voice, even when it was raised in anger. He smelled nice – nicer than Master Odoma." She raised her chin as she spoke, as if expecting Ko to argue with her. Instead, Ko asked, "Why was he there?"

Emiko bowed her head again, her fingers nervously tapping at her cane. "I – I did not hear that. I was ushered out into the rain. But I did not wish to get wet so I… dallied." She paused again, as if waiting for a rebuke. When none came, she continued, "I heard shouting. And then… Master Odoma screamed."

"Screamed what?"

Emiko shook her head. "In pain, my lady."

"The Kaeru guards?"

"They – they went in and then… silence." Emiko hunched tight, making herself small. "I fled, then. Into the rain, away. I did not want them to – to…" She trailed off. Ko studied her for a moment longer then turned to one of the Kaeru who'd escorted her.

"What is there to report?" she asked.

"All dead," he replied. "Odoma, his woman, his guards and ours. Someone took a sharp blade to them. Someone who knew what they were doing."

"A professional, you mean."

"The Hiramori," one of the auditors muttered.

The Kaeru nodded, his expression grim. "A trained swordsman. Quick, too. No signs of a real struggle but one of our people found this caught on a splinter near the vats." He held up a scrap of blue cloth. Ko took it wordlessly. It was thin, torn possibly from a sleeve or the hem of a robe. She ran her thumb across it. Silk. Fine quality.

Shin.

She took a deep breath. "Send riders downriver. We need to try to catch Lord Aoto, if possible. He needs to return to the city immediately." She looked at the auditors. "You are free to go with them, if you wish."

They looked at one another. Then, the taller one said, "No, my lady. Lord Aoto ordered us to aid you in any way we could. That means we go where you go."

"Fine. But from now on, if I wish to hear your opinions, I will inquire about them. Remember that, and we will be friends." She turned to Ina. "Ina, I want you to escort Master Sanemon to Saibanshoki. Find Lord Azuma." Ko looked at Sanemon. "You are to tell him everything, do you understand? Just as you told it to me. It is imperative that he knows what we found and that Lord Shin is the one who directed us to it. And tell him where Lord Shin has gone, as well."

"What about you, my lady?" Ina asked. "If you are not returning with us ... ?"

"I intend to speak with the one person who might be able to unravel all of this." Ko slapped her fan into her palm.

"I must talk to a paper-seller named Ito."

CHAPTER TWENTY-NINE
Two Hill Station

The morning sky was the color of slate, and the clouds rolled with a feral oiliness. The grasslands of Shinten Province stretched away to either side of Shin in rainswept waves. The storm had redoubled its strength in the night, and its reach was greater than just the city. The sheer emptiness of the grasslands, contrasted against the bleak sky, served to sour Shin's mood even more than it already was.

He and Kasami rode in the van of a small Ide caravan, bound for Laketown in the Kawabe Province, there to pick up a cargo of pearls – or so Konomi had explained. They were dressed like simple traders, in plain robes fit for travel. Shin's distinctive hair was hidden beneath a straw hat, though Kasami had been allowed to keep her swords. Their horses were from the Iuchi stables, and trotted gaily along the hardscrabble road. He kept tight hold of the reins, not trusting his mount not to bolt at the first scent of sweet grass. Kasami rode more easily, chewing on a barley stalk as she kept a wary eye on the Ide.

Shin left her to it. The events of the previous day had begun to settle in, leaving him in his usual state of moody self-reflection.

The adrenaline of the moment had faded, leaving only questions and the ache that came from witnessing too much death. Foolishly, he'd once believed that he might grow used to such things, the way Kasami or Sanki seemed to be. Even Kitano had a stronger stomach, when it came to violence.

Worse, he was beginning to wonder if that was a sign that he was unsuited to the role he'd chosen for himself. Perhaps Aoto was right, and a quiet country estate might suit his talents better. He had a number of potential innovations in regard to irrigation and seed rotation that he could implement and test in such a place; the sort of things that might benefit the Crane as a whole. He frowned, annoyed by the idea that Aoto might have been right as much as the fear that he himself had been wrong.

"You look tired, Shin," Konomi said, urging her horse toward his own. She and Hachi looked none the worse for wear, despite the fact that the ride had taken the better part of the morning, and the rain had accompanied them the entire way.

Shin peered at her suspiciously from beneath the brim of his umbrella. "When you said that your estates were in the country, I assumed they'd be – I don't know – not quite so… rural." He indicated the rolling hills with his fan. Looking at them for too long made him queasy. Or maybe that was just being on horseback.

Konomi smiled at him from beneath her own umbrella. "Rural? We are within a day's ride of the city, Shin. Less, by boat. This is hardly the wilderness."

"Oh?" Shin looked around. "Looks like the wilderness to me. Smells like it, too. Even with the rain." He grinned at the expression on Konomi's face. "Not that I'm complaining," he added. "Last place anyone would expect to find me, I suspect."

"That was my thinking," Konomi said. She nudged her horse

forward and the animal obligingly clopped ahead. Shin tried to urge his own forward, but it ignored him, preferring to maintain its steady pace. He tried again.

"Come on, blasted beast," he muttered. "Move."

"You do not speak with authority," Kasami chided, guiding her own steed past and down the road. She whistled sharply, and Shin's horse jerked into motion and followed the others. Shin wobbled awkwardly on its back, startled by the abruptness of its motion. He glared at her. She frowned and took the barley stalk out of her mouth. "You are still thinking about Odoma," she said.

"Yes."

"You think whoever was smuggling the weapons killed him."

"It seems obvious. Don't you agree?"

Kasami grunted and turned away. "I think it is a good thing he is dead. One less problem for us." Shin watched as Konomi rode to the head of the caravan, likely to speak with the caravan master. From what she'd told him, they'd be separating from the caravan proper sometime soon, in order to make their way to the local Iuchi estate, the bucolically named Two Hill Station.

"In the scheme of things, he was only a little one. However, I fear the difficulties which remain might be beyond our abilities to overcome." Shin gnawed his lip, thinking about Odoma and the sound of the shamisen, playing out in the dark. He couldn't be sure, but he thought he'd heard that tune before. The memory rested on the surface of his mind like a snake sunning itself on a rock. "Aoto won't care about smuggled weapons. As far as he's concerned, that'll be someone else's problem. Which means we're the ones who have to deal with it."

"Are you certain?" Kasami asked. "You have made certain Ko will know of it and she will no doubt inform Lord Azuma. They will investigate, and we are safe here. Lord Aoto will eventually have to return home when he can't find you and..." She trailed off.

Shin shook his head. "Aoto won't give up that easily, and you know that as well as I do. He'll eventually work out where we are, and come storming in. Konomi's influence won't keep him at bay for long. But, if we can find the answer to the question before us, we might also find a way of extricating ourselves from this difficulty."

He hauled back on his reins as Konomi rode back toward them. Even in the hazy light of a downpour, she was lovely. She rode like one born to the saddle, and the joy on her face warmed his heart, despite all his reservations. "We'll take our leave of the caravan now. The road to Two Hill Station is close. In fact, you can see the hills themselves from here."

She pointed and Shin saw a pair of gentle slopes emerging from the grasslands, close as siblings. They were taller than the rest, with a few trees scattered across their crests, and it was hard to tell where one began and the other ended. To Shin, they resembled nothing so much as a section of bunched cloth. "How picturesque," he said.

Konomi laughed loudly. "Wait until we get close. Then you'll see."

As she'd promised, their destination was close. Even so, by the time they reached the hills, Shin was ready to drop from the saddle. He'd never ridden longer than it took to get from inn to teahouse in his life, much preferring the stolid dependability of boats to the questionable loyalty of horses. His rear was going to ache for days.

However, all thought of aches and pains fled his mind when he saw what awaited him in the lull between the two hills. It resembled the interior of a cup, complete with some dark liquid gathered at the bottom. "A lake?" he said, in some surprise.

"One of many out here. They hide in the lees of the hills, unseen unless you bother to look." Konomi pointed to a streak of darkness slithering away from the lake. "And there, a tributary leading to the river. When we got here, it was barely a trickle of mostly stagnant water. A haven for mosquitoes and kappa and not much else. But over the years, we widened it and straightened its course. Made it large enough to sail down. Now, Ide traders coming from the city will stop here for refreshment and to allow Iuchi toll officers to inspect their caravan's load, before it continues downriver or up to Laketown." She spoke with pride. "Who says the Unicorn are not builders, eh?"

"Not me, I assure you." Shin leaned forward in his saddle. A structure that could only be the station rose from the center of the small lake like a flower of wood and stone. It consisted of a central keep nestled amid a blossom of short, chunky stone bridges covered by artfully decorated roofs. At the end of each bridge was a storehouse, with a small wharf. The storehouses, like the keep, were circular and seemed to rise from the waterline. "Are the islands artificial?" he asked, intrigued.

Konomi grinned. "I wondered if you'd notice – yes. Took years, I'm told. They started with wooden pylons, driven into the muddy bottom, and then added alternating layers of woven reeds, dried mud, and loose stone to create solid ground capable of holding the weight of the storehouses. It was all trial and error, according to the records. Lots of collapses and sunken storehouses until they finally got it right."

"Fascinating," Shin murmured.

"In the high summer, when the water level drops, you can actually see the most recent of those failed attempts. As a girl,

I walked the old timber bridges and explored the crumbled storehouses." Her expression softened. "I sometimes miss those days. Simpler times." She shook herself slightly and smiled at Shin. "What do you think of it?"

"Magnificent," Shin said. Though the rain made it hard to pick out details, he could see that the walls of the central building, constructed from stone, were modestly steep. Violet tiles studded the circular roof of the keep, the rooftops of the buildings at the ends of the bridges, as well as the bridges themselves. All in all, it was as if the Iuchi had taken a part of their district from the city and deposited it here. "And you say you widened the river to accommodate trade?"

"Among other things. The tributary runs right into the lake here; no name, I'm afraid. Or maybe it does have one but I don't know it." Konomi gestured to the iron-gray waters. "The lake started as a place to take on cargo bound for the city. It would be floated downriver from Laketown, and then shipped on to the city. A chancy business, though. We lost quite a lot of cargo to smugglers and sticky-fingered fishermen." She patted her horse on the neck, causing it to whicker softly. "So, we built toll-stations along the tributaries; most are tiny – no more than crude wharfs with some huts attached, really. But this one has been my personal project for some years now."

"Oh?"

"Oh yes. Two Hill Station is the largest of them; the center of the web, so to speak. I oversaw the addition of the central keep," Konomi said proudly. "Before that, it was simply a barracks for the toll officers, and a poorly maintained one at that. I took responsibility for all of it after none of my brothers showed any interest."

A wide, flat bridge connected the shore to the central keep.

Two wooden portcullises served to cut the bridge into easily defended thirds. There were few visible guards, however. Kasami sniffed. "I do not think the Unicorn take security as seriously as the Lion," she murmured. Shin nodded, though he wondered if that was simply due to the rain. Any guard with sense would be indoors and dry on a day like this.

Beyond the second portcullis was the entrance to the keep itself; the gate was open, and Konomi led them inside a small courtyard, where attendants waited to take their horses. Servants flocked to lay claim to their small amount of luggage, occasionally squabbling over who got to carry what. Guards armed with horsetail-decorated spears were positioned unobtrusively on the walls above, and at the internal doors.

Shin looked around. The courtyard was a semi-circle of packed stone, broken at intervals by shaggy willow trees. He noted with interest that, in places, the roots of the trees had spread under the stones of the courtyard and through the walls. Konomi noticed his interest. "Cuttings from Saibanshoki itself, or so my father claims. Given as peace offerings by the Miya, when they assumed governorship of the city."

Small boats, barely larger than fishing vessels, were docked at several of the wharfs and loads of cargo were dropped off or loaded on for delivery farther downriver. The storehouses themselves were but pale imitations of the vast structures that dominated the waterfronts of the city. Even so, there appeared to be a substantial amount of cargo passing through them, and on a regular basis. Shin snapped open his fan to better disperse the smell of wet horse. "So, everything bound for Unicorn land from the city comes through here?"

"Almost all of it, yes. Why?"

Shin fluttered his fan, considering the likelihood that more of the smuggled weapons might have come through Two Hill Station. If there were more weapons. If the shipment under the theater hadn't been the first and only. But he feared that wasn't the case. No, something told him that it had been going on for a long time – longer than he cared to admit to himself. "No reason, merely speculating."

"Well, stop it. It's annoying."

He laughed and looked at her. "Your father must be proud of what you've done."

Konomi laughed. "Not in the least! He still holds out hope I will settle down with some worthy suitor and provide him healthy grandchildren."

"I don't see why you can't do both."

Konomi grinned at him. "Neither do I." A toll officer approached, bowed low and handed her a set of papers. Konomi scanned them at a glance and handed them back. "Later, Bao. Our guests come first." She paused and smiled. "I've had them prepare lunch for us. Something warming, after a brisk ride in the rain."

"You call that brisk?" Shin asked.

Konomi laughed. "Oh, Shin, I don't think you'd last a day as a Unicorn – then, I suspect I'd be devoured within moments of setting foot into a Crane court." She caught hold of his robes and gave him a gentle peck on the cheek. "Come. We'll find you some dry robes of suitable quality." She started toward the doors. Kasami caught up with him.

"You have that look," she murmured.

"What look?"

"The one you get when you think you've done something clever." Kasami paused. "What is it? What are you thinking?"

Shin leaned toward her, covering his mouth with his fan.

"You heard Konomi. All goods come through here. That includes our smuggled weapons, possibly." The thought wasn't a pleasant one; he doubted Konomi would react well to such a discovery. But that was a problem for later – and possibly not even a problem at all, if his suspicions were incorrect.

"How do you know?"

"I don't. Which means I need to have a look."

Kasami frowned and looked around, taking in the guards. "That will be difficult."

"Not if you help me."

Her frown deepened. "I do not like the sound of that."

Shin smiled and tapped her on the chest with his fan. "Trust me. Have I ever steered us wrong?" He paused. "Don't answer that."

She snorted and gave him a discreet shove. "Get inside, fool. The rain is picking up."

Shin hurried toward the doors, already planning the best way to get to the storehouses. He was hoping that he'd find nothing but rice and fish, and hoping, deep in his soul, that for the first time in a long time he was wrong about everything.

CHAPTER THIRTY
Paper-Seller

Kitano knelt nervously beside Ito, his eyes on the door. "You're sure?" he asked. "Maybe they won't bother? They have to have realized that he's innocent."

"According to a little bird of my acquaintance, they will be here soon," Ito said, steeping the tea. He'd laid out a tray of barley cakes as well. "Unpleasant, but we must muddle through if Lord Shin is to have any hope of escape."

"He didn't do it," Kitano protested. Ito sighed.

"It doesn't matter. If the Daidoji say that he did it, he did it. History is simply another narrative – one written by the victors." Ito sat back and looked at Kitano. "Our opinions on the matter are surplus to requirements."

"It's not fair."

Ito chuckled. "Little in this world is fair, my friend. Especially for people like us."

Kitano grimaced and glanced toward the window. "We could sneak out."

"And go where?"

"Chobei would hide us." Kitano looked at the merchant. "He'd do it for Lord Shin."

"I'm sure he'd do more than that, if asked," Ito murmured. He peered at Kitano. "If you want to run, run. I won't think less of you. It is the nature of the fox to flee the hunters. But I'm too set in my ways to abandon my little patch just because a few nosy birds decide to circle overhead." A bell sounded, signaling that someone had entered the shop below. Ito stretched. "Too late now. Gird yourself, Kitano. Our duel begins."

Kitano nodded, knowing that to flee now would risk him being spotted, or worse, caught. The auditors weren't likely to look kindly on him making the attempt. They might even kill him, just for trying. Ito was right – better to stay and brazen it out. He touched the dice hidden in his robes, hoping there was enough luck left in them to see him through.

Ito's servant girl knocked lightly and opened the door. "Master," she began. Ito silenced her with a gesture.

"Show them in, please," he said. "And take the rest of the day for yourself. I will close up when I am finished here." She flushed, pleased, and bowed. Ito glanced at Kitano. "No sense letting them question her as well."

"Smart thinking."

"I have my moments," Ito said. He fell silent as the sound of the creaking floors outside reached them. Ito listened and held up three fingers. Three of them, then. Bad odds, Kitano thought. He glanced again at the window, but any chance of escape had passed. Lord Shin had said Ko was smart – she'd probably have people on the street, watching Ito's shop.

And then, the door was opening, and Ko was there. From Shin's description, Kitano had been expecting someone more like Lady Konomi, but Ko was... small. Not just short, but compact. She moved lightly into the room without waiting for Ito's invitation, her fan fluttering as her eyes roamed, taking in every detail, and filing it away. Kitano had seen that look before on Lord Shin's face and he winced inwardly, hoping that Ito had tidied away anything incriminating. The ledgers were safely under the floorboards where they would remain until Ito decided to hand them over.

Behind Ko came two of the Crane auditors. They weren't like Kenzō; these two made no attempt to hide their capacity for violence the way he had. They were not obviously armed, but something about the way they moved put Kitano's hackles up. Kasami moved the same way, like a snake looking for a place to strike or a hawk circling its prey.

"Tea?" Ito said, without preamble. He indicated the small table, and the waiting cups.

"You were expecting us," Ko said, as she sat. The Cranes hesitated, but followed her example. "Some might think that suspicious."

"Merely good planning, I assure you," Ito said, as he poured the tea. "You have set this city all atwitter with your hunt for Lord Kenzō's murderer, and now Lord Shin. Word travels fast and you have a hundred eyes on you at any given moment."

"And some of those eyes belong to people in your employ, I assume," Ko said.

"They might."

She sniffed the tea and set it down without taking a sip. "Does my presence here worry you?" she asked. Ito paused, as if considering the question.

"No," he said, finally. "You have come to ask me something, I expect. But have some tea, first. It is quite good." He gestured. "My own blend."

The Crane sipped; good manners counted, even in situations like this. Ko refrained. Kitano took his own sip. The tea was spicy, a hint of ginger burning at the back of his throat. Ito was a man of many talents. He hunched over his cup, trying not to meet the cold gazes of the auditors. They reminded him of a flock of cranes watching a frog.

"You are younger than I expected," Ko said.

"Youth is a matter of perception," Ito said smoothly. Kitano felt a flicker of unease. How could the little man be so calm?

"You are a seller of paper."

"I am."

"And a spy."

Ito shrugged. "All men are spies. We all take note of our own observations and store them for future use. We gossip, trade information, and share stories. Is that espionage?"

"Yes." Ko flicked her fan, dismissing his words as if they were flies. Kitano was starting to understand where Shin had learned some of his odder behaviors. "That is, in fact, the definition of espionage." She took a small sip of her tea and nodded. "Ginger?"

"A touch," Ito said.

"I do not care for ginger."

"My apologies."

"Watch your tone, merchant," one of the auditors growled. He was tall, with a face like a reed-cutter's hatchet and eyes that were as flat and cold as an iced-over pond. Plenty of scars on his cheeks and neck; shrapnel, Kitano thought. Lun had similar scars, from where a mast had shattered and sprayed splinters into her face. "You are a servant of the Daidoji. It is only through their beneficence that you are allowed to hawk your wares in this city."

"And I am ever so grateful for that kindness," Ito purred.

"Indeed, I am always quick to proclaim the generosity of the Crane to any who listen."

Ko was watching Ito as the auditor spoke, and Kitano was watching her just the way Shin had taught him. Her accusation had been calculated aggression, designed to provoke. Shin did the same, albeit without the accompanying muscle… unless you counted Kasami. Ito likely knew that game as well; it was no wonder then, that he didn't appear perturbed. Kitano began to relax. It was a stalemate. That was good. A stalemate bought time.

He blinked. Ko was staring at him. He cursed inwardly, wondering if she'd seen something in his face. "You are Lord Shin's servant," she said, addressing him for the first time since she'd arrived. He hesitated, and then nodded jerkily. "Why are you here?"

Ito glanced at him. "He is helping me."

"He is armed," Ko said, indicating the knife in Kitano's belt with her fan.

"For eating and other mundane chores," Ito said.

"I would like to examine that knife."

Kitano's hand went immediately to his knife. The auditors tensed. "Hand it over hilt-first… slowly," the big one grunted. Kitano grinned obsequiously and did as they demanded. Ko took the blade and placed it horizontally across her fan, as if to test its balance. Then she ran a finger across the hilt, scrutinizing the weapon from tip to haft.

"Have you ever killed anyone with this knife?" she asked, not looking at Kitano.

Kitano hesitated. Then, with a shrug, "Yes."

She nodded. "There is dried blood where the blade meets the hilt. It is old, however. A year, maybe more. I am told you used to be a professional gambler."

"My luck ran out," Kitano said, indicating his prosthetic finger.

She raised an eyebrow. "Lord Shin?"

"His bodyguard," Kitano said.

"Why?"

Kitano shifted uneasily. "I… tried to kill him."

Ko's expression didn't change, though both Cranes looked outraged. "Why?"

"I thought he had cheated me."

"Had he?"

Kitano found his mouth suddenly dry and took another swallow of tea. "I am not sure." He felt like a traitor even as he said the words. "If he did, I deserved it," he added, quickly. "I was not above a bit of cheating myself, when it came to it."

"Scum," the larger auditor said. Kitano ignored him. Ko handed him back his knife.

"You are loyal to Lord Shin," she said.

Kitano nodded jerkily. "He has been good to me."

Ko's gaze flicked to Ito. "And you?"

"As I said, I have prospered in the shadow of the Crane's wings," Ito said, humbly, bowing his head. Again, Kitano marveled at his calm. Ko frowned.

"That is not an answer."

Ito's lips twitched. "Is it not?"

"Your license can be rescinded, merchant," the second auditor said sharply. She was a short woman, round in body and face, but without any softness to her. Her hair was dyed white, after the fashion of the Daidoji, but Kitano figured her for a Fujihiro, given the family crest he'd glimpsed tattooed on her inner wrist.

"So your comrade implied only moments ago," Ito said, still calm. He fixed Ko with a steady look. "I am happy to continue the dance, if that is your wish. But we could save time by being direct. You came for the ledgers."

"I came for answers."

Ito chuckled. "I have few of those."

"You undersell yourself, Master Ito." Ko rattled off a list of names. "Tell me, what do you know of the individuals I just named?"

"Shaiban was a common smuggler. Taoka was a gangster and of no notice to someone of Lord Shin's status, save as a nuisance. Hiroto and Dari were merchants, yes, but neither imported anything in Lord Shin's portfolio–"

"I did not mean in a business sense," Ko interjected softly. Ito paused.

"Ah." He paused. "They are all dead."

Ko leaned forward, expression intent. "Lord Kenzō saw some link between the victims – a conspiracy…"

"Is that what you call it?" Ito asked, his tone implacably mild. Almost bored.

"What do you know of the tunnels beneath the Foxfire Theater? According to Lord Kenzō's notes, you were instrumental in Shin's purchase of the building."

Ito tapped his fingers against his knees. "Do you wish to see the ledgers or not?"

Ko waved this aside. "It may interest you to know that Master Odoma is dead. Slain by a professional killer. Lord Shin has been implicated. Odoma was the previous owner of the theater, was he not?"

"He was, yes," Ito said.

"Did you know of the tunnels before you advised Lord Shin to buy the building?"

"I did, yes."

Ko was silent for a moment. She looked perturbed, as if something were gnawing at her. "The day Lord Kenzō died – before he visited Odoma, he went somewhere else. Do you know where?"

"I do." Ito smiled thinly and took a sip of his tea. He cut his eyes toward Kitano, and the latter wondered if that was amusement he saw in the merchant's eyes. "He paid me an unscheduled visit. And I served him some of my best tea."

Ko was about to speak when the taller auditor suddenly gave out a strangled grunt and collapsed in a twitching heap. A moment later, the second auditor rose to her feet, lurched sideways and fell onto her face, her body contorting in grotesque fashion. Ko swayed where she knelt, shaking her head. "What…?"

"Poison," Ito said. "The correct dosage this time." He glanced at Kitano. "Don't worry; it was in the cups, not the tea." He rose swiftly to his feet and, before Kitano could react, he reached over and jerked the gambler's knife from his belt. "Pardon me, but I require the use of your blade." Even as Kitano scrambled to his feet, Ito was lunging for Ko. She scrambled back, but not quickly or gracefully. She groaned and fell, Ito atop her.

"What are you doing?" Kitano wailed as Ito made to drive the knife into the investigator's chest. He sprang over the tea table and caught Ito by the back of his robes. "Get off her!" He hurled the paper-seller across the room – or would have, if Ito hadn't caught his arm and smoothly thrust the knife into Kitano's side. It took a moment for the pain to reach him, but when it did, he cried out.

"I should think that was obvious," Ito said, as he shoved Kitano back. "I intend to kill her. The stupid woman barely touched her tea. She got less than half the dose needed." Kitano tripped over his own feet and fell, clutching his injured side. The knife had gone in deep; he felt like someone had inserted a hot needle into his guts.

Ito turned back to Ko, who was crawling toward the doors. He sighed and prowled after her. "It's my own fault, really. In my arrogance, I forgot that clever people are like grains of rice in a bushel. Kenzō, Shin – you..."

Ignoring the pain in his side, Kitano forced himself to his feet and lunged for the paper-seller, hands outstretched. If he could just get a grip on the man's throat–

Ito spun on his heel and drove the knife into Kitano's chest. Kitano caught the other man's wrists and dragged him backwards. Ito's eyes widened and then rolled up as their skulls connected with a solid krump. Ito slumped with a groan and Kitano fell back onto the floor. His limbs felt heavy and he was having trouble breathing.

With blurring vision, he watched as Ito rolled upright, rubbing his head. The look on the other man's face was odd, frustrated and sad. "I wasn't going to kill you, you fool. Why did you force my hand?" Kitano tried to reply but all that came out was a wheeze. The knife was still in his chest and he fumbled at it, trying to pull it loose. Every time he touched it, the world seemed to quiver.

Ito stepped over him and went to one of the lanterns burning in the corner of the room. Kitano's vision wavered and went black. When sight returned, the room was ablaze. Fire crawled up the paper walls and crisped the ceiling. There was no sign of Ito, but he spied Ko, laying near the door. She was coughing weakly. Still alive, but not for long. Like him. The thought of death did not bring peace, only panic. Urgency warred with numbness.

Kitano tried to push himself upright – failed – tried again. Everything was spinning and the edges of his sight were limned in red. He staggered toward Ko, thoughts tattered and confused. Lord Shin was counting on him. And Kasami would be angry with him, so angry.

He had failed – couldn't fail – *mustn't*. His dice were in his hand – when had that happened? He knelt – stumbled – and pushed them into Ko's. "For luck," he mumbled, as he dragged her to her feet, and the fire closed in.

Time for one last roll of the dice.

CHAPTER THIRTY-ONE
Conversation

Shin sighed and fanned himself. He knelt on the balcony of the keep, shielded from the rain by the edge of the overhanging roof, watching the rain strike the surface of the lake. The day had gone from a dull gray to a deep slate. The weather made any thought of leaving the keep ridiculous, though Konomi had offered to give him a tour of the storehouses.

He couldn't help but wonder how things were going in the city. Ko should have found the tunnels by now. She might even have been alerted to Odoma's death. He wondered whether the killer was still in the city, or had already departed for greener pastures. He glanced to his right, where Kasami knelt, her gaze turned inwards. He was tempted to ask her opinion, but decided to leave her be for the moment.

Instead, he pondered the knot that had landed in his lap. He'd obviously been used to disassemble Odoma's organization, and he didn't care for the feeling one bit. The question at the center of the knot was the identity of his manipulator. He had a few suspicions in that regard, but his mind shied away from contemplating them too closely at the moment.

In a way, he hoped it was someone unfamiliar – a stranger, who had fastened upon him as a useful fool. The alternative was too painful to contemplate.

He thought back to when he'd found Kenzō's notes, and the names. Dead men, but not killed by Odoma, as he'd first thought. Now Odoma himself was dead. It was plain to Shin that someone was cleaning up after themselves, trying to remove any link between themselves and the weapons he'd found, by killing anyone who might identify them. But that same person had had the opportunity to kill him – and hadn't. Why?

He thought he knew the answer, and he didn't care for it at all. Yet, his mind circled back to the ledgers again and again. The answer was in them, he was certain of it. What had Kenzō seen in those discrepancies, in those names? How had he managed to link them together? And who was really responsible for his death? Odoma, like Shin, had been nothing more than a dupe for an unknown party. He might have struck the fatal blow, but it had been directed by another hand.

The same hand that Shin had detected in other events – incidents meant to sow confusion and discord among the city authorities. But why? To cause war? Or simply to provide a convenient smokescreen for less ideological activities? Maybe both. Some individuals saw chaos as a means of advancement. Fools, mostly. Promotion based on disorder was akin to building a house on sand.

Kasami stirred, and Shin smiled. "Hello, Konomi."

"You are sulking again," Konomi said, from behind him.

"I am pondering."

"You are sitting in the rain, fretting." Konomi strode out onto the balcony, her hands folded into her sleeves. "Violet is a good color on you."

Shin looked down at his borrowed robes, helpfully provided by Konomi. He plucked at them and forced a smile. "Yes, and they're not scratchy in the least."

"I am glad to hear it." She looked out at the rain. "A poor day for riding, I suppose. Are you sure I cannot tempt you with a tour of our storehouses? You seemed interested in them earlier."

"Professional curiosity."

Konomi sighed. "There are no weapons here, Shin. Other than those in the hands of the guards, that is. Come, let me show you."

"I don't recall saying anything about weapons," Shin said, as he rose to his feet. Konomi planted a hand against his chest and stopped him.

"You didn't have to, Shin. I can read you like one of those pillow books you're so fond of. You're wondering if there might be more smuggled weapons hidden in the cargo stored here. So – let's go look. Let's soothe that burning curiosity of yours."

Kasami rose. "She is right. It is better to be invited than to sneak about."

"She understands," Konomi said.

"Very well. Lead on, oh mistress of Two Hill Station."

They left the keep and proceeded across one of the curved bridges that connected the main structure to the storehouses, protected by umbrellas in the hands of Konomi's servants. Shin looked down into the water as they passed over it, noting how dark it looked. "How deep is this lake?"

"I'm not certain. Deep enough." Konomi glanced at him slyly. "That isn't really what you wanted to ask me, is it?"

"No. Do you keep records for all incoming and outgoing cargo? I assume so, but one likes to be certain. Is there any way I could see them, if so?"

"Try again, Shin," Konomi sighed.

Annoyed, Shin looked at her. "Very well. Why don't you tell me what question I should be asking? What have I missed, in your opinion?"

Konomi met his gaze squarely. "Your problem, Shin, is that you are distracted by your own plight. You see everything as a whole, when it might simply be dissimilar events, occurring in close proximity. My father has a saying: 'Not every enemy action is attributable to strategy'. Do you understand?"

Shin snorted. "I think so. You're saying I might have tied this knot myself."

"It's possible. You've become obsessed with learning what Kenzō might or might not have known. What if that had nothing at all to do with his death? What if he died because he was in the wrong place at the wrong time?"

"He was poisoned," Shin pointed out.

They reached the storehouse and several men hastened to open the doors for them, at Konomi's gesture. "An accident, perhaps. Maybe he ate something that made him ill." She looked at him. "Have you considered that at all?"

Shin frowned. He hadn't, as a matter of fact. It seemed an obvious question now. So why hadn't he asked it? Konomi nodded, as if reading his thoughts. "You are distracted, as I said. You are not thinking clearly, and haven't been for some time." She poked him between the eyes, and he batted her hand away in annoyance.

"Fine. Say you are right. Suppose I am. How should I proceed?" He looked around the storehouse. It wasn't large. The building was cylindrical, made from stone, and braced with carefully placed timbers that kept everything from collapsing. There were two stories – a ground floor and an upper, smaller space. The bulk of the cargo was clearly stored on the ground floor.

Konomi smiled. "Let us begin with the root of the issue."

Shin inspected a pile of sealed wicker baskets, loaded with salt. "Which is?" He prodded a basket with his fan, but saw no signs of anything hidden within.

"Your grandfather."

Shin blinked. "What?"

"Your grandfather, Shin. Clearly much of what troubles you is his doing."

"I'm not so certain of that. Aoto said – well. Suffice to say, my grandfather may not occupy the same lofty position he once did." Shin paused, thinking of the old man.

"Tell me about him."

Shin almost demurred. But instead, he cleared his throat and said, "He is… complicated. He is not a courtier, but he plays the game better than most. Deposit him on a battlefield, whether it be physical, social, or fiscal, and he will soon adapt his strategies to best claim victory." Shin sat back. "As a child, I admired that sort of formidability. The idea that nothing could defeat him was a potent one."

"What changed?" Konomi asked.

Shin peered at a nearby line of barrels, noting the duty stamps on them. All from the city; all from the wharfs his own goods passed through. "I got older. I learned to fight in my own way, and I had no use for his strategies. He took offense. So, I began to take delight in making a fool of myself, in order to teach him a lesson." He glanced at her, a self-deprecating grin on his face. "He did not learn it, insofar as I know."

Konomi chuckled. "You mean this whole act of yours was simply a means to annoy an elderly relation? And you call Aoto the spiteful one."

Shin winced and turned away. "Yes, well… I suppose you

could see it that way." He picked at a roll of leather. Something about it caught his eye and he discreetly used one of the steel tines of his fan to slice through the edge of the roll. He positioned himself so that no one could see what he was doing. "In another sense, you could say I was finding my own path. Much as you have done."

"You'll pardon my frankness, but you don't seem satisfied with it."

Shin paused. "No. Perhaps not. Then, satisfaction is an elusive thing."

"So I am told."

"Are you satisfied, then?" Shin asked, continuing his efforts. There was definitely something concealed in it. Something flat and metal. His heart sped up. Osho had been a leather importer. Had this been one of his?

"Never. No matter my accomplishments, my path has already been determined in the minds of my family and my clan. Just like you, Shin. We are two of a kind, you and I. Both disregarded by those who should be thanking us."

Kasami grunted softly and Shin turned. Several Iuchi guards had entered the storeroom and fanned out, covering the exit. Shin tapped the roll with his fan. Something was wrong. He looked at Konomi. She had a sad expression on her face. As if simultaneously resigned and disappointed. "I have never thought of it like that," Shin said slowly. "Is something amiss, Konomi?"

"What have you found, Shin?" she asked, in a low tone. "Something of interest?"

"No," Shin said, turning away from the leather. "Just a rumple in the material."

"Are you certain?" There was a hint of challenge in her voice.

Shin licked his lips and looked at Kasami. Her hand was close to the hilt of her sword, and her eyes were on Hachi. He, in turn, looked distinctly uneasy. Shin forced a smile. "Well, as a matter of fact, I have found something. It seems some criminal has concealed a set of spearheads in this roll of cloth." He reached back and extricated one of the flat triangles of steel. The guards tensed slightly as Shin brandished it. "How embarrassing for your toll officers. I do hope nothing else is hidden in all this cargo."

Konomi looked at the floor for a moment, and then said, "I can explain."

"You can try." Shin paused. "Tell me this was not you, Konomi. Tell me that it is all a mistake and I will do my best to believe you."

"I wish I could," she said, and he believed her.

He shook his head. "It was all there in front of me. You were the one who planted the thought of the theater in my head. You were the one who sent me to Hisatu-Kesu, where I nearly died. The one who inspected my ledgers and no doubt altered them, tried to steal blackmail material from my lead actress… the one who encouraged me to leave the city, making myself look guilty." He ticked off the points on his finger as he spoke. "But I cannot think of why you bothered, when my death would solve all of your problems."

Konomi was silent for long moments. Then, "Can't you?"

Shin paused. For a moment, uncertainty reigned. He had hoped his suspicions were wrong. That Konomi was not involved. That they might – but no. He pushed the thought aside. "Why weapons? Smuggling, I understand. But this is something else. Why risk it?"

Konomi took a deep breath. Her eyes were not on him, but

something else. "The Unicorn are iron," she said softly. "And I am rust."

Shin stared at her, a sinking sensation in his gut. After a moment, he said, "In Hisatu-Kesu, I met a certain group. A group determined to upend what some call the natural order of things. The sort of group who would put Lion weapons in the hands of Unicorn enemies, in order to set the clans at each other's throats. They wanted me to join them."

"You said no."

"Yes. But I have the feeling they are not the sort to take no for an answer."

There was a soft sound from behind him – the whisper of steel, parting the air. Then a blade was against his throat.

"No," said a horribly familiar voice. "We are not."

CHAPTER THIRTY-TWO
Awake

Ko awoke with a start. She sat up, and immediately regretted it. Everything hurt, inside and out. But she was alive, which was unexpected given her disordered recollections of her visit to the paper-seller. She clutched her stomach, which felt empty and cored out, as if she had swallowed burning embers and tried to spit them out again.

She remembered the fire and the feeling of someone helping her – carrying her – down the narrow steps and out through the shop as the heat washed over them and the smoke coiled about them like a great black serpent. She remembered the auditors falling, convulsing… dying. She realized that she had not even known their names. Now they were gone, their bodies no doubt burnt to a crisp.

Someone else had been there… two men. They had fought? One of them had tried to kill her, and the other… had saved her? She clutched her head, trying to recapture the memories of those last frenzied moments. Someone had tried to kill her. Someone had stopped them. And now she was – where?

She looked around and recognized her room at Saibanshoki.

She closed her eyes in relief. When she opened them, Aoto was standing in the doorway, peering at her. "Are you awake, then? I am told they feared the worst."

"They?" Ko asked, waving him in.

He slid the door shut behind him. "The Kaeru physicians. Battlefield surgeons, mostly. If they can't sew it, lance it or set it, they are at a loss. I can send for my personal physician, if you like."

"No, thank you. How long… ?"

"It is morning, though you could not tell for the rain." He came and knelt beside her pallet. "Apparently you vomited up the contents of your stomach after they found you. They claim you showed some sign of poisoning, though I cannot imagine what they would know about such things." Aoto said it offhandedly, as if such things were common in his experience. Maybe they were.

"It was the same poison used on your auditors. And on Kenzō."

"He was stabbed," Aoto protested.

"And poisoned, as I told you before. There is more going on here than either of us suspected, Lord Aoto." She relaxed, trying to muster enough breath to continue. "You got my message then. That is why you are here?"

"I am here to see how you are feeling. But… yes." Aoto frowned and tugged on his earlobe. "Kaeru riders caught up with us at Willow Quay. You were right – it was a diversion, nothing more. It seems Shin wished a clear path to his enemies. You heard about the slaughter?"

Ko nodded weakly. "The Snakeheads attacked the theater, for reasons that still elude me. Shin was defending himself. There is no fault there."

"A matter of opinion," Aoto said.

"Fact," she said. She closed her eyes, trying to organize her hazy thoughts into something approaching sense. "I was – there was a fire. What happened?"

"You were found on the street next to that disreputable servant of Shin's. Someone had stabbed him." Aoto hesitated. "Witnesses saw him carry you out of the fire. I suppose we should be thankful that Shin's servants show more spirit than he does."

"Is he–?"

"Dead? Yes, and good riddance. Never liked the look of him."

Ko pushed down the flare of anger and asked, "What about Ito?"

"Ito?" Aoto leaned forward. "That was his shop, then? What were you doing there?"

"Looking for Shin's ledgers."

Aoto's eyes widened. "What? Why?"

"Because Shin gave them to the man for safekeeping. Apparently Shin did, in fact, deign to associate with his subordinates, despite your assertions to the contrary." Ko coughed and propped herself up, with some difficulty. To her relief, Aoto did not offer to help. "You warned him. Wanted him to hide his ledgers… because you thought he was guilty."

"I did." Aoto admitted it with barely a flicker of hesitation. "Those ledgers are property of the Daidoji Trading Council. As such, they are outside your purview."

"If you thought he was guilty, why–?"

"Because some things transcend guilt or innocence. No matter what crimes he may have committed, Shin still understands that. Though I did not imagine he would turn them over to a – a servant for safekeeping. How like him."

Ko realized that Aoto still thought Shin was guilty. Or maybe he simply didn't care, so long as it gave him an excuse to do what he had come to do. "But I have just told you…"

He cut her off with a lazy gesture. "It does not matter. How did the shop come to be on fire? Was it Shin's servant?"

Ko shook her head, and the world swam momentarily out of focus. "No. No, it was Ito. The paper-seller." Her thoughts were starting to clear. "He claimed to have killed Kenzō. He… laced our cups with something. Your people died first. They got more of a dose, I think. When I didn't die, he… came at me with a knife."

"You fought him off," Aoto said approvingly.

She shook her head again. "No. Shin's servant – he tried to stop Ito." It was coming back in bits and pieces. "Ito stabbed him. Then he – he set the fire. He left me there. I think – I think he thought I was dead." She took a deep breath. "Then the other man – Kitano – he somehow managed to drag me downstairs. I don't know how." Her voice softened. "He must have been in great pain."

Aoto was silent for a moment. "I suspect he had already passed beyond pain. A shame – a man like that would have made a worthy servant for someone," he said, in contrast to his earlier comment. "I might have taken him on myself, had he survived. Then, he was one of Shin's… no doubt he was guilty of some crime. Probably several."

"He saved me," Ko said.

"One good deed does not erase a soul's burden of debt," Aoto said, piously. "It is obvious to me that Shin was behind the whole thing. He no doubt ordered this Ito to defend the ledgers and Ito did. Poison is a coward's weapon, but then one cannot expect better of an old merchant I suppose."

"He was not that old," Ko said. "Where is he now? Do you know?"

"No one has seen him." Aoto shrugged. "I have no doubt he is running to his master even now. I expect we will find them together."

"You know where they are," Ko said. Of course he did. She realized suddenly that he was here to gloat, as much as he was to check on her.

"Lady Iuchi Konomi, it seems, has something of a soft spot for Shin. Fortunes know why. They left the city with an Ide caravan yesterday, heading for someplace called Two Hill Station. An odd name for a country estate, but then, the Unicorn are peculiar. Apparently, she hoped to hide Shin there, until matters were resolved here. No doubt she is unaware of just how vile Shin truly is."

"Konomi," Ko murmured. The only one other than Ito to see the ledgers; the one who had avoided her summons. An old flicker of suspicion reignited, and she began to fear that Shin had not found sanctuary, but instead handed himself over to danger. There was no evidence, of course, but maybe – was that why Shin had been so foolish as to leave the city? Was he still following the trail he'd laid down for her?

"Yes. I'm told she's a difficult woman. Apparently a foolish one as well, if she is so silly as to help someone like Shin. I have assured her father she will come to no harm, and in return, the Iuchi have wisely provided me with the location of the estate. It is along the Ide trade road running upriver, into Unicorn lands, no more than a few hours ride from here. After I leave here, I intend to take my auditors and the Kaeru warriors helpfully provided by Lord Azuma, and arrest them all."

Ko shook her head. And her heart sank. It seemed her efforts had been in vain. "All of them? Why?"

"Because of the weapons, of course."

"The ones under the theater," she said. Ina had clearly gotten the information to Azuma, and Azuma had obviously seen fit to inform Aoto. That complicated matters.

Aoto nodded. "The very ones! This afternoon one of Shin's servants – a fat fellow named Sanemon – came to Saibanshoki to report that the theater was being used as part of a smuggling operation." He smiled brightly. "I have him, Ko. He is caught now, and there is nowhere to run. Still, we will have to arrest everyone until it is all sorted out to the satisfaction of the local authorities."

"Shin is the one who uncovered this crime," Ko began, and then broke off into a coughing fit. Though the poison was hopefully out of her system, she could still feel the scratch of smoke in her lungs and the heat of the fire on her skin.

Aoto frowned. "Do you need the physician?"

"No. Shin is innocent of this."

Aoto grimaced. "Shin is trying to make it seem as if he is the hero in all of this, as he always does. But not this time! This time I have him and no one can save him. Not even you, Investigator Ko." He hesitated. "Whatever your feelings for him, surely you must see that he is not worth tarnishing your reputation for."

"I have no feelings for him," she protested. "This is about facts!"

"As I said to you when we first met, facts can be shaped to fit whatever narrative is desired. The facts here are in my hands now, and your services are no longer required. I'm sure the governor will agree when I inform him of that. Shin is finished. His time here has come to an end – as has his freedom." He rose to his feet. "I came to tell you this as a courtesy, nothing more." He paused. "I hope your recovery is timely. Good day."

He was gone a moment later, a definite spring in his step. She wondered whether he intended to do as he said, whether Shin might resist and what might come of it. Aoto was spoiling for a fight, and she suspected that Shin might well give him one.

She winced and sat up. Even that small effort winded her, but she needed to get a message to Lord Azuma. They needed to be there when Aoto made his arrest, or things could go very badly for all concerned.

Especially Shin.

CHAPTER THIRTY-THREE
Duel

Kasami cursed and turned. Shin's captor had moved so silently that Kasami had only noticed her when it was too late. She half-drew her own sword, and Hachi and the Iuchi guards tensed. Hachi, especially, looked unhappy. Then, he'd sparred with her enough to know how any duel between them would invariably go.

"Let him go," Kasami growled. She recognized Shin's captor, though only faintly. The blind shamisen player they'd encountered in Hisatu-Kesu the year before. An assassin and a fanatic. Despite her blindness, she was a cunning swordswoman. Dangerous.

Shin stood frozen with a blade pressed lightly to his throat. Behind him, the blind woman, clad in plain robes, a shamisen slung across her back. She held a bamboo cane close to her chest, and the concealed blade she'd drawn from it to Shin's throat. She tilted her head, her half-closed eyes fixed on a point somewhere just past Kasami's head. "No," she said.

Konomi took a deep breath. "She is right. Let him go, Emiko."

The blind woman turned her head slightly, following the

sound of Konomi's voice. "No. Not until she discards her sword."

Kasami bared her teeth. "No."

"Shin, tell her to put her sword down," Konomi said.

"Would Hachi there listen to such a command?" Shin asked.

Hachi said nothing. Kasami snorted. "Not if he is half the guard that he believes himself to be," she said. There were half a dozen guards scattered around the storage area, not counting Hachi. All but two had spears; they had bows. That worried her some, given her lack of armor. One archer she might have been able to rush, but two – there was too much uncertainty for her liking. Battle was about control; control of the field, control of your opponent's actions… control of the flow of battle.

A slow pageant unfolded in her head: different possibilities. Move left, this happens. Move right, that. Strike down two men, leave herself open to a third. A process of give and take, that only ended in one way – Shin's death. Hers as well, but that didn't matter. If she could simply get him clear, he might stand a chance of escape.

She expelled a slow breath, gauging the distance between herself and Emiko. She could remove the other woman's hand before she sliced Shin's throat. Arrows would follow, but they would be aimed at her, not Shin. That would give him enough time to flee.

Kasami met Shin's eyes – anxious, but not frightened. He was calm. She would be the same. A pool of water, ready to flow in whatever direction chance – or Shin – provided.

Shin sighed theatrically. "Kasami would not heed such an order, in any event. She values the reputation of the Hiramori – and the Daidoji – more than our lives."

"Then we are at an impasse," Konomi said.

"No. We are in a negotiation. What do you want?"

Konomi's gaze sharpened. "What do you mean?"

Shin folded his hands before him. "What do you want, Konomi?"

She was silent for several moments. Then, "How long have you known?"

Shin smiled. "For certain? Not until just now. But I've had my suspicions for some time." Kasami forced herself not to look at him. That, she was sure, was a lie and nothing less. "I needed to see it with my own eyes…"

"And now that you have, a reminder: you owe us," Emiko said pointedly. "We aided you in Hisatu-Kesu and all we ask in return is that you… say nothing of this. Let this go. Walk away. Return to Crane lands, marry, and forget about all of this."

"Emiko…" Konomi began.

Shin chuckled, and Kasami felt a flush of pride. He was brave, there could be no doubt of that. "Oh, that is a pretty trap, I admit," Shin said. "The bait is lovingly spiced, the scent intoxicating. But if you recall, I saw what bargains like that cost men like me, in Hisatu-Kesu. I turn my back here, and sooner or later you will ask me to do it again, on threat of revealing my duplicity. And then again, and again, each instance another stone piled atop me until I am buried in a grave of your making."

"You would rather die here, then?"

"I think if you wanted us dead, you would have killed us in the city. That was you, at the White Frog Inn? And then later, at Odoma's brewery? I thought I recognized the sound of your shamisen. Were you following us – or someone else?"

"It does not matter now," Emiko said.

"I think it does, actually."

Kasami glanced at Hachi. He refused to meet her gaze. The

guards looked nervous, uncertain. She doubted they understood what was going on. They had their orders – but how long would that be enough? Her eyes flicked to Konomi. There was the knot to be unraveled. Lady Konomi was the one holding the reins of this frenzied horse, desperately trying to maintain control.

Konomi took a deep breath and spoke. "If you suspected, why put yourself in my power? Why the charade, Shin?"

Shin looked at Konomi and Kasami knew the answer – because he had not wanted to believe what all his observations were telling him. The pattern had resisted him not because it was convoluted, but because a part of him had not wanted to see it. But instead of saying any of that, he said, simply, "I needed to see the evidence with my own eyes."

"And now that you have?"

"You have a choice to make," Shin said. Kasami frowned. He was picking at the knot, right in front of them. Loosening it with every statement. "Kill us to save yourselves, or throw yourself on the mercy of Governor Tetsua. Given your father's reputation and influence, I have no doubt you will be treated with leniency."

Emiko laughed throatily. "And what of me? Will I be given leniency?"

"That depends," Shin said. "Why, exactly, are you here?"

"To ensure my good behavior," Konomi said flatly. Emiko's smile could have parted flesh. Kasami suspected that she might cut Shin's throat simply for the fun of it. "She represents–"

Shin flicked open his fan, and Kasami followed its movements. He was up to something: a plan? Maybe. "The Iron Sect, yes, I recall," he said. "But I had not imagined to find her this far from the mountains. Unless… the weapons. Of course. You are here to ensure their delivery."

"Very good," Emiko murmured.

"The weapons are intended for your compatriots in Hisatu-Kesu, then?"

"Some, not all," she said. "There are many who might find a use for them, in Unicorn lands. Many who yearn for freedom from the tyranny of the celestial burden placed upon us by distant generations." She tilted her blade, so that it kissed his neck. Kasami felt anger thrum through her, but did not move. Emiko was attempting to provoke her. The assassin shrugged. "In any event, I do not decide such things. I am here merely to see that Lady Konomi upholds her end and that our transaction was not endangered in any way."

"Is that why you were following us, then? To make sure we didn't interfere?" Shin hesitated. "Or were you told to follow us by someone else?" He glanced at Konomi. "How long have you been in their thrall, exactly?"

Emiko chuckled. Kasami ignored her and kept her eyes on Konomi, trying to read her expression, but she had as much experience masking her emotions as any courtier. Better than Shin even, in some ways. "It was… a game, at first," Konomi said, after several moments. "A calculated rebellion against my father, my family… the limits they imposed on me. If the Unicorn was determined to be my enemy, then enemies we would be." She attempted a smile. "I am not good with boundaries, as you know." She looked at her hands. "Most of my – of them – were dilettantes; children, playing at conspiracy. Poets and courtiers, with not an ounce of steel between them. But if the players were boring, the game at least interested me."

"Game," Shin repeated.

"The greatest game," she said defensively. "You've played it yourself."

Shin said nothing, and Kasami knew what he was thinking. Every courtier knew the game; it was the one they were born to play, after all. But this was something else – something worse than a simple war of influence. Finally, he said, "Not against my own clan – my own family."

Konomi frowned. "Haven't you? You refuse to play the role they set for you, and in doing so you weakened your grandfather's position on the Trading Council. Or so rumor has it. Why do you think he was so desperate to see you married?"

Shin didn't flinch. "There is a difference between ignoring one's duty and actively harming one's own people and you know it." He gestured loosely to one of the barrels. "You are delivering tools of death into the hands of those who will use them against your family."

Konomi closed her eyes. "That was not my – I did not intend it to come to this. By the time I realized the true nature of the game I was playing, it was too late to deal myself out. Not without risking my life, and worse, my reputation."

Kasami grunted. Konomi wouldn't be the first noble to make such a mistake, foolish though it was. Though she'd thought better of Lady Konomi. From the look on his face, Shin was thinking much the same. "Were you behind the Poison Rice Affair as well?" he asked.

Kasami blinked. She hadn't even thought of that. That incident had been the instigating factor in Shin and Konomi's friendship. Konomi took a deep breath. "Shin, are you asking if I sought your company because you thwarted me?"

"Answer the question," Shin said harshly. Kasami had only rarely seen Shin genuinely angry, and almost never because of something directed at himself. Insults rolled off his back like water off a turtle's shell. But this was different. The look on his face – so stiff and sharp… it reminded her of the stories she'd heard about his grandfather. A fury as cold as the wind over the Carpenter's Wall, they said.

Konomi looked away. "I cannot claim that it was not… a factor." She looked back at him. "But we are friends, Shin. You must believe me!"

"Must I?"

Konomi flinched. She drew herself up, her expression as flat as still water. "If we were not, you would have been dead a dozen times over. It was only my influence that kept you safe upon your return from Hisatu-Kesu, Shin. Tell him, Emiko."

"I could have killed you many times since our last meeting," the latter purred. "Your powers of observation are not as impossibly potent as some claim." A sharp smile passed across the assassin's face. "But our partners insisted you had some use."

Partners. Kasami caught the plural. Shin did as well. "Who else is involved?" he asked. "I deserve to know that much, I think."

Emiko ignored the question and tilted her head. "I have not heard a sword drop, yet."

"That is because I have not dropped it," Kasami said.

"Then you leave me no choice," Emiko said. She brought her blade closer to Shin's jugular, clearly preparing to slice it open. Another provocation – an obvious one, even. Shin was too valuable to kill out of hand. It was Kasami herself who needed to die. But rather than give them the opening they wished, she did nothing. Simply waited. Still, and ready.

Emiko frowned at the delay. "Does his life truly mean so little to you?"

"She's just looking forward to saying I told you so," Shin said. He met Kasami's gaze and winked – a bad sign. Then, he stumbled back and jammed an elbow into Emiko's chest. Her sword twitched, drawing a red weal on the side of his neck as she staggered and he leapt aside. Kasami cursed and launched herself toward the assassin.

"Idiot," she barked. Her blade met Emiko's own, as the assassin somehow intercepted her blow. Emiko used the momentum of her parry to push herself away from Kasami. The guards scattered, shouting in alarm. Out of the corner of her eye, Kasami saw Konomi wave Hachi back. At least she wouldn't have to worry about him. She pushed the thought aside and tried to concentrate on the movements of her opponent.

Emiko moved in an odd, sinuous fashion. One halting step, followed by several quick ones – almost like a dance. Abruptly, Kasami realized that her opponent was listening to the rustling of her robes, and the rattle of her sword.

Then – the hiss of an arrow. Kasami spun, cutting it from the air. A shuffle of feet behind her alerted her to Emiko's attack and she turned back, just in time to block a blow that would have opened her throat to the bone. Another arrow cut through her sleeve as she retreated before Emiko's almost-frenzied assault.

Kasami spotted Shin, surrounded by a ring of spears held by nervous looking Iuchi. There was blood on his neck and the collar of his robes, but he seemed otherwise unharmed. She lost sight of him as she was forced back. The assassin moved like a wild beast, hopping and slashing – not erratically or madly, but with a feral precision. Kasami couldn't help but wonder how the fight looked inside the other woman's head – was it a thing of patterns, or something more esoteric? Blooms of sound, traced in steel?

A third arrow plucked at her thigh and whistled past into the darkness of the store house. A fourth kissed her knuckles as she blocked a blow meant to spill her intestines on the straw-covered ground. Then – pain. Sharp and piercing. An arrow jutted from her side.

Kasami staggered, turned… another arrow caught her high in the chest. She took a step back, nearly dropping her sword. Emiko circled her warily, sword hand braced against her cane. The assassin wasn't smiling; she showed no expression save concentration.

Kasami tightened her grip on her sword and brought it up in both hands. The pain made a red fog at the corners of her vision. A third arrow punched into her hip, but improbably, she didn't lose her footing. She heard Shin shout something and duck under the ring of spears. He knocked the feet out from under one of the soldiers, making enough of an opening to hurl himself at the closest of the archers.

She wanted to curse him for an idiot, or even praise his bravery. Instead, she used her fast-draining strength to aim a slash at Emiko's head. She'd hoped to split the assassin's skull. Instead, her blow was intercepted by blade and bamboo cane, both of which spun from Emiko's hands. She fell back, knocked off balance by the force of Kasami's blow. Kasami felt the world swim about her as she raised her sword over the dazed assassin.

Red faded into black, and her world narrowed to the blind woman's face. Her expression was one of startlement – and perhaps a touch of fear. Kasami felt some grudging satisfaction in that, even as her sword fell from her suddenly-numb grip. Annoyed with this show of weakness, she swayed on her feet. A fourth arrow struck her in the small of the back and she hissed in pain as she sank to her knees. A few moments later, she collapsed and joined her weapon on the ground. As her vision constricted to a blur and the hungry darkness swarmed in, she watched as Shin was jerked to his feet and bound.

She had failed.

And because of that, Shin would die.

CHAPTER THIRTY-FOUR
Explanations

Shin sat in the center of the small room, pondering his options. They were limited and all bad. Escape was impossible; Kasami might have made it, but Kasami was indisposed. He swallowed and closed his eyes. The sight of her falling had driven him mad, if only for a few moments. He'd lunged for her attackers, his mind lost in a frenzy of rage. The Hiramori called it 'the killing mood' – the moment when fury overtakes discipline, and the world bends to the arc of a blade.

He'd never been that angry before, and it frightened him to think of such a loss of control. From the look on their faces, it had frightened his captors as well. He'd knocked two of them flat before Hachi had intervened, and he'd nearly wrestled the bodyguard's sword from him before Emiko had caught him a blow to the side with her cane. The bamboo had connected with his ribs and knocked the air from him. It still hurt.

The only thing that made it bearable was the knowledge that Kasami wasn't dead. Badly hurt, but not dead. Not yet. She was being held as a hostage to his good behavior, he suspected. An injured Kasami ensured that he stayed put.

He bowed his head and tried to control his breathing, to center himself as he'd been taught as a boy. To find the calm in the storm and set his roots so deep that nothing could shake him. He would need that equanimity soon, he feared. He had been outwitted and tricked; played for a fool from the first. Luck had been his only saving grace. But would it be enough to see him and Kasami through? No answer was forthcoming.

The door slid open, and Hachi entered. He said nothing, merely stepped aside so that Konomi could enter. "How are you, Shin?" she asked softly.

"If Kasami dies, I will be most upset," he said, in a studiously composed tone.

"She will not die," Konomi said. "My people are tending to her as if she were one of their own. I have given orders that she is to be kept safe."

"So long as I behave," Shin said, still not looking at her. Instead, he stared at the wall. The Unicorn, and the Iuchi especially, had no talent for interior decorating. The walls were plain, with no art to obfuscate what was on the other side. He could see the faint outline of someone in the corridor. Emiko, perhaps. Eavesdropping on his and Konomi's conversation. "I will hold you to that, Lady Konomi. I will take it as a promise."

Konomi flushed slightly. "If you had just surrendered…" She fell silent, as if realizing that he was in no mood to hear it. "It doesn't matter now, I fear."

"We were waiting for someone, I take it. Not a rider – by boat?"

Konomi nodded jerkily. "Yes. My… comrade in this endeavor is on his way. He will be here with the evening tide."

"Accomplice, you mean."

Konomi sighed. "Yes."

Shin looked at her. "Why?"

"I had to. The Iron Sect has me trapped, Shin. Hoisted by my own hubris." She spoke quickly, as if desperate to explain. Maybe she was.

"Not that," Shin said, dismissively. "Why are we waiting for your partner? What is the point? Is my execution to be a ceremonial affair, requiring witnesses? Or is there some other reason?"

Konomi drew back. "He is the one who spun this web. Earlier you accused me of being behind the poison rice delivery to the Lion last year. That was him – all of it has been him, Shin. He is your enemy, not me." Then, in a small voice, "Never me."

"He is a member of the Iron Sect, then?" He wanted to ask for a name, but he thought he already knew the answer. Three people had had access to his ledgers; one was dead; one was here; and one… He closed his eyes as his poise threatened to desert him. How could he not have seen it? It had been right before him, the entire time.

"No," Konomi said. "They are fools. Like me. Dangerous, but – but they – we – had goals, Shin. What we – what I did, I did for what I thought were good reasons. This world is not fair, and it is not fair in a way that can be changed, if only some of us had the courage. I thought I had the courage." She looked at him. "I thought, I hoped, that you might as well."

Shin took a deep breath. "If he is not one of you, what is he?"

"A ghost," Konomi said. "A hungry ghost. A shadow. He has no interest in politics or in the struggles of his fellow man. He wants power, but not to elevate himself. He wants it because it makes it easier for him to play his games." She looked away. "When I first met him, I thought he was one of us, but in the days and months since, I have learned better." She glanced back at the door. "I warned them. Told them that he couldn't be trusted."

The door slid open and Emiko stepped in, tapping at the floor with her cane, a thin smile on her face. "From our perspective, it is you who are the untrustworthy one. Like the unlamented Lord Shijan, whose foolishness almost cost us so dearly in Hisatu-Kesu, you have endangered us by insisting that this Crane be left alive. That he be wooed, rather than plucked. I wonder, is your judgement compromised? Should we cut our losses?"

Hachi's hand fell to his sword, and Emiko tilted her head. The smile never left her face. "Then, the chance of having two on the hook is worth a bit of inconvenience, is it not, my lord Crane?"

"Surely you must realize that your plan is in tatters," Shin said. "The tunnels and the weapons have been discovered and the authorities informed. I have no doubt that by now, Lady Konomi's father as well as Akodo Minami will have been told of the plot. Were I you, I would seek to put as much distance between myself and the City of the Rich Frog as possible. Yet you dally – why? Not for me, I think."

"For you," Emiko said. "But also for our ally in the city. He has requested sanctuary. We will give it to him, provided he can still honor his end of our bargain."

"And if he can't?" Shin paused. "No, I think I can guess. You aren't here just to ensure Konomi's compliance, but his as well. And so far, I imagine you are very disappointed. Or am I wrong about this as well?"

Emiko's smile slid into a frown. "No. You are not wrong."

Shin chuckled. "Do you intend to kill this ghost of Konomi's?"

"If it comes to that."

Shin shook his head, though he knew she couldn't see the

gesture. He looked at Konomi. "Your life might be forfeit as well, you know. The simplest thing would be to kill all of us, take the weapons and go."

From Konomi's expression, he could tell that this was not new information. Emiko was smiling again, as if heedless of the armed man within sword length of her. Was the blind woman simply that confident, or was there some other reason she didn't fear retaliation? "What hold do they have on you?" he asked, looking at Konomi. "Letters? Documents?"

"All that and more," Konomi said. "I was not always as circumspect as I am now. I have recovered some, bargained for others. They are my payment."

"But every act you undertake on their behalf only puts you deeper in debt," Shin said.

Konomi nodded and Emiko chuckled. "If it helps, consider it the price of your unearned privilege." She lifted her chin. "He has arrived, by the way. I heard his boat dock some minutes ago. No doubt he is waiting in the receiving room by now."

Konomi turned to the door. "Then let us go meet him, by all means."

Emiko gestured in Shin's general direction. "Bring him."

Konomi hesitated. "I do not think that is necessary."

"I disagree," Emiko said. Konomi hesitated, and then gestured for Hachi to get Shin to his feet. The bodyguard did so. Shin briefly considered some token show of resistance, and then decided against it. He wanted to see this ally with his own eyes. To hear him explain himself, the way Konomi had tried to do. If nothing else, it was information and information was valuable. But if the newcomer was who he suspected, there would be precious few answers in whatever he learned.

The house was silent as they proceeded to the front rooms.

They had not bound him, but there were guards stationed in unobtrusive spaces, alert and ready. Shin took note of their placement and number as he was escorted to the receiving room. "Eight in the house, another ten outside," Konomi murmured, into his ear. "A small garrison, by my father's standards. There are also five clerks and three servants."

Shin glanced at her, and saw something in her eyes. A warning? Why warn him now, unless … ? His eyes strayed to Emiko, who felt her way along behind them. Perhaps Konomi had plans of her own – ones that did not include playing facilitator to an assassin.

The thought gave him some hope, however small. Maybe, just maybe, things weren't as certain as he'd feared. Maybe he had one ally left, at least. He clamped down on the thought even as it formed, and kept his features composed and serene. Whatever came next, he would have to be ready.

The receiving room was small, and decorated in the Iuchi fashion: racks of weapons on the walls, picture banners depicting triumphal charges across the grasslands or the wastes of the Burning Sands. At the center of the room, kneeling in the position of supplicant and guest, was a familiar bent figure.

"The weather has become truly horrendous," Konomi's guest said. "I feared I might drown before I got here." He bowed obsequiously to Shin, as the latter knelt opposite him. "It was only luck that saw me safely from the city."

"Ito," Shin said.

Ito smiled. "Hello, my lord. So good to see you."

CHAPTER THIRTY-FIVE
Shadow

Ito smiled. "I confess, I expected a bit more bewilderment, my lord. Like something from one of those kabuki plays you so enjoy. Yet, you do not seem surprised to see me."

Shin kept his features composed, letting no sign of the anger he felt show on his face. He didn't intend to give the man any satisfaction. "Would you believe me if I said I wasn't?"

"Possibly." Ito rose to his feet and looked at Konomi. She still stood near the door, along with Hachi. Emiko had taken a seat along the far wall, and was quietly plucking at the strings of her shamisen. "What happened?" Ito asked, as he glanced at the assassin. He didn't seem unduly perturbed by her presence. A sign of confidence, or hubris?

"I thought it best to take him into custody," Konomi said. "He did not react well to finding the weapons." She glanced at Shin, and he looked away, unwilling to see the regret and pity in her eyes. "As I warned you both would be the case."

"Of course," Ito murmured, walking over to examine a rack of weapons along the far wall with evident appreciation. His hands were clasped behind his back, and his expression was... mild.

Everything about him was familiar; unthreatening. And yet something in his eyes was different. Not predatory or gloating, but – hard. Cold.

"Then why suggest I bring him here?" Konomi demanded, taking a step toward him. "Why play this game with him? With us?"

Emiko stilled the strings of her shamisen. "A good question and one I would like an answer to as well, merchant." Her sightless eyes fixed on Ito. Not for the first time, Shin wondered just how good the blind woman's hearing was. He'd seen her fight, of course, and knew first-hand how lethal she could be. But even so, the way she pinpointed a person by the sound of their voice unnerved him.

Ito grunted. "I suggested it, because I wanted you to see his reaction with your own eyes. To understand that he is not the sort of man to throw over his beliefs simply to save his own skin. As you insisted that he was."

"I don't know about all that," Shin said. "I am very attached to my skin."

Ito chuckled. "See? He jokes. Surrounded by death, and he makes light. The perfect courtier. Iron to the core."

"Iron rusts," Emiko said softly. Ito glanced at her.

"Yes." He smiled. "Their rule is iron, and we are rust. That is the saying."

"Very catchy," Shin said.

"Needlessly grandiose, in my opinion," Ito said. "Then, our friends in the Iron Sect do have a high opinion of themselves, don't they, my lord?"

"And you do not?" Konomi said pointedly.

Ito laughed and turned his attentions back to Konomi. "It was a good idea, my lady. A fine plan – win him over to your cause, and gain a voice on the Trading Council. But as I said when you first suggested it… it was doomed to fail. I wanted you to understand that. Still, we will get some use out of him, before the end."

"I'm to be the necessary sacrifice, then?" Shin said. "You'll place the blame for it all on my head, and then I will conveniently disappear. The Crane will hunt for me, but they will never find me, leaving you free to fill the void left by Odoma's death." He glanced at Emiko. "Speaking of which, nicely done, Emiko. I assume it was you."

"It was," she said. "You arrived sooner than I anticipated."

"My apologies."

"It is of no matter. The deed was done, in the end."

Shin smiled coldly, though he knew she couldn't see it. "Of course, I am not the only one looking into this matter. Investigator Ko–"

"Will not be an issue," Ito said. "Unfortunately, she has suffered an accident in the course of her duties."

Shin felt a sudden tightness in his chest. "What sort of accident?"

"A fire." Ito sighed. "She and several of your cousin's auditors were caught in the blaze, as well as your servant, Kitano. They didn't make it out."

"Kitano," Shin began, feeling a dull grayness settle over him. The other man wasn't lying. Kitano was dead. Ito had killed him. Shin had sent Kitano to protect Ito – had sent him to his death. Because Shin hadn't been smart enough to see what had been in front of him the entire time. Guilt flooded him and his hands clenched into fists as they rested on his knees.

"I'd hoped to avoid his death, but he was determined to see things through. Much like yourself." Ito went to the weapons rack and lifted a sword from it. "He was tougher than anyone gave him credit for. Smarter, too." He gave the sword an experimental swing, and Shin could see that he was no stranger to a blade. "I did my best, but… he insisted."

"You killed him," Shin said, watching the blade dance in the light. Ito was moving through a set of practice positions as if he'd been born to do them.

"Let us say that his luck finally ran out." Ito spun suddenly, moving quickly, the sword curving out in a tight arc. Shin froze as the blade came to a halt within a finger-flick of his jugular. "He was a better servant than you deserved. Loyal to the last. Then, you are an easy man to give loyalty to. As nobles go, you are… tolerable. A fool, but a benign one, with your love of puzzles and charitable sentiments." Ito paused. "Which is why you do not have to die, unless you wish it."

"What?" Shin asked, startled. Emiko clearly felt the same, for her head came up and her expression tightened. Thankfully, she said nothing, however.

"I admit, killing you would sever the knot neatly. But I am not a butcher like our friend Odoma, killing for the sake of expediency. No, we have in our possession a rare opportunity. With a bit of compromise, we could all emerge from this with reputations intact and bargains fulfilled."

Shin blinked. Then laughed. "Of course. That is why you came. You need me just as much as the Iron Sect does. A pawn, to – what? – help you become head of the merchants' association, perhaps?"

Ito smiled widely. "I knew our minds worked in similar fashion. Yes, with the backing of the city's favorite Crane, newly cleared of all charges and ensconced once more in his seat of influence, I could step into the void left by Odoma."

"Is that why you had me kill him?" Emiko asked, in a dangerously mild tone. "So that you might advance in society?" She set her shamisen aside, and pulled her cane close.

Ito laughed. "Yes. And also because he was an impediment, both to myself and your organization. Odoma was a spiteful creature. Once he realized who his actual enemy was, he'd have never stopped coming. And he had some dealings with his opposite number, Honesty-sama, in Hisatu-Kesu. Imagine if that fine fellow knew of your little sect, eh?" He pulled the sword away from Shin and set it across his shoulder. "It needed to be done, as much for you as me."

Shin grunted. Moments collided in his mind, disparate facts lining up like soldiers at attention. Suddenly, Ito was... not Ito. He stood differently, held himself erect, even his face was not the same. It was as if something had lain dormant in him and now come to the surface. A hungry ghost. That was what Konomi had called him. "You poisoned Kenzō," Shin said. "Why? What did he find?"

"The ledgers," Ito said. "The discrepancies."

"The dates," Shin said. "Of course!" Everything clicked into place. The missing thread. He pulled it and the knot at last unraveled. "The dates in Kenzō's notes corresponded to days when deliveries from Osho and the others arrived. Only those deliveries did not appear in my own ledgers... because you altered them, in order to hide the cargo, so that you could then smuggle them via the tunnels."

Ito nodded slowly. "Yes. He paid off a few fishermen to watch the wharfs. He noted the deliveries of goods from the Lion waterfront, compared them to your accounts and realized – well."

"He realized that someone was lying about something. And

you knew it was only a matter of time until he knew that you were the common factor. So you poisoned him."

"Sadly, the dose wasn't strong enough to kill him." Ito swung the sword out and examined the blade. "I admit, I panicked slightly. Kenzō was very close to figuring it all out. He was a much better investigator than any of us gave him credit for. I sent him to Odoma, hoping that he might succumb on the way. But… well."

"But Odoma killed him instead."

"Not Odoma," Emiko said, still frowning. "His courtesan. I suspect she stabbed him while he was speaking to Odoma. She was very quick. Nearly caught me." She tapped the side of her neck, where a faint red line, already healing, stood out against her flesh. "He probably never saw her coming."

Ito stepped back, the sword resting once again on his shoulder. "And Odoma, as was his wont, proceeded to overcomplicate things by accusing you of murder."

"Because you convinced him that I was trying to take over his business," Shin said.

Ito frowned. "Yes. I thought – I assumed – that Odoma would be cowed by your status. Instead, it infuriated him. So I did what I could to mollify him. I made him think I was sympathetic…"

"The complaint was your idea," Shin said. He paused. "You hoped I would be recalled. That the Trading Council would replace me."

Ito gave him a small smile. "That was the idea, yes. But once again, you defied expectation." He shook his head. "Such a surprising fellow you turned out to be."

"Why help me, all those times? Why aid me in any of my endeavors – outside of the ones you turned to your advantage, obviously?"

"It was all to my advantage, Shin, in one way or another. But the simple fact is, I like you. You are… interesting. Entertaining. Watching you pick at the threads, knowing I could crush you in an instant – it was the most fun I'd had in ages." His eyes sparkled with a bleak joy as he spoke, and Shin felt a curious chill crawl along his spine. Who was this man?

"A bad reason to risk our enterprise," Emiko said flatly. "We told you he was dangerous after that one sent him to us, so that we could test him." She waved a hand in Konomi's general direction. "Too dangerous to be allowed to live."

"Danger is the spice of life," Ito said, circling Shin slowly. "Think about it, my lord. Odoma is the obvious culprit in all of this. Why, he even tried to murder me. Sadly, he only managed to kill the Kitsuki investigator, and your servant. Luckily, I was coming to you, in order to tell you what I had found – how he had somehow inveigled to use our merchants to smuggle his weapons." He turned to Konomi. "And Lady Konomi, of course, was helpful in locating those weapons that had already left the city."

"And who killed Odoma, in this scenario of yours?"

"Why, his angry business partners of course," Ito said, pointing his sword at Emiko. "They no doubt slew him because of his failures, as criminals are wont to do. Sadly, they escaped. But the scheme was undone and the true culprits punished, if not by the law."

"A pretty story," Shin said. "It lets everyone escape with reputations intact."

Ito nodded. "Does that mean you have seen sense?"

Shin was silent for a moment. Finally, he sighed. "No. I'm afraid not. In fact, I believe the only way to resolve this is for one of us to die." He unfolded and rose smoothly to his feet, so that he was facing Ito.

"Strong words, but– eh?" The clang of an alarm bell interrupted Ito's reply. He frowned and turned in the direction of the sound. "What is that? What is going on?"

The door to the room was flung aside as a servant stumbled in, a look of panic on his face. "My lady – we we are under attack!"

CHAPTER THIRTY-SIX
Miscalculation

Konomi shot to her feet as a guard stumbled in behind the servant. "It's the Kaeru, my lady," the guard cried, clutching a bloody arm. "We are under attack by the Kaeru!" He stumbled against the wall and slid down, clutching his injury.

"They came out of the rain like – like ghosts," he continued. Konomi crouched beside him, ignoring the blood that stained her robes. She tore a strip from her sleeve and began to wrap the guard's arm. "I don't know how many. They've taken one of the wharfs."

As Konomi treated him, she turned to Shin. Something in her eyes, the set of her jaw, told him that she was indeed planning something, as he'd thought. He decided to help as best he could, if only to ensure his own survival. So, he laughed. As he'd hoped, Ito turned to him. "Some comment on the situation, my lord?" Ito drawled.

"You miscalculated – again. Miscalculation upon miscalculation." Shin tapped his lips with a finger. "There is a saying among the Daidoji, about how strategy is nothing more than a straw that often breaks upon the stone of the enemy. Let me guess… you poisoned Ko before you set the fire. But did you get the dosage right this time, or did she, too, manage to stumble away?"

Ito stared at him for a moment. Then, he chuckled. "I confess, poison has never been a friend to me. Too much or too little, never enough." He shrugged. "I have always preferred to handle things in a more direct manner." He extended his sword, and peered at Shin over its length. "But subtlety was the art required of me, and I did my best."

"It was not enough," Shin said. From somewhere outside came the crash of a gate, and the sounds of men dying. He felt a flicker of concern for Kasami, then quashed it. There was nothing he could do for her here.

"It rarely is," Ito replied agreeably. "Emiko, a favor if you please…"

The blind woman rose smoothly to her feet. "Finally. But once it is done, we will have a reckoning of our own, merchant." She raised her cane and slid the concealed blade loose, even as she crouched. Then, she was in motion – arrowing directly for Shin.

"Hachi!" Konomi shouted. Her bodyguard lunged to his feet, hand flying to the hilt of his blade. He spun as Emiko raced past him, his sword in hand. There was a wet sound, and Hachi stumbled and sank to his knees, one hand pressed to the swelling tide of redness at his throat. Emiko slid to a stop, but did not turn. Hachi forced himself to his feet and swung around to face her. Before he could take another step, his head rolled free of his neck, and his body collapsed, geysering blood.

Shin glanced toward Ito, but the man was already gone. Emiko stood in the center of the room, head tilted, listening. Shin realized that she was trying to pinpoint the sound of his breathing. Panic momentarily threatened his equilibrium, but his training took over and his eyes fixed on Hachi's fallen sword. If he could reach it–

As if sensing his intent, Emiko sidled between him and Hachi's body. She said nothing, simply listened. Shin tensed… then, relaxed. He had never been good at silence. Instead, his talents lay in conversation. "It seems a waste, to me."

Emiko paused, but didn't reply. Shin strode a few paces to the left, his hands behind his back. "Yes, a great waste. All this effort – and for what? Chaos and death. A shame."

"Not chaos," Emiko said. "Freedom."

"For whom? Not you, because you will certainly die."

Emiko frowned. "Then I die in service to a worthy cause."

"That doesn't seem satisfying somehow."

"I would not expect you to understand," she said. Her head turned, following him. The bloody blade in her hand scraped the floor as she took a step in his direction. "You are not blind, but you refuse to open your eyes."

"Ito has already fled. He left you here."

"Yes," she said.

"It doesn't bother you that your compatriot has abandoned you?"

"We both serve the same end, in our own way. He is a sower of chaos; I am its reaper. And if he fails to do as he has promised… well. There are others. Clever men are like rushes on the riverbank. Cut down one, two more will take their place."

Shin forced a laugh. "How droll. Still, a few clever men might make a difference where you and your compatriots are concerned. I've often wondered whether I made a mistake in not saying anything about your Iron Sect to someone, but I comforted myself with the thought that you were largely incompetent."

She paused, smile fading. Shin pressed on. "I mean, really. Lion weapons are easy enough to acquire on the black market. And forge markings can be faked – or declared fakes, by the right experts. Your ploy was – well – somewhat amateurish at best. Then, I would expect nothing less from such a lot of bumbling incompetents."

Her cheek twitched. Shin stepped back, drawing her in. "How fools like you expect to replace your betters is beyond me, especially if this is the best ruse you can muster. It's insulting, frankly. Even the Lion could come up with a better scheme."

Emiko hissed, "Quiet."

"No," Shin said bluntly. "Honestly, I sometimes wonder whether you really want to upend the celestial order – or whether you just want to complain about it."

Emiko slashed at him, interrupting him, and forcing him back. "Quiet, I said!" She stretched out her sword, angling it slowly. "Your bodyguard was good. She almost had me. I wonder… has she taught you anything?"

As she spoke, she sprang forward, moving like a whirlwind. But Shin was ready. He'd been ready since she'd started talking. She was too quick, too lethal to try and match blade-to-blade. Something else was required.

Something sneaky.

His palms snapped together, trapping her blade mere inches from his face. Emiko's face twisted into an expression of surprise and Shin allowed himself a grin. "A few things, as it turns out," he said, twisting her blade away from his face. It wasn't easy, and she fought him every bit of the way, but if he could wrestle the weapon away from her, he might stand a chance. If not – well, that didn't bear thinking about.

As it turned out, however, he didn't have to worry. Their

struggle was interrupted by the sound of Emiko's shamisen slamming against the back of her head. The wood shattered, and the assassin crumpled to the ground in a heap. Konomi looked down at her and then at the broken instrument in her hand. "I never cared for the shamisen anyway," she said, as she met Shin's astonished gaze. "What?"

"Why did you do that?"

"She killed Hachi." Konomi looked down at the assassin. "She insulted me in my own home. And a variety of other, very good reasons." She tossed the ruined shamisen aside. "The Kaeru's arrival is your doing, I assume."

"Yes. I made sure the right people knew where we were. Just in case."

"Just in case," Konomi murmured. "As clever as ever, Daidoji Shin." She sighed. "I suppose I should tell my soldiers to surrender."

"That would be wise." Shin tightened his grip on Emiko's sword. It felt odd in his hand. At once too heavy, and too light. "And you are wrong. I am not clever enough. Not by far. Otherwise, I would have known better than to trust you, or Ito."

Konomi flinched. "I deserve that. But I meant what I said. None of this was my intention, Shin. Not your troubles, not Kasami being injured…"

Shin froze, suddenly fearful that Ito might try to get to her. Konomi, reading his expression, said, "Go, Shin. I will see to her, and our captive assassin here."

Shin hesitated. "Konomi, I…"

Konomi smiled thinly. "Go." Her smile faded. "If I were Ito, I would be heading for the wharfs. There are a number of small boats we use for unloading that only require a single pair of hands to crew. If he gets to one, he could slip away in the confusion."

"He'll never make it," Shin said. But he knew he was wrong. Ito was far more adept than he'd realized, as well as more dangerous. Who knew what other talents he had?

Konomi nodded. "Go on, Shin. I will still be here when you return."

Shin paused for only a moment longer. Then, he was out the door and on the hunt. Anger thrummed in him like the pulse of a drumbeat. Anger for the death of Kitano and the others, for Kasami, but mostly for himself. For how foolish he'd been, and how easily they had turned his own weaknesses against him. Perhaps Aoto was right after all. Perhaps he'd brought all of this on himself. But if so, that meant only that he was the one to fix it.

He stepped carefully into the courtyard, careful not to make a target of himself. It wouldn't do to die here and now to some overzealous Kaeru's arrow. Outside, the dark of early evening was full of the sounds of death and confusion. Soldiers clashed in the rain, and there were bodies in the mud of the courtyard.

No flames though, thankfully. Not yet, at least. It wouldn't take long for Aoto to have things under control, especially if Konomi kept her word to have her men surrender. That just left Ito. He couldn't have gotten far, and Shin intended to be the one to catch him.

One way, or another.

CHAPTER THIRTY-SEVEN
Darkness

Shin caught up with Ito at the closest storehouse bridge.

A Kaeru lay dead at the entrance, slumped against the rail, blood pooling in the rain. At the far end, two more Kaeru confronted Ito, who moved with an incongruous implacability. He seemed larger, somehow, amid the increasing fury of the storm. It was as if his form swelled with every step. His shadow, in the leaping lantern-light, was long and hungry looking.

Shin hesitated at the sight, and in that instant, a second Kaeru died. Ito was a better killer than Shin had feared, better even than Emiko. As the paper-seller closed in on the third man, Shin stepped onto the bridge. "Ito," he shouted.

As he'd hoped, Ito paused and turned. The Kaeru stumbled back, shouting for aid, his words lost in the drumming of the rain. Ito turned back, as if to pursue, then shrugged and swung back around to face Shin. "Well, we have a few moments, it seems," he called out. "What shall we discuss?"

"Why, Ito?" Shin asked, approaching the other man warily. Emiko's sword felt heavy in his grip. "What was it all for? Money? Power? Tell me, please."

Ito shook his head. "I have all the money I could want, and power is in the eye of the beholder." He smiled at Shin. "Why do you do what you do? There is your answer."

"I do not accept that," Shin said. He didn't want to fight Ito. He wasn't certain he'd survive. But the merchant couldn't be allowed to escape.

"No? Maybe it's simply a darkness in the blood," Ito said, glancing into the shadowed waters below them. "That's what the Crab nobleman called it, when he burnt my village." He looked at Shin, and in the rain, his face seemed as smooth as a pebble. "I don't remember who I was, before I was Ito." His voice had a dreamy quality that nonetheless carried through the rising howl of the storm. "I cannot recall my father's voice, my mother's touch. All I remember is shadow and rain, and the cool darkness beneath the trees, as I fled…" He glanced up at the willows that loomed over the bridge. "And here we are again, in the rain, under the trees."

"Ito," Shin began, confused. What was all this? What was he trying to say?

Ito shook his head and looked again at the lake. "The water is very dark. I have spent so much time in the shadows that sometimes I fancy that they speak to me. Do you ever find yourself thinking that?" He looked at Shin, and for an instant, his eyes seemed as black as the water. Shin froze in alarm. Then, Ito's eyes were as they always had been, and he said, "We are, both of us, slaves to fate. I am bound by mine, as you are trapped by yours. Were it up to me, we would have played our little game for many years. But instead, it ends here, on this narrow span." He raised his sword. "I'm sure there's some poetry in that, but I'll be damned if I can see it."

He moved so quickly that Shin barely saw it coming. He

managed to interpose his own weapon, but only just. Ito shoved him back, beat his blade aside. His sword scraped across Shin's chest, cutting through his robes, and opening a shallow cut on his chest. Shin staggered back, one hand against the wound, his sword extended.

Ito pursued him, his expression flat and empty. Again and again he attacked, keeping Shin on the defensive and unable to retaliate. The drenched state of his robes didn't seem to slow him down, the way it did Shin. They circled and stamped, splashing across the slick stones, back and forth, until Shin's foot slid too far and he fell back against the side of the bridge. Ito was on him in a moment, and Shin's sword flew from his grip to vanish in the waters of the lake below. He rolled aside as Ito struck, and narrowly avoided losing his head. He scrambled to his feet and backed away, looking desperately for something – anything – that could help him.

"Shin!"

Shin heard the shout and turned instinctively. Aoto was there, spear in hand, flanked by half a dozen Kaeru. As Shin watched, his cousin cocked his arm and hurled the spear – toward Shin. "Catch," Aoto cried. Instinct took over. Shin's hand snapped out and he felt the haft of the spear slide against his palm as he caught the weapon and spun back toward Ito, who, though startled by Aoto's presence, had started toward Shin once more.

It was like he was a boy again, back on the training fields with Aoto. The spear was a familiar weight in his hand as he whirled it up and around and then – Ito lunged – Shin bent to meet him – the spear blade glanced against Ito's sword in a spray of sparks – then… impact.

Shin stared into Ito's eyes. The merchant was smiling. Gently. Kindly. Then, blood slipped from between Ito's lips as he took a step back, pulling the spear from Shin's nerveless fingers. The flat of Ito's sword slipped from Shin's shoulder and then the weapon clattered to the ground. Shin felt bewildered. Ito had had him. So why hadn't he struck?

Before he could ask the question, Ito took a two-handed grip on the spear and tugged it from his stomach. "Well – well struck, Shin," he gurgled. He cast the spear aside and stumbled back against the rail of the bridge, where he slid down to sit. "A g-good ending, I think. Not the one I'd hoped for, b-but good enough."

Shin took a step toward him, but Aoto caught his arm. "No, Shin. Stay away from him. He might have another weapon."

"I do," Ito said helpfully. He drew a knife from within his bloody robes and gestured with it. "Though I have only ever used it to cut paper." He fixed Shin with a placid look. "It doesn't hurt, you know."

Then, he was gone.

Shin and Aoto stared down at the dead man. Aoto spoke first. "That is not Ito," he said quietly. "According to our records, Ito is an old man. Decrepit. He's been in the city for longer than either of us have been alive."

"What?" Shin looked at his cousin. "But this man – he..." He trailed off as the implications crashed down on him. "Surely my predecessor would have noticed."

"Maybe she did," Aoto said. He grunted and looked away. "Or maybe it is simply an error. Maybe he truly was a – a spy. Maybe..." He looked at the body. Shin followed his gaze, and felt a sudden uneasiness as he studied the slack features of the dead man. In that moment, they did not seem peaceful, or even relaxed. And the shadows around them suddenly seemed all too deep.

"I wonder who he really was," Shin said softly.

"Does it matter?" Aoto said. "He is dead, and whatever foolishness he was up to has died with him." He reached down, retrieved his spear, and turned to face Shin.

"Now then, cousin – we have some business to settle, you and I."

CHAPTER THIRTY-EIGHT
Resolution

Shin sighed. Once more, he was confined to a room in Two Hill Station, awaiting his cousin's convenience. He knelt on the floor, rubbing his aching chest. Everything hurt and he wanted to go home. He doubted Aoto would be sympathetic.

He'd been taken into custody immediately, and bundled into confinement. Nor was he the only one. True to her word, Konomi had ordered her guards and servants to surrender. They'd all been confined to quarters.

By the time the rain had finally ceased, the Iuchi toll house was fully under the control of the Kaeru and the Crane. There were fewer bodies than Shin had feared there might be; a testament, perhaps, to the efficiency of the Kaeru in such matters. Nothing was on fire, and the lingering smell of the rain hid the odor of blood.

Two auditors stood sentinel on the other side of the doors, talking quietly to one another. From what he'd overheard, Shin gathered that the Iuchi were unhappy with how things had escalated and were even now sending a troop of warriors to retake possession of the station. The Kaeru had already made it clear to Aoto and his followers that they were quite happy to turn the station – and all its contents – over to its rightful owners. Aoto was, of course, protesting this for reasons which escaped Shin. Stubbornness, perhaps.

Footsteps sounded in the corridor, and Shin straightened, assuming a docile expression. The time had come at last. Now that it was here, he found he didn't fear it quite so much as he might otherwise have. So long as no one else suffered on his behalf, he was content. He hoped Kasami would be allowed to return to her people. Perhaps she could find a new, less aggravating lord to serve, when she recovered.

The door slid open and Aoto entered, looking as unhappy as ever. "Here to kill me, then?" Shin asked, as if he were inquiring about the weather.

Aoto laughed harshly. "I do not intend to kill you, Shin. That would be too easy. No, I came to take you home so that you could fulfill your duty to our family."

Shin noted his use of past tense, and felt a thready pulse of anticipation. "But something has changed, has it?"

Aoto stared at him. "Damn you," he said. "I have always thought you a fool, but perhaps you are more clever than I gave you credit for."

"Meaning?"

"It has come to my attention that all of this…" Here, Aoto waved a hand as if to encompass recent events. "Was, in some respects, your doing. That you are to be thanked." He grimaced, as if the words pained him.

Shin frowned. "By whom?"

In reply, Aoto stepped aside so that Ko could enter. Shin nearly sagged in relief to see her alive, if a bit battered and moving unsteadily. "Ko," he said.

"Investigator Ko," she corrected, but not unkindly. She looked pale and wasted, and the skin on her neck and cheek was raw, as if she had strayed too close to a fire. But she was alive, and his heart leapt to see her. "I would be dead, if not for your manservant." Her voice softened. "He used what strength he had left to save me, rather than himself."

Shin bowed his head. "He was a better man than he gave himself credit for." The shock of Kitano's death was no less sharp than it had been earlier – another mistake on his conscience. He pushed the thought aside, trying to focus on the here and now. "Why are you here?"

"I am here to stop your cousin from making a mistake and embarrassing both himself and the Daidoji – as well as the Crane as a whole," Ko said, glancing at Aoto. "It seems we have had the wrong fox's tail from the beginning." She looked at Shin. "You have been ahead of us from the start, doing your best to root out the true criminal behind all of this. Without your efforts, more lives might have been lost. Lord Azuma agrees… as does Governor Tetsua."

Shin glanced at Aoto, who was looking distinctly dyspeptic. "Does this mean you do not intend to drag me back, after all?"

"It means, if I were to attempt it now, the governor would lodge a formal protest and perhaps retract the various trading concessions that the Crane have garnered here. The Lion, among others, have also put forth a request that you be allowed to remain, at least until the full accounting of this incident is made public." Aoto glared at him, as if this were some betrayal of Crane principles. "I suggest you use the time wisely, Shin. This reprieve is only temporary. You have earned yourself a few weeks. Nothing more."

Shin hesitated, and then rose and bowed respectfully to his

cousin. "Thank you, Aoto." He turned to Ko and bowed again. "And thank you, Lady Ko."

"Investigator Ko," she corrected him again, but smiled. She leaned close as he straightened. "I would advise you to choose your friends more carefully in the future, Shin. Next time, I won't be here to keep you out of trouble."

Shin smiled and stepped back. "That's what you said last time." He bowed his head. "I mean it… thank you. You had no reason to help me. I would have understood, if you'd chosen to leave me to my fate."

"That you think that was a possibility is proof you never really understood me," Ko said softly. She shook her head. "I am sorry about your – about Kitano, Shin. I'm sorry for all of it. I wish…" She trailed off.

Shin smiled sadly. "I know. I am, too." He took a breath and looked at Aoto. "I wish to see my bodyguard, if you please."

Kasami's room was at the far end of the house. She lay pale and groggy on her pallet, wrapped in pink-stained bandages, looking somehow shrunken. As if all the vitality he associated with her had been suddenly snatched away. He dismissed the servants who were watching over her. They had things to discuss in private.

When the servants were gone, she cracked an eye and said, "Is it true? The gambler is dead?"

"Yes." Shin hesitated. "It was my fault. I should have seen through Ito from the beginning."

"Yes," Kasami croaked.

Shin frowned. "I'm glad you agree."

She gave a weak, gurgling laugh. "If you were not so lazy, you might have. Then, maybe he was just cleverer than you."

"That is a definite possibility. Then, I cannot help but wonder how much of my own cleverness has been nothing but good timing and luck." He reached for her hand, but fell short of taking it. "When I thought you had died, I…" He trailed off, unable to say the words, though he had practiced them. Kasami snorted, though without her usual vigor.

"I saw you charge the archers, Daidoji Shin. You are a fool, and a courageous one. I will fight anyone who swears different."

Shin laughed softly. "There's a list of people who would gladly argue with you."

Kasami closed her eyes. "As soon as I am healed, I will begin shortening it."

Shin was silent for a moment. He did not think she was asleep. Finally, without opening her eyes, she said, "What of Lady Konomi?"

"Under arrest. Given what I know of Unicorn justice, she will likely be executed and her family removed from their various positions of authority. The Iuchi will want to hide any hint of such a catastrophic occurrence."

"And how do you feel about that?"

"How should I feel?"

Kasami sniffed and winced. "I do not know. That is why I asked."

Shin looked away. "She betrayed me – us."

"Yes."

"You nearly died."

"Yes."

"But if she is to be believed, it is only because of her that we aren't already dead. Me certainly, at least." Shin looked up at the ceiling beams, seeking answers in the wood grain. "She may have saved our lives."

Kasami said nothing. Shin gnawed his lip, turning it over

in his mind. "I do not wish her death on my conscience," he said, finally. "But I do not think simply vouching for her good intentions will be enough. Something drastic is needed – a change of circumstance…" He trailed off as he noticed the steady rise and fall of Kasami's chest. She was asleep.

He smiled, pleased that she was resting, and rose. "A change is as good as a rest, they say," he murmured, as he made for the door. The threads of an idea wound through his mind, and he carefully wove them together. It would be risky, and not just for him. But, if reason were applied by all parties, they would see the obvious benefits. Satisfaction for all, save possibly a stubborn few. Aoto, for one. But that would be a problem for later.

Even so, the plan, such as it was, made him distinctly queasy. He had resisted so long, but to surrender now was the only way to save not just his own life, but that of Konomi as well. There had been too much death already.

There would be complaints, of course. Arguments for and against. The Trading Council would likely be beside itself, until they paused to consider the amount of potential remuneration such an act might bring to their coffers. It would also please the Iuchi to no end. Another link between the Unicorn and the Crane would be welcomed by both clans. But would it be welcomed by Konomi?

When Shin reached the room where they were holding her, he gestured for the Kaeru soldier at the door to let him pass. The man nodded and stepped aside, sliding the door open as he did so. Shin waited until the door was shut once more before he spoke. "I understand Emiko escaped. How careless of you." He'd overheard that unpleasant bit of news while confined.

Konomi looked up. Her hair was unbound, and her robes loose. Anything that could be used as a weapon or means of escape had been taken from her, on Aoto's orders. He obviously had no intention of letting Konomi escape justice in the usual fashion open to those of the nobility. She had not been crying, Shin was pleased to see. Rather, her expression was one of stoic resignation. "I must not have hit her hard enough," she said apologetically.

"At least you broke her shamisen. That's not nothing."

Konomi chuckled. "It did feel good, I admit."

"How did it come to this?" Shin blurted, as he sank to his knees before her. It wasn't the question he'd intended to ask, but it was good enough.

"I told you – youthful folly." Konomi gave a brittle smile.

"If you'd told me, I might have been able to help you."

"If I'd told you, they would have sent Emiko to cut your throat in your sleep. She is one of the most dangerous individuals I have ever encountered, and she believes wholly in the sect's teachings. I suspect that they only still exist as an organized cell because of her."

Shin grunted. "It's a shame we couldn't take her captive."

"Yes."

He hesitated. Then, "Did you let her go?"

Konomi looked away. "If I did?"

Shin was silent. He wasn't sure how to answer that. In fact, he wasn't sure about anything, anymore. The whole world seemed topsy-turvy and he felt out of sorts. Nervous. "She nearly killed me. Nearly killed Kasami, if you hadn't stopped her."

Konomi looked at him. "Have you checked on Kasami? Is she… ?"

"Alive. Angry. In pain. Which makes her even angrier."

Konomi sighed. "Good." Another pause. "I am… sorry it came to that. Please pass along my apologies to her."

Shin flicked open his fan. "Somehow, I don't think she's going to be in the mood to accept your apologies any time soon." He took a deep breath. "Nor am I, honestly. Kitano is dead, Konomi. You saw him only as a servant, but to me he was that and more. He is dead because of us. Kenzō as well. We share responsibility for them."

Konomi bowed her head. "What would you have of me, Shin? I have apologized. I will pay with my life for my lapse. What else is there?"

Shin was silent for several moments. Then, "Would you be willing to find out?"

Konomi looked up, her expression one of puzzlement. "What do you mean?"

"Death is permanent – and unfulfilling. If you lived, you could make restitution every day, by helping thwart the very evil you perpetuated." Shin looked around the room. "It would require some compromise, of course. On your part – and mine – if you agreed."

Konomi frowned. "Shin… what are you saying, exactly?"

Shin took another deep breath, trying to steady his racing heart. "Aoto still intends to drag me home, so that I can be forced into marriage. But, if I were to declare myself already engaged, he would have no reason – no excuse – to do so. And if you were to be wed to someone, say, on the promise that your part in this affair was explained away, then you would be spared from death."

Konomi stared at him. "Are you… proposing?"

Shin gestured absently with his fan. "In a sense. You and I – that is to say, we – have a… fondness for one another, yes? And you were right – we are alike. Neither of us fits into the pattern woven by our families. So, it stands to reason, in this instance, that it might behoove us to, as they say, strike down two snakes with a single blade. Your life and reputation will be preserved, and my situation will become… tenable."

"I tried to have you killed."

"And failed. Intentionally, if you are to be believed. If that isn't affection, I don't know what is, frankly. My mother has tried to have my father killed on at least three occasions and, frankly, he seems to find it something of an aphrodisiac. She is – was – a Scorpion, my mother. A Yogo, to be exact. Though, I suppose that's neither here nor there." Shin realized his words were tumbling over one another and he paused. "Nevertheless, I am already planning to tell the governor that you were only involved in this matter as a favor to me – my spy in the Iron Sect's camp, as it were."

Konomi climbed to her feet. "You mean you're going to claim that this was all – what? An investigation to uncover the conspiracy?"

Shin nodded. "In a sense. Kenzō was working on my behalf, and there is no one to say otherwise. I will simply… omit a few details, and fabricate a few others."

"Why, Shin?"

Shin hesitated. "The truth is, we were all fooled, all used. This way, at least, some good will come of it."

"Not that. Why me? Why this offer?" She leaned close to him, so close he could smell the scent of her hair, of her sweat. He looked into her eyes, and for once could not see the wariness that had always unnerved him before. There was only confusion and something that might have been hope. It mirrored the feeling in his own heart.

"Because I do not want you to die," he said, after a moment.

She swallowed. "Why?"

Shin took her hands, and ran his thumbs over her knuckles. She had strong hands, brown against his pale fingers. A strong mind, as well – and when it came down to it, a code that he could not entirely fault. After all, only a fool could deny that the empire – that the way of things – was flawed to its very core, in some ways. Under different circumstances, at a different time, wouldn't he have made the same mistakes? He sighed. "Why? Because I do believe that I am in love with you, Iuchi Konomi. Perhaps that is all there is to it, in the end."

Konomi took her hands from his and placed them against his cheeks. Her eyes glistened with unshed tears. Tenderly, eagerly, she kissed him. After a few moments, they broke apart. "It will not be so easy as all that, you know. My father…"

"Your father will be pleased," Shin said confidently. "As will my own kin. With this, we turn a potential tragedy into a victory for the Unicorn – and the Crane. The governor will agree with my version, if only because it maintains the status quo. But truthfully… this will satisfy everyone with any interest in seeing the matter settled."

Konomi nodded, but asked, "What about Emiko, and the rest of the Iron Sect?"

"That is a problem for tomorrow," Shin said softly. "Today, let us be happy." Not a command or a plea. A prayer. *Let us be happy.*

"Yes," Konomi said, and kissed him again. Harder. Fiercer. And he returned that ferocity with his own as a weight he had not previously noticed seemed to lift from him. She broke away and smiled at him.

"I think we will be, Daidoji Shin. I think we will be."

CAST LIST

Crane

Daidoji Shin – *Crane nobleman and detective*
Hiramori Kasami – *Shin's long-suffering bodyguard*
Kitano Daichi – *Shin's servant; former gambler*
Ito – *merchant; Crane spy*
Junichi Kenzo – *Crane auditor; murder victim*
Daidoji Aoto – *agent of the Daidoji Trading Council; Shin's cousin*
Crane Auditors – *terrifying*

Other

Iuchi Konomi – *Unicorn noblewoman*
Odama – *soy magnate; leader of the merchant's association*
Ichiro Gota – *Badger merchant*
Nagata Sanki – *doctor; grumpy*
Akodo Minami – *Lion noblewoman*
Kaeru Azuma – *Kaeru nobleman and magistrate*
Lun – *ship's captain; former pirate*
Chobei – *fisherman; Shinobi*
Miya Tetsua – *Imperial governor*
Tonbo Kuma – *Dragonfly priest*
Kitsuki Ko – *investigator; Shin's former lover*
Three Flower Troupe – *Kabuki troupe; Shin's employees*

ABOUT THE AUTHOR

JOSH REYNOLDS is a writer, editor and semi-professional monster movie enthusiast. He has been a professional author since 2007, writing over thirty novels and numerous short stories, including *Arkham Horror, Warhammer: Age of Sigmar, Warhammer 40,000,* and the occasional audio script. He grew up in South Carolina and now lives in Sheffield, UK.

joshuamreynolds.co.uk
twitter.com/jmreynolds

Gorgeous illustrations from the realms of Rokugan.

AVAILABLE NOW IN HARDCOVER & EBOOK

ACONYTE

ACONYTEBOOKS.COM // LEGENDOFTHEFIVERINGS.COM